Leaves from the Note-Book of a New York Detective

Leaves from the Note-Book of a New York Detective

The Private Record of J. B.

John Babbington Williams

WESTHOLME
Yardley

First published in 1865 by Dick & Fitzgerald

Westholme Publishing, LLC
Eight Harvey Avenue
Yardley, Pennsylvania 19067
Visit our Web site at www.westholmepublishing.com

First Printing: October 2008
10 9 8 7 6 5 4 3 2 1

ISBN: 978-1-59416-080-6
(ISBN 10: 1-59416-080-5)

Printed in United States of America

Contents

Contents

Preface

More than twenty years before the publication of Sir Arthur Conan Doyle's first Sherlock Holmes story, *A Study in Scarlet* (1887), the casebook of a New York City detective who solved crimes through the powers of observation and deductive reasoning appeared in print. This book, *Leaves from the Note-Book of a New York Detective: The Private Record of J. B.*, has been known until now only by a handful of specialists; it stands, however, as both an entertaining collection and an important milestone in the history of detective fiction. Frank Wadleigh Chandler observed in *The Literature of Roguery*, that the combination of the analytical detective—represented in the works of Edgar Allan Poe and Émile Gaboriau—with sensationalism created a new type of story with the "purpose to gratify the reader's taste for the ghastly, the tragic, or the criminal, and at the same time to propose a mystery whose solution shall exercise intellectual ingenuity." Chandler continues: "the supreme example of this mingling of the sensational and analytical is to be seen in the stories concerning Sherlock Holmes; but as early as 1864 the *Autobiography of a London Detective* and the *Experiences of a French Detective Officer* by 'Waters,' combined the two. Such French and English adventures were supplemented in 1865 by an American contribution—*Leaves from the Note-Book of a New York Detective*—detailing the episodes in the career of James Brampton, whose powers of quiet observation and analysis were especially emphasized." Ellery Queen noted that, "in the seventeen years that followed the first edition of Poe's *Tales* (1845), not a single book was published in the United States that contained a detective story." (*Tales* includes Poe's detective masterpiece, "The Purloined Letter," one of the three stories featuring his French detective, C. Auguste Dupin.) In 1863, "two books finally cracked the long silence." One was was an anonymously written collection of "Curiosities of Crime" by "a retired member of the detective police;" while the second was a collection by Harriet Elizabeth Prescott, which contained a single detective story. But it was two years later, in 1865, when Dick & Fitzgerald published *Leaves from the Note-Book of a New York Detective*, containing "no less then twenty-two exploits of detective James Brampton" wrote Ellery Queen, that America had its first home-grown detective hero.

What sets Brampton apart is that, like the great Sherlock Holmes, Brampton's exploits spanned more than just two or three stories; the character is sustained over a series of individual cases and portions of his biography and personality are revealed. Like Holmes, Brampton employed disguise during some of his investigations. It is interesting to note that detective Brampton's cases were ultimately edited and published by a medical doctor, a similar service rendered by Dr. Watson for Holmes. However, all of Brampton's cases are written in the first person, not third, allowing the reader to follow the mind of the detective as each case unfolds—his hypotheses, assumptions, reasonings, and observations—to its ultimate solution. The cases take place in the mid-nineteenth century, so the stories also reveal the details, atmosphere, and social conventions of the times, from onmibuses on the streets of New York City to the once universal propriety of offering food and shelter to any traveler who requests. The cases take Brampton to cities and places along the East Coast, including Philadelphia, Baltimore, and Georgia, and as far as Chicago, the "capital of the West," Iowa—and even to France.

The author wrote no more James Brampton mysteries, but this book was published well before the detective genre began to take off later in the century. This is the first modern reprint of Dr. John B. Williams's "Private Record of J. B." Of the twenty-nine "leaves" most feature Brampton, but following leaf eighteen, Brampton's casebook includes "adventures of various personal friends," inserted by the detective for their peculiar interest. For those who enjoy Edgar Allan Poe, Wilkie Collins, and Sir Arthur Conan Doyle, the following will provide a satisfying journey into the life and times of the first American sleuth: James Brampton.

Introduction

Some few years ago I was travelling in the South. By some misadventure I missed the train at Augusta, Georgia, and was compelled to spend a night in that rather slow town. I patronized the best hotel in the place, and after having partaken of an early supper I thought I would go and explore the city until bedtime.

Half an hour, however, was amply sufficient to see all the lions of the place, and at the end of that time I returned to my hotel, weared and ennuied.

I listlessly entered the reading room which was also the bar-room; and taking up a paper that had been issued in New York four days previously, composed myself to read the shipping intelligence. Not that I had the remotest interest in that species of news, but it was the only part of the paper I had not perused.

While thus engaged, a slight cough drew my attention from the arrivals and departures and I raised my eyes. Seated at the further end of the room was an individual I had not noticed before. He was a man, I suppose, between forty and forty-five years of age. There was something very peculiar in his features which immediately arrested my attention. I do not know how to describe it, but it gave me the idea that he possessed in an eminent degree the power of analysis. This impression was further increased by his movements. They were quick; and it was plainly to be perceived that he did not allow the slightest circumstance to escape him. I am not naturally inclined to make friends with strangers, but there was something in the man which attracted me to him. I drew my chair more closely to his, and commenced a conversation.

"A pleasant evening," said I.

"You are right, sir, " he replied; "it is very pleasant indeed, considering the time of year. One would expect to find it hotter than it is so far down South."

"I should judge from your remark you do not reside in Augusta," I ventured.

"No I am from New York."

At that moment the door of the bar-room opened, a young man entered and walking rapidly up to the bar asked for a glass of ale.

"I will wager anything," said the stranger to me in a whisper, "that the young man who has just entered, has, a few minutes since, robbed his employer's till."

"How in the world do you know that fact," I asked. "He appears to be a very respectable young man."

"As far as dress goes, certainly, but I'll bet two to one he has just taken some money out of the till. If my supposition is correct, he will pay for his glass of ale with a piece of gold."

The stranger was right; the clerk, for such I judged him to be, threw down a five dollar gold piece in payment. The bar-keeper, however, had not time to give him the change before a policeman hurriedly entered and arrested the young man. He was at once taken before a magistrate.

"Did you ever see that young man before?" I asked as soon as the excitement occasioned by this little episode had subsided.

"Never in my life," replied the stranger.

"How in the name of all that is extraordinary could you tell that he had robbed his employer, and that he would pay for his glass of ale with a piece of gold?"

"Simply by observation and analysis. When that young man entered the room I noticed three things. First, that he glanced nervously at the door after it was closed on him. Secondly, that he took in every person at a glance; and Thirdly, that he held something clutched tightly in his hand. There must have been a reason for all these three things. The most probable reason for glancing at the door as he came in was the fear of being pursued. If he was afraid of being pursued he must have done something contrary to law. He examined every person in the room for the same reason; he did not wish to be recognized by any one he knew. The something he clutched in his hand was more probable to be money than anything else, and the fact that his fingers were not bulged out, showed that it must be a single piece, how natural then to suppose that it must be gold. The chain was immediately formed; he had taken the piece from the till; he was afraid that it might be marked, and he wanted to get it changed as soon as possible. It was evident by the anxious manner that he thought he might be suspected, and hence his anxiety to get rid of that which might compromise him.

"But is it possible that you could make out all that chain of reasoning during the time he took to walk from the door to the bar?"

"Certainly; it is merely a matter of education. By educating the powers of observation it is perfectly astonishing how they may be developed. It is only of late years that this species of knowledge has been perfected. Perhaps I have done more towards detecting crime than any other living man.

"Indeed! then you have made a profession of it."

"For twenty years."

"Is it possible? will you forgive my inquisitiveness if I ask you your name?"

"My name is James Brampton, known among thieves and rogues as J. B."

"What! James Brampton, the famous detective officer?"

"The same at your service. Even now I am tracking a defaulter, who has made off with a large amount of funds from one of the New York banks. I have traced him as far as this place, and I have but little doubt that I shall ultimately capture him; I have traced him as far as here by means of a Provence rose."*

I was delighted to meet Mr. Brampton. His name had been prominently before the public in many instances. He was a man of extraordinary sagacity, and had succeeded in discovering the perpetrators of crime, where to ordinary men all clue appeared to have been lost. His faculty in this respect was evidently owing to his keen observation, his acute mental analysis and determined perseverance. No difficulty daunted him; in fact, his powers seemed to increase in proportion as the case was enveloped in mystery. He was a man of great courage, and, what is still better for his profession, extraordinary coolness.

*The reader will find in one of the leaves the full particulars of the part this Provence rose played in this particular case, so I need not repeat the explanation given me by Mr. Brampton.

With the assistance of a cigar and a good bottle of sherry I soon became quite at home with him.

"I suppose you have kept a record of the cases in which you have been engaged."

"The more important ones."

"Have you any objection to have them published?"

"I have concluded to retire from business in two or three years time. I shall have no objection to have them published then. My detective experience embrace every species of adventures, and I assure you that every word is true. I have a MS book of the principal cases in which I have been engaged, which I shall be happy to place at your disposal to publish when I retire from my present occupation."

"I am much obliged to you," I answered, "and accept your offer with gratitude. Might I ask you one question?"

"Certainly, a hundred if you like."

"Did you embrace your present profession from choice?"

"I may say I embraced it from choice and necessity combined, but let us light a fresh cigar and I will give a history of my first case."

We drew our chairs closer to the table, and he told me the following story, which I repeat exactly in his own words without making the slightest addition or alteration.

I was born in New York city. My father was a respectable merchant, and he bestowed upon me the best education that money could procure. He wished me to embrace the medical profession and for that purpose sent me to read with a physician who lived in a village on the Hudson River. This physician was a particular friend of his.

I liked the study of medicine pretty well and remained several years in the physician's office. But a terrible accident happened to my father, in fact, he was burnt to death, and he left his affairs so embarrassed, that my mother could not afford the means necessary for me to complete my medical studies. I therefore determined to seek for some more renumerative employment.

I was one day seated at home in my mother's house, when the servant girl entered the room and informed me that a gentleman wanted to speak with me. I told the girl to show him up.

A moment afterwards a young man entered the room whom I immediately recognized as an old schoolmate of mine John Millson.

I shook hands with him cordially, and was really delighted to see him.

"Brampton," said my friend, "I am in great distress of mind, and have come to you for assistance."

"My dear fellow," I replied, "I will do any thing in the world for you in my power. What is it?"

"Have you read the papers this morning?"

"Certainly."

"Then you doubtless read about the murder committed in Williamsburg yesterday. A young lady, Miss Emily Millwood has been arrested on suspicion."

"I certainly read the account in the papers," I replied, "and it seemed to be a case which admitted of no doubt."

"I know the evidence is very strong against Miss Millwood," replied Millson, "but if you knew Emily as well as I do, Brampton, you would be morally certain that she is incapable of this act."

The young man spoke with such warmth that I looked at him somewhat curiously.

"Why, Millson, this Miss Millwood is no relation of yours, is she?" I asked.

"Well, the fact is, Brampton, we are engaged to be married. I have known her from a child. Her heart is pure and noble. She could not injure a worm much less murder her aunt and benefactor."

"Well, but my dear fellow, what can I do in the matter?"

"I want you to help me to prove Emily innocent. I remember at school how you used to point out all mysteries almost intuitively. The moment I heard you were in town, I determined to apply to you, for to tell you the truth I would rather trust the case in your hands, than in those of the best detectives in New York."

"You are very complimentary, Millson—but you know I am a perfect amateur in such matters, and I would strongly advise you to consult some one who makes a business of ferreting out crime."

"Then you refuse to assist me?"

"Not at all. I will do my best if you insist upon it. I assure you I feel great interest in the matter, and will proceed at once to Williamsburg."

Millson then entered into particulars from which I gathered substantially as follows:

Mrs. Weldon, an old inhabitant of Williamsburg, lived in a small frame house at the further end of Grand street, at that time very sparsely built up. A niece and a servant girl were the only persons residing with her. The former appeared very much devoted to her aunt, and attended to her wants with filial assiduity. The domestic had lived with Mrs. Weldon for five years and was considered a good servant.

Mrs. Weldon was a widow lady of ample means in the shape of an annuity which was to close with her death. She was rather miserly in her disposition, and accustomed to hoard money. Her husband at one time lost a considerable amount by the breaking of a bank, and since then no one could persuade her to have anything to do with any bank. It was supposed that this hoarding propensity was known only to the niece. Miss Millwood, and the servant girl, Hannah.

On the morning of September 14th, 1840, the inhabitants of Grand street were electrified by the report that Mrs. Weldon had been discovered murdered in her bed; and that strong proofs of guilt existed against Miss Millwood.

Such was the substance of the information given me by my friend Millson. He then bade me good-bye, promising to call the following day to learn the result of my enquiries.

I hurried through my breakfast and proceeded at once to Williamsburg to visit the scene of the crime. I found the apartment in much the same condition as it was when the body was first discovered.

Mrs. Weldon occupied the front bedroom on the second story—and in all probability was sleeping when the deed was committed. She had been discovered lying on the floor of the chamber with a fearful wound in her left side that had evidently penetrated the heart. The bed and carpet were stained with blood.

The servant girl had been the first to discover the crime and had given the alarm. All the doors and windows were I fastened on the inside, for Hannah had given the alarm from the window.

An examination was made of the premises. This resulted in the apprehension of Miss Millwood as the perpetrator of the deed. She had been arrested while in bed. In the pocket of her dress which hung on the back of a chair a large sum of money was found, together with some old fashioned jewelry which was known to have belonged to the deceased. But there was even more damning evidence than this. In her trunk a sharp pointed knife was found, smeared with blood, and which exactly filled the wound by which the deceased had come to her death. This trunk was found locked and the key in the pocket of the accused with the valuables.

I examined the chamber occupied by the deceased at the time of her death. A few minutes convinced me that the young lady was innocent. My reasons for this conclusion were these. The wound was too deep to have been inflicted by the hand of a woman, and whoever had struck the blow must be left handed. While searching the chamber, I found on the floor a vest button, it was rather peculiar being made of blue porcelain. I put it in my pocket.

I then went to see Miss Millwood, and having been admitted to her by an order from her attorney, I explained my business and stated that I had been engaged by John Millson. I found her a very pretty girl, but very delicate and frail. After conversing a little while with her on the subject, I asked her to tell me all she knew about the matter.

"I know but little, Mr. Brampton," she replied. "My aunt retired to bed early that night. I had a head-ache, and about two o'clock took a cup of tea. I then grew very sleepy and went to bed. I slept all night without waking. In fact I was asleep when the officers of justice entered my room."

"Did you sleep more soundly than usually?"

"Now you remind me of it, I did indeed. I scarcely ever remember to have slept so soundly before, and even when awakened I was unaccountably drowsy."

"Who gave you the tea you drank the night before?"

"The servant, Hannah."

"Do you suspect she could have committed the deed?"

"Impossible! a better servant, or one more kind to my aunt could not be found than she is."

After a little longer conversation I bade her adieu. I must confess I was all at sea. I felt perfectly convinced of the young lady's innocence but I was no nearer to the discovery of the real perpetrator of the crime than before. I next determined that I would visit the servant Hannah. She was confined as a witness.

I found a good-looking girl, about twenty-two years of age. Her countenance was an open one, but there was an expression of deceit about her lips that I did not like. I have not much faith in physiognomy, so I put it down for as much as it was worth.

Hannah's story was satisfactory enough. She stated that on the night of the murder she retired to bed about eleven o'clock at night, and had heard no noise in the house. She got up early in the morning as was customary with her, and on entering her mistress's bed-chamber had discovered the fearful tragedy. She had at once opened the window and screamed out "murder." She also testified to the great affection Miss Millwood entertained for her aunt, and it was her opinion that the latter was entirely guiltless of the crime imputed to her!

I soon found this Hannah was what is called a *smart* girl. She gave her answers readily and without any hesitation—almost too much so to please my fastidious taste.

I had already said it was no woman who had committed the deed—this, of course, precluded the possibility of Hannah being the guilty party. The question then arose if neither of the women committed the deed, who was the murderer? Then I must acknowledge I was completely at fault. All the doors and windows being fastened inside precluded the idea of the house having been entered from without.

I felt annoyed at being baffled, and started to walk to the ferry as night was fast approaching. I had not proceeded many steps down Grand street, when my eyes were attracted by the gleaming show bottles of a drug store.

No saying is truer than that great events spring from little causes. The fact of my eye having caught the glass of a druggist's show bottles in all probability saved an innocent person from dying on the scaffold. I naturally glanced in the window and saw a cigar box. The druggist then sold cigars. I thought I would like to smoke one, so I entered the store.

Two or three people were inside imbibing soda water. The owner of the store and a customer were conversing about the recent murder. "There can be no doubt about Miss Millwood's guilt," said the druggist, "but Lord! I should have thought she would have been the last person in the world to have done such a deed as that she is such a nice spoken young lady."

"You know her, then?" asked the customer.

"Certainly, I know them all. Why only the very evening of the murder, the servant, girl, Hannah, was in my store."

I pricked up my ear but no further conversation passed between them. The customers were soon all served and I was the only one left. I immediately accosted the druggist.

"You stated just now that Mrs. Weldon's servant girl Hannah was in your store on the night of the murder. May I ask what she bought?"

"Let me see," ventured the druggist; "it was morphine—she stated that she had the tooth-ache."

I said no more, but left the store. I had now the first clue—it was a faint one to be sure, but I felt certain that Hannah knew more about the murder than anybody else. I remembered Miss Millwood's extraordinary drowsiness on the night in question, and to this I added the fact, she had partaken of a cup of tea prepared by Hannah, and that the latter had purchased morphine that same evening at the drug store. But then my first conviction rushed into my mind, no woman had committed the deed. The first link of the chain was found, however, and I was hopeful. I resumed my walk towards the ferry determined to sleep upon it.

During that memorable walk down Grand street something else also attracted my attention. It was a tailor's shop, outside of which various garments were exposed for sale. Amongst them I noticed some vests, the buttons of which struck me; they were made of blue porcelain.

I began to examine the things as if I wanted to purchase. An obliging shopman came outside to try to sell.

"What do you ask for one of these vests," I demanded.

"Two dollars," was the reply.

"They are something new are they?" I inquired.

"Quite new; we have not sold more than two or three of them. We have not had them in the shop more than three or four days."

"I saw a man with one on yesterday." I said.

"You mean Bill Holsley, hostler at the Eagle Tavern."

"Yes, that was the man," I returned. "Good evening, I don't think I will buy one to-night."

To make my way to the Eagle Tavern was the work of a very few minutes. I asked to see the hostler, and was directed to the stable.

I approached it with a cautious step, and peeped in the door. The hostler was cleaning down a horse with his left hand, By and by, he turned round, and he wore the famous vest, with the middle blue porcelain button, wanting. I knew I stood in the presence of the murderer.

I determined on practising a *ruse.* I suddenly advanced, and seizing him by the arm, exclaimed:

"William Holsley, I arrest, you for the wilful murder of Mrs. Weldon. Your confederate Hannah has made a full confession."

The murderer turned deadly pale; his limbs shook and his countenance betrayed the most abject fear.

"I will confess all," he exclaimed. He was immediately removed to jail, and that night made a full confession, which amounted to as follows:

He had been engaged to be married to Hannah, and was only waiting until he earned enough money to support a wife. Hannah, who it seems was a thoroughly bad woman, was tired of the delay, and proposed to him that they should rob her mistress. It was finally agreed that Hannah should drug Miss Millwood's tea with a powerful opiate, and after she was asleep she let in Holsley.

They then decided it would be better "to put the old woman out of the way," and throw the guilt on the niece. Holsley committed the deed, and after having robbed their victim they proceeded to Miss Millwood's chamber, and placed a portion of the money and the old fashioned jewelry in the pocket of her dress which hung on the back of a chair. They then took from her pocket the key of her trunk and unlocking it placed the instrument with which the deed had been committed under her clothes. This done, they re-locked the trunk, and replaced the key from where they had taken it. Holsley left the house, and Hannah fastened the door after him. The deed was skilfully planned, and had Hannah been only concerned, a guiltless party might have suffered; but Holsley was by no means a courageous man and wanted presence of mind.

They were both tried, found guilty, and in two months from the committal of the deed, Holsley was hanged, and Hannah condemned to the State Prison for life.

Six months after this occurrence, I one day received an invitation to a wedding. It was that of Emily Millwood and her faithful lover. I have seen them quite lately, they are as happy as it is possible to be, and have a fine family of children to add to their felicity.

Such was my first experience as an amateur detective, and although I could not lay claim to any great sagacity in unravelling the mystery, my success made a great sensation, and I received overtures to join the detective force, which was then being organised in New York for the first time. I was out of employment, I liked the business, I accepted the offer and became a detective police-officer, which calling as I have before told you, I have followed for twenty years.

Mr. Brampton here finished his story; it was now late and we retired to bed.

The following morning we each departed on our respective business.

I heard no more of Mr. Brampton until a month or two ago when I received by Adams Express Co., a MS book, and the following note from him.

> New-York, Jan., 6th, 1864.
>
> My Dear Sir:
>
> I have decided to retire from my profession, and herewith forward you a history of some of the principal cases in which I have been engaged. You are at liberty to publish them as soon as you please. I wish it to be distinctly understood, that, with exception of some of the names being altered every word is true. Of course I shall leave it to you to render them fit for publication. You know I am not much accustomed to composition for the press, and they may require considerable alteration to render them ship shape.
>
> Yours, very truly,
>
> James Brampton
>
> *To Dr. John B. Williams.*

Having thus received permission to publish the contents of the MS book, confided to me, I now present them to the public, hoping they will be as much interested in their perusal as I have been.

Leaf the First

The Silver Pin

I had not been settled long in New York, before I was engaged in a large number of cases, and, fortunately for me, I was successful in by far the greater portion of them. I became very popular, and there was not a single case of importance in which there was any doubt, but what I was consulted in it.

One day I was walking at a rapid pace down Broadway when I suddenly felt some one tap me on the shoulder. I turned quickly round, and who should it prove to be but my old school-fellow, Harry Markham.

"Why, Harry, my boy," said I, "how are you?"

"Why, Jem," he replied, shaking me cordially by the hand, "I little expected to find you in New York. I thought you were in Stansfield buried among your medical books."

"I have left physic, and turned detective officer," I returned, and then I told him in a few words what had passed. "But you, Harry, what are you doing?"

"I'm in luck," he replied. "I have got a situation as private secretary to a Mr. Percival, a gentleman of wealth, living near Washington. He gives me a thousand dollars a year, and my board and lodging, I am to take charge of his money matters. I think it is rather an easy place."

I congratulated Markham on his good luck in having secured such a good situation. He was to leave for Washington the next day, and we agreed that we would meet again at five o'clock and dine together.

At the appointed hour we met at Delmonico's, and had a capital dinner. We talked over old times, and passed in review all our schoolboy days, and really enjoyed ourselves very much. We did not separate until a late hour, and when we did so, we parted with mutual regret.

When I returned to my lodgings that night, I thought on all that had passed during the day. I had always liked Harry Markham, and at school had frequently been his champion. Harry, however, had not turned out as well as had been expected of him when he grew up to man's estate. He had chosen surgery as his profession, but after having graduated he retired from the profession in disgust, and for a year or two had wandered about without aim or purpose. It was no wonder, then, that I felt pleased that he had obtained such an excellent situation, and hoped that it would prove a stepping stone to fortune.

A few days after our dinner, I received a letter from him, informing me of his safe arrival at his destination. He expressed himself as very much pleased with his situation, and alluded more than once to Miss Amy Percival, the only daughter of his employer. I replied to his letter but he did not write again.

About a year afterwards, on a cold November morning, I got up, as the saying is, "wrong side foremost." The fact is, I had been unsuccessful in unravelling a case in which great interests were involved, and was in no very amiable mood of mind. It was a miserable, wet day; the rain pattered against the window, and the street was a mass of slush and mud. To add to my annoyance, my breakfast was not ready when I came down stairs, and I walked to the window, and looked out into the cheerless thoroughfare. If it was disagreeable out of doors, it was comfortable enough within. A cheery coal fire burned in the grate, a snowy cloth was spread on the table, and a delicious scent of rashers of bacon saluted my nostrils. I had not waited very long before my landlady, Mrs. Hobbs, brought in in my breakfast. She just glanced at my face, and perceiving the scowl on it, did not utter a word, for she knew my humor. She placed the coffee, toast, bacon and boiled eggs on the table, and then suddenly vanished, just deigning to say, as she slipped from the door, "Breakfast is ready, sir."

I sat down to my breakfast, and began to eat mechanically. I tried at first to find fault with my fare, but could not in reason do so. The eggs were cooked just as I liked them; the bacon was done to a turn; the coffee was excellent. While discussing my breakfast, I thought over the matter I had in hand, and a sudden light gleamed upon me, and I saw a clue to all the difficulties that had bothered me so much before. In a moment my ill-temper vanished, and I became the amiable Jem Brampton, as my acquaintances all called me.

When I was about half through my breakfast, my room door opened, and the form of my respectable landlady, Mrs. Hobbs, appeared on the threshold.

"*Herald*, sir," said she, holding the newspaper in her hands.

I took it from her very graciously; she appeared to be surprised at my change of demeanor.

"Mrs. Hobbs," said I, "this is very nice bacon."

"I am glad you like it, sir," said she, dropping a curtsey as she left the room.

Having made the *amende honorable* to my worthy landlady, I drew my chair to the fire, and opening the paper, began to peruse it with that sense of satisfaction a man feels when he is surrounded by comforts. The very first paragraph that met my eyes absolutely took my breath. It runs as follows:

> MYSTERIOUS DEATH.—Yesterday morning Mr. Percival, of Washington, was found dead in bed. It appears that he retired to bed perfectly well the evening before. It is suspected that he came to his end by foul play, but the motive for any one to commit the dead, and the mode of death are entirely wrapt up in mystery. There can be no doubt there will be the strictest investigation made into the affair.

I immediately thought of Harry Markham, and pitied the poor fellow that he would be so soon deprived of his situation. But, selfish mortals that we are, my own business soon engrossed my attention, and I forgot all about the Percival affair and Harry Markham.

That same evening when I had got through my business for the day, and was enjoying a quiet cigar by my own fire-side, there was a violent peal at the bell. Almost immediately afterwards, Mrs. Hobbs came and informed me that two gentlemen wished to see me. I told my landlady to show them to my room. She returned in a few moments with a young man about twenty-five years of age, and one about ten years older.

They introduced themselves to me, the younger as Mr. Stephen Massett, the elder as Mr. Edward Morton.

"I believe I have the pleasure of speaking to Mr. James Brampton," said Mr. Massett.

"That is my name," I returned.

"Mr. Brampton," continued tho speaker, "I have heard of your skill as a detective officer, and I have come to consult you on a very delicate matter. A mysterious death has lately occurred in Washington and—"

"Do you allude to Mr. Percival," I asked.

"What! have you heard about it?" asked Mr. Massett, in surprise.

"Nothing more than I read in the papers this morning."

"I came from Washington yesterday, I am a nephew of the deceased, and I think the matter ought to be investigated. I want you to go to Washington to-morrow morning, and if, from the observations you make, you come to the conclusion that my uncle came to his death naturally, we shall be satisfied."

"But," said I, "why not let a surgeon make a *post mortem* examination?"

"Oh! that has been done," replied Mr. Percival's nephew.

"Well, what was the report?"

"Well, the doctors use so many scientific phrases, that it is hard to understand what they do mean, but from what I can make out, they say that he had some disease of the aorta."

"But do they say he came to his death by foul means?"

"No they do not say that—on the other hand, they appear to imply that he died from natural causes."

"Then, what the necessity for any investigation in the matter?"

"Well, his relatives are not satisfied, and would much prefer that you should investigate the matter. I believe I speak the wishes of Mr. Edward Morton, who is the deceased's first cousin."

"Certainly," replied the elder of the two visitors.

"Well, gentlemen, since you desire it, I will start to morrow."

"Here is a five hundred dollar note for your services," said young Massett.

I made no scruple in taking the money, although it was a very liberal sum. After the conversation had been prolonged a little, my visitors left me.

Early next morning I started by the Camden and Amboy Railroad for Washington, at which place I arrived about seven o'clock in the evening.

My first proceeding was to ask for Mr. Harry Markham, and I was introduced to him in Mr. Percival's study where he was engaged, in writing.

"Why, Brampton," said he, in a rather flurried manner, the moment he saw me, at the same time rising from his, chair—"is it possible it is you? Why, what in the name of all that extraordinary, brings you down to this part of the country?"

"I am here on business, Harry," I replied, and then I told him all that had transpired between Mr. Massett and myself.

"What egregious folly!" he exclaimed, when I had finished. "The physicians have distinctly stated that Mr. Percival died from aneurism of the aorta. You had better see them at once, and it will save you a world of trouble."

I thought with Markham, that if the surgeon who made the *post mortem* examinations, really stated that the deceased had really died from aneurism, it was a waste of time to make any further investigation in the matter. But I had received my pay, and determined to do my duty.

"Mr. Percival's death was very sudden, was it not?" I asked.

"Of course it was—death by aneurism always is; the moment the sac bursts death ensues, but I forgot you have perhaps forgotten your medical studies. Let me explain. Aneurism of an artery is the rupture of one of the internal coats. A sac is formed, which gradually increases until the remaining coats of the artery give way; death is then instantaneous."

I thanked him for his information, and after some further conversation with him, I asked to see the body. He immediately took up a lamp, and led the way to the chamber where the dead body lay. It was a dark gloomy chamber, being hung with heavy curtains and a grave-like odor pervaded the room. The coffin was placed beside the bed, but the body had not yet been placed in it, but lay on the bed.

He must have been a strong, hearty man when alive. I brought the lamp to bear on his face, but saw nothing there but the ordinary face of a corpse. I then opened the night-dress and examined the region of the heart. At first I saw nothing, but on examining more closely, I discovered a little blue mark, not larger than the head of a pin, exactly over the space where the heart was.

"What a curious mark," said I, pointing it out to Harry. "Where?" said Markham.

"There," I returned, bringing the lamp to bear upon it.

"That is only a mark of decomposition," said Harry.

I thought such might be the case, and said no more about it. I made a careful examination of everything in the apartment, but it amounted to nothing. I went to see the surgeon who had made the *post mortem* examination, and he assured me in a very pompous tone that there could be no doubt as to the cause of his death.

"It was a very peculiar case of aneurism," said he. "Scarpa, you know, made a distinction between dilatation and aneurism, applying the former name to the expansion of the whole of the arterial coats for a limited extent, the latter to an expansion of the exterior coat, occurring in consequence of a solution of continuity in the inner and middle. But in this particular case there was a rupture without any evidence of a solution of continuity having existed before, or even a dilatation. A very peculiar case, sir—a very peculiar case, indeed."

"But, doctor," said I, without the faintest idea what he meant by a solution of continuity, "did Mr. Percival die from what is commonly known as a natural cause?"

"Certainly, my dear sir, certainly, but still it was a very peculiar case—very peculiar, indeed. I intend to write a history of it for a medical journal."

I next interrogated the servants, but discovered nothing to raise the slightest suspicion. It is true, I discovered that Mr. Percival had more than once given utterance to his disapprobation of the intimacy existing between his daughter Ada and his secretary, but as he was a fretful faultfinder, little notice was paid to it. I also found that all his large wealth was left to Ada during her life, with the exception of a legacy of five thousand dollars to young Massett; if she married, it was settled on her children; if she had no issue, she was at liberty to will it to whom she pleased.

There was nothing left me now but to return to New York, which I did the next morning. Mr. Massett called on me, and I entered into full particulars as to the result of my inquiries. He appeared perfectly satisfied and left me.

Four months passed away, and I had forgotten the whole circumstance, when one morning I received by post an embossed envelope, containing wedding cards, with the names of Mr. and Mrs. Harry Markham engraved on them. In the corner of the lady's card was Miss Ada Percival. The address given was No. 121 State street, Boston. From what I had heard of the relations existing between Miss Percival and Markham, this marriage did not surprise me, but I thought their haste was very unseemly.

Six months had now elapsed, and I had heard and seen nothing of Markham. I had written a letter of congratulation to him, and our correspondence had ceased. One morning, however, just as I was about to leave the house, who should come to the door but Henry Markham. I was struck with the great change that had taken place in his appearance. His once handsome face was bloated and blotched from the effects of strong potations, his hands trembled, and he looked a wreck of his former self. Still he addressed me in the friendly tone of other days. I asked him in, and I soon found that he lived very unhappily with his wife. He had evidently taken to drinking, and what was still worse, gambling. He stayed with me three or four days—but his visit was anything but an agreeable one; I did not ask him to prolong it, and he returned home.

About eight weeks after this, I one morning received another visit from Mr. Stephen Massett.

"Mr. Brampton," said he, as soon as he entered, "you may remember about a year ago, I asked you to investigate the cause of my uncle's, Mr. Percival's death. I have now come to you on a similar errand."

"Indeed," I returned, "who is dead?"

"My cousin."

"What cousin?"

'You remember Mr. Percival's daughter, do you not?"

"What? Mrs. Henry Markham?"

"Exactly."

"Well, she is dead!"

"Dead!" I exclaimed, scarcely able to believe the statement. "Impossible?"

"It is true. She died yesterday, and under circumstances just as mysterious as her father. I want you to investigate the matter thoroughly, for I am satisfied there is some foul play in the matter."

"Is any one suspected?" I asked.

"No one. In fact, I believe the surgeon who made the *post mortem* examination, gives it as his opinion that she died of some peculiar kind of aneurism."

"The same disease that her father died of then?"

"Yes, the same."

"I will leave for Boston at once. I agree with you now, that this matter requires the fullest investigation."

Mr. Stephen Massett left me, and I immediately made preparations for my journey. I must confess that I was at first amazed beyond expression at what I had heard. The thought struck my mind that Henry Markham might—but I did not allow myself even to finish the thought.

In a few hours, I was at Markham's house in State street, Boston. I frankly told him my business. He appeared to be plunged in the deepest grief, and expressed himself as very anxious to have every investigation made. My first proceeding was to make inquiries as to when Mrs. Markham died. The particulars I gained amounted to substantially as follows:

Mrs. Markham had retired to bed at night in perfect health. She and her husband had occupied separate rooms for several months—but within the last two weeks a species of reconciliation had sprung up between them, but not sufficient to cause them to change their mode of living apart. The house-maid had gone to Mrs. Markham's chamber, and as was usually the case, found it locked. She knocked, and knocked again and received no answer. She became alarmed, and summoning her master, whom she found fast asleep, she told him of the condition of things. He immediately got up, and finding that knocking did not really succeed in awaking his wife, he procured the assistance of a neighbor or two, and they broke open the door. The key was found inside the lock. When they entered the bed-chamber they discovered Mrs. Markham lying in bed, stone dead. Death appeared to I have been very sudden, for the clothes were not in the least disturbed. Nor was there the slightest mark of violence apparent on the body. Mr. Markham, when he saw the dead body of his wife, appeared to suffer the most terrible agony. He threw himself on the body, and wept and cried like a child. He was obliged to be removed from the apartment at last by gentle force. A coroner's inquest was summoned, as is usual in the case of sudden death, a *post mortem* examination was made, and the verdict given was "died by the visitation of God."

Such was the statement made to me; and it was my duty now to see if it were correct. I visited the chamber of death, and, first of all, examined the apartment narrowly. It was evident that the door had been fastened on the inside, thus precluding the idea of any one entering the room by that means. I next went to the window, and it looked out on the back part of the house. The room itself was in the third story, and there were roofs of back buildings that came exactly under the window. Hanging from the roof a short distance from the window was a broken lightning rod, much thicker than usual. But the end of it appeared to be such a long distance from the roof underneath, that it entirely precluded the possibility of any one entering the apartment by that means.

I now proceeded to examine the body of the deceased; the face was perfectly natural, and except it being very livid, she might have been supposed to have been asleep. I do not know what impelled me, but it appeared to be almost an instinct, I opened the night-shirt of the deceased. The moment I did so I started back, and would have uttered a cry had I not exercised the most determined self-command.

There was a distinct blue spot, the size of a pin, exactly over the region, of the heart.

This could not be a coincidence; this same mark could not occur in both father and daughter exactly in the same spot, without having been caused by something. I hastily closed the night-dress, and turned the sheet back again. I did not know what to think or what to do. As was my usual custom whenever in perplexity, I determined to think over the matter an hour or two before I made another move. I left the chamber and proceeded to a room which served as library and study. I sat down at the table, and leaning my head on my hands tried to study out the case, as I called it. But it was to no purpose, I could make nothing out of it, and upon reflection, I was compelled to admit the only suspicious thing about the whole affair was the blue mark over the region of the heart. I knew some little about medical matters, and this, after all, might be natural. At all events, I determined I would consult the surgeon about it, and I rose from my seat for that purpose. I was about leaving the room when I saw lying on one of the shelves a French medical journal. I took it up mechanically, and turned over the pages. The book opened of itself in one particular place. I can read French well. The reader may imagine my astonishment and horror when my eyes fell on the following paragraph:

> PAINLESS EXTINCTION. Monsieur Velpeau on Wednesday last read a very interesting paper before *L'Academie de Medecin* on painless extinction. He states that if a silver pin be placed exactly over the arch of the aorta, and then be suddenly driven in, death ensues instantaneously. There is not the slightest disfiguration of the body, nothing being apparent after death than a little blue spot, the size of a pin's head. Monsieur Velpeau suggests that this method of taking away human life should be used on criminals condemned to public execution instead of the guillotine.

I no sooner read this paragraph than I saw the whole affair in a moment. In two minutes, more I was in Harry Markham's chamber. I found him plunged in the deepest grief.

"My dear friend," said he, holding out his hand, which I did not take; "have you finished your investigations?"

"I have," said I.

"I am very glad to hear it. I suppose you have come to the conclusion that the surgeon was right as to the cause of it?"

"No, I have not."

"Why, what do you mean?" said Markham, turning almost as pale as the corpse up stairs.

"What I mean is, that your wife was murdered!" I replied, looking him sternly in the face.

"Murdered!" he exclaimed, "impossible!"

"It is true," I replied. "Come, Markham, I have got a painful duty to perform, and I must do it. Give me that 'Silver Pin' with which you committed the deed."

I shall never forget the expression of Markham's face when I uttered these words. His features were actually convulsed. It was the most fearful sight I think I ever beheld. I saw him instinctively put his hand on his coat pocket. I knew that I was sure of my man—for he had the instrument with which he committed the deed in that pocket. He appeared to reflect a moment, and then his countenance assumed a calmer expression.

"Brampton," said he, "I see it is no use denying the charge, by extraordinary means you have found out how the deeds were done. I say deeds, because Mr. Percival was killed by the same means. A few words will explain everything to you. You never knew my real character—under a calm exterior and genial manners, I possess the heart of a demon. When I went to Mr. Percival's I immediately fell in love with Ada. Mr. Percival discovered our liaison, and calling me into his study, told me I must leave next morning. That night I killed him by means of a Silver Pin—"

"As recommended by Velpeau," I interrupted.

"Ah! I see now how you have discovered it, but no matter. Ada, of course, knew nothing of the crime. Four months after her father's death I persuaded her to marry me. But, as you know, we lived very unhappily together. My crime preyed on my mind. I took to drink and gaming for pure distraction. At last the breach between my wife and myself grew so wide that we lived entirely separated. All my wife's property was settled on herself by her father's will. I made an effort to be reconciled, and so far succeeded, that she made a will in my favor, in case she should die without leaving children. I then made my preparations to kill her. Two weeks after she had signed the will I concealed myself in her bed-room, and as soon as she was asleep, I drove the fatal pin into the arch of the aorta; and then escaped from the window of the chamber by means of the broken lightning-rod on the roofs of the back buildings. I felt so certain that my crime would not be detected that I courted inquiry, but Man proposes and God disposes. I have nothing more to say. I am determined, however, that I will not suffer an ignominious death—

"And before I could utter a word, he drew from his waistcot pocket, a long and slender silver pin, fixed in a short handle; he placed it against his chest, over his heart, and leaning forward, pressed the handle against the edge of the table. It entered his flesh, and he fell dead to the ground without uttering a single groan.

I summoned assistance immediately, but the vital spark had fled. The whole matter was thoroughly investigated, and the coroner's jury brought in a verdict in accordance with the facts.

Leaf the Second

The Mysterious Advertisement

The nature of my profession brings me in contact with every description of person. I have formed through its agency many pleasant acquaintanceships, to which my memory often reverts with pleasure. Some years ago I became acquainted with a Mr. Norval, a wealthy merchant, who resided in West Fourteenth Street. He was a widower, and the only persons living with him were two in number, a niece and an only son. Mary Norval, his niece, was a beautiful girl, about twenty years of age when I first became acquainted with her. She was tall and gracefully formed. Her hair was a dark brown, and her eyes a heavenly blue, shrouded with long eye-lashes which gave a dreamy expression to her lovely, oval face. Her complexion was as white as the driven snow, and her form was gracefully rounded. Her neck and shoulders might have served for a model to a sculptor, they were so exquisitely chiselled. When she moved it was with that undulating grace so charming in the other sex.

Such was Mary Norval when I first knew her. Had I not been married and possessed of the best wife in the world, she would have been just the woman I would have chosen for a wife, for her natural disposition, the cultivation of her mind, and the amiability of her character fully equalled her physical beauty. She had so won upon her uncle's heart that he loved her better than he did his son. This, however, might be accounted for, from the fact that Charles Norval was a most dissipated young man. He had long ago exhausted his father's affection for him by a dissolute life, and was only permitted by sufferance to be an inmate of his house.

One day Mr. George Norval invited me to dine with him. I accepted the invitation, and we passed a very agreeable hour together at the social meal. After dinner, being something of an invalid, my host excused himself for half an hour while he went to lie down. I amused myself in the meantime examining some illustrated works placed on the drawing-room table. The apartment in which I was seated was only separated from an adjoining one by folding doors. I should have stated that Miss Norval had also excused herself, under the plea of having some letters to write. Left alone to my reflections I fell into a reverie, which I suppose ended in a doze, for I was suddenly awakened to consciousness by the sound of voices in the adjoining apartment. The evening was somewhat advanced, consequently the noises in the street had almost entirely ceased. Owing to this fact I heard distinctly every word that was said. It was Mr. Norval's son Charles's voice that had awakened me.

"Mary, listen to me," he exclaimed, with a peculiar thick utterance which showed that he had been drinking; "You know I love you. Yes, dear girl, I adore the very ground you walk on. Your beauty is so transcendent that you appear more like a fairy creature of the brain than a human being."

"Have done with your senseless compliments, Charles," returned Mary. "Why do you persecute me so? I have already made known my decision to you. It is irrevocable."

"Dear girl, do not say that. O, if you did but know how deeply your image is engraven on my heart! My every thought is for you; every pulse of my heart beats for you—angel—smile on me!"

"Charles, you are intoxicated. How dare you address yourself to me in this manner?'

"Dearest cousin, I adore you, and by Heaven, you shall be mine!"

"I pity your condition, and I beg, sir, you will leave my presence."

"Never, my charming cousin, until you say that you love me. I would sell my soul for one kiss from those ruby lips. I could sit all day and gaze wonderingly into those glorious orbs. Dearest, darling—lovely Mary, be mine, be mine!"

It was evident the young man was working himself into a passionate frenzy.

"Mr. Norval, unless you leave the room I will call for assistance."

"No, you shall not. It is true you have supplanted me in my father's love. It is true he has left you the bulk of his fortune, while he has only bestowed a miserable pittance on me. Not content with having effected all this, you despise my love—but by the great heavens above us you shall be mine."

I could hear the rustling of a silk dress, by which I knew that Mary had risen from her chair, doubtless to ring the bell.

"Mary, you shall not escape me thus," continued the young man. "I repeat it, you shall be mine. Dearest girl, come to my heart—let me fold you to my breast."

A half suppressed scream now reached my ears; and I heard the infatuated young man rush towards her. I thought it was high time to interfere. I ran to the folding doors, threw them wide open, and just saw the inebriate seize the shrinking girl in his grasp. When he saw me, he loosened his hold, a demoniacal expression lighted up his features, and he hurried from the room, shaking his fist in my face as he made his exit. I caught the fainting girl in my arms and conveyed her to a sofa. A few simple restoratives soon brought her to consciousness, but it was some time before I could make her believe that the danger was past.

I thought it my duty to acquaint Mr. Norval with the whole transaction, that proper means might be adopted to prevent a recurrence of this persecution. Charles Norval was forbidden the house.

About a month after this occurrence, business took me to a southern city, where I was detained a week. The very night I returned to New York, I received a visit from Mr. M——, the famous attorney.

"Brampton," said he, when he entered the room, "I have been here to see you a dozen times to-day. Thank God, you have come home at last!"

"Why, what's the matter, Mr. M——?"

"I am in great trouble, and I want you to help me out. You knew Mr. Norval, I believe?"

"Certainly, I know him well—he is a particular friend of mine, but why do you use the past tense?"

"Are you not aware that he is dead?"

"Dead! is it possible?"

"Yes, he died yesterday."

"Is there any suspicion connected with his death?"

"None at all, he has been ailing for some time. He died of disease of the heart. A post-mortem examination has settled that question satisfactorily. You are aware, perhaps, that I was his lawyer; and you also know the terms on which he lived with his son. About three months ago Mr. Norval sent for me to make his will. As I have before said, he had been in failing health for some time past, and did not know how soon he might be called away from this earthly scene; I drew up his will as he requested; by its provisions Mary was made an heiress, a small pension payable at certain intervals being only left to his son. This will was properly signed and attested."

"Excuse me for interrupting you," said I, "but was Mr. Charles Norval cognizant of the provisions of his father's will?"

"Not that I am aware of, but now you come to mention it, I distinctly remember at the time of witnessing it, a sudden rustling was heard at one end of the apartment, and a door opening into an adjoining room was heard to close, but no notice was taken of the circumstance at the time."

"Exactly, that must have been the young man who was listening, for I have reason to know that he was aware of the contents of his father's will."

And I then related the conversation I had overheard between Mary and Charles Norval.

"This may be very important," said M——, as soon as I had concluded; "but let me conclude what I have to say. The will I had drawn up was confided to my care. I placed it in an envelope and locked it up in my private desk. The moment I heard of his death, I opened my desk and took out the envelope in which I had placed the will. Judge of my surprise and horror when I found it contained only a blank sheet of paper!"

"A blank sheet of paper! The will had been abstracted, then?"

"Exactly. When I made the discovery I was completely thunderstruck. I could neither speak nor act. I sank down into a seat utterly prostrated both in body and mind. After a little time I somewhat recovered my faculties, and then began to turn over in my own mind the best course for me to pursue under the circumstances. Fortunately I was alone."

"Do you suspect any one?"

"I don't know whom to suspect. But from the conversation you have related to me, it is very probable that Charles Norval has something to do with it. Still it is utterly impossible that he could have obtained access to my private office and desk."

"How many clerks have you?" I asked.

"I have three clerks, and they all enjoy my most implicit confidence. In the first place none of them knew the will was there. They have been with me many years, and I cannot entertain the slightest suspicion against them. Long intercourse with the world has taught me, however, to be cautious, and I determined to keep my own counsel, so I have not mentioned the fact to them at all. I closed and locked my desk again, and went about my business as usual."

"You did quite right. Did the desk show any evidence of having been looked into?"

"Not the least in the world. Who ever entered it must have possessed a duplicate key."

"And you have discovered no reason to suspect your clerks since?"

"No—when they entered I watched them narrowly, but could not detect any evidence of guilt in their manner. I then determined that I would apply to you, Brampton. I assure you I have eaten nothing since the fatal discovery. The thought that Mary Norval will be reduced to penury is horrible to me."

"Leave the matter in my hands, I will do what I can. If the will is not already destroyed, I trust I shall be able to restore it to you."

M—— took his leave. I then threw myself back in my easy chair and tortured my mind for some means to discover the missing will. I formed half a dozen different plans, but was at a loss to know which to adopt, for the case was involved in much difficulty. While I was thus engaged, my eye fell upon a copy of the *New York Herald* which lay on my desk. I mechanically took it up, without, however, intending to read it. My eyes rested on a column of advertisements. Suddenly they were arrested by the following, under the head of "Personal:"

> "A strong will can overcome overcome ever obstacle. Eight o'clock to-night. Love and joy await you!"

I started from my chair like one bereft of his senses. A sentiment which I can never explain told me that I had found a clue. The mysterious advertisement seemed to me as plain as daylight. "A strong will can overcome every obstacle," evidently referred to the missing document. "Eight o'clock to-night," was the the time appointed for a rendezvous. "Love and joy await you," meant that the place of meeting was to be Lovejoy's hotel.

I was very much pleased with this discovery, for, besides my wish to oblige M——, I really felt great esteem for Mary Norval, while on the other hand I knew her cousin to be a worthless young man. I felt perfectly certain that he was at the bottom of the conspiracy, and that he had in all probability bribed one of M——'s clerks. I almost fancied that I had the will again in my possession, and pictured to myself M——'s joy at recovering it again from my hands. My mind was immediately made up what to do. I determined that I would visit Lovejoy's hotel, and be present at the interview.

I sat watching the clock until the hour should arrive. How slowly the time passed! At last the hand pointed to half-past seven. I rose up, put on my overcoat, and departed on my errand. It was a bitter cold winter's night. The snow was drifting directly in my face, but still I pressed on. I soon reached the hotel and entered one of the private supper rooms. These rooms, as every frequenter of Lovejoy's knows, are divided only by a thin partition from each other, so that a conversation carried on in the adjoining apartments, can, by attentive listeners, be overheard. I ordered my supper, and while pretending to eat it I kept my ears open. Some time passed and no sound reached me. At last I heard the sound of a door shutting, and one person entered the room on my right; a few minutes more elapsed, and again the door shut. The first person had been joined by another. I crept cautiously up to the partition and fixed my ear to it.

"Mr. Norval," exclaimed a voice which I did not recognise, "I am glad to see you."

"And I assure you, Mr. Mills, I am more pleased to see you. I saw your advertisement in to-day's *Herald*, and am here in consequence."

I knew Mr. Mills was M——'s confidential clerk. The other speaker was of course Charles Norval.

"Yes, I worded it as agreed," continued the clerk. "I was almost afraid, however, you might have forgotten it, and feared it would be too obscure. But it was necessary, you know, to blind others' eyes."

"O, yes, I understand all about that. When did you get hold of the precious document?"

"Only yesterday. You know he has left the will in his private desk, and it was only by chance that I obtained the key. The moment I did so, I seized the document, and put in its place a piece of blank paper."

"Do you think he has discovered the loss yet?"

"O, no, I am certain he has not. I have watched him well all day."

"Well, then, now to business," said young Norval. "How much do you want for the will?"

"It is a very valuable paper, Mr. Norval," replied the villainous clerk. "I suppose you know its provisions?"

"O, yes, I overheard M—— read it over after he had drawn it up. I know father has left my cousin Mary everything, while on me, his lawful heir, he has only settled a miserable pension. When that document is burned I will bring her haughty spirit down. She will cringe and fawn on me then. But come, what am I to give you for it?"

"You shall give me your note of hand for $5000, payable when you come into the property."

"Agreed—agreed! Here, I will write it on the spot."

I could hear them arranging some papers on the table. I cautiously left the apartment, and crept noiselessly to the door of the room where this worthy pair were seated. I applied my eye to the key hole and saw that Norval was in the act of writing a promissory note. This done, he handed it to my clerk, who, after examining it, placed it in his pocket-book. He then drew out the will and handed it to Norval. The latter eagerly perused it, a smile of gratification overspreading his features.

"Now," said he, "my fair cousin, Mary, you are in my power—and, by heavens, I will teach you how to love me. So, so, you are a beggar, now! and I am the wealthy Mr. Norval. They say money can buy anything. I will see if it cannot buy your smiles. But I will not marry you, that idea has passed. To the fire, then, I commit the only thing between me and my rightful property."

So saying, he placed his hands on the will in order to cast it into the flames but at that moment I burst into the room and pinned the legal document to the table with my hand. My motion was so rapid that the two conspirators must have thought it was something supernatural.

"Hold!" I exclaimed in a loud voice; "your villainy is not yet perpetrated."

I shall never forget the look of horror revealed on the countenances of the two villains. I quietly folded up the will and transferred it to my pocket. M——'s clerk rushed from the room, and from that day to this I have not seen him. I have heard, however, that he is in Australia. Young Norval was completely crest-fallen, and left my presence without uttering a word. That same night I restored the will to Mr. M——'s possession, and the delight with which he received it was beyond all bounds.

Mary Norval had no difficulty whatever in proving her right to the property, in fact there was no one to dispute it. It was her desire that her cousin should not be prosecuted for the part he had taken in the nefarious transaction. She increased his allowance to double the amount that had been left him by his father. He did not live long, however, to enjoy it, for he died of delirium tremens a year after his father's death. Mary was soon after married to a wealthy Bostonian; I had the pleasure to be at her wedding. She is now the mother of a happy family, and beloved by all who know her in her new home. M—— was so much delighted with my share in the transaction, that he became a staunch friend of mine, and materially increased my business by recommending me to all in want of the services of a detective officer.

Leaf the Third

The Club Foot

One cold January night I was seated cozily by my fireside, enjoying a cup of tea which my wife knows so well how to make, when a violent ring at the front door bell disturbed the reverie in which I was indulging, and made my wife spill the sugar she was in the act of putting into my cup.

"I do hope, James," said my wife, "that this is no one to take you out tonight."

"I hope so too," I returned, "but if it should be, I must obey. Business must be attended to, my dear."

"But it is snowing so fast, and you work so hard."

"Everybody, my dear, has to work hard to obtain a livelihood," I returned, philosophically.

Our conversation was interrupted by the entrance of our servant girl, who stated that a young lady wished to see me on important private business. My wife, who is in no wise of a jealous disposition, discreetly withdrew, and the party wishing to see me was immediately ushered into the parlor. I rose as she entered, and handed her a chair.

My visitor was a very handsome young girl of about eighteen years of age. She was dressed with great taste, and evidently belonged to the upper ranks of life. She appeared somewhat embarrassed, as if she were at a loss how to begin the conversation.

"Have I the pleasure of speaking to Mr. James Brampton?" she said, at last.

"That is my name," I replied.

"You are a private detective officer, are you not?"

"I am, madam."

"O, sir," said she, "I am in great trouble, and I have come to seek your assistance."

"Anything I can do, I am sure I shall be very happy to oblige you," I returned.

"My name, sir," continued the young girl, gaining courage, "is Eliza Milford."

"Milford," said I, "what the daughter of the gentleman who has lately so mysteriously disappeared, with the account of which the papers have been so full for the last few days?"

"The same, and it is on that very business that I have come to consult you. You are perhaps aware that a young man has been arrested on suspicion of having taken his life?"

"Yes, a Mr. Henry Waring, I believe?"

"Yes, sir, that is his name—that young man is innocent."

"Indeed!"

"I will make a plain statement of the facts of the case, and then I am sure you will agree with me. My father's name, as you are aware, is Mr. Herbert Milford. We live on the banks of the North River, about twelve miles from New York. My father was devotedly attached to me, and we lived as happily as possible together. He gratified my every wish, and for years not a single cloud obscured my calm and peaceful existence. About a year ago, I was introduced to the son of a gentleman living in the neighborhood, and mutual love sprang up between us. My father did not oppose our union, and as it was a desirable match on all sides, it was to be settled that we were to be married next spring. Things went on in this way for several months. Henry Waring visited my father's house every night. But suddenly our dream of happiness was dissipated, and that, too, by an extraordinary circumstance. Henry was early one morning found in the garden attached to our house in a half senseless condition, his clothes and hands were covered with blood, and my father had mysteriously disappeared. Every search was made for him, but without avail, and Henry was arrested on the charge of having murdered him and concealed the body somewhere."

"That was a very strange conclusion to come to," said I, interrupting her.

"Yes, but you have not heard all," she replied. "My father's watch and purse were found in Henry's pocket at the time he was arrested."

"How does Mr. Waring account for that?" I asked.

"I don't know," returned Miss Milford, "for I have not been permitted to see him. He has been removed to the county jail, and his case has not yet been investigated, owing to the fact of my father's body not having been discovered. But to suppose that Henry could be guilty of murder and robbery, is too preposterous to be believed for a moment.

"Such would certainly appear to be the case," I returned; "but did the place where Mr. Waring was arrested reveal nothing?"

"O yes, a terrible struggle had evidently taken place there. The flowers and roots were torn up, the shrubbery broken, the ground in various places was covered with blood, and a knife was found which was proved to have belonged to Henry, was also stained with the vital fluid."

"Do I understand that your father imposed no obstacle to your marriage with him?"

"Not at all, sir, in fact my father loved him."

"How long ago is it since your father was missing?"

"This is the fourth day. My motive, Mr. Brampton, in applying to you, is to free Mr. Henry Waring from the imputation of a crime of which I am sure he is as innocent as I am."

"It does indeed seem very improbable that he committed the deed. There appeared to be no possible motive for it. The first thing I must do is to see Mr. Henry Waring, and hear what explanation he has to give."

"Thank you, sir," replied Miss Milford. "When shall I come and see you again?"

"Are you staying in New York?"

"Yes, sir. I am staying with an aunt, at 115 East Broadway."

"Very well, when I have anything to communicate to you I will call."

She then wished me good evening and took her leave. When she had gone I reflected a few minutes on the strange case, for to tell the truth, at first glance, I did not know what to make of it. The whole affair appeared to be involved in mystery. Of course, I did not for a moment suppose that Henry Waring was guilty of Mr. Milford's death. The utter absence of motive, and the fact that he had everything to lose and nothing to gain by the death of the father of his betrothed, satisfied me that he could not be the guilty party. Then the thought naturally arose in my mind was Mr. Milford murdered at all? I passed several hours in these vain conjectures, and was no nearer a conclusion after all.

The next morning I started for the town of L——, situated on the Hudson River railroad, in the prison of which place Mr. Waring was confined. I had some little difficulty in obtaining admission to the prisoner, but when I stated that I was a detective officer, an order was reluctantly given me.

The moment I entered his cell, Mr. Waring advanced to meet me. In a few words I told him of Miss Milford's visit to me, and that I was acting by her instructions.

"The dear girl," he replied, "I knew that she could not think me guilty of this foul crime."

"Mr. Waring," said I, "it is necessary that you should state exactly what occurred to you in reference to yourself. You are aware that suspicion points very directly at you as having committed the deed. You were found on the night Mr. Milford disappeared in the grounds attached to the house. Your clothes were covered with blood. Evidences of a struggle were apparent, and the old gentleman's watch and purse were found in your possession, to say nothing of the concealed knife which was proven to be yours."

"I own the circumstantial evidence appears to be very strong against me," he replied, "and I am afraid my plain unvarnished story will not do much towards disproving it. But the following are the simple facts of the case. On the night in question I visited Mr. Milford's house as usual. I stayed there until eleven o'clock and then took my leave. I was accustomed to return home by the garden at the back of the house, as I saved something in distance by so doing. On the night I refer to, I was about a dozen yards from the back gate when two men started up from behind some bushes, and seized hold of me. Before I had time to defend myself, one of them struck me a violent blow on the head which knocked me down senseless. When I recovered it was daylight, and I must have been there all night. I found my hands and clothes covered with blood, and my knife which I carried for self-defence abstracted from my pocket. I had scarcely risen to my feet when I was seized and accused of having murdered Mr. Milford."

"But how about the watch and purse?"

"I assure you no one was more surprised than myself when they were taken from my pocket."

"How long a time had you parted from Mr. Milford when you were assailed in the garden?"

"Mr. Milford usually retired at ten o'clock, leaving Miss Milford and myself up together."

After a little more conversation with the prisoner, I withdrew, not very well satisfied with the result of my visit. It is true it served to confirm me in the opinion I had formed of Waring's innocence, but I was no nearer discovering the truth than before.

My next proceeding was to make a strict examination of the premises lately occupied by Mr. Milford, and especially the spot where Mr. Waring had been assailed. The house afforded us no clue, but the garden convinced me that the disorder there had been made after the young man had been struck, and that it was not occasioned by any real struggle that had taken place, but to induce the belief that such a struggle had occurred. There was too much regularity in the uprooting of the flowers and roots, and the shrubbery was broken too systematically not to set this point at rest to the eye of the detective.

I discovered that the most minute search had been made for Mr. Milford's body, but without any success. After making these investigations, I returned to New York, and saw but little hope of being able to unravel the mystery.

Three weeks passed away, and I had not discovered one single link in the chain I was seeking to find. One day Miss Milford called on me again. In a few words I told her, that up to the present time my researches had all been fruitless. She looked disappointed.

"Have you heard," she said, "that my uncle, Mr. Oliver Milford, is occupying Linden Manor House?"

"Your uncle occupying Linden Manor House?" I exclaimed, in a tone of the greatest surprise.

"Yes, he appeared there two weeks ago, and claimed all my father's property by virtue of a will which he exhibited, and by which he was made sole heir to all my father's estate."

"Are you sure the will is a genuine one?" I asked, a ray of hope entering my mind.

"There can be no doubt that it was signed by my father," she replied.

"But who is this uncle of yours? I never heard you mention him before."

"I had almost forgotten his existence, for the fact is, my father and he were not on good terms, and his name was scarcely ever mentioned."

"And you are left nothing in this will?"

"Nothing."

"Is it not very strange, Miss Milford, that your father should have left your uncle all his property?"

"It is, indeed, very strange," replied the young lady. "They have not spoken to each other for years. My father could not bear to hear the name of his brother Oliver mentioned, and he always spoke of him as a bad-hearted man."

"And yet you say the signature to the will was in your father's hand-writing?"

"Yes, sir, I am perfectly satisfied of it, so much so, that when urged by some of my friends to contest the validity of the will, being firmly convinced that my father really did sign it, I refused most positively. I care nothing about my father's wealth, and it is not to regain this that I ask your assistance, sir; my simple wish is to obtain Mr. Henry Waring's release."

"Has the will been proved?" I asked.

"O yes," she replied, "my uncle has taken full possession."

"And what have you been doing since?" I asked, more out of curiosity than anything else.

"I have obtained some music pupils, and I am doing very well. I have no concern about myself."

"Have you any letter or document with your father's signature attached to it?"

"I have a number at home," she replied; "by-the-by, I think I have a letter of his with me now, written to me some six years ago, when he was in Albany."

So saying she took from her reticule the letter in question, and handed it to me.

"Will you allow me to retain possession of this?" I asked.

"Certainly," she replied; "but I can assure you that if you suppose the will to be a forgery, you are mistaken. The will is undoubtedly genuine."

"Well, my dear young lady," I returned, "I do not doubt your word, but you may be mistaken. At all events I should like to judge for myself."

I then bade her good morning, and expressed a wish to see her again that day week. When she had gone, I immediately put on my hat and coat, and directed my stops to the Recorder's office, for the purpose of examining the will. Aided by the index I found it readily, and read every word of it.

It was by no means a long document, but went on to state that he, Mr. Herbert Milford, being of sane mind, did thereby bequeath unto his beloved brother all his personal and real estate, etc., etc.

The document appeared to be drawn up in a perfectly legal form, and the most captious special pleader could take no exception to it. At last I came to the signature. I took from my pocket the letter Miss Milford had given me, for the purpose of comparing the signatures. There could be no doubt whatever but the signature was genuine; the letters were formed exactly the same, and were evidently written by the same hand. Still there was a marked difference between the two. That attached to the letter was bold and firm, while that attached to the will was weak and tremulous. The will was witnessed by John Dorsey.

The fact of this difference in the signatures immediately aroused my suspicions. A person's signature rarely differs except when the mind is influenced. But then again I reflected that time might impair a person's writing, and I compared the date of the will with that of the letter. What was my astonishment to find that they were both dated on the same day, namely, January, 1st, 1840. I next held up the document to the light, for the purpose of seeing if their was a water mark on the paper. I found such was the case, and the words, "Connecticut Mills, 1843," could be made out-most distinctly.'

Here was a will purporting to have been signed in New York on the 1st January, 1840, by a man who was in Albany on that very day, and on paper that was made three years afterwards. And yet there could be no disputing the fact that the signature was a genuine one. The whole truth in a moment flashed across my mind, and I immediately set about unravelling the web. I went to work with a good heart, for I had but little doubt of success.

My first proceeding was to make inquiries as to the exact date of Mr. Milford's disappearance. I discovered that it was on the 10th day of January, and that Oliver Milford had come to take possession of the property on the 21st. I also made inquiries as to the past life of the heir of the property, and found that in Boston, from which city he came, he bore a very disreputable character, and that no one would trust or believe him. I then returned to L——, and putting up at the country tavern, I called the landlord to one side.

"Mr. Adams," said I, "do you know any one of the name of Dorsey living in this neighborhood?"

"Yes, sir, there's a Mr. John Dorsey who lives over the river."

"What kind of a man is he?" I asked.

"He's a very tall, strong man," he replied.

"I mean what kind of a character does he bear?"

"Well, I can't say much in his favor, so I would rather not say anything."

"I suppose he is not very much liked by his neighbors?"

"You may well say that. Ever since he attacked poor Mr. Milford so savagely, nobody speaks to him."

"He attacked the late Mr. Milford, did he?"

"Yes, sir, a most unprovoked assault. It seems that Mr. Milford offended this man in some way, and one day there was a sale in town, and Mr. Milford and Dorsey both bid for the same article. It was knocked down to the former, and it was after the sale that the assault was committed."

"Was Dorsey prosecuted for it?"

"Yes, he was imprisoned for a year, and had to pay a heavy fine."

I learned all I wanted to know, and changed the conversation. I now determined I would visit Linden Manor House again. My purpose was to have an interview with the new proprietor, so that I might observe him well, and perhaps gain a few points by my scrutiny.

I soon reached the dwelling, and ringing boldly at the bell, demanded an interview with Mr. Oliver Milford. After some delay I was admitted into his presence. I found him to be a gentlemanly man enough, but with rather a forbidding cast of features. I noticed two things in particular about him; one was that he had a club foot and a restless manner.

"Mr. Milford," said I, "I have been informed that you wished to dispose of Linden Manor House; if that is the case I should like to purchase it."

"Who the deuce told you that?" said Mr. Oliver Milford, an angry flush mounting to his face.

"A friend of mine," I replied.

"He told you a lie, then."

"If I have been misinformed, I apologize," I replied.

Mr. Milford was somewhat mortified, and I bade him good morning. When I left the house I determined to visit the stable, for a reason the reader will discover by-and-by. I found two very fine horses, and the hostler, a good-humored Irishman there.

"Fine horses, there," said I, as I entered the door.

"Sure, an' you may well say that," replied the hostler, proud of my notice.

"You keep them well groomed, too."

"Faith, and it's but little grooming they require."

"I suppose they can travel pretty fast?"

"You've just hit the nail on the head. You should just have seen them the day they came down here from New York. Why, they didn't sweat a hair, and it's a good twelve miles, too."

"Indeed! they did not belong to the late Mr. Milford, then?"

"No, indeed. Sure an' Mr. Oliver Milford brought them down with him when he came."

"They were not at all distressed, you say?"

"Divil a bit! they looked as fresh as if they had just come out of the stable."

"Did Mr. Milford arrive here in the day time or night time?"

"It was dark night."

"I see you come from the old country; here's a quarter to drink my health. Good day."

"Good day, and God bless you, sir—may the holy saints preserve you!"

I made inquiries at the tavern as to the exact spot where the witness of the will lived. I learned that it was across the river on a small island, the whole of which he owned. I procured a boat and rowed directly across—the river was not very broad. I then skirted along the shore until I came to a landing place. After I had proceeded a quarter of a mile, I reached a spot where the marks of horses' feet were plainly to be traced on the snow. It was evident that horses had been embarked at this point on a boat or raft, and had been conveyed to the other side at the point from which I had started.

I made my boat fast and looked about me. I found that the island was small, and so thickly studded with evergreen trees that I could see but very little in advance of me. Taking, however, the horses' hoofs for my guide, I came upon an old dilapidated stone building which had evidently been built long anterior to the revolution. It seemed to be entirely unoccupied.

I walked all round the house, but could not find a living soul visible, but I was rewarded with a sight which made my blood tingle in my veins, for it served to substantiate my theory with respect to clearing up the mystery, and this sight was nothing less than the impression of a club foot many times repeated, near the front entrance of the house, thus showing conclusively that Mr. Oliver Milford was a frequent visitor at Mr. Dorsey's.

I rung the hall bell, but receiving no answer, I opened the door which was unfastened. It was evident that Mr. Dorsey lived by himself, for there was only one room furnished, and that but meagerly. The first thing that I noticed was a candle and box of lucifer matches on the table in the room. Although it was daylight I lighted the candle and began to explore the house. I first of all examined the upper portion of it, but found nothing. I then examined the ground floor with the same success. I did not feel discouraged, for I was almost satisfied from the fact of the candle being there that such would be the result.

I next proceeded to examine the cellar, and had not descended half a dozen steps before I heard a faint groan. I rushed forward, and entered a spacious vault. In a corner of this damp, dark and dismal dungeon, reclining on a heap of straw, with manacles on his wrists and ankles, I saw an old man whom I was satisfied was Mr. Herbert Milford. I held the candle over his head and saw that he was sleeping. At that moment I heard the sound of footsteps behind me, and turning round, saw that it was Mr. Oliver Milford advancing towards me with all the ferocity of a tiger. A terrible struggle ensued, but I was the younger man of the two, and finally succeeded in overpowering him, and in fixing the manacles with which he had loaded his poor brother, on his wrists and feet.

The joy of the poor old man at his release, knew no bounds. In a very few words he informed me of all that had passed. On the night of his disappearance, he was seized by his brother and Dorsey, and conveyed to this prison without being able to give the slight alarm. While there he had been compelled, under threats of instant death, to sign a document, the purport of which he did not know. His brother or Dorsey visited him every day, bringing him a supply of food, but he could not have lasted much longer, as he was fretting weaker and weaker every day.

Everything turned out exactly as I expected. The trembling characters of the signature to the will, and the fact that it had been antedated, convinced me that it had been obtained by force. I then argued that Mr. Herbert Milford was not dead, but in some place of confinement. This place I was satisfied must be near Linden Manor House, as it would be impossible to convey him any long distance without detection. I was also satisfied that Mr. Oliver Milford must have been in the neighborhood long before the time he was supposed to have come from New York, and it was to discover if my opinion were a correct one that I paid a visit to the stable.

The poor old gentleman was conveyed back to his own residence, and was soon gratified by his daughter's presence. Young Waring was immediately released from confinement.

I may add that in a month or two Eliza Milford and Henry Waring were married. Oliver Milford died after four years incarceration in the State Prison, where he had been condemned for life. Dorsey escaped. By some means he learned that his victim had been discovered, and at once started for New York. I need scarcely add that it was Dorsey and Oliver Milford who had made the attack on

Waring, and placed the watch and purse of their prisoner in his pocket, for the purpose of causing him to be suspected of having murdered the old gentleman.

Leaf the Fourth

The Accusing Leaves

It is astonishing what a small circumstance will sometimes serve to detect a criminal. I have known the most simple thing, which in itself seemed so trivial as to be deemed scarcely worthy of notice, in more than one instance, serve to clear up a mystery and bring a criminal to justice. The history I am about to relate is a case in point.

Some six years ago there lived in a good substantial dwelling, about a mile from Hoboken, a gentleman of the name of Palmer. His household consisted of himself, an only daughter, and a servant girl. I became acquainted with Mr. Palmer in a rather curious manner.

I was at the theatre one night, and noticed an old gentleman seated in front of me, who was very vociferous in his applause. This appeared to annoy a young man who sat by his side, and he several times made some disparaging remark at the old man's expense. This at last became so annoying that the latter took it up, and high words ensued between them. At last the young man rose from his seat as if to strike the old gentleman. It was then that I caught sight of his face for the first time, and recognized in him a noted pickpocket. I thought it was now time for me to interfere. I laid my hand gently on the young man's shoulder, he turned sharply round, but the moment he saw me he turned pale, and could not utter a word.

"Don't you think you had better leave the theatre, Emory?" said I.

"Certainly, Mr. Brampton, if you say so," he replied, completely cowed by my presence.

"Go then?" I exclaimed, pointing to the door.

Emory took up his hat and walked out without saying a word. When he was gone the old gentleman introduced himself to me as Mr. Palmer, and thanked me for my interference in his behalf, although he could not understand the power I exercised over his antagonist. This, however, I soon made clear to him by relating to him the nature of my profession, that the occupation followed by the young man who had insulted him.

Mr. Palmer invited me to occupy the seat beside him, and we were soon engaged in a most interesting conversation. I found him to be a very intelligent man, well read, and with an extraordinary knowledge of theatrical matters.

In the course of conversation he told me that he had a fine collection of old plays at home, and invited me to visit him to examine them. This was a temptation I could not resist, and I promised to visit him the following week. When the theatre was over we separated, mutually pleased with each other's society.

The next week I kept my promise, and visited Mr. Palmer at his house. He treated me most hospitably, and introduced me to his daughter, a charming young girl about eighteen years of age. He then took me over his grounds, which were kept with remarkable neatness and order.

"What tree do you call that?" I asked, pointing to one isolated from the rest.

"That is an almond tree," replied my host. "It was planted by my father, and I prize it above all others in the garden."

I never had seen an almond tree before, and examined it attentively. I was particularly struck with the beauty of its leaves. After dinner he led me into his library, and spread before me his fine collection of old plays. I was soon deeply absorbed in Wycherly, Congreve, Dryden and Beaumont and Fletcher. It was quite late when I returned to New York, after promising to renew my visit at an early date.

About a week after this visit I was walking down Broadway, when I met Hardin, a brother officer of mine, with whom I was on terms of intimacy. We stopped and shook hands.

"That was a terrible murder last night," said he, after we had passed a few remarks upon the weather.

"What murder?" I returned. "I have heard nothing of it."

"Is it possible? Are you not aware that Mr. Palmer of Hoboken was found early this morning murdered in his garden?"

"Mr. Palmer!" I cried, in the greatest astonishment. "Impossible!"

"I assure you it is true. News came to the office of the chief-of-police at seven o'clock, and Lewis has been sent over the river to investigate the matter."

"I shall go myself," I returned. "This Mr. Palmer was a friend of mine."

"You will find Lewis there." After a few more words we separated, and I hurried through my business, and by twelve o'clock I was at Mr. Palmer's residence. I met Lewis in the parlor.

"Well, Lewis," said I, "what do you make of it?"

"Did the chief send you here?" was his reply.

My success in the P—— case where he had so signally failed, had rankled in his heart, and he was not on the very best of terms with me.

"No," I returned, "this Mr. Palmer was a friend of mine, and I am not here in a professional capacity at all."

"If you are here only as a friend to the deceased, I don't mind answering your questions. The person who murdered Mr. Palmer is arrested."

"Indeed!" I returned. "I am glad you have been so successful."

"Yes. I think I am legitimately entitled to take great credit to myself for the way I have worked it out."

"Who is the murderer?" I asked.

"Guess."

"I haven't the most remote idea."

"What would you say to Miss Charlotte Palmer?"

"Who?" I exclaimed, not believing my ears. "Miss Charlotte Palmer, the daughter of the deceased?"

"Ridiculous!" I replied.

"Of course, I expected you would say that," replied Lewis. "I tell you what it is Brampton, you think there is nobody as clever as yourself."

"My dear fellow," I returned, in a good natured tone, "rely upon it, you have found a mare's nest."

"You can think as you please, but the proof will be made manifest on the day of trial who is right."

"The idea of Miss Charlotte Palmer murdering her own father is to me so supremely ridiculous, that I cannot entertain it for a moment. But I would be much obliged to you, Lewis, if you would relate to me the particulars of the proofs you have against her."

"Certainly, I have no objection to do that. Mr. Palmer's body was discovered very early this morning under the almond tree in his garden, with his throat cut. The man who discovered the body—a carpenter living in Hoboken—immediately went to the house to give the alarm. He found all the house fastened up, and knocked for sometime without being able to arouse the inmates. He then immediately left for the city, and brought information to the chief's office. I was immediately sent over. I made a strict examination of every thing connected with the case. I soon discovered the strongest proofs that Miss Palmer was the perpetrator of the deed. I traced drops of blood from the front door to her room. When she was awakened her bedroom window was found open, some drops of blood were on the window sill, and underneath her window in the long grass was found the knife with which the deed had been committed. She had evidently thrown it out of the window after committing the deed."

"That is a strange conclusion to arrive at," said I.

"How so?" he returned.

"Why in the name of all that's wonderful should she take the weapon back with her to her bed-chamber after committing the deed?"

"In the excitement of the moment she doubtless forgot she held the knife in her hand, and only found it out when she reached her own chamber."

"But what could be her motive for committing this deed?"

"That I have not discovered yet. I have heard it whispered that Mr. Palmer opposed her marriage to a young man whom she loved."

"Where is Miss Palmer now?" I asked.

"She is in custody, of course."

"But where?"

"In Hoboken."

"Well, Lewis, strong as you think the proofs are against the young lady, I assure you, you have made a mistake. I would stake my life she is innocent."

"You would lose it, Brampton, for she is guilty of this murder as sure as I am standing here. Just examine the proofs yourself, and I am sure you will be of my opinion."

Lewis a few minutes afterwards returned to New York, and left me a clear field for action. Before even I began my examination I was perfectly convinced of Miss Palmer's innocence. Everything was against, it. In the first place I knew that she loved her father devotedly, and under no circumstances could she possibly commit such a deed. A single glance at the wound by which the deceased met his death satisfied me that she had not physical strength enough to have inflicted it. No woman's hand had dealt that blow.

I proceeded to visit the spot where the body had been found. It was in the midst of November, and the ground was strewn with the leaves of the almond tree, for a violent wind had been blowing on the night the deed was committed. There appeared to be no evidence of any struggle having taken place, for with the exception of a pool of blood of considerable size, the place presented its natural appearance.

I inquired which was Miss Palmer's bedroom, and found that the window looked out into the garden where the deed had been committed. That side of the house was covered with a thick grape vine which ascended to the very roof. I examined this grape vine very minutely, and was soon rewarded for my trouble, for I discovered distinct marks of some one having recently clambered up it. On some of the branches the pressure of the foot was plainly to be seen. I came at once to the conclusion that whoever had committed the deed had entered Miss Palmer's apartment by the window, no doubt for the sole purpose of fixing the guilt on her. I then traced the stains of blood which Lewis had considered such a positive proof of the young lady's guilt. To my mind they proved her innocence, for just outside her chamber door they were plentiful and grew less as they descended, until at the front door they were scarcely discernible. If Miss Palmer had been guilty, the exact reverse would have been the case. It was perfectly evident to me that the murderer had descended the stairs from Miss Palmer's chamber, and then ascended them again, and escaped through the window by which he had entered. The fact of the window being found open strengthened the hypothesis.

My next proceeding was to visit the young lady in custody. My profession procured me an order instantly, and I was shown into her presence. I found her naturally in a state of great excitement, but she immediately recognized me and pressed my hand warmly. I commenced the conversation by expressing my firm conviction of her innocence. She could not restrain her tears, but wept bitterly.

"Thank God!" she exclaimed through her sobs, "there is at least one person who believes my innocence. I cannot at present realize the fact that I am accused of murder. I fancy I am suffering from some hideous nightmare. I repeat to myself the question over and over again, 'can it be possible I am arrested for murder, and the murder of my own father?' No, no, it cannot be!"

"Miss Palmer," I returned, "unless we can set aside the evidence, I know not what we must do. To the vulgar mind the evidence is strong against you. Let me hear your statement."

"I have no statement to make. I retired early to bed last night leaving my father up. I slept all night through without waking. In fact I was asleep when the officers of justice entered my room."

"Has your father had any quarrel with any one lately?"

"Not that I am aware of it."

"There is a rumor abroad that your father opposed your marriage with a young man whom you love."

"There is not a word of truth in it, Mr. Brampton—in fact it is exactly the reverse. A young man named Charles Butler has for some time past been persecuting me with his address, but I have always disliked him. His persecution at last became so annoying that I was obliged to appeal to my father for protection. He called to see him, and I have only met the young man once since that time."

"When was that?"

"It is about a week ago. He always used to be loitering about our house. After tea in the evening in question, I left the house to take a short stroll by moonlight. I had scarcely gone a dozen yards when he presented himself before me."

"What passed at that interview?"

"He was extremely violent. He informed me that father had called on him, and forbade him ever addressing me again, but that he would be revenged on both of us. I told him that I despised his threats. He left me in a towering passion, and I have never seen him since."

"The information is of very great importance," I returned.

"You cannot surely think that he could have been guilty of my poor father's murder?"

"There is no telling what a man will not do for revenge. Where does the young man live?"

"He lives about two miles from my father's house. His father was a miller."

"Well, I shall call and see him."

I now took my leave, promising to see her again as soon as I could. I immediately directed my steps to the residence of Mr. Charles Butler, and had strong hopes of being able to obtain some important information from my visit.

In about an hour's time I had reached the dwelling in which the young man's father lived. It was in an old mansion, and beside it was the mill, which stood on the banks of a rapid stream of water. The mill was enclosed by a fence, and the entrance was by means of a stout gate. I tried to open it, but I found that it was secured by a large block of stone being placed on the other side, the lock having been broken. I pushed at the gate for some moments, but found I could not move the stone. I then rattled it violently. This summons brought out an old German, who appeared to be in charge of the building.

"Good morning," said he, when he saw me.

"Good morning," I replied. "Can't you let me in? I want to speak to you about grinding some corn."

"In a minute, mein Herr, you see dat de lock is broken. Mr. Karl, he broke dat mit his foot."

"Mr. Charles broke it with his foot, did he?" I replied, while the old man was moving the stone away; "how was that?"

"Mr. Karl, he came home very late last night, and he found de gate locked, then he kick him open mit his foot."

"Mr. Charles must be a very impatient young gentleman," I observed.

"You may well say dat, mein Herr—he be one wild boy."

"He must have been out late last night," I said.

"Ya, ya, he be come home very late, it be four o'clock in de morning."

"Where had he been?"

"Das weis ich nicht—but he be very pale—like a ghost."

"What time did he go out last night?" I asked.

"He left his home at ten o'clock for I see him go."

This information was very important to me, and I continued to interrogate the old German, but he began to grow suspicious of my questions, and at last declined to answer any more of my interrogations. But I had heard sufficient for my purpose.

"Is Mr. Butler at home?" I asked, of the old man.

"Ya, mein Herr—he and his son be in de house yonder."

"Well, perhaps I had better see them about my business?"

"Mebbe you had," said my German friend, very glad I am sure to get rid of me.

I left the old man and went to the house, and ringing the bell asked to see Mr. Butler on business. After a little delay, I was ushered into a parlor where both father and son were sitting. The former was a fine old man, about sixty years of age, the latter was a young male about two-and-twenty.

He was decidedly handsome, but there was a restlessness about his eyes which immediately struck me. I also noticed that he was very pale. He was in his shirt sleeves, but his coat hung on the back of a chair.

"Mr. Butler," said I, when I entered the room, "could you grind me fifty bushels of corn to-morrow?"

"Certainly," replied the old gentleman, "send it in, and I will do it to your satisfaction."

"Your neighborhood has been the scene of a terrible tragedy," said I.

""Fearful," returned Mr. Butler, senior, "but there can be no doubt but that the unfortunate man's daughter committed the deed."

"The proofs are very strong against her," I returned, glancing at Mr. Charles Butler.

He was very uneasy, and moved restlessly about the room.

"It seems to me very extraordinary that she should have committed this deed," said the old gentleman—"the father and daughter always appeared to me to live on the best of terms together."

She must have had some secret motive for the act—perhaps she was actuated by a feeling of revenge.

As I uttered the last word I fixed my eyes on the young man's face.

He could not stand my gaze. His face assumed a livid hue, and he turned away his head.

"It was a very windy, dark night, just fitted for such a crime," said Mr. Butler, senior.

"I believe it was, but your son can better answer that question, as he was out nearly all night."

"My son out last night—you make a mistake—he went to bed before I did."

"The gentleman is in error," said the young man with a ghastly smile. "I was not out last night."

"You have forgotten," I replied quietly. "You left the house at ten o'clock, and did not return until four in the morning. When you wanted to enter the gate leading to the mill you found it locked. You then knocked the gate with your foot and broke the lock."

"Is this true?" said the father, gazing sternly on his son, who stood trembling in every limb, unable to utter a word.

"Is this true, I ask?" repeated the old man in a more peremptory tone of voice.

The young man made a violent effort over himself, and replied in a broken voice:

"Yes, I believe I was out last night, now I come to think about it."

"It is very strange you should ever forgotten it," returned the old man; "pray what were you doing out last night?"

"I went to Jersey City on business," replied the son, with a determined air.

"To Jersey City on business, in the middle of the night?" repeated the old man in a tone of astonishment and incredulity.

"Your son makes a slight mistake," I observed; "he did not go quite so far as Jersey City."

"What do you mean?" said Mr. Charles Butler, gazing fiercely on me, for he was evidently getting desperate.

"I simply mean that you went no further than Mr. Palmer's," I returned.

The young man staggered, while his father looked at me, with surprise most intensely marked on his face.

"I—I—don't—understand you," stammered Mr. Charles Butler.

"O, yes you do," I returned,"you understand me very well. I may as well tell the truth at once, gentlemen. I am a detective officer, my name is Brampton, and it is my painful duty to arrest Mr. Charles Butler, charged with the willful murder of Mr. Palmer."

"It is a false charge," exclaimed the accused, assuming a kind of bravado.

"Your denials are of no avail, young man," I replied. "The proofs are only too evident against you. Your case is a black one. Not content with taking the life of that poor old man, you must endeavor to fix the guilt on his child. For that purpose you ascended to her window by means of a grapevine, and took the trouble to drop the blood from her chamber to the front door."

"Who is the witness against me?" said the young man, his bravado giving way when he saw that all was known.

"The Almighty," I returned, advancing to the spot where his coat hung on the back of a chair. "Examine the back of your coat. Do you see those two leaves from the almond tree sticking to it? They are fastened there by the blood of your victim. The high wind blew them after you, as you had in all probability turned to leave the spot, and there they are, a damning proof of your guilt."

Charles Butler fell back in a chair, buried his face in his hands, and did not utter a word.

The moment I had entered the room, I had noticed the almond leaves on the back of his coat, and I knew that I stood in the presence of Mr. Palmer's murderer. Mr. Butler senior was utterly overwhelmed by the accusation made against his son. He saw in a moment from the young man's manner, that he was really guilty, and gave way to his feelings by a paroxysm of grief.

I immediately procured assistance, and removed the murderer to prison. He maintained an obstinate silence, but proofs in addition to what I had already discovered were soon forthcoming. A witness was found who had seen him loitering about Mr. Palmer's premises; a dealer in cutlery recognized him as the man who had purchased the knife with which the deed had been committed—in short the evidence of his crime became perfectly overwhelming.

Miss Palmer was at once set at liberty. In due time Charles Butler was tried and convicted. He did not, however, die on the scaffold, for a week before the day fixed for the execution, he was seized with a violent fever which carried him off in three days.

Lewis's chagrin at having made such an egregious mistake can be more easily imagined than described. He was so indignant with me for having "over-reached him," as he called it, that it was some weeks before he would speak to me.

Leaf the Fifth

The Struggle for Life

News was one day brought to the office of the chief-of-police, that the residence of George Templeman, Esq., situated in Union Square, had been burglariously entered and completely sacked of its valuables. A large amount of money had been stolen as well as all the plate and jewelry. The family were out of town at the time, and the house was left in charge of three servants, a footman, housemaid, and cook. They had heard no sounds in the house on the night of the robbery, and were very much surprised to find every room ransacked when they awoke in the morning.

Some policemen were immediately despatched to the spot, and made an examination of the premises, but they discovered no clue to the perpetrators of the robbery. It was then that I was consulted.

I found that an entrance had been effected by the rear of the dwelling, and a single glance was sufficient to tell that it had been the work of experts, in fact, I at once came to the conclusion that it was the work of English burglars.

The gate leading in the yard was studded on the top with sharp spikes, and on one of these spikes I found a piece of cotton handkerchief, with a red ground and blue spots. It was evident that the housebreaker had raised himself up by it, and that it had given way, leaving a portion of it remaining on the spike. This little piece of handkerchief, then, was the only clue I had. I carefully preserved it.

It is a well known fact that the English burglars are the most expert in their calling. An experienced detective can at once recognize their handiwork, and they are generally so careful that they leave nothing behind them by which they can be traced. I could only account for this piece of handkerchief being left behind by the fact that the night on which the robbery was committed was very dark and in all probability the burglar was not aware that his handkerchief had been torn.

My proceeding was plainly to find out to whom the handkerchief belonged, and to effect this, I determined I would visit the haunts always to be found in great cities where criminals congregate together. I disguised myself as well as I could, and plunged into the classic regions of the Five Points. The first place I entered was a wretched low tavern, and calling for a glass of ale and a pipe, I sat down to watch every one who might enter.

I had not been there long when a noted English burglar named Bristol Jem came in, accompanied by a woman. They took a seat some distance from me, and began to converse in a low tone. I kept my eyes fixed upon them without really appearing to notice them. I soon had the satisfaction of seeing Bristol Jem pull a handkerchief from his pocket, which had a red ground covered with blue spots. I felt certain now that I had the robber of Mr. Templeman's house before me; but I knew also it was necessary that I should receive some further proof of his crime in order to convict him, and I waited patiently.

After conversing together in whispers for some time, Bristol Jem and his companion began to quarrel about something. Their tones grew loud and furious, and at last the woman having made some bitter remark, the ruffian struck her on the side of the head, and knocked her senseless on the floor. He then rose up and left the tavern. I immediately ran to the woman, and rising her up succeeded after a little time in bringing her to her senses.

"Where is that villain?" were her first words.

"He is gone," was the reply.

"The scoundrel! I will pay him off for this."

"It was Bristol Jem, was it not?"

"Yes. How dare he strike me when he knows he is in my power?"

"If you want your revenge you can have it now. I am a detective officer. I know that he was concerned in the recent robbery of Mr. Templeman's house, but I want proof against him."

The woman wrung her hands and scarcely seemed to heed what I was saying.

"To think only how I have watched him when he has had his awful fits. Many and many a time he would have been buried alive had it not been for me," said she, as if speaking to herself.

"What do you mean?"

The woman explained to me that her companion was subject to cataleptic attacks, in which condition he appeared exactly as if he were dead, and that several times he has been in great danger of being interred prematurely. This Bristol Jem was a noted character. He was one of the most fearful villains that as yet had escaped justice. He had several times been tried, but had always managed to escape punishment. It would be a great feat for me if I could manage to bring this crime home to him.

"I saw his assault on you," said I, to the woman," and I was disgusted at his infamous behaviour. I am surprised that you should take up with such a miscreant as that."

"Yes, he struck me as he would a dog; but, by heavens, I will have my revenge. I loved him once, but now my love is changed to the bitterest hatred, and before to-morrow dawns, he shall feel the weight of my vengeance."

"You have an opportunity of being revenged at once. Did he not commit the burglary at Mr. Templeman's?"

"He did," returned the girl. "I know all about it, and will put you on the right track, where you can obtain all the evidence you require."

She then entered into full explanations respecting the matter, informing me that a greater portion of the booty had been conveyed to Mother Adams, a noted fence house, and that the rest was concealed in a mattress in his lodgings, which was in a miserable dwelling in Water Street. After a little more conversation we separated. When she was leaving me, she stated her determination never to see him again, and hoped he would meet his deserts.

I immediately procured the assistance of three police officers, and we proceeded to the house in Water Street, which we entered, and found the plate hidden in the mattress, but Bristol Jem had not yet returned. We waited till next morning, and yet he did not come back. I sent one of the men to get some information about him. He soon returned, and stated that he had traced the burglar to the New York and Erie railroad depot, and he had no doubt he had gone off in the early train.

I was very much vexed to think that he had escaped us. But by some means he had received information that we were on his track. I have since thought he must have detected me through my disguise when in the tavern, for I was aware that he knew me well in my professional character. Be that as it may, it was certain he had left New York.

My professional pride was wounded at letting the criminal escape through my fingers. It is true, all the stolen property was discovered, for the remainder was found at Mother Adams. My mind was soon made up what to do. I determined to follow him, and if possible bring him to justice. I had an idea that he had gone to Minnesota, as I knew he had relatives in that State. I arrived there without delay, and there received information that the burglar had visited his relatives, but had left for Davenport, Iowa. To Davenport, accordingly, I directed my steps.

In due time I reached it, and found a long straggling town, not half built up. I need not detain the reader with an account of the search I made. Suffice it to say I was entirely unsuccessful. I believe almost, every town and village in the territory was visited by me. Many times I received descriptions which made me believe that I had at last got on the right track; but perhaps after a journey of a hundred miles, I would find myself as far off the scout as ever.

Two months were wasted in this manner, and I gave up the matter in despair. I must acknowledge I felt considerably crest fallen. It was the first time I had ever been foiled, and I hated to go back again to New York and run the gauntlet of the jeers of my companions, whom my previous success had already made very jealous. But there was no help for it, and one fine morning in August I started on horseback from Dubuque in the direction of Iowa City. I should say that I was habited in the garb of a farmer, which disguise I thought the best for my purpose. I had concealed on my person a revolver and a bowie knife, so that I had no fear from my single antagonist; but I determined to keep out of the way of the numerous Indian bands who were traversing the whole territory.

My road lay through a magnificent prairie, and I travelled for hours through the vast undulating ocean of grass, without a single tree or shrub to be seen, as far as the eye could reach. The day was intensely hot, and both my poor beast and myself began to feel the effects of it. I have no idea how many miles I travelled that day. I had been told on leaving Dubuque that I should reach a tavern after I had proceeded twenty miles on my road. But I was certain that I had ridden more than twenty miles, and no house made its appearance. Nothing but the same unbroken sea of prairie grass as before. I then became conscious that I had lost my way, for the road, from being a well broken track, every hour showed less signs of travel, and by-and-by I found myself floundering in the midst of the long rank grass, without a sign of any human foot having passed that way before.

I am not naturally of a nervous or timid temperament, but it was impossible to shut my eyes to the danger of my situation. The day was now closing, and it was in vain I looked for some sign of human habitation. There was nothing before, behind, on each side of me, but a vast unbroken desert. I stood as it were in the centre of an immense round plain, bounded everywhere by the fiery horizon. To add to my discomfort, I began to suffer horribly from hunger and thirst, and the poor animal I bestrode doubtless suffered from the same cause, for its tongue lolled out of its mouth, and it every now and then uttered a most distressing sound.

The sun sunk slowly beneath the horizon, and intense darkness soon followed. The wind began to rise, which was very grateful after the intense heat of the day. The stars were soon also obscured by clouds, and a distant rumbling presaged a coming storm. At last it came upon us with the most intense fury. The thunder roared and the lightnings flashed, but strange to say it did not rain.

Even in the horrors of my situation, I could not but be struck with the grandeur of the lightning as it descended in distinct blue streaks from the heavens to the earth. At one time it appeared a considerable distance from me. At another time it came directly in front of my horse and for a moment blinded me by the vivid glare.

My situation now was perfectly horrible. I saw no prospect before me but death—and a fearful death, too—death from thirst, hunger and exhaustion. My tongue felt as if it were swollen enormously. My throat was dry and husky, and when I spoke to my horse, I was astonished at the harsh, grating sound of my voice. My head, too, began to grow dizzy, and I could scarcely keep my seat. My faithful horse, however, still continued his course. At the very moment when I had given up everything as lost, we entered a clearing, in the midst of which was a hut. I immediately dismounted, led my horse to the hut and knocked at the door. It proved to be the very tavern I was in search of. My summons was answered by an old woman.

"I want lodging for the night," were the first words I uttered. She invited me in, while her husband took charge of my horse. I found myself in a dreary looking room which was feebly lighted by a single tallow candle. The only thing that looked at all cheerful was a stove, in which the wood burned brightly. The furniture was of the most meagre description, consisting of a deal table and two or three chairs. About ten feet from the stove, and standing about three feet apart, were two trestles on which was placed a flat board. On this board lay something evidently bulky, which was covered over with a white sheet.

After I had had a copious drink of water I felt considerably revived, and asked the old lady if she could give me something to eat. She immediately spread on the table the best that her house afforded, which was not much, but hungry as I was it tasted perfectly delicious. Soon afterwards the tavern-keeper entered, having watered and fed my horse.

"By the way, stranger," said he as he sat down, "are you afraid of a dead man?"

"Afraid of a dead man? What do you mean?"

"I ask you the question because you will have to have one for a companion to-night."

"Indeed!" I replied, glancing at the board placed on the trestles; the something on the top of it I now recognized as a corpse.

"Yes, this is the only room we have to spare. This morning a traveller arrived here, and he was seized with a fit and died. He now lies there waiting for the coroner's inquest. It will meet to-morrow morning."

"I don't suppose a dead man will do me any injury," I replied, "and as I have no option, I must be content to pass the night with him."

We now turned the conversation to other subjects. I found my host to be quite an intelligent man. We discussed the crops, the state of the country, and the future destinies of Iowa. At last he and his wife rose up (the latter had prepared me a bed on the floor) and lighting a candle, left me.

I must confess when I was alone with the corpse I felt an involuntary shiver running through me, which I was ashamed to confess even to myself. The confined, heavy atmosphere of the apartment appeared to exert a depressing influence on my nervous system, and I almost repented that I had not asked the landlord to contrive a bed for me in some other room. I strove, however, against this silly feeling, and reasoned with myself that a dead body was nothing but a collection of gasses. I succeeded at last in dispelling in a measure my uncomfortable feelings.

I threw myself back in my chair, and lighting a cigar, began to puff at it furiously, and tried to persuade myself that I was very comfortable. All at once a sudden desire seized me to go and examine a dead body. I tried to combat it, but it was irresistable. I felt that I must see what my companion was like. The candle had gone out and the fire was very slow, giving but a very feeble light to distinguish his features.

I advanced to the bier and turned down the sheet which covered the body, but there was not a sufficient light to distinguish his features. I could tell however, that it was a strong, powerful man that lay before me. I passed my hand over his face, and its icy coldness sent a chill through my blood. I could also distinguish that his face was very black as if it were congested with blood.

I re-seated myself by the side of the stove with my back to the body, and endeavored to think of something else, but he haunted me still. I almost fancied he was sitting upright on his bier. The supposition, was too hideous, and I moved my chair so as to face the body again. I had forgotten to replace the sheet over him, and the moment I turned round his black congested face met my eye. By a strong effort I rose up and again advanced to the body. I took up the covering which had fallen to the ground, and replaced it over his head; while doing so the peculiar form of his hands arrested my attention. They were exceedingly long and bony, each of his fingers showing that his hands had been endowed with great strength.

I returned to my seat beside the stove and endeavored to think of something else. I remained musing there an indefinite length of time, for I became so much wrapped up in my thoughts that I could not tell whether it had been ten minutes or an hour. At last I thought it was time to go to bed. I threw a couple of fresh logs on the fire, undressed myself and threw myself on the pallet.

I soon fell asleep, but how long I slept I cannot tell, for I was awakened by a dream. I fancied that the corpse came to life again and rose up from the bier. When I awoke the logs of wood I had thrown on the fire were burning brightly, shedding quite a vivid light through the apartment.

I instinctively turned my eyes to where the corpse lay, and fancied that I saw the sheet move. No, it could not be, it was only an hallucination of my senses, and I endeavored to chase away the idea. Again I thought I saw the covering move—there was no mistake about it this time—the fact was plainly visible to my senses. I gazed horror-stricken. The movement in the cover continued. O, heavens! what was it that I saw? One of his long bony hands projecting beyond the sheet, the fingers convulsively opening and closing in the palm of the hand! I was benumbed and could not move hand nor foot, but could only gaze in mute horror at the terrific spectacle.

Slowly the body of the corpse rose to a sitting posture and glared round the room. His horrible features seemed familiar to me. But I did not at first recognize them. In a moment the truth flashed across my mind—it was Bristol Jem, the burglar, that I saw. He had had one of his cataleptic fits, and had been supposed to be dead. He was a powerful man, possessing three times the strength that I did, my clothes in which my weapons were concealed were on the other side of the room. The hideous monster had found me out. When he saw me the devilish smile which crossed his features told me that he had recognized who I was, and he gibbered and glared at me like a maniac. He continued to work his hands convulsively. I remained spell-bound and could not utter a word.

The burglar continued his hideous contortions for some minutes, when, imagine my horror, to see him slowly getting on the board on which he had been placed. Yes, I could see his leg emerge from the sheet. He endeavors to reach the floor—he succeeds. He slowly draws his body after him, and stands erect in the middle of the room. Good God! he approaches me with outstretched hands—he is walking towards me. I utter a cry of horror, and starting up from my bed move away. The burglar follows me, his eyes all the time fixed on me with a basilisk's glare. I endeavor to turn my eyes from him, it is in vain. He still approaches. I dart round the room—he follows me with a horrid laugh. He gains upon me. I can feel his hissing breath on my cheek. His hand is on my shoulder. I sink exhausted to the ground. The demon raises another mocking laugh and clasps my neck with his long bony hand. His grasp tightens—I am suffocating—I am dying! can feel my eyes protruding from their sockets. I can no longer breathe.

At this critical moment I heard a crash followed by a blow, and the grasp was released from my neck. I looked round and saw my host with a thick club in his hand and Bristol Jem extended his full length on the floor.

To bind him securely was but the work of a few minutes. I then entered into full explanation with the tavern keeper. The next morning Bristol Jem was on his way to New York, and in six weeks he was tried and sentenced to the State Prison for life.

Leaf the Six

The Bowie Knife Sheath

My wife possessed a very dear friend named Ellen Braddock. They were school-fellows together, although my wife was considerably the elder of the two. There is quite a romantic episode connected with the life of this young girl, in which I played quite a conspicuous part and which I am about to relate to the reader.

Ellen Braddock's father resided at Athens, just opposite the city of Hudson. He was a very wealthy gentleman, but very proud and aristocratic. It is but right that I should inform the reader that I married considerably above my station, and it was owing to this fact that I could claim acquaintance with Ellen; as for her father I had never seen him, nor do I suppose he would have noticed me even if I had ever been introduced to him; with his daughter, however, it was different, whenever she came to New York, she called to visit us, and spent many hours in our company. She was a charming girl and beloved by all who knew her. One day she called on us, and informed us that she was to embark for South America, where she was going for the benefit of her health.

She sailed in the *Irene*. A twelve-month passed away, and nothing was heard of the vessel. It was supposed that it was lost and that all hands had perished, I need not tell you how deeply affected my wife was to hear the news.

It was about two weeks after all hope of the *Irene* had been given up, that I was down town riding in a buggy, near the Battery, when the wheel of my vehicle came in contact with a hackney coach. There was a considerable shock, and both vehicles stopped. I got out of my buggy, and advanced to the door of the hack for the purpose of apologizing for the accident. I found it occupied by a young lady and gentleman.

"Madam," said I, "I beg to apologize,"—I suddenly stopped and gazed at the young lady very earnestly—"why surely I know that face," I continued; "yes, it is—it must be Ellen Braddock!"

"Why, as I live, it is Mr. Brampton," returned Ellen, holding out her hand. "Allow me to introduce you to Mr. Leonard Bartlett."

I shook the young man cordially by the hand.

"Why what does this mean?" I asked; this is indeed a joyful surprise.".

"It is a long story to tell, Mr. Brampton," replied Ellen; "the first opportunity that occurs, you shall know all."

"Where are you going now?"

"We propose going for the present to the St. Nicholas. To-morrow, I shall start for Athens." returned Ellen; "I shall telegraph, at once to my father to let him know of my safe arrival."

"How overjoyed he will be. Do you know we all gave you up for lost—but I won't detain you any longer now. I shall take the liberty of calling on you at the hotel in an hour or so, and will bring, my wife to see you."

"O do! I shall be delighted to see my dear, dear old school-fellow."

There was another shaking of hands all round and we separated. I hurried home, and in a few words related to my wife the joyful surprise I had met with. Mrs. Brampton was rejoiced at the idea of meeting her old companion, and acting upon my suggestion, at once put on her bonnet and shawl and we started for the hotel.

"We found the young couple seated in one of the drawing rooms. The meeting between the old school-fellows was affectionate in the extreme. Ellen told us a fearful story of shipwreck, privation and danger. It appeared that Leonard Bartlett was first mate of the *Irene*—that the vessel had been lost, and all had perished on board of her excepting the young sailor and the fair passenger. They had at last been driven on a desert island in the Pacific, and had been picked up by an American ship.

"And this gentleman," said Ellen, in conclusion, "is my preserver—to him I owe my life over and over again." While she spoke, I thought she cast on Bartlett a look revealing devoted love.

"I assure you, Mr. Brampton," returned the young man, "Miss Braddock overrates my poor exertions. I consider myself fully as much indebted to her for my preservation; for, had it not been for her courage, her noble heart and hopeful disposition, I should have thrown myself into the sea in despair."

"I can believe all you say of her; she is the same noble-hearted girl she was at school," returned my wife. "Every one was in love with her, from the servants in the kitchen to the professors themselves."

"Hush, you flatterer," replied Ellen, putting her hand before her friend's mouth, "you will make me vain."

And the conversation continued for some hours. I was very favorably impressed with Leonard Bartlett. I found him extremely intelligent, and the discourse became animated in the extreme. Several subjects were started, in which young Bartlett felt himself quite at home and shone to great advantage. The clock struck eleven without our having any idea how rapidly the time had passed. My wife and myself at last rose from our seats, we bade our friends a cordial adieu, and we returned, to our own home.

"Have you much to do to-day?" said my wife, as we sat at breakfast a week after the above interview took place.

"Not a great deal, I shall get through about mid-day. Give me another cup of coffee, my dear. By-the-by, where's the *Herald*? I have not seen it this morning."

"How stupid it is of Mary," returned my wife; "I cannot get her to leave it on the breakfast table."

She rung the bell and the paper was soon forthcoming. I opened it carefully, and glanced first at the leading articles. I then read the congressional intelligence, which, however, did not interest me much. I was still less interested with the proceedings of the state legislature. At last I came to the telegraphic intelligence. I ran my eye half down the column, when the following paragraph met my eyes:

> HORRIBLE MURDER—A terrible murder was committed in Athens last night. Mr. Braddock, a wealthy gentleman was the victim. The murderer is a young man, named Leonard

> Bartlett. He is in custody, and the evidence against him is most conclusive.

"How shocking!"exclaimed my wife, after I had read it aloud to her.

"Bartlett, Bartlett?" said I, trying to recollect where I had heard the name; "why that must be the young man we saw with Ellen. Certainly, it was, I remember his name distinctly now. Is it possible that he can have murdered the old man? Well, I will give up my belief in phisiognomy, for if ever there was a countenance more opposed to any act of violence, it was his."

"Poor Ellen!" exclaimed my wife, "what a fearful trial for her! Do you know, James, it struck me that she was very fond of that young Bartlett."

"I fancied the same thing myself. It is very strange about the murder; I wish they had given some particulars. I have—"

The door here opened, and who should appear but Ellen herself. She had just arrived by the cars. In the midst of sobs and tears she entered into full particulars of the fearful catastrophe. Her information amounted as follows.

She had returned home the day following her arrival in New York. She had related to her father all the obligations she was under to Robert Bartlett. He immediately insisted that the young man should be sent for, that he might thank him personally for saving his daughter's life. Leonard went, and was received with the utmost cordiality by the old gentleman. Leonard Bartlett and Ellen Braddock had not been thrown so long together without the usual result following—they were both deeply in love with each other.

Two days before Ellen's visit to me, the young man ventured to ask Mr. Braddock to give his consent to his marriage with his daughter. To his great surprise he was received with contempt, opprobrium and insult, and although it was night, turned at once out of the house. He left, utterly overwhelmed with despair, he could not leave the premises without having a last interview with Ellen. He took refuge in a barn for the night, hoping to be able to see the young girl the next morning. Mr. Braddock retired to rest, and never rose from his bed alive. That night he was assassinated. The next morning, a servant went up to call his employer as usual, and found there was blood on the handle of the door. She entered the room, and a fearful spectacle met her eyes. Hanging from the bed, the long white hair draggling in a pool of blood, was the dead body of Mr. Braddock. By the position in which he was placed, a hideous gaping wound in his throat plainly showed how he had met his end. He had evidently not struggled much. The bed clothes were very little discomposed, and the furniture in the room was scarcely displaced at all. The murderer, whoever he might be, had undoubtedly taken the old man unawares, and had done his work quickly. It was immediately suggested by some one, that the young man who had had a quarrel with Mr. Braddock the evening before, must have committed the murder. An immediate search of the premises was made, and young Bartlett was discovered in the barn covered with blood, and the knife with which the deed had been committed was found concealed in a truss of hay. The young sailor was immediately arrested, although strongly protesting his innocence.

"Mr. Brampton," said Ellen, in conclusion, "I have come to you as the only friend I have in the world. I am as firmly satisfied that Leonard is innocent as I am that I am now living. I have heard it said that you have extraordinary talent in tracing a matter out. You see exactly how Leonard is situated. Appearances are frightfully against him, but I have a conviction that if you will take the trouble to investigate the matter, you will prove his innocence."

"You say he was discovered covered with blood; how does he account for that?"

"He says his nose bled during the night I am certain, you can prove that he is innocent of this foul crime."

"My dear Ellen," I returned, "I am afraid you rather overrate my power; but rest assured I will do my best to find out the truth, and however strong the circumstantial, evidence may be against him, if he is really innocent—"

"O, Mr. Brampton, I know it I feel that he is innocent," interrupted Ellen.

"I have, no doubt in the world you do, my dear; but unfortunately the jury will require some stronger evidence of his innocence than feeling. I repeat, if he is truly innocent, I have but little doubt we shall be able to prove it."

"How, you re-assure me! What course do you intend to pursue?"

"That will require a little consideration; the first thing to be done is to visit the scene of the sad catastrophe. I think you told me the room where the murder was committed had not been disturbed?"

"With the exception of the removal of my poor father into another apartment, the room has not been touched."

"Well, my child, leave all to me, and with God's blessing, I will yet bring your preserver off scatheless, that is, if he be really innocent. Now, my dear, you had better return home at once. I will visit Athens this evening. Above all things, don't let the servants touch a single article in that fatal chamber."

"I will see that everything shall be observed as you wish," returned Ellen. "O, Mr. Brampton, how can I ever repay you for your great kindness?"

"Nonsense, my dear. Good-by! I must be off, and get my business finished so that I can be free by night."

I shook hands with the young girl, and we separated. I transacted my business, partook of an early tea, and by five o'clock in the evening, I was at the Hudson River depot. In due time I reached my journey's end, and proceeded to the residence of the late Mr. Braddock. I was received by Ellen, and no remark was made on account of my visit, as it was supposed that I had come to attend the funeral.

I proceeded at once to the chamber where the deed had been committed; the first thing that struck me was that it was evident the old man had been taken unawares, for the room showed no evidences of any struggle having taken place. I searched the room very minutely, and found on the floor a small piece of thin paper, apparently very old, on which was inscribed, in a mercantile hand, *"S. V. Barnard, Pres."* This I carefully deposited in my pocket.

I next proceeded to view the body, and noticed the moment I saw it, that the skin round the mouth of the deceased abraded. A few hours afterwards the funeral took place, which I attended. I found myself alone with Ellen when the ceremony was over for the first time since my arrival. The noble-hearted girl looked inquiringly into my face, as if she would read there the result of my investigations.

"You would ask me," said I, "what my opinion is?"

"You have guessed right."

"Well, be of good cheer, the young sailor is not guilty of this murder."

"O, thank you, thank you—but what made you adopt this opinion?"

"I will explain it to you. On the night this murder was committed, no sound was heard to emanate from your father's apartment!"

"None."

"It follows, then, whoever committed the deed must have done it instantaneously to prevent the victim from crying out. He must, at the same time, have placed one hand over the old gentleman's mouth, while with the other he gave the fatal blow. Had he not done this, however deep the wound might have been, it must have elicited a cry. But then in this case we meet with a great difficulty; from the position of the wound, no one man could possibly have done this. And yet it is evident that a hand was placed over the mouth, for the marks of the fingers were still to be traced on the face of the deceased when I saw it. My theory is, that two persons were concerned in this murder."

"Two! Can it be possible?"

"Had but one person committed the deed, the wound must have taken a different direction, and the bed would have been saturated with blood. Such, however, was not the case; the blood was on the floor, and the sheets were unstained. I can tell exactly how the deed was committed, but I am afraid to shock you by repeating it."

"O, Mr. Brampton," replied Ellen; "I have undergone enough to bear anything now. Do tell me if it will exonerate Leonard in any way."

"Well, my dear Ellen, the manner was simply this: Two persons entered your father's chamber while he was fast asleep. One of them immediately placed his hand over the victim's mouth, and dragged him half out of the bed. The other inflicted the fatal wound."

"But, Mr. Brampton, what motive could they have? The house was not robbed."

"Has your father no enemies?"

"No one that I know of, except Captain Larkin."

"Captain Larkin who is he?"

"He lives two miles from here. He was captain of a privateer in the war of 1812. My father and he have a very important law-suit pending about some property. They never spoke to each other for months, but lately they have been more friendly, and on the very evening before the murder, the captain paid my father a visit."

"This may be important, I will just make a note of it," I returned, entering the information I had just received in my note-book. "With respect to Leonard Bartlett, he was certainly watched. He must have been seen to retire to the barn. After the murder was committed, one of the murderers must have stealthily entered the barn, and hid the knife among the hay in so careless a manner that it might easily be found. What made me first suspect that young Bartlett could not be the murderer, was that the proofs of his guilt were too glaring. A man must be mad who would commit a crime and then quietly retire to an outhouse on the premises of his victim, and conceal the evidence of his guilt, bloody as it was, in a truss of hay, and in such a manner that it might be detected by the first person who entered."

"True, true, this never struck me before."

"I know more—one of the murderers wore a ring on the middle finger of his right hand, and one of them paid a sum of money to the other after the deed was committed."

"How can you possibly know this?"

"The mark of the ring was distinctly visible near the mouth of the deceased, and while searching the room, I found this little piece of paper," I replied, taking from my vest pocket the piece before referred to. "You see it has the name "*S. V. Barnard, Pres.*" written on it. Now, it so happens, that I know this Mr. Barnard. He is president of the Bank of America. This scrap of paper is a portion of a bank bill, which must have been accidentally torn off while being passed from one to the other."

"But how do you know it was given after the deed was committed?"

'From the simple fact, that there is a slight stain of blood on it, as you see."

Ellen shuddered, but recovered herself immediately.

"Have you discovered who are the guilty parties?" she asked.

"I have my suspicions as to one of them, but no proof at present. In spite of all I have told you, unless I can bring home the crime to some one else, it will go hard with the young sailor. You must excuse me, Ellen, for the present. I must devote every minute of my spare time before the trial searching for proof. I must see the prisoner, visit some one in the neighborhood, and then return to New York. You may expect to see me again in a few days at farthest."

So saying, I hurried from the house. I was very quick in my movements, and in a very short space of time I had procured an order for admission to the prisoner, and was alone with him. We conversed together for half an hour, and although in the interview I did not gain any more proofs, it confirmed my previous opinion. I parted with young Bartlett after having infused hopes and comfort in his heart, but without letting him know my suspicions.

When I left the prison in Hudson, I re-crossed the river, and directed my steps to the residence of Captain Larkin. I soon arrived there, and giving my name to a servant, I was shown into the parlor. In a few minutes I was ushered into his bed-room, for he had had an attack of the gout the day before, and could not leave his chamber. I found Captain Larkin to be a man about sixty years of age, very hale and hearty looking, but evidently very fond of the good things of life.

"Captain," said I, as I entered, "I am a detective officer from New York, and have come down here to make inquiries concerning this recent murder. I thought perhaps you could give me some information about it."

"What information can I give you?" growled the captain.

"Did you not visit the deceased on the evening of the day he was murdered?"

"I did."

"What passed at that interview?"

"Nothing particular. Mr. Braddock informed me that he had had a row with a young man named Bartlett, and had turned him out of doors."

"That is very important testimony," I replied; "for it proves a motive for the deed on the part of the prisoner."

"They tell me the proof is perfectly overwhelming against him," said the captain, with something like exultation in his voice.

"Beyond all cavil," I replied, glancing furtively, round the apartment. My eyes rested on the sheath of a bowie-knife which lay on the bureau. There was no weapon in it."

"When is the murderer to be tried?" he asked, carelessly.

"The court opens in about four or five days," I returned, "I suppose he will be tried then."

"Shall I be summoned as a witness?"

"I should suppose so," I returned, "as I before said, your evidence is most important."

I had now got all the information I required, and rose to go. My hat was placed on the bureau near the empty sheath. I picked up my hat, and while addressing some remarks to Captain Larkin, put it down again, taking care, however, to bring the sheath next to me, my hat being between it and the man I suspected. By this means I managed to pick up the sheath and convey it to my pocket without being seen.

I then took my leave, shaking hands with Larkin. I noticed particularly at this moment, that the latter wore a plain gold ring on the middle finger of his right hand.

I again crossed over to Hudson, and easily obtained permission to examine the knife with which the deed had been committed. As I suspected, I found it fitted exactly into the empty sheath which I had abstracted from Captain Larkin's residence. I immediately bent my steps to the railway depot. I congratulated myself on my good fortune, for I felt certain I had discovered one of the murderers; at the same time I was fully aware that unless I could discover the other, the case would not be complete.

The next day, as soon as I had breakfasted, I proceeded immediately to the Bank of America, situated in Wall Street. The bank had just opened.

"Is the president in?" I asked of the cashier, whom I knew quite well.

"You will find him in his private room," replied the officer; "you know the way."

"Yes, thank you," I returned, and walked straight up to the door and knocked, and was told to "come in."

"How-are you, Mr. Barnard?" said I, shaking hands with a fine gray-headed old man.

"How are you, Brampton?" returned the president. "I suppose you want to make another investment?"

"Not exactly," I returned, laughing; "I don't make my money quite so fast; my business is of a very different description. I wish to know, in the first place, if within the last day or two, you have had a note presented at your bank for payment, with the name torn off?"

"I will inquire; but why do you ask?" asked the banker, looking very much surprised.

"Give me the information first, and then I will explain everything."

The bank president left the room, and returned again in a minute or two.

"There has been no such bill paid," said he, as he entered the room.

"I am rejoiced to hear it," I returned, taking from my vest pocket the scrap of paper I had picked up in the bed-chamber of the murdered man.

"Do you recognize that writing?" I asked, giving it to Mr. Barnard.

"Certainly, it is my signature, and by two dots at the end, I know it was originally attached to a hundred dollar bill."

"Well, then, the man who possesses the other portion of this bill is the murderer of Mr. Braddock, the account of which you must have read in the papers; he will present the bill for payment soon. I want you to detain him when he does so, and send for me."

"I will do so willingly—but explain?"

I entered into full explanation of all matters connected with the murder, and my own suspicions, cautioning him, however, to be secret. When I had finished, I left the bank and returned home.

Three days elapsed, and I received no communication from the banker. But I was not idle during this time. In the first place, I obtained the very best counsel I could procure in New York. The fourth day dawned and I began to grow nervous. I could find no trace of the party I was seeking, and young Bartlett's trial was to begin next day. About eleven o'clock, however, I received the following note:

> Bank of America, Wall Street. December, 18— .
>
> Dear Sir—The note has just been presented. We have the man in custody. Come at once. Yours truly,
>
> S. V. Barnard.

I jumped into a carriage, and was whirled at a rapid pace down Broadway to Wall Street. I entered the bank, and was at once shown into the private room, where I found the man seated who had presented the note, and two policemen in plain clothes on each side of him. He was a rough-looking man, who had evidently been a sailor. He said his name was Martin. The man looked dogged and determined. His features were contracted into a scowl, and he seemed angry at being detained.

"What am I here for, I should like to know?" he exclaimed, in a gruff voice "I'll make you smart for this, I can tell you—you'll just see if I won't bring an action against you for false imprisonment, that's all."

The policeman made no reply, but handed me the note which the man had presented for payment. I examined it closely and found a small portion at the bottom of it had been torn off. The portion I had found in the murdered man's chamber exactly supplied the deficiency. Martin watched me scrutinizing the note.

"Is the bill a bad one?" said the ruffian. "Perhaps that's what you are keeping me for; if so, I can tell you who gave it to me."

"We know that already," said I carelessly.

"Come now, that's a whopper! I dare bet you what you like, you can't tell me who gave me that note."

"To show you that we know more than you suspect," I returned, "I will tell you that Captain Larkin of Athens gave you that $100 bill."

Martin turned pale, and seemed uneasy for a minute or two—but he recovered himself.

"Come that's a good guess," he replied, with bravado. "Perhaps you would like to know what he gave it me for?"

"We do know," I replied, quietly.

"How-—what?" stammered Martin.

"I repeat, we know that he gave you it for assisting him to murder Mr. Braddock. Ah, you start! To show you how much we know, I will detail to you how you did the deed. In the first place he provided the knife—you both managed to get into the house without being heard. You entered Mr Braddock's bedroom; Larkin seized the unfortunate old man, and placed his hand over the mouth of your victim, while you committed the deed. Captain Larkin, then and there, with the bloody corpse of your victim looking you full in the face, paid you a portion of the wages of your crime, in shape of this hundred dollar bill which I hold in my hand. You then proceeded with cautious steps into the barn where you had previously seen Leonard Bartlett enter. You entered without awakening him, and thrust the bloody instrument with which you had committed the crime into a truss of hay in such a manner that it might easily be discovered; and now, John Martin, I arrest you for the wilful murder of Mr. Braddock."

As I proceeded to describe the manner in which the deed was committed, a fearful change came over the ruffian's face. He turned as pale as death, and when I had concluded he fell back in his seat apparently deprived of consciousness. In a few minutes he recovered a little.

"I will deny nothing—I will confess all," replied Martin, completely cowed. "I acknowledge I did the deed, but it was at the instigation of Captain Larkin. Answer me one question, has he confessed?"

I paused a moment before replying, at the same time scrutinizing Martin very closely, as if I would read his very soul. I saw that the villian's eyes were gleaming with unconquerable hate, and I immediately made up my mind what course to pursue.

"He has not," I replied; "nor does he even know that his crime is discovered."

A gleam of satisfaction shot through Martin's eyes.

"Then how did you find out all the particulars?" he asked.

"Never mind how we found them out, suffice it to say that we know all."

"I see you do. Then Captain Larkin has no suspicion that all is discovered?"

"None in the world."

"Then lead me to a magistrate that I may make a full confession—and if I can only hang that wretch, I will die willingly myself."

This was exactly what I wanted, and I lost no time in acting on the suggestion. We all adjourned to the nearest magistrate's office where Martin made a full confession which was duly signed and witnessed.

From it, it appeared that Larkin had Martin in his power, from the fact that years before the latter had forged his name to a note. The law-suit, the loss of which would be the yielding up of nearly all Captain Larkin's estate, would undoubtedly have been decided against him, if Mr. Braddock were not disposed of before the day of trial. Larkin, who scrupled at no crime, made the desperate resolve to kill him, and sent for Martin to do the deed for him. He determined, however, before proceeding to the last extremity, to pay a visit to his intended victim, and see if he could by any means effect a compromise with his opponent. He found, however, that Mr. Braddock was too much excited to enter on any business matter, he having just turned young Bartlett out of his house. When Larkin returned home he found Martin waiting for him; he proposed at once that the latter should murder the old gentleman, and throw the guilt on the young sailor. He promised to give Martin $500 in five monthly payments of $100 each. The sailor would not consent unless Larkin would himself assist in the murder. This, after some hesitation, the captain consented to do, and they both of them went to Mr. Braddock's house. It was yet too early for the accomplishment of their purpose, and they waited and watched. While lying in ambush, they saw the young sailor enter the barn, and immediately surmised that he had taken refuge there for the night. They then waited until all the house had retired, and then committed the deed exactly in the method I had traced out.

After Martin had made this confession he was conveyed to the Tombs. Armed with this confession, I immediately left for Hudson. I had it in my power to stay the trial, but I determined to allow it to proceed to a certain point. That same night I was closeted until a late hour with the young sailor's counsel.

The town of Hudson was in a state of great excitement, on the morning of the trial of Leonard Bartlett, for the wilful murder of Mr. Braddock. Not that any one had any doubt about the matter, for the whole community looked on Leonard's guilt as certain. But the wealth of the victim, the youth of the offender, and the supposed motives which had caused him to commit the act, had all made a deep public impression, and at an early hour the courtroom was crowded to excess.

As to Leonard himself, he saw the time for his trial approach with something like apathy. He was entirely ignorant as to the defence to be adopted, but he felt strong in his own innocence, and calmly waited until that innocence should be made manifest. For public opinion he did not care one groat. He knew that Ellen believed him guiltless, and that was sufficient for him.

Ellen Braddock was more nervous and anxious than any one else. I had not told her my discovery, but in order to assuage her fears, I had hinted very strongly that the young man would be acquitted. Still there appeared to be some doubt about the matter, and until that was satisfied, she felt considerable anxiety. At last, the court was opened, and the prisoner's counsel declared he was quite ready for trial. The prosecution was conducted by two lawyers of eminence, and one of them immediately opened the case.

He spoke in a calm, dispassionate manner; disclaiming all oratory, he gave a plain statement of what he expected to be able to prove. He traced the prisoner from his first entrance into the house. He dwelt particularly on the quarrel, and the words which the young man had been heard to utter. He then gave a vivid description of the finding of the body, and the tracing to the place where the prisoner had secreted himself. He managed the speech in such a manner, that he left the motive to be implied rather than distinctly stated.

When he had concluded, a murmur ran through the court. The jury looked convinced already, and everybody wondered what possible defence could be made against so plain a case. Leonard himself was astonished at the fearful array of circumstantial evidence against him, and glanced at his counsel as if he would read from the expression of their faces whether there was any hope for him. But he could learn nothing from them; they looked grave, but perfectly impassable. As for Ellen, when she heard the counsel's opening address, her heart sunk within her, and she gazed in mute despair on her lover.

The first witness called was Bridget Murphy. She deposed that she was a domestic, in the employment of the late Mr. Braddock; that on the evening of the day of the murder she carried candles into Mr. Braddock's study, and at the moment she opened the door, she heard the prisoner at the bar exclaim in a loud and excited voice, "Mark my words, sir, as sure as you now live, you will repent your conduct." She also deposed that as he left the room, he repeated, "You will bitterly repent this infamous proceeding."

When the counsel for the prosecution had obtained the foregoing evidence, he sat down, expecting that his witness would have to undergo a severe cross-examination; but, to his great surprise, the counsel for the defence declined to cross examine.

Several witnesses were now called one after another, who deposed to the finding of the body, and the knife with which the deed had been committed, and the tracing of the blood to the barn where the prisoner was discovered asleep. To the supreme astonishment of all present, the prisoner's counsel did not put a single question to any of these witnesses.

The curiosity of the counsel for the prosecution became very great, to know what line of defence they would adopt; they almost imagined they had given up all idea of defence at all.

When the constable who had made the arrest deposed to a speech made by the prisoner, in which he asked, before anything about a murder having been committed was mentioned, "if they meant to accuse him of having committed murder?" the judge threw down his pen as if it were useless to go on further.

"Have you any more witnesses for the prosecution?" asked the judge, of the prosecuting attorney.

"One more, your honor," replied the lawyer.

"Is it necessary to call him?" returned the judge. "I do not see how you can make your case stronger."

"We purpose to show by him, the motive the prisoner had in committing the murder."

"Well, as you like."

"Call Captain Larkin," said the attorney, to the clerk of the court.

The name was called, and there was a profound silence in the court. The name, position and wealth of the witness had raised everybody's curiosity. The name was called a second time; a slight movement became perceptible in the body of the court, and Captain Larkin slipped into the witness box. He looked rather pale, but appeared perfectly self-possessed.

"Your name, I believe, is Robert Larkin?" said the prosecuting attorney.

"It is."

"Where do you live?"

"Near Athens, about two miles from the residence of the deceased."

"Did you pay a visit to the deceased, on the day that he was murdered?"

"I did."

"Relate what passed at that interview."

"He told me that the prisoner had the audacity to ask him for his daughter's hand, and that they had a violent quarrel, and that he had dismissed him from the house."

"That will do, sir, you may stand down," said the counsel for the prosecution.

"Stop, sir!" said the counsel for the defence, rising for the first time. "I have a few questions to ask you."

An expression of surprise ran through the whole court, in which even the judge participated. It seemed so strange, that the counsel for the defence should fix upon such an unimportant witness to cross-examine, when they had not put a single question to any of the others.

"Captain Larkin," said young Bartlett's lawyer, "will you please to tell the court and jury the motive of your visit to Mr. Braddock on that day?"

"I went to see him about a lawsuit in which we were concerned."

"You were opposed to each other in this lawsuit were you not?"

"Yes."

"The case was to come up for trial immediately, was it not?"

"Yes."

"Mr. Braddock's death will put an end to the suit, will it not?";

"I refuse to answer impertinent questions, and appeal to the court to support me," replied the witness.

"This examination appears to me to be quite foreign to the issue" said the judge; "and the witness is at liberty to answer the question or not as he thinks fit."

"Well, it is not material. I have another question to ask, however, which I insist on being answered. Do you know a man of the name of Martin?"

Captain Larkin grew pale and livid.

"I decline to answer the question," he stammered at last.

"I insist on an answer, it is material to the defence."

"What do you expect to prove by it?" asked the judge.

"I expect to be able to prove," said the lawyer, in a loud voice, that the prisoner is the victim of a base conspiracy, and finally, I expect to be able to fix this crime on the guilty parties."

The most intense excitement ran through the court. No one had the least idea what was to come.

"You had better answer the question," said the judge.

"I do know a man named Martin," replied Larkin.

"Did not this man, Martin, visit you at your house on the day of the murder? And did you not there and then make him a pecuniary offer, to do a certain piece of business for you?"

"I decline answering any of these questions," said Captain Larkin, who was now pale and gasping.

"The court must support the witness in this case," said the judge; "the witness is not bound to criminate himself, and the court further observes that he cannot see what all this has to do with the matter in question. Even supposing all this to be true, it does not exonerate the prisoner at the bar from having committed the murder."

"Of course, I submit with deference to the opinion of the court, and will leave this part of the subject. I will now ask the witness one or two more questions, and then I have done. "Does this sheath belong to you?" continued the lawyer, holding up the sheath I had abstracted.

The willy villain gazed on the evidence of his guilt with a fixed glare. His face assumed a greenish hue; he saw himself hemmed in and vainly tried to extricate himself. He gasped, but no sounds issued from his lips.

"I will not detain the court longer by an examination of this witness," said the attorney for the defence. "I beg to hand in a confession made by one John Martin, and duly attested, in which the said John Martin confesses he is the murderer of Mr. Braddock, aided and abetted by Captain Larkin!"

The witness no sooner heard this, than he uttered a loud groan, and fell into the witness box insensible. A scene of indescribable confusion followed, in the midst of which the judge directed the jury to return a verdict of "not guilty," which was at once done.

The same moment that Leonard Bartlett left the felon's dock, Captain Larkin was conveyed into a felon's cell.

I shall not attempt to describe Ellen's joy at the release of her lover. Leonard at that moment was the happiest man in tho world—all his troubles had melted into the air, for he was the accepted lover of the noblest, the best and the most courageous girl in the United States—at least, that was his opinion.

Captain Larkin was in due time brought to trial, condemned and executed. Martin was imprisoned in the State Prison for life. A year afterwards, my wife and myself received an invitation to attend the marriage ceremony of Leonard Bartlett and Ellen Braddock.

Leaf the Seventh

THE NIGHT OF PERIL

Of course it is to be expected that in a life like mine I should often be exposed to danger of a personal character; it is the lot of all detective officers, and I have been no exception to the rule. In the course of my life I have been subjected several times to extreme peril. In the following pages I am about to give an instance of such peril to the reader.

One day I was sent for by the president of the Bank of Commerce. When I arrived there I found the whole bank in a state of consternation. The safe had been broken into during the night, and all the specie abstracted. I immediately proceeded to examine the safe, and found that the locks had been forced; but a single glance was sufficient to show me that it had been forced after it had been opened, or in other words, that whoever had taken the money had wished to convey the impression that it had been forced open from the outside. Of course I came at once to the conclusion that some one connected with the establishment had taken the money. While examining the spot, I found on the ground a single leaf of a white Provence rose. It is the observation of small things that makes a good detective, for it is often the most trivial circumstance which supplies the first link in the chain. I did not pick up this rose-leaf, nor indeed appear to notice it. After the scrutiny was over, I went to the president's, Mr. Cameron, apartment.

"Well, Brampton," said he, "what do you make out of it?"

"Do you suspect anybody connected with the bank?" I asked.

"Certainly not? It is impossible that any body connected with the bank could have committed the robbery; it must have been the work of burglars. Did you visit the cellar where the robbers entered?"

"Yes, and found that the bars had been filed from the inside."

"Indeed!—but what do you make out about the safe?"

"That the lock was forced after the safe was opened."

"What do you infer from that?"

""That some one connected with the bank is guilty of the robbery; and he has endeavored to make it appear that it is the work of professional burglars. But he has done his work very bunglingly."

"You must be mistaken," replied the president. "I would answer for all in the employ of the bank with my life."

"I am afraid you would lose it," I replied, with a smile, "for there can be no doubt about the truth of my assertion."

"But how will you prove it?"'

"That remains to be seen. How many have you in the employ of the bank?"

"Twelve, including the porter."

"Who has care of the safe?"

"Mr. Charles Munsel."

"Have any of your clerks a special fondness for flowers?"

"That is a strange question. But since you ask it, I remember that Munsel generally has a flower in his buttonhole."

"Who is this Munsel?'

"A very worthy young man. You surely do not suspect him?"

"I shall be very much surprised if he does not prove to be the robber."

"You astonish me! He has the reputation of being very pious."

"Well, we shall see. Where does he live?"

"No.— East Broadway."

" What time does he go to dinner?"

"At two o'clock."

"Just point him out to me as I go through the bank, and I will see you again to-morrow morning."

Mr. Cameron did as I requested. The young man I suspected was about twenty-five years of age. He was quite handsome; it might have been my fancy, but I thought there was a hypocritical look about his face. I glanced earnestly at him, so that I might engrave his countenance in my memory, and then passed into the street.

I directed my steps at once to East Broadway, and calling at the clerk's residence I found that it was furnished in gorgeous style, far beyond his means. The door was opened by a shrewd old woman. I asked to see Mr. Munsel but was of course told that he was not at home. But my purpose was answered by my visit, for in the hall, I saw a quantity of choice flowers in pots, and among them a fine Provence rose. I employed the rest of the day in making inquiries as to the private life of Mr. Munsel, and found that he was very extravagant in his habits, and also discovered that on that very day he had deposited a large sum of money under a false name in the Manhattan Savings Bank. The next morning I went to the bank for the purpose of reporting progress to the president, and to advise the immediate arrest of young Munsel.

"Well, you were right about that young man," said Mr. Cameron to me, the moment I entered his private room.

"You have come to that conclusion, have you?" I replied.

"Yes; after you had gone yesterday, I caused his accounts to be examined, and found a terrible deficit, amounting to $30,000. I called him into the room, and asked for an explanation—"

"The worst thing you could have done," I interrupted.

"You are right—he has escaped."

"I expected as much. Where has he gone?"

"He left last night by the Southern train—at least, so we suspect. He has an uncle living about fifteen miles from Augusta, Georgia, and it is very likely he has gone there. Now, Brampton, you must follow him."

"If you had left the matter in my hands, he should have been arrested without any trouble."

"I acknowledge I am in fault, and I am the more anxious to have him captured. Come, I will pay you well. Say you will go."

It was the middle of summer, decidedly not the best time to travel in. But the affair was imperative, and I was obliged to undertake the journey. That same afternoon at five o'clock I had started on my expedition.

Railway travelling in July! Who is there that has experienced it that does not vividly remember its discomforts. The hot glaring sun, the dust, the intolerable thirst, and the warm water in the coolers, are all evils of such magnitude, that they make an indelible impression on the mind. Why, at the very thought of it at this moment, my throat feels choked up, and I feel the pricking of the flinty dust in my skin. And then the view from the car window; how hot and glaring everything looks. The poor cows are panting in the meadows, the dogs at the stations appear to be on the verge of hydrophobia, everybody and everything is lazy, excepting the flies; and it appears to be their particular province to keep passengers from dozing, so that they (the passengers) may not lose any of the beauties of the scenery.

The longest journey must eventually come to an end, and after three days really hard work, I reached the pleasing town of Augusta, in Georgia. I was, however, in a very bad humor. I was annoyed at the banker's want of thought in allowing his dishonest clerk to escape. Now, when a man is in a bad humor with a journey he is obliged to take, he is very apt to consider the town at which he is compelled to stay as the most odious place in the world. I was no exception to this general rule. I hated Augusta, I detested it, I abominated it, I—but I cannot just now think of any other word to express my abhorrence of that unoffending Southern city. I went to the best hotel in the place, and entered my name in the most savage manner, actually blotting the book in the act, much to the disgust of a precise looking clerk, who stood looking at me while I made the entry.

At last I partook of supper, and I must confess after that genial meal "a change came over the spirit of my dream." After all, Augusta was not such a very bad place. I actually began to think that it possessed some fine streets and elegant houses. A cup of tea will sometimes work a marvel. I determined I would go and explore the city till bedtime, and make inquiry after the absconding bank-robber.

This young man's fondness for flowers seemed to be the greatest misfortune that could befall him. I have mentioned that a single bud remained on the rosebush in his hall. During my investigations this bud had blossomed. When he absconded from New York he took this flower with him. By means of it I had no difficulty in tracing him to Augusta. There was something peculiar about the rose; it was a large white one, and fortunately attracted the attention of all the conductors on the route. My business now was to visit all the hotels in the city, to see if he had been there the very first one I entered immediately settled the question in my mind that Munsel had left Augusta, and this, too, before I made a single inquiry.

I entered the bar-room, and the first thing I noticed was a faded Provence rose on a chair. On the back of this chair was a newspaper. I took it up, and my eyes at once fell on a paragraph containing an account of the bank robbery in New York; but I was immediately struck with the fact that where the person of the defaulter was described the paper was mutilated, seemingly accidentally, but sufficiently so as to mar the description. This paper was the *New York Herald*, and from its date I knew it had only been delivered in Augusta that morning. I walked up to the bar and called for something to drink. While the barkeeper was preparing it, I said to him, carelessly:

"There was a young man here this morning with very black hair and dark eyes; he was of medium height, but stooped a little."

"I suppose you saw him here," replied the bar-keeper. "He did not stay long, however, but left with Mr. Theodore Munsel of Parkville."

"You know Mr. Theodore Munsel, then?"

"Yes, indeed."

"What sort of a man is he?"

"A very rough customer."

"How do you mean rough?"

"He's been tried for his life twice, but managed to escape."

"You say he lives at Parkville?"

"No, that's the post town; but he lives in the woods five miles from the village."

"How can I get there?"

"You had better drive to Parkville, which is twelve miles off, and then inquire your way—his house is rather hard to find."

The next day I got a horse and buggy and drove to Parkville; the horse, however, fell dead lame just as I entered the village, and could proceed no further. I drove up to the tavern, and determined to proceed the rest of the way on foot. After making particular enquiries, as to my road, I set off on my five miles walk. I did not suppose that I was known to Munsel, and my intention was to verify his actual presence, and then return the next day with the proper officers to arrest him.

It was a beautiful July evening, just cool enough to render walking a pleasant exercise. It was dark when I started, and I had not walked a mile before it became quite dark. But I had informed myself so well as to the right road, that I thought I could not mistake it. It soon, however, became apparent to me that a great change had taken place in the scenery around me. Instead of the road being clear and open, as it was when I first set out, large trees, loomed up on each side of me, and the road became very bad—entirely different from the smooth gravelled surface I had first passed over. But I still pressed on, not suspecting that I had mistaken my way. I began to get tired. I must have walked at least two hours before any doubt entered my head.

By this time the broad road had degenerated into a narrow path I knew, then, that there must be something wrong, for the people of the town, of whom I had enquired, had informed me that the road to Mr. Theodore Munsel's house was pretty good all the way. I paused, for a moment irresolute, and did not know whether to retrace my steps or press forward. It had now become pitch dark, and I determined to go on, well assured that I could never find my way back. I had not proceeded many steps before I became convinced that I was wandering about in a forest. The underbrush began now to seriously impede my progress, and I found great difficulty in keeping on my feet.

My position was anything but agreeable—in the midst of a forest on a dark night. I cannot tell how I passed the three ensuing hours—they appeared three centuries to me. I suppose I must have walked the same path over and over again. I was at last completely overcome by physical fatigue, and sunk exhausted on the stump of a tree.

I rested my head upon my hands, and determined to pass the night there, being now certain that it was perfectly futile endeavoring to find my way till morning. While in this stooping position I thought I saw a light glimmer through the trees. I looked earnestly, and became convinced such was really the fact. I immediately determined to make for it, hoping to find shelter for the night. I advanced in that direction, and soon reached a dilapidated house built entirely of wood. It was a miserable looking abode, and had it not been for my tired condition, I should have hesitated seeking its shelter. But anything was better than spending the night in the forest, so I resolutely knocked at the door. My summons was for some time unheeded, and it was not till I had knocked again and again, that the door opened, and a gruff voice asked what I wanted.

"Can you give me lodging for the night?" I replied.

I was told to come in, and found myself in a room of moderate size, miserably furnished. A log-fire was burning on the hearth; and two persons occupied the apartment. The one that opened the door to me was a man about fifty years of age, very stoutly built, and possessed of a very sinister expression of countenance. The second occupant was none other than the absconding clerk. I then knew that I was in Mr. Munsel's house, and I congratulated myself on my good fortune. I noticed that as I entered he cast a scrutinizing glance at me; but as I felt assured he did not know me personally, I experienced no alarm.

"I have lost my way in the forest," said I, in answer to their looks of interrogation, "and if you will afford me shelter for the night, I shall be happy to repay you for your hospitality."

"Be good enough to sit down," said Mr. Theodore Munsel, his eyes sparkling when the word "repay"was used. "Where, are you going?" asked his nephew, fixing, another searching look on my face.

"I am going to Centerville. I left Parkville at six o'clock, but I suppose I mistook the road, for I have been wandering about the woods ever since."

"You are fifteen miles from Centerville," said the uncle with a kind of leer.

"You do not belong to this part of the country?" said the banker's clerk.

"No," I replied, "I from Virginia."

"What is your business?"

"I am collector for a house in Richmond."

"I should have taken you for a Yankee," said the young man.

"No, indeed," I replied, with an attempt to smile.

The uncle and nephew now left the room, and I could hear them whispering together in the next apartment. Still I did not feel any uneasiness, for I relied on the fact that I was unknown to the absconding clerk. They soon returned to the apartment where I sat.

"We have only one room in the house," said the uncle as he entered; "if you will not mind sleeping with a son of mine, you can have part of his bed."

I, of course, immediately consented, glad enough to find any place, where I could rest my weary limbs.

After a pause of a few minutes, I pulled out my watch, and said I should like to go to bed. I noticed at the time significant looks pass between the uncle and nephew when they saw my watch. It was a fine gold one—a real Cooper—and had been presented to me by an importer of watches for services rendered.

"You will find my son next the wall," said the uncle. "You will have the goodness not to awaken him, for he has been sick lately, and has to get up very early."

I replied that I would certainly avoid waking him. The uncle took up a candle, and showed me to a room upstairs; it was the only habitable sleeping room in the house, and was situated over that in which we had been seated. Cautioning me to put out the light as soon as I was in bed, he left me.

I found myself in a room the exact counterpart of the one below, excepting that this one contained a bedstead. Snoring on the bed next the wall was a man some years younger than myself. I cautiously brought the light to bear on his face. The first thing that struck me was, that the man below had deceived me when he had told me his son was sick. He was undressed and wore on his head a night-cap.

A vague sensation of uneasiness crept over me. I regretted having entered the house, and looked round the room for means of exit. There was only one door in the room, that by which I had entered. Opposite to the door was a window. I walked up to it, and endeavored to peer through the outside darkness, but could distinguish nothing. I tried to reason away my forebodings, and succeeded in doing so to some extent.

I began to prepare for bed, and had already taken off my coat and waistcoat, when I fancied I heard a step on the stairs. I immediately extinguished the light, and waited with breathless anxiety; the door gently opened, and the uncle cautiously thrust forward his head. In the gloom of the chamber he could not perceive me; and finding the light extinguished, I suppose he thought I was in bed, for he closed the door very softly and descended the stairs again.

I was now worked up to the highest pitch of excitement. I felt certain that something was going to happen. I remembered my lonely situation—the inquisitive questions of the men below. There was no possible means for me to escape, except in going through the room in which they were seated—and such a course I knew would be perfect madness. I summoned up all my philosophy, and determined to wait the *denouement,* and tried to persuade myself my fears were groundless. But when I thought of the significant looks that passed between the men when they saw my gold watch, I must confess that the effort was a failure. And then the thought suddenly struck me, if, after all, the clerk had recognized me, it was certain that he would never let me leave that place alive. Five long minutes passed away, and I heard nothing. At that moment a light flashed before my window. I went directly to it and saw the uncle with a lantern digging in the garden. I watched him with eager eyes; he was digging a hole about six feet long and three broad.

"Good God!" I exclaimed to myself, "he is digging my grave."

"I now felt certain that the young man had been left in the room below to prevent my escape. But I determined to satisfy myself if such were the fact or not. I opened the door noiselessly, and stole cautiously down stairs in my stocking feet. I glanced through the keyhole of the door which opened into the room, and saw that my suspicions were well founded, for the absconding clerk sat beside a table with a revolver all ready cocked within his reach. I returned to the bedroom again.

I again took my position at the window. Five minutes more of agonizing suspense ensued. I had nothing with which to defend myself, and was completely at their mercy. A sudden calmness now took possession of me. I suppose it was the calmness of despair, but withal my faculties were perfectly clear, and I turned over a hundred plans to escape the doom that awaited me. All this time I was eagerly watching the actions of the uncle.

The soil was very light, and he soon succeeded in opening the hole to at least four feet. He then threw down his spade and entered the house again. I expected every moment to hear them ascending the stairs, and made up my mind to sell my life as dearly as possible, when a purring sound attracted my attention.

I now perceived for the first time that the light from the room below penetrated through several chinks in the floor. I lay down on the ground, and looking through one of the cracks, found that I could perceive everything in the apartment. One of the men was sharpening a large knife on a grindstone, and it was this that made the purring sound that I had heard. He felt the edge, and finding it sharp enough, discontinued his employment. They then began to converse. I could hear every word they said.

"Are you certain, Charles, that this is the detective?" said the uncle. "Perfectly certain!" returned the clerk. "I know Brampton as well as I do you."

"It is certain he must die then. I suppose he has plenty of money with him besides his gold watch."

"Yes, he must be well provided with funds, and his business here is evidently to arrest me."

"Come, then, let us finish the business at once," said the uncle.

"Do you think he is asleep yet?" returned the clerk.

"No matter if he is not, he'll sleep well enough afterwards, anyhow."

The clerk laughed—hideously, I thought.

"Will you do it, or shall I?" said the nephew.

"O, you may go; but be sure you make no mistake. Bill, you know, lies next the wall; he has a nightcap on, the detective has none. Leave the light outside the door, for fear of waking Brampton; and above all, be quick about it."

In a moment my plan was formed. Bill was fast asleep. I gently turned him over to the outside of the bed, and pulling off his nightcap, put it on my own head. I accomplished this without waking Bill. I then cautiously laid myself in his place next the wall. The agony of the next few minutes was intense—my, heart seemed ready to cease beating. I heard a step on the stairs; it advanced, the door opened softly, the floor creaked with the weight of a heavy tread. The murderer approached the bed. I could feel his hot breath on my cheek. I had presence of mind enough to imitate a snore. I felt his hand passing over my head—it rested on my shoulder. O, agony of agonies, he had found out my *ruse,* and was about to kill me! My whole body was bathed in a cold perspiration.

Suddenly I heard a heavy thud on the bed, which was followed by a groan, and then all was still. The blow had been struck, and I was not the victim. A pause of some moments ensued, and then I heard the uncle ascending the stairs. They wrapped the body of the unfortunate Bill in a sheet, and conveyed it at once into the garden. They had no sooner left the house than I leaped out of bed and ran to the window. They had evidently not discovered their mistake, for the body was already in the grave prepared for it, and they ware filling it in.

I lost not a moment to put on the rest of my clothes, and creeping quietly down stairs, escaped through the front door. I ran as fast as I possibly could, and by chance the right road. In less than an hour I was at Parkville. I roused the whole village, and in a few hurried words told my story. A large party of men immediately set off for the scene of the tragedy accompanied by myself.

When we entered the house we found the front room still occupied by the uncle and nephew. When they saw me they turned deadly pale, and I really believed they thought that I had risen from the grave, for they had not yet discovered that they had sacrificed Theodore Munsel's son. When they saw that I was really alive, they assumed an air of bravado, supposing that I had only come to arrest the clerk for the bank robbery. Their dream, however, was soon dissipated, for in a few moments the body of the murdered man was exhumed, and they were confronted with their bloody work.

It was shocking to see the uncle's agony when he discovered that his son had been murdered. Neither of the criminals attempted any defence. Three months afterwards they were tried, convicted and executed.

Leaf the Eighth

Stabbed in the Back

I had been engaged in my profession about a year, when rumors reached New York that a small town in the extreme western portion of the State was the theatre of crimes. Several atrocious murders and robberies had been committed there, and not the slightest clue had been found as to the perpetrators of these deeds. At that time there was no telegraph or railroad to the town in question, therefore, the reports that reached the metropolis were in the first instance vague and contradictory, but they soon assumed a more decided character, and a full endorsement as to their truth was received in the shape of a letter from the local authorities of the police department, begging that a most skilfull detective might be sent down, to ferret out the real criminal.

A brother officer of mine, Mr. George Lewis, was despatched to the theatre of these events, and he went with the full assurance that he would be successful. George was a good fellow, and a capital hand at discovering ordinary criminals, but he did not possess the subtlety necessary to make a first rate detective. He was too frank, too boisterous, too conceited, to deal with refined villainy. He was fully acquainted with all the ordinary modes practiced in such cases, such as disguise in dress, decoy letters, and tracing out a chain of circumstantial evidence when the first link was found, but he was deficient in the power of analysis, so that when he had to do with a more acute mind, than his own, he was generally foiled.

I was not surprised to learn, then, that after he had been absent a week, a letter was received from him, to the effect that all his efforts had been entirely fruitless. On receipt of this letter the chief-of-police sent for me, and desired me to go at once and take Lewis's place. My instructions were written out, and the next day I started on my errand.

In the first place I provided myself with a book of patterns, clothed myself in a suit of chequered cloth, assumed a certain jaunty air, and was for the occasion transformed into a drummer or commercial traveller, travelling for a large commercial house in the cloth line.

I had to travel by stage, in order to reach the town where the crimes had been committed. It was a cold day in February; the wind blew from the northeast, and the inside of the stage was by no means the pleasantest place in the world on such a day. But when I am engaged on special business, I never allow myself to think of my own comforts, and being also something of a philosopher, I made the best of it.

After a tedious journey of two days, I saw the spires of the two churches that the town of P—— contains; and we were borne, bowling along the well paved street, for the town consists of only one long thoroughfare.

We stopped at the Eagle Hotel, and I was shown into the parlor where I found a bright fire burning; After supper I went to seek for Lewis, who was staying at the Fountain, the rival inn to the Eagle. I found him there, and told him he must go back to New York and leave the business in my hands. He did not like it much at first, but of course he had to obey orders. He then gave me the information he had gathered, and the particulars of the various crimes which had caused such consternation in the little town of P——. Divested of all verbiage, the facts were simply as follows:

About two weeks before Lewis's visit, the inhabitants of P—— were one morning startled and horrified by the report that a fearful murder had been committed during the previous night. Jasper Copman, a night watch employed by Russell & Son, the bankers of the town, was discovered stabbed in the back. The murderer had evidently approached him from behind, and the blow had been so surely given, that the unfortunate victim did not appear to have made the slightest struggle. The safe of the bank had been forced and the contents rifled, amounting to some $10,000.

The town of P—— does not consist of more than three thousand inhabitants, so that the consternation spread by this murder may be easily imagined. Every effort was made to discover the assassin, but without the slightest success. Three days afterwards, before the excitement attending this frightful deed had subsided, the dwelling-house of a retired merchant, who lived on the outskirts of the town, was broken into and robbed of its valuables. The inmates, consisting of an old man and two female servants, had heard and seen nothing although it appeared the robber or robbers had actually entered the sleeping apartments, picking the locks in a most dexterous manner.

Four nights after that another fearful crime was committed, which raised the public excitement and fear to the highest pitch. A widow lady residing in the heart of the town was discovered murdered in her bed. She, too, had been stabbed to the heart. The house had been rifled, and in spite of every effort of the local authorities, not the slightest trace or clue could be discovered. It was then that a detective officer from New York had been sent for.

Such was the substance of the facts told me by George Lewis. He then entered into particulars of what he had done, which amounted to nothing. He had caused several worthless characters to be arrested, but they were immediately released for want of evidence against them. I found it to be Lewis's opinion that a band of men had been concerned in those atrocities.

George had told every body his business, and had shown but little tact in conducting his investigations. He left for New York by the night mail, and I returned to my inn, debating in my own mind the best way to begin my investigation. Everybody was talking of the recent murders, but I mingled very little in the conversation myself.

The next morning I paid a visit to the house of the late victim, the widow lady. It was a small dwelling, situated on the main street, and it really appeared surprising how such a deed could have been committed without alarming the neighbors. I saw in a moment, that I had a most difficult case to contend with. The villain or villains were no ordinary persons. The first thing that struck me was the noiselessness with which the deed was committed. No one had heard a sound. As I have said, the same person who had committed this deed had entered the merchant's chamber while he slept, without awakening the owner of the house who was lying in bed asleep at the time.

Here then was my first point. The question next presented itself to my mind, that for a man to have accomplished this he must have some soft covering to his feet. In minutely searching the apartment, I discovered clinging to a nail in the floor, some shreds of white woolen of very thick texture. I immediately surmised that the murderer must have worn thick woolen stockings over his boots, for the purpose of deadening the sound of his footsteps. I made the experiment myself, and found that I could move about in them without eliciting the slightest sound.

I also made the discovery that the murderer (for I had made up my mind that only one man had been concerned in the crime) was a small man and had light hair. I came to this conclusion from the fact that the opening through which he had entered the widow lady's house was a small one, not allowing a full sized man to enter. This opening had been made by the removal of an iron bar. Attached to the fragments of this iron bar were two long hairs of a very light brown.

My next proceeding was to go round to all the dry goods shops in town where they sold the peculiar kind of stockings to which I have refered, carelessly making inquiries as, to who had purchased woolen stockings there during the last two or three weeks. Trade in that particular article appeared to have been dull for some time past, for in the first four shops I inquired at, I found they had sold none for the last two or three months, but I was more fortunate at the fifth and last shop in town. Here I learned that a certain gentleman, whose name I shall not at present reveal, had recently purchased three pairs there. On inquiring, I found the purchaser to be a little man with light hair.

Here was a most important point gained. The simple fact of the man buying three pairs of woolen stockings was not in itself very suspicious, but the fact that he was small and had light hair was proof positive to me that I had found out my man. There was one thing, however, which to any one else might have proved sufficient to dismiss such an idea as soon as it entered the mind. The gentleman who had bought those stockings was a most respectable, wealthy, and influential man, and had I breathed my suspicions to any body, I should have been laughed at as the veriest blockhead that ever lived.

By the time I had made all this investigation it was late, and I returned to the hotel, determined the next morning I would make my grand *coup*. I retired to bed very well satisfied with myself, and slept as soundly as if the murderer were already in jail. The next morning I was awakened by a tap at my door.

"Come in," said I

"The door opened, and the chambermaid made her appearance with a pitcher of hot water. She looked as pale as a a ghost, and trembled violently.

"Why, what's the matter, Mary?'" I asked.

"O, sir, haven't you heard the news?"

"Why, what news could I possibly have heard?"

"Well sir, another terrible murder was committed last night."

"What!" I cried, starting up from my chair.

"Mrs. Adams, of the Elms, was murdered last night."

"Mrs. Adams!" I almost screamed out, for the name was perfectly familiar to me.

"Yes, sir, she was found in her husband's study stabbed dead, and the house was robbed."

"And Mr. Adams, was he injured?"

"No, sir, they say he is almost distracted. It appears that he went to bed first, as is often his custom. He fell asleep and knew nothing of the murder until this morning."

Mary continued to converse for some minutes on the last fearful tragedy. At last she left the room, and I finished dressing as quickly as possible. This last crime caused me the greatest surprise. I could not comprehend it—it upset all my calculations, and left me wandering about in a sea of doubt and uncertainty.

I went down to breakfast. Consternation and fear were depicted in every face. Public excitement had now reached the highest pitch. Persons appearing to he afraid to walk alone even in the day time. In the street groups were conversing together. Every face wore a pale, anxious expression. On the dead walls of the town I saw a handbill convening a public meeting on that day at noon, to decide what was best to be done for the protection of the town.

Mr. Adams, the husband of the hurt victim, was a most respectable gentleman, living in a large house called the Elms, about half a mile from town. He was reported to be very wealthy, and had recently made some heavy purchases in real estate. The unfortunate woman, his wife, was about twenty-five years of age, and it was stated by all who knew her that she was kind, affable and generous. She was very talented and had made some contributions to the literature of the country.

The Adams's had not been long residents of P——; not long, more than two or three months at most, but they had brought with them excellent letters of introduction, and had at once been admitted to the very best society of the place. The family consisted of Mr. Adams, his wife, and two or three servants. The husband's grief at the loss of his wife can be very well imagined; it was stated that he was almost distracted.

The moment I had finished my breakfast I determined that I would return to the scene of the tragedy. I had more than one motive for doing this.

I found the Elms to be a large building, evidently erected prior to the Revolution. It was surrounded by a high wall, on the top of which were placed broken glass bottles, a very common method in that part of the country for preventing the ingress of interlopers. The entrance was by means of a massive gate.

A large crowd had already assembled in the court yard, seeking for admission, but watchmen were at the door, and refused entrance to all except friends of the deceased

Before entering the house, I made a thorough examination of the exterior. I found the wall was so lofty, and so well defended by the broken glass, that entrance except through the gate was almost impossible. I next proceed to inquire if the lock had been forced, and learned that the gate was still locked when the murder was discovered. I now went to the main entrance, but was refused admittance, and it was not until I told them who I was that I could obtain it. I would rather not have done this, but there was no help for it.

The room where the young woman had been killed remained exactly in the same condition as when the deed was first discovered. She had evidently been seated at the table writing, and had been utterly unaware of the assassin's approach. There was not the slightest evidence of any struggle having taken place; no disorder was apparent in the room, and the victim could not have uttered a single cry. She, like the others, had been stabbed in the back. On the floor were strewn some small pieces of paper, as if a letter had been torn up and thrown there.

In the ashes under the grate were also some pieces of paper, half consumed. I gathered them carefully together, and made out the following detached sentences:

"Fearful discovery——a felon's doom——my husband——life a burden——O, God!——what to do?——my husband——horrible! Horrible!"

I made inquiry concerning the deceased of the servants, and learned that the whole of the previous day she had been in the lowest possible spirits, that she had kept herself shut up in the room all day, and had spoken but a few words.

I then asked to see the bereaved husband, but was told that he was too deeply plunged in grief to be seen. I begged the messenger I sent to inform Mr. Adams who I was, and that the ends of justice demanded that I should see him. After some little delay I was admitted into his presence. He had on a morning gown. He was fearfully pale, and appeared to be plunged in the deepest grief.

I conversed with him a few minutes concerning the late occurrence, and learned that he had retired to bed about ten o'clock, and his wife told him she would follow him in a few minutes. He had fallen asleep, and did not awaken until morning, and it was then, that after a servant had entered the study the dreadful truth had become known to him.

When I had heard this statement, I left him, and going to the watchmen guarding the door, I begged that they would accompany me to perform a disagreeable duty. The men started as if not comprehending what I said.

Accompanied by the watchmen, I returned to Mr. Adams's chamber, and knocking at the door, I informed him that I wished to ask him another question. As soon as the door was opened, I entered, and placing my hand on Mr. Adams's shoulder, I exclaimed:

"Mr. Adams, I arrest you for the wilful murder of your wife! I also accuse you of having murdered Mrs. B——, the widow lady, and the watchman in the employ of Russell & Son, bankers." The man turned livid.

"What do you mean?" he said; "are you mad?"

"No, sir, not exactly; thank God, I am in full possession of my senses, or I might not have succeeded in discovering the perpetrator of these fearful crimes."

"Where is your proof?" he exclaimed.

"Here are the stockings," I replied, going to a corner of the apartment, and taking from it a pair of woolen stockings—"which you wore over your boots, and here are some small pieces of paper still adhering to them with which the floor of the study was strewn when you entered. I have also discovered a letter which your wife was writing at the time you stole behind her."

"That letter was destroyed," exclaimed the assassin.

"You see," I replied, turning to the watchmen, "he virtually confesses that he destroyed the letter after having committed the deed. What a pity it is that these clever murderers sometimes forget themselves. "Here," I continued, pointing to his dressing gown, "is a spot of his wife's blood still on his wrapper."

The assassin saw that he had committed himself, and sunk down in his chair speechless. The moment I saw him I knew that I stood in the presence of the man who had committed those fearful deeds. I saw the woolen stockings in one corner of the apartment, and Mr. Adams was a small man with light hair.

He was removed to jail, and that same evening confessed his crime. It appears that he had the reputation of being wealthy, when he was really straightened in circumstances. He became desperate, and determined he would recruit his fortune by burglary. By some means his wife became acquainted with her husband's crimes, and accused him of them. He made a faint denial, and determined to sacrifice his wife. How he affected his purpose the reader already knows. While the lady was in the act of writing a farewell letter to her husband, the fatal blow was given. After the deed was committed, Adams tore up the letter and threw it on the fire where it had been partially consumed. The only way to account for the husband sacrificing his wife, is that the fear of detection became stronger than his love. Six months after, the wretched criminal was executed in the gaol-yard of the town.

Leaf the Ninth

The Masked Robbers

Some six or eight years ago I received a requisition from the mayor of a small town in the interior of the State of New York, to visit that place for the purpose of discovering the perpetrators of various highway robberies which had been committed in the neighborhood. I soon reached my destination, and found Elliotsville, the name of the town in question, consisted but of one long, straggling street, containing the usual number of stores, taverns, etc., which are to be found in all country places. The neighborhood, however, was very pretty, and I was not surprised to learn that in summer time it was the favorite place of resort for the dwellers of cities.

My first duty was to call on the mayor, and receive from him the particulars of the crimes he had referred to in his letter to me. I found "his honor" to be a smart, little man, who in a few minutes put me in possession of all the facts he knew, which amounted to simply that for two or three weeks before my arrival, scarcely a person left the village at nightfall that was not dispossessed of all his money and valuables. All the robberies had been committed by two men who wore cape masks. No violence had been done to any person who made no resistance; but one or two individuals, who had disputed the robbers' right to their property, had been dreadfully beaten. It appeared that every effort had been made to discover the offenders, but every scheme had proved in vain, and even a detective officer from a neighboring city, who had been engaged to ferret out the criminals, had returned home, giving it up in despair.

An hour after my interview with the mayor (whom I desired to keep my visit a profound secret), I was seated in the bar-room of the Congress House, the chief hotel in the town. It was the middle of the month of December, and intensely cold, so that I was very glad to draw my chair close to a large stove used for heating the apartment. A considerable number of town's-people were assembled there, discussing the events of the day. It was really very amusing to hear their conversation, embracing as it did a hundred different subjects. Politics, religion, Farmer Jones's pigs, were all touched upon but at last it came to the grand topic, the recent robberies. On this exciting theme every one had something to say, but I gained no further information than what had already obtained from the mayor.

By special invitation I went to spend the evening at his honor's house, it being specially understood that I was to be introduced as a Mr. Clark, a New York merchant—that being the name I had thought fit to assume for the occasion.

I found Mr. Dobell, the mayor, surrounded by his family. The worthy official was disposed to be very hospitable, and soon made me feel perfectly at home. At the tea-table I was introduced to his family, consisting of his wife, two grown-up daughters, and a confidential clerk of his, named Jasper Barton, a young man about thirty years of age. The latter I found to be very intelligent. He was from the New England States, and could converse on almost every subject. At the tea-table the subject of the recent robberies was started. Mr. Jasper Barton was very indignant that such outrages should be perpetrated in the midst of a civilized community, and offered to make one of a vigilance committee to put a stop to them. I was half inclined at first to impress him into my service; but after conning the matter over in my own mind, I determined to keep my own counsel, and trust to my own unaided efforts to discover the robbers.

I passed a very pleasant evening at the mayor's house. After tea we had music, and I soon saw that Jasper was paying his addresses to the eldest daughter of my host, and that they were favorably received by the young lady and her parents.

"Do you play chess, Mr. Clark?" suddenly said Mr. Dobell, after a pause in the conversation.

"I play a little," I replied.

"Suppose that we adjourn into the dining-room, and leave these young people to amuse themselves as they please," said the mayor.

"With all my heart," I replied, rising from my chair and following Mr. Dobell into an adjoining apartment, where a splendid hickory fire was burning on the hearth. The table was drawn near the fire, the men were placed, and we commenced the game. I soon found that my opponent was not very strong, and that I could easily beat him, so that I was able to think of other things, besides the game.

"That Mr. Barton appears to be a very fine young man," said I, while waiting for my adversary to move.

"He is indeed," replied Mr. Dobell. "I may say he is quite a treasure to me."

"Has he lived with you long?"

"He has not been with me more than six weeks, but he has proved more attentive to business than any clerk I have ever had. He is a great favorite with all my customers."

"And a favorite with others beside," said I, smiling.

"Yes, he is very attentive to Emily and he is such a worthy young man that I do not know that she could do much better. It is true he is poor, but I am pretty well to do, and in case my daughter should decide to accept him as a husband, why, I can take him into partnership. Riches do not make happiness, you know."

"That is a truism that cannot be disputed," I replied. "He appears to be a remarkably intelligent young man."

"Yes, our parson says he has few equals. Would you believe it, he can speak French and German like natives of those countries!"

"Indeed!" I returned, continuing my game.

"We played two or three games, two of which I allowed my adversary to win; for I have long since discovered that nothing sets a man more against you than beating him half a dozen successive games at chess. Mr. Dobell, whom I have before said was a short fat man, decidedly apoplectically inclined, began to grow sleepy, so that his attention was no longer fixed on the chess-board.

He proposed that we should discontinue playing, and smoke a social cigar together. I seconded the proposition, and some exquisite Havanas and a decanter of brandy were placed on the table. We made ourselves a tumbler of punch each, and were soon enveloped in the blue wreaths of smoke from our cigars.

We conversed on several subjects, but by degrees our conversation grew more and more interrupted, until at last Mr. Dobell replied only by mono-syllables to my remarks, and at last made no reply at all—for he was fast asleep.

I sat for some time gazing on the burning logs, smoking my cigar, and thinking of nothing in particular. At last I began to feel tired, and rose up for the purpose of taking my departure, when I was attracted by a lot of gaudily-bound books placed on a table at the other end of the apartment. Now if I have one weakness more than another, it is the fondness of turning over new books and reading their title-pages. I could not resist the temptation before me, and going to the table, I sat down beside it and began to examine the books on it. This table was placed near the folding-doors, which separated the dining from the sitting-room. When I first sat down I heard a confused murmur of voices, which, however, grew more distinct, and without listening I was enabled to hear the conversation going on in the next apartment. Perhaps I was in honor bound to move away, but my profession as a detective officer had in a measure blunted these nice punctilios of honor, and I always made it a rule to know everything I possibly could—for I frequently found information, apparently the most unimportant, bore upon the particular case I might be investigating, at the time. The speakers in the next room were evidently Jasper Barton and Miss Emily Dobell.

"I have the greatest respect for your father," I heard Jasper say, "but forgive me, dear Emily, if I say that I have more ambition than to become a partner in a grocery business, respectable though it be. When you are my wife, I want you to shine in the world as a lady of fashion, and not bury yourself in this little town—"

"But Jasper—"

"I know what you would say, dear," interrupted the young man. "I am fully aware that my present position makes my ambition appear very foolish, but you do not know all. I have already considerable means saved, and have good expectations of being rich very soon."

"I thought your parents were dead," said Emily.

"So they are, but I have other relatives living, and rich ones, too. I hope—"

Here his words grew so indistinct that I lost them. For some moments a confused murmur of voices followed. Then their voices grew distinct again.

"Dear Jasper," I heard Emily say, "you never told me how you lost the middle finger of your left hand."

I had noticed at the tea-table that the young man's hand was minus this finger.

"Did I, not?" replied Jasper. "I thought I had told you. When I was a boy—"

I could not hear his explanation, for the reason that he suddenly sunk his voice, and the worthy mayor at that moment waking up, I heard no more of the conversation going on in the adjoining room, which, to tell the truth, did not interest me at all. Rising from my seat, I shook Mr. Dobbell cordially by the hand, and returned to my inn.

I immediately went to bed, and, as is my usual custom on retiring for the night, I began to turn over in my own mind the best course for me to pursue. I recapitulated in my own mind all that had been told me concerning the robberies, and the first conclusion that I arrived at was that the perpetrators of them resided in Elliotsville; for it appears that the persons who had been robbed were always addressed by their real names. After a few minutes thought on the matter, I made up my mind as to the best course of action for me to pursue, and that was to allow myself to be robbed.

The next day I went through the town and stated to everybody I met, that it was my intention to leave for Albany that night. When the landlord of the Congress House heard my determination, he earnestly advised me not to go, stating that he was certain I should be robbed if I did so. This only made me the more determined, for it was the very thing I wanted. I was inflexible in my resolution, stating to him that, whether I was robbed or not, I must go, as my business was imperative. Among other persons I called on Mr. Dobbell, and told him of my determination. I found him alone in his store.

"My dear sir," said he to me, when I told him what I intended to do, "let me persuade you to give up the idea. You will never detect the criminals that way, and you may be seriously maltreated."

"I have thought the matter over, Mr. Dobell," I replied, "and have concluded that it is the best course for me to pursue; and when once I have made up my mind, nothing can turn me."

"Well, you know best. I must leave the matter entirely to yourself."

"Where is Mr. Barton this morning?" said I. "I do not see him here."

"He has just gone down to the bank."

"You have said nothing to him as to my real character?"

"No, indeed—not a soul in this place knows who you are excepting myself."

"That's right! Be good enough to keep my secret until you see me again."

So saying, I bade him good-by, and left the store. I had not gone a dozen rods down the street, before I met his confidential clerk, Mr. Jasper Barton.

"Good morning, Mr. Clark!"said he, shaking my hand.

"Good morning!" I returned; "or rather I should say, good-by."

"What, are you going to leave us?"

"Yes, I leave for Albany to-night."

"Are you not afraid?"

"Afraid of what?"

"The robbers."

"I had forgotten all about them—no, I am not afraid of them, though perhaps I ought to be, for I often carry considerable funds with me."

"By the by, can you tell me where the bank is? I wish to change some money."

"The bank?—O, yes! Take the first turn to the left, and you will see a brown stone building—that is the bank."

I thanked him, and hurried on. I soon transacted my business at the bank and then returned to the inn. When it was quite dark I ordered my horse, and putting two ten dollar bills in my purse, both of which I carefully marked with red ink in one corner, I started on my journey. As I intended to make no resistance, I had provided myself with no weapons of defence.

It was a bitter cold night, and intensely dark. The sky overhead was covered with thick, murky clouds, through which not a single star penetrated; the wind, which was from the northeast, blew a cutting blast in my face, but I pushed on, animated by the hope that I should discover some clue to the perpetrators of the robberies. I soon left the lights of the town behind, and entered upon an open country road. For two or three miles nothing occurred to arouse my suspicious, and I began to fear I had made my journey for nothing. But suddenly I felt my horse's rein seized, and saw the bright barrel of a pistol gleam before my eyes.

"I want your money, Mr. Clark," said a rough voice.

"Ah, you know me, then!" said I.

"Yes, you are the stranger who has been staying at the Congress House."

"I am," I returned, scrutinizing the robbers closely, for I now discovered there were two of them.

"Come, hand over your money!" said one of the men, touching me on the arm.

"Certainly," I replied; "it is no use resisting, for I am unarmed. I have not much money with me, but what I have you are welcome to."

So saying, I handed to one of the robbers the purse containing the two marked ten dollar bills. He opened it and appeared very much disappointed.

"You have more money than that about you," said he.

"No indeed, that is all I have."

"You were seen to go into the bank at Elliotsville this morning."

"True, but that was to send money away, not to receive it."

"Well, we must search you."

"Very well; as I said before, I cannot resist."

The robbers searched me very expeditiously, turning my pockets inside out. At last they were compelled to come to the conclusion that I had spoken the truth.

"I suppose you expected that you would be stopped, and that is the reason you did not bring your money with you," said one of the men.

"That is exactly the truth," I replied.

"I was told that I should be certain to be robbed; and although I thought that perhaps I might escape, I thought it better to be on the safe side."

"Well we can't get blood out of a post, so I suppose we must be satisfied. Good night!"

"Good night! You have spoiled my journey, though. It is of no use to go on to Albany without any money. I shall have to return to Elliottsville."

"We are sorry to have inconvenienced you. Good night."

"Good night!" I repeated, and turning my horse round, started back for the town I had so lately quitted.

While I was conversing with the highwaymen, I had done my best to endeavor to penetrate their disguise, but all my efforts had been entirely unavailing. The masks they wore had entirely concealed their faces, and their voices were quite strange to me. In fact, owing to the darkness of the night, I had not been able to catch the slightest glimpse of the form of one of the men, and the other I felt certain was an entire stranger to me. I began to be afraid that my plan would fail, but still I did not wholly despair.

I soon formed my plan of action. I felt assured that the robbers must be inhabitants of the town, and I made up my mind that I would go to the entrance of the town and watch for their return, and then follow them home. I soon reached the first house, and concealed my horse in a neighboring thicket, and then returned to the cottage of which I have just spoken.

It was evidently an old building, and its dilapidated condition informed me that it was unoccupied. The upper windows were all boarded up, the chimney was in ruins, and the yard attached to it looked the picture of desolation. I walked round the house, but not the slightest sound greeted my ears. The thought then struck me that it would be an excellent place to watch from, and I determined to enter it. I tried the door, and to my joy I found it unfastened. I entered, and found myself in a moderately-sized apartment, with a low ceiling, and entirely destitute of furniture. My first proceeding was to examine the room minutely. I found in a recess a large cupboard, but nothing else in the apartment merited any notice.

I now approached the window, and opening the shutter, found to my joy that no one could pass along the road without my being cognizant of the fact. I threw up the window, and determined to await there the issue of events.

Perhaps an hour elapsed and I began to feel rather tired and sleepy. The wind blew very keenly through the open window, and pierced my very bones. As time passed I had serious thoughts of giving up my expedition as a failure; and yet the knowledge that there was no other entrance into Elliotsville, and the firm conviction that the robbers must be inhabitants of that town, made me hold out a little longer. At last I heard the sound of footsteps on the hard ground.

Every minute they grew more and more distinct, and I felt certain that the robbers were approaching. In a moment or two I saw their dusky forms in the distance—but to my extreme surprise and consternation, I saw them crossing the road and making directly for the door of the uninhabited house in which I was watching. It did not take me a moment to creep away from the window; in less than a minute I was safely concealed in the cupboard which I have before mentioned. I had scarcely entered it before the front door opened, and the two robbers advanced into the room.

"Not much luck to-night," said one of the robbers.

"We can't expect it to rain gold every night," said the other. "Taking all things into consideration, we have done remarkably well during the last week."

"Not so bad, that's a fact! You must own there is a good deal of credit due to me for planning our expeditions. There is not the slightest suspicion attached to us."

"Yes, I must say you have managed things well. People little think when they are talking to me of the robberies, that I am the man who relieved them of their superfluous cash."

"How miserably cold it is here!"said the other, changing the conversation. "Where are the matches?"

"They are on the shelf in the cupboard," replied his companion.

This was by no means pleasing information to me; to tell the truth, I really felt afraid. In spite of the cold weather, my body was bathed in perspiration, when I heard one of the robbers approaching my place of concealment. I drew myself into the smallest possible spare, and could actually hear my own heart beat. The robber opened the cupboard, and I held my breath. My good fortune, which has so often befriended me, did not forsake me this time; for the first thing he put his hand on was the box of matches, and I was, comparatively speaking, safe. In another moment or two I saw a light gleaming through the chinks of the cupboard door.

"What, in the name of fortune, did you leave the window open for?" said one of the men.

"I didn't leave it open," replied the other.

"Yes, you did."

"No, I didn't!"

"What is the reason it is open now then?"

"How should I know? You left it open yourself, I suppose."

"Well, it's no use arguing about it; it's open now," said the first speaker shutting it down.

I was very glad to find that they did not suspect any one of having entered during their absence, and I began to hope that I might get out of my difficulty scot free. I did not forget the end I had in view, and bringing my eye in close proximity to the key-hole of the door, I distinctly saw the two men. One of them was tall and powerfully built, the other was much shorter. I confidently expected that they would remove their masks, but I was disappointed, for they kept them on, and I was no nearer recognizing them than when they were in the dark.

"Now, then, let us proceed to business," said one of the men. "What is our booty to-night?"

"Well, there's that twenty dollars we took from that Mr. Clark, the New York merchant; a gold watch we took from farmer Johnson, and the two rings we took from his wife."

"We will pursue our usual custom," said the taller of the two robbers; conceal the watch and rings, and divide the money."

"That's soon done; there's one of the ten dollar bills, and now to conceal the other things."

The robber handed his companion one of the ten dollar bills, which I noticed he placed in the side-pocket of his vest; and then going to a particular plank in the floor, he raised it up, and I saw a deep hole, which appeared to be filled with valuables. He concealed the watch and rings in this hiding-place, and then replaced the plank.

"We have got a pretty good haul in there, said he, as soon as he left the place. "When are we to divide?"

"I think it will be safe to continue this game a week or two longer, and then we must vamoose."

"But before we do that, we ought to try some of the houses in the town; there's old Dobell, for instance—he keeps lots of money always at his house."

"Yes, that's easy enough got at; but that must be the last thing done."

"I agree with you—but where's the brandy? I am as thirsty as a dog—let us have a drink."

"The brandy's in the cupboard on the top shelf. I'll get it," returned the robber's companion.

I now thought it was all up with me. The robber approached the cupboard with the lamp. A sudden idea entered my head—it was the only thing left for me to do; it might, or it might not, prove successful. The moment the cupboard opened, quick as thought, I blew out the light before the man had time to look in.

"Confound the draught!"said the man, stamping his foot angrily on the ground.

Again I held my breath. Without waiting to re-light the lamp, the man groped about on the shelf, and to my joy found the bottle he was seeking. He closed the door again, and again the lamp was lighted.

I now hoped they would remove their masks for the purpose of drinking, but again I was disappointed; they merely lifted them up, and I did not catch the slightest glimpse of their features. But when the tallest robber took the bottle in his hand, I saw something that set the blood dancing through my veins.

After drinking a considerable quantity they took up their hats and left the house. When they had been gone half an hour, I also left; and finding my horse in the same place that I had left it, I proceeded at once to my inn, and entered as if nothing had happened.

In reply to the interrogation of my landlord, I merely informed him that when I had got some distance on the road, I had changed my mind, and determined to put off my journey to Albany for the present.

I went to bed and slept soundly that night. The next morning I sauntered down to Mr. Dobell's store. I found the owner and Mr. Jasper Barton there; they both appeared to be extremely surprised to see me.

"Why, Mr. Clark," said Mr. Dobell, "you back again! I thought you were at Albany."

"I might have been," I replied, "but I had the misfortune to be robbed just outside of the town."

"How shameful!" said Mr. Barton. "Can nothing be done to stop these outrages?"

"I think there can," said I; "and my business here this morning is for that special purpose." And then advancing to Mr. Barton, I laid my hand on his shoulder, and said, "Mr. Barton, you are my prisoner! I accuse you of having robbed me last night!"

"You are mad, sir!"said Barton, as pale as death.

"Not quite," I returned; and before he was aware of it, I dived my fingers into the side-pocket of his vest, and drew from it the bank-note for ten dollars with my private mark in red ink in the corner. I had seen him place it there himself, so I knew where to find it. Mr. Barton had revealed himself to me when he raised the bottle to his mouth to drink. I then detected the absence of the middle finger of the left hand, and was sure of my man. The accused at first stoutly denied my accusation; but when he learned that I had been concealed in the cupboard in the room where he had concealed his dishonest gains, he confessed all, revealing the name of his accomplice, who was a hostler employed at one of the inns of the town.

Mr. Jasper Barton and his companion are now undergoing a sentence of imprisonment in the State prison. Most of the property that had been taken was discovered in their secret hiding-place, and returned to their rightful owners.

The fact of the other day receiving wedding cards from Miss Emily Dobell, who has lately married a Mr. Theodore Johnson, the son of a wealthy farmer, recalled the circumstances of this affair to my mind, and I determined to make it public.

Leaf the Tenth

The Lottery Ticket

I was one day walking quietly down Broadway, thinking that I would buy a present for my wife, for the following day was her birthday, and she and I have always kept up the good old fashion of making each other presents on these occasions. I was debating whether it should be an article of jewelry, or a new dress, when I felt some one suddenly tap me on the shoulder. I turned quickly round, and found myself face to face with a gentleman of about sixty years of age. He was dressed in black, and wore a portly watch-chain, from which hung two or three seals, and was altogether a very respectable-looking individual.

"I believe I have the pleasure of speaking to Mr Brampton?" said he.

"That is my name," I returned.

"You have been mentioned to me very favorably by Mr. M——. I wish to consult you in a very delicate matter. Can you accompany me to my house?"

I looked at my watch, and finding that I could spare a quarter of an hour, I agreed to accompany him. We jumped into an omnibus which was passing up town, and in a short time stood before his residence, which was situated in Bond Street. He took me into a small room which evidently served him for a study. A library table stood in the middle of the apartment, which was covered with magazines and papers. He invited me to be seated.

"My name is Morton," said he; "I am engaged in no business, having sufficient to live upon comfortably. I possess considerable property in houses, and collect the rents myself. Yesterday was my collection day. Last night when I returned home I placed five thousand dollars in that safe which you see yonder, intending to take it to the bank this morning; but when I opened it for that purpose it was gone. Whoever took it must have had duplicate keys not only of the safe but of the house door."

"Was the safe locked this-morning?" I asked.

"Yes."

"Do you suspect anybody?"

"I am at a complete loss to know whom to suspect. Mr. M——, lawyer, whom I consulted in the matter mentioned your name to me as having extraordinary talent in ferreting on crime. I determined I would apply you before taking any further steps in the matter."

"Who are the inmates of your house?"

"There is no one but my wife and two servant girls."

"Do you not suspect the girls?"

"O, dear no, they have lived with us for many years. It must have been somebody from the outside that committed the robbery."

"You say that the house had no appearance of having been broken into?"

"No; when the servants rose this morning all the doors were locked as usual."

"It is rather a strange case," I returned. "I must first of all make an examination of the premises."

The old gentleman took me over the house, and I found after an attentive examination that there was only one way of entering the house from the outside—excepting, of course, the front entrance and that by means of a garret window which opened on the roof, which communicated with several houses in the same block. I made a great many inquirie making notes of everything I thought bore upon the case. I then left, promising to call the next morning.

When I got home, I what I call "studied out the case," by which I mean I shut myself up, lighted my meerschaum, and perused the notes I had made. My mind was soon made up with respect to one point. I was certain that whoever had committed the robbery had entered by means of the attic window, that is, provided no one in the house was the guilty party. Early that next morning I made inquiries as to whom lived in the houses on the right and left of Mr. Morton's residence. These inquiries resulted in the fact that the house on the left hand side was occupied by a family of the name of Carpenter, and that a nephew of Mr. Morton frequently visited there. In fact he had stayed there all night the very same night that Mr. Morton was robbed, and what is more, he occupied the attic room looking on the roof.

After I had made these investigations I again called on Mr. Morton for the purpose of making some inquiries concerning this nephew. I was at once shown into the old gentleman's study, and who should be with him but the very young man in whom at that moment I was so much interested. He was a handsome young fellow of about twenty-one years of age. He had a fine open countenance, and there was nothing at all in his face which would lead me to suspect that he could be guilty of robbing his uncle. He was exceedingly well dressed, in fact I might say he was over-dressed, and I judged him to be a bit of a fop. They were conversing on the subject of the robbery when I entered, and the young man expressed himself exceedingly concerned at the loss his uncle had sustained.

After conversing a little time he took his leave, and I was left alone with Mr. Morton. He immediately asked me what conclusion I had come to with respect to the robbery.

"Before I answer your inquiry," said I, "will you he good enough to answer me a few questions?"

"Certainly," he returned.

"How many keys of the safe do you possess?"

"Only one."

"Had you in your possession on the night in question?"

"Certainly. I always put it into the drawer of the bureau in my room. I did so on that occasion, and found it there the next morning."

"I think I understood you to say that no one lives with you but your wife and two servants?"

"Yes. But my wife was absent—she is visiting Baltimore," he returned. "She has been there for the last three weeks."

"Then on the night of the robbery there was no one in the house but yourself, and two servant girls?"

"Exactly."

"Now I want you particularly to carry your mind back to that night. Did any sound disturb you?"

"Well, now you call my mind to the fact, I remember about three o'clock in the morning I fancied I heard a step in my room. I listened attentively, and not hearing it again I felt convinced I was mistaken, and fell asleep."

"And in the morning you found the key in the same place that you had left it the night before?"

"I did."

"I see your front door closes with a night latch, how many keys have you to that?"

"Two. I have one, my wife the other."

"That is the only fastening you have to the door, I believe?"

"The only one. It is a patent nightlatch, and perfectly secure."

"Before I proceed any further I should like to see your two servants. Be good enough to call them in."

The old gentleman did so, and in a minute or two they were in my presence. I addressed various questions to them, but all that I could gain was the fact that about four o'clock in the morning the cook thought she heard a step on the stairs. I dismissed them.

"Mr. Morton," said I, when we were again alone, "there was a young man here just now. May I ask his name?"

"His name is Edward Legrand; he is a nephew of mine."

"What is his occupation?"

"He is clerk in a wholesale store down town."

"What salary does he receive?"

"Eight hundred dollars a year. But I can't see what all these questions have to do with the robbery."

"You will see by-and-by; you must allow me to conduct this investigation in my own way."

"Certainly. I did not mean to give any offence by the observation I made."

"I understand that. Your nephew, I believe, is on terms of intimacy with your neighbors, the Carpenters, who live next door?"

"Yes, he is paying his addresses to the eldest Miss Carpenter."

"On the night of the robbery he slept in their house."

"Very likely; he frequently stays there all night."

"I suppose you have implicit confidence in your nephew?"

"The most implicit in this world. I would trust him with untold-gold. You surely do not suspect him?"

"The salary he receives, you say, is eight hundred dollars a year?"

"Yes, and on that he supports a widowed mother and sister."

"Is it not strange that with such a moderate remuneration he should wear such an expensive diamond ring?"

"Diamond ring!"said Mr. Morton, in a tone of surprise; "he wears no diamond ring!"

"Excuse me, sir," I returned. "I particularly noticed it when he was in the room just now. I am something of a judge of the value of precious stones. I assure you the brilliant he wears on the little finger of the left hand is of the first water, and could not have cost less than five hundred dollars."

"What does it mean? It is very extraordinary! Perhaps he has not yet left the house," said the old gentleman, making a step towards the door.

"Stop, my dear sir, stop!" I exclaimed, seizing him by the arm, "you would spoil everything. We must be very cautious in investigating this matter. There is enough evidence for us to suspect this young man, at the same time we must not be precipitate. If you see him again, act towards him just the same as usual, and above all do not let a hint escape you that he is suspected. I shall now go and make further inquiries. But first tell me if you can identify any of the bank notes that were stolen?"

"I cannot; there was a good deal of it southern money. I remember distinctly amongst it was a considerable quantity of Baltimore bank notes."

"Where does this young man reside?"

"He lives with his mother and sister, No. 144 West Twenty-First Street."

After having made a few more necessary inquiries I took my leave, promising to call the next day, or before, if I discovered anything conclusive. When I reached the street I turned the whole affair over in my mind, and was compelled to acknowledge the affair looked black against the young clerk. I felt sorry for him, for there was something very prepossessing in his appearance, and then I thought of his poor widowed mother and sister. A detective, however, must not indulge in the luxury of sympathy, or he would soon be rendered unfit for his duty. I therefore dismissed all these feelings, and at once decided as to the course for me to pursue.

I knew there were only two retail stores in New York likely to keep such expensive rings as the one worn by Mr. Legrand, namely, Ball, Black & Co., and Tiffany and Co. I determined I would call on the latter first. I soon reached their magnificent jewelry establishment. I entered the store and asked to be shown some diamond rings. An obliging clerk soon spread a variety before me. I remarked one which I thought resembled Mr. Legrand's, and asked the price.

"That is worth five hundred and twenty dollars," was the reply.

"It is a beautiful stone," I remarked. "I perceive it is the only one of the kind you have left."

"Yes; we had two of them, but sold one of them yesterday."

"Exactly," I returned; "the young man who purchased it was rather tall, handsome and exceedingly well dressed?"

"That was the very person."

"He paid you in southern money?"

"He did so," returned the clerk, "chiefly Baltimore funds. The bills are in the cash-box now."

"Thank you. Can I see the proprietor, if you please?"

I was at once shown into his private office and explained my business to him. He promised to aid me all in his power and to retain the bills until he heard from me again.

Proofs of young Legrand's guilt were now accumulating thick and fast. My next duty was very clear, I must go and examine the house in which he lived. I jumped into an Eighth Avenue omnibus, and was soon set down at the foot of Twenty-First Street. I found the house to be about the middle of the block. It was a small, genteel-looking dwelling, and was scrupulously clean on the outside. I rung the bell, the door was answered by an elderly lady in a widow's cap, whom I at once concluded was Legrand's mother. I requested to speak with her privately. I was immediately conducted into a neatly furnished parlor.

"Madam," said I, "you are doubtless aware that your brother has been robbed of a large amount of money."

"O, yes," she replied, "Edward told us all about it. What a dreadful thing!"

"Your son is in possession of a very fine diamond ring, is he not?"

"Yes, his uncle gave it to him. But what can that have to do with the matter in question?"

"I am a detective officer," I returned. "In a case like this it becomes absolutely necessary that wherever there is the slightest suspicion a search should be made. Will you be good enough to show me up to your son's bedroom, that I may make an examination of his effects?"

"Surely, sir, you cannot suspect my son?" said the old lady, tears gushing into her eyes.

"My dear madam, restrain your feelings; an innocent party is never injured by a search."

"Of course, sir, you are welcome to examine his room; but I must confess I feel grieved that my brother should allow the slightest, suspicion to enter his mind. But come, sir, follow me."

So saying, the old lady led the way into her son's bedroom. It was a small apartment, comfortably furnished. A large trunk was placed on one side of the room. I commenced my search with this. I found it locked, but soon succeeded in opening it. It was filled full of books, papers and drawing utensils. I took each article out one by one, and laid it on the floor after I had examined it thoroughly. I proceeded in this manner until the trunk was completely empty. I had found nothing. I was about closing the lid when I fancied part of the lining of the bottom was slightly elevated. I ripped it up, and pulled out a large quantity of bank bills. They were most of them on the Merchants' Bank, of Baltimore. The whole amount discovered was four thousand two hundred dollars. Mrs. Legrand stood aghast when she saw this money. She wrung her hand in consternation, and could only utter:

"He is not guilty! He is not guilty!"

To add to the painful character of this scene, Legrand's sister, a beautiful girl eighteen years of age, entered the room. When she learned what had occurred, she added her lamentations to those of her mother. She, however, soon recovered herself.

"Mr. Brampton," said she, for she had learned my name, "I acknowledge appearances are against my brother, but do not judge hastily. I am perfectly convinced that he is innocent of the crime imputed to him. I cannot account for this money in his trunk; but rest assured he will be able to give a satisfactory statement. He will be here in a quarter of an hour to dine. Wait until he comes, and then interrogate him."

I had already made up my mind to do so, and bowed acquiescence. Soon afterwards he entered the house. He certainly did not seem guilty from his bearing, for he was in the best possible spirits, and entered the parlor singing. When he saw me, he appeared somewhat surprised, but evinced no evidence of guilt.

"Mr. Legrand," said I, "a painful duty devolves upon me. I am compelled to arrest you on suspicion of robbing your uncle, Mr. Morton."

"Robbing my uncle!" exclaimed the young man, in a tone of surprise. "You are jesting."

"No, indeed," I returned, "and I must tell you the evidence is fearfully strong against you."

"Stuff!" he replied, "I can immediately prove my innocence. I should as soon think of committing, murder as robbery. You have made some mistake. What are the grounds of your suspicions?"

"Well, young man," I replied, "I am not obliged to tell you; but I feel an interest in you, and I assure you no one will be more pleased to find you innocent than myself. The evidence against you up to the present time amounts to as follows. Two days ago Mr. Morton's safe was robbed of five thousand dollars, chiefly in Baltimore money. In the first instance no suspicion at all was entertained of you. It was supposed that some one had possessed himself of a key which would open the safe, and by some means he had obtained access to the premises. I was consulted in the matter. After examining the premises I came to the conclusion that the robber must have entered the house by the attic window. I also discovered that you slept at Mr. Carpenter's on the night the robbery was committed, and that you occupied the very room which opened out on the roof. This morning when I called on your uncle you were with him. I noticed something about you which immediately struck me. When you left the room I inquired what salary you received; I was told then that it was eight hundred dollars per annum."

"That is the truth," interrupted the young man; "but what was it you noticed curious about me?"

"Well, I thought it rather curious that a young man on so small a salary should possess such a magnificent diamond ring."

The young man turned deadly pale, and tottered into a chair.

"I have since learned that you told your mother that your uncle made you a present of it."

"I did say so, fool that I was!" stammered the young man.

The faces of his mother and sister evinced the greatest surprise when they heard this. I continued:

"I this morning discovered that you yesterday purchased that ring at Tiffany's for five hundred and twenty dollars, and that you paid for it in bills on a Baltimore bank. Suspicion was now fearfully strong against you. I next examined your bed-room, and concealed in the lining of your trunk, I discovered—"

"Money to the amount of four thousand two hundred dollars," interrupted the young man, striking his forehead with his hand.

"Exactly; and more, this money is also in Baltimore bills."

"Great God!"exclaimed the young man, starting from his seat, "what a fearful array of circumstantial evidence!"

"Edward, you are not, you cannot be guilty of this crime?"exclaimed his sister, clinging to him.

"No, Clara, I am not guilty; the only fault I have committed is in stating that my uncle gave me this diamond ring. I bought it at Tiffany's as Mr. Brampton states."

I could see a shadow of suspicion creep over the features of both his mother and sister. But their love would not allow it to rest there, for their countenances cleared, and his mother asked:

"But the money, Edward, explain how you came in possession of it."

The young man paused a moment and then said:

"I am almost afraid to do so, for fear my statement should not obtain belief. The simple truth, however, is as follows. About two weeks since I accompanied a friend into the reading room attached to the St Nicholas Hotel. I mechanically took up a paper and found I was perusing the *Sun*, published in Baltimore, Maryland. Among other things the advertisement of a lottery on the Havana plan caught my eye. It was to be drawn in about a week, and the tickets were ten dollars each. I have not the slightest faith in lotteries, but it entered my head that I would purchase a ticket and try my luck. I then and there wrote to the party advertising, and enclosed ten dollars for a ticket. In two or three days I received it. What was my surprise to find, when the list of numbers which had drawn prizes was published, that my ticket had drawn a prize of five thousand dollars? I immediately wrote to the agent, of whom I had purchased the ticket, for the amount, requesting that he would send me Baltimore funds in preference to a draft on New York, for you must understand I was a little ashamed of the transaction, and determined to reveal it to no one. Yesterday I received the agent's letter, containing the amount. I thought I would treat myself to a handsome diamond ring; I devoted a portion of the funds for that purpose, the rest I concealed under the lining of my trunk. This is the simple truth, so help me God!"

"It is true! It is true!"exclaimed both mother and sister, embracing him.

"Mr. Legrand," I exclaimed, "your explanation will be perfectly satisfactory if it can be proved to be true. You have the agent's letters of whom you purchased the ticket?"

"No, I have not; unfortunately I destroyed them. I have already told you I was ashamed of the transaction, and determined to destroy all proof of having been engaged in it."

"You at least remember his name?" I asked.

"Indeed, I have forgotten it; it began with an M, I think."

"Well, you remember the number of the ticket which drew this prize of five thousand dollars?"

"I do not even remember that I put it down on paper when I sent to claim the amount. But after I received the money I destroyed that paper also. I only remember it was seventeen thousand and something, but for the life of me I cannot recollect the exact number."

"Mr. Legrand," said I, in a grave tone, "you must accompany me to a magistrate. Your explanation may be true, but I am afraid, unless you can bring some corroborative evidence, it will not avail you in a court of justice. To tell you the truth, there is an air of improbability about your whole story."

"Well, sir, time will prove. I am ready to accompany you. I feel conscious of my own innocence, and feel satisfied God will not allow me to be punished unjustly."

He embraced his mother and sister, and we left the house together. We immediately proceeded to a magistrate's, and Edward Legrand was that same night fully committed to the Tombs, to await his trial.

When I returned home that night I must confess I was not satisfied. Although suspicion was so strong against the prisoner, and his own explanation so lame, yet I thought it might be true. And then his handsome face haunted me. I asked myself the question over and over again, if it could be possible that he could be guilty? Wearied with conjecture, I lighted a cigar, and was almost dozing to sleep when I was aroused by a ring at the bell. In a few moments afterwards my fellow-officer, Hardin, entered the room.

"How are you, Brampton?" said he, shaking me by the hand.

"How are you, Hardin? When did you get back?"

"I got back this morning. Not seeing you at the chief's office all day, I thought you might be sick, and so I thought I would just drop in to see you."

"I am quite well, I thank you. Take a cigar. What luck have you had?"

"O, I bagged my game. But I tell you I had a wily customer to deal with. I thought once he would escape me. The proofs I had against him were very meagre; but I stuck to them like a leech. Two nights ago he left Philadelphia for New York; but I was too deep for him, for I got in the same car with him. He returned to Philadelphia by the next train, and I went back too. At last I was convinced I had the right man and he is now in the goal at Philadelphia."

This conversation had reference to a defaulter whom Hardin had been employed to arrest.

"He seems to have kept you running about; to take you from Philadelphia to New York and back again the same night was too bad."

"Yes, but I met with an adventure in the cars which served to amuse me a good deal."

"Indeed, what was it?"

"It did not amount to much; but anything, you know, serves to pass time. The fact is, I met with an extraordinary *lusus nature'*, a silent woman."

"A silent woman! What do you mean?"

"You must know when I got into the cars in Philadelphia there were very few passengers. Among them, however, was a lady dressed in black, who wore a very thick veil. I wondered for a long time if she were handsome or not, and at last I determined to try and make her raise her veil. An opportunity presenting itself, I addressed some commonplace remark to her, but not a word could I get in reply. I made several fresh attempts, but met with no success. At last I gave it up in despair."

"She doubtless thought you intrusive, and did not want to converse with you."

"That was my opinion at the time; but I am now certain she had some special reason for remaining silent."

"What makes you think so?"

"I told you the man I was watching stayed only two hours in New York, returning to Philadelphia by the next train. Well, would you believe it? The silent woman did the same thing, for there she was in the cars again. I again endeavored to commune with her, but with no better success than before. Now I think it very strange that a woman travelling alone should only visit New York for two hours in the middle of the night."

"Did you catch a glimpse of her features?" I asked, eagerly.

"No, she kept her veil down all the time. I noticed, however, that she took the southern train."

A light began slowly to enter my mind. I turned the conversation to some other topic, and in a few minutes Hardin took his leave. After he had gone I settled my course of action for the following morning, and then retired to rest, and slept as only a detective can sleep; when he thinks he possesses the clue to a mystery which has bothered him for some time.

I was up very early the next morning, and having settled some business, found myself at eight o'clock at the Jersey City depot. I had determined to take a run down to Baltimore for the good of my health. At half past four in the afternoon I reached the Monumental City, after a very pleasant trip. I installed myself in Barnum's Hotel, and having taken my tea, I determined I would go out and explore the city. I commenced with Baltimore Street, and walked slowly up this busy thoroughfare. When I reached the corner of St. Paul and

Baltimore Streets, a large printed bill fastened to the front of a lottery office attracted my attention. It ran as follows:

"This is the lucky office. No. 17,512, sold here a few days ago drew a prize of live thousand dollars! Walk in and try your luck."

I walked in as requested, and found a middle-aged man behind the counter.

"Good evening," said I, as I entered.

"Good evening," returned the lottery office keeper. "What can I do for you? Two little beauties to be drawn to-morrow—the lucky little 'Patapsco,' and the 'Maryland Consolidated'—tickets only one dollar. Let me sell you some; chose your own numbers if you like."

"Well, I don't know," I replied, putting on as country a looking air as I could. "I don't believe much in lotteries. Why, there's Jem Randall, of our town, has tried his luck ever so many times, and he never got a prize. And, by golly, I never heard of anybody winning anything."

"My rustic friend, you are mistaken," returned the lottery-office keeper. "I very frequently sell large prizes. Why, only last week I sold a prize of five thousand dollars on a venture of ten."

"O, yes, it's very easy to say that. I don't say that you don't tell the truth; but—"

"Here is the ticket that drew the prize," replied the man. "And here are the letters of the young man who purchased the ticket. He lives in New York, and his name is Edward Legrand."

So saying he handed me the letter in question. One glance at them was sufficient to prove that young Legrand's statement to me was true in every particular, and it followed as a matter of course that he was innocent of the robbery. I had just finished reading the letter when a lady dressed in black entered the office. She handed the man a large bundle of tickets. He looked them all over very carefully.

"I am sorry to inform you, madam," said he, "that you have been unlucky again—you have drawn no prize."

She wore a thick veil which concealed her face; but I could see her tremble.

"I have almost determined I will not try again," said she. "I have already lost nearly five thousand dollars. However, here are two hundred more, this must be my last venture."

"You will very likely draw a big prize this time, which will make up all your losses," replied the office keeper, banding her a quantity of tickets for the money she had given him.

The lady left the store. I followed her, and saw her enter a house in Courtland Street. When she had been in ten minutes, I went to the same door and rang the bell.

"I wish to speak with Mrs. Morton," said I to the servant who answered my summons.

I was shown into a parlor, and found the lady in black there alone.

"Madam," said I, "I have come to inform you that your nephew, Mr. Edward Legrand, is in prison, charged with the robbery of five thousand dollars from your husband's safe."

She turned as pale as death, and trembled so violently that she could scarcely support herself.

"He is innocent!" she murmured at last.

"I am aware of it, madam, and I come to you to do justice to him. It was you that took the money from your husband's safe. On the night of the robbery you left Baltimore, and surreptitiously entering your husband's house, you went to his bedroom, took the key of the safe from the bureau drawer, and appropriating the contents, you replaced the key, and returned to Baltimore by the next train. You have spent the whole of this money in the purchase of lottery tickets."

"I acknowledge I am guilty," returned the woman, covering her face with her hands. "I have been mad—crazy; but I had hopes of getting back what I had lost, and then I intended to confess everything to my husband."

"You must make that confession in writing now, madam. I need scarcely tell you that your husband cannot proceed against you, and that in the eyes of the law you are guilty of no crime, but it is necessary that Edward Legrand should be immediately exculpated."

"I will do anything you wish."

At my dictation she wrote out a full confession. It appeared that when she first came down to Baltimore, out of curiosity she bought a lottery ticket. With this she won a small prize. The passion for gaming was developed in her mind, and she risked all the money she had in her possession. Maddened at her loss, she determined to return to New York and procure more. She knew where to find the key of her husband's safe. She abstracted the money, and then returned to

Baltimore, and lost all the money she had taken in the purchase of lottery tickets.

Edward Legrand was of course immediately liberated, and a few weeks afterwards I had the satisfaction of learning that he had been admitted an equal partner in the house in which he had served as clerk.

Mrs. Morton's husband forgave her for what she had done, and the last I heard of them was that they were living happily together.

Leaf the Eleventh

The Coiners

During the year 1848 the West was flooded with counterfeit coin. It was so well manufactured that it passed readily. The evil at last became so great that the United States authorities requested a skilful detective might be sent to ferret out the nest of coiners. I was fixed upon to perform the duty.

I had nothing to guide me. The fact, however, that Chicago was the city where the counterfeit coin was most abundant, led me to suspect that the manufactory might be somewhere, within its limits. It was, therefore, to the capital of the West that I first proceeded. I spent five weeks in that city, but without gaining the slightest clue of the counterfeiters.

I began to grow discouraged, and really thought I should be obliged to return home without having achieved any result. One day I received a letter from my wife requesting that I would send her home some money, as she was out of funds. I went into a bank and asked for a draft, at the same time handing a sum of money to pay for it, in which there were several half dollars. The clerk pushed three of the half dollars back to me.

"Counterfeit," said he.

"What," said I, "do you mean to tell me those half dollars are counterfeits?"

"I do."

"Are you certain?"

"Perfectly certain. They are remarkably well executed, but they are deficient in weight. See for yourself."

And he placed one of them in the scales against a genuine half dollar on the other side. The latter weighed down the former.

"That is the best counterfeit coin I ever saw in my life," I exclaimed, examining them very closely. "Is all the counterfeit money in circulation here of the same character as this?"

"O, dear, no," replied the clerk, "it is not nearly so well done. These are the work of Ned Willet, the famous New York counterfeiter. I know them well, for I have handled a great deal of it in my time. Here is some of the money that is in circulation here," he added, taking several half dollars from a drawer. "You see the milling is not nearly as perfect as Ned Willett's, although it is pretty well done, too."

I compared the two together, and found that he was right. I supplied the place of the three counterfeit half dollars with good coin, and returned the former to my pocket again.

A few days after this I received information which caused me to take a journey to a village about thirty miles from Chicago. I arrived there at night and took up my quarters at the only tavern in the place. It was a wretched dwelling, and kept by an old man and woman, the surliest couple I think it has ever been my lot to meet. In answer to my inquiry as to whether I could have lodging there for the night I noticed that the host gave a peculiar look at his wife, and after some whispering I was informed in the most ungracious manner possible that I could have a bed.

I have frequently in the course of my life been obliged to put up with wretched accomodation, so I did not allow my equanimity of temper to be destroyed by the miserable fare set before me, and the still more miserable sleeping apartment into which I was ushered after I had concluded my repast.

The chamber was of small size, and was certainly well ventilated, for I could see the stars peeping through the roof. The bed was simply a bag of straw thrown into one corner of the room, without sheets or covering of any kind. This last fact, however, was not of much consequence, as it was summer time, and oppressively hot.

I stood for more than an hour gazing out of the opening which served for a window. Before me was spread an immense prairie, the limits of which I could not see. The tavern in which I had taken up my abode appeared to be isolated from all other dwellings, and save the croak of the tree frog and the hum of the locust not a sound reached my ears. It was a beautiful moonlight night, and so bright that I could see to read the smallest print.

At last I began to grow weary, and throwing myself on my pallet I was soon plunged into a deep slumber. How long I slept I know not, but I was awakened by a dull sound, which resembled some one hammering in the distance. I suppose it was the peculiarity of the sound which awoke me, for it was by no means loud, but conveyed to me the idea of some one striking iron with a muffled hammer. I rose up from my bed and went to the window; the moon was low in the western horizon, by which fact I knew that it must be near morning. The sound I have before refered to, reached me more distinctly than when in the back part of the chamber. It appeared to come from some outhouses which were situated about a hundred yards from the house.

Now I am naturally of an inquiring mind, and this sound, occuring as it did in the middle of the night in such a remote, out of the way place, piqued my curiosity, and I felt an irrepressible desire to go out and discover the cause of it. This desire, as the sound continued, grew upon me with such intensity that I resolved to gratify it at any price.

I put on my boots, the only article of attire I had discarded, and cautiously opened the door of my chamber, noiselessly descended the rickety staircase. A few steps brought me into the lower apartment, which I found entirely deserted. I crept quietly to the door, and unfastening it without making the slightest noise, was soon in the moonlight.

Not a soul was visible, but the sound still continued, and grew much more distinct as I approached the place from whence it proceeded. At last I found myself before a long, low building, through the crevices of which I could perceive a lurid glare issuing. I stooped down and peered through the keyhole, and to my extreme surprise, I saw half a dozen strong-looking men with their coats off, and sleeves turned up, performing a variety of strange occupations. Some were working at a forge, others were superintending the casting of moulds, and some were engaged in the process of milling coin. In a moment the whole truth burst upon me. Here was the gang of counterfeiters I was in search of, and the landlord and his wife evidently belonged to the same band, for in one corner I perceived them employed—the man polishing off some half dollar pieces, just turned from the moulds, while the woman was packing the finished coin into rolls.

I had seen enough, and was about to return to my apartment again, when suddenly I felt a heavy hand placed on my shoulder, and turning my head round, to my horror found myself in the grasp of as ill-looking a scoundrel as ever escaped the gallows.

"What are you doing here, my good fellow?" he exclaimed, in a gruff voice, giving me a shake.

"Taking a stroll by moonlight," I replied, endeavoring to maintain my presence of mind.

"Well, perhaps you'll just take a stroll in here, will you?" returned the ruffian, pushing open the door and dragging me in after him.

All the inmates of the barn immediately stopped work, and rushed towards us when they saw me.

"Why, what's this!" they all exclaimed.

"A loafer I found peeping outside," said the man who had captured me.

"He's a traveller that came to the tavern to-night and asked for lodgings; the last time I saw him he was safe in bed," said the landlord.

The men withdrew to a corner of the apartment, leaving one to keep guard over me. I soon saw they were in earnest consultation, and were evidently debating some important question. The man keeping guard over me said nothing, but scowled fiercely. I had not uttered a single word during all the time I had been in the barn. I was aware that whatever I might say, would in all probability only do more harm than good, and it has always been a maxim of mine to hold my tongue when in doubt. At last the discussion seemed to be settled, for the blackest and dirtiest of the whole came forward, and without any introduction, exclaimed:

"I say, stranger, look here—you must die!"

I did not move a muscle, nor utter a word.

"You have found out our secret, and dead men tell no tales."

I was silent.

"We will give you ten minutes to say your prayers, and also allow you the privilege of saying whether you will be hanged or shot."

Suddenly an idea struck me. I remembered something that might save my life. I burst into a violent fit of laughter, in fact it was hysterical, but they did not know that. They looked from one to the other in the greatest amazement.

"Well, he takes it mighty cool, anyhow," said one.

"I suppose he don't think we are in earnest," said another.

"Come, stranger, you had better say your prayers," said the man who had first spoken, "time flies."

My only reply was a fit of laughter more violent than the first.

"The man's mad!" they exclaimed.

"Or drunk," said some.

"Well, boys," I cried, speaking for the first time, "this is the best joke I ever seed. What, hang a pal?"

"A pal—you a pal?"

"I aint nothing else," was my elegant rejoinder.

"What's your name?"

"Did you ever hear of Ned Willett?" I asked.

"You may be certain of that. Aint he at the head of our profession?"

"Well, then, I'm Ned Willet."

"You Ned Willet!" they all exclaimed.

"You may bet your life on that," I returned swaggering up to the corner where I had seen the old woman counting and packing the counterfeit half dollars.

Fortune favored me. None of the men present had ever seen Ned Willett, although his reputation was well known to them, and my swaggering, insolent manner had somewhat thrown them off their guard, yet I could plainly saw that all their doubts were not removed.

"And you call these things well done, do you?" I asked, taking up a roll of the money. "Well, all I can say is that if you can't do better than this you had better shut up shop, that's all."

"Can you show us anything better?" asked one of the men.

"I rather think I can. If I couldn't I'd go and hang myself."

"Let's see it," they all cried.

This was my last *coup*, and one on which I knew my life depended.

"Lookee here, gentlemen," I exclaimed, taking one of the counterfeit half dollars from my pocket which had been rejected at the bank, "here is my last job, what do you think of it?"

It was passed from hand to hand, some saying it was no counterfeit at all, others saying that it was.

"How will you prove that it is a counterfeit?" asked one of the men.

"By weighing it with a genuine one." I replied.

This plan was immediately adopted and its character proved.

"Perhaps he got this by accident," I heard one of the men whisper to another.

"Try these," said I, taking the other two from my pocket.

All their doubts now vanished

"Beautiful!" exclaimed some. "Very splendid!" said others.

"When they had examined it to their satisfaction, they all of them cordially shook me by the hand, every particle of doubt having vanished from their minds. I carried out my part well. Some questions were occasionally asked me, involving some of the technicalities of the business; these, however, I avoided, by stating that I was on a journey of pleasure, and would much rather drink a glass of whiskey than answer questions. The whiskey was produced, and we made a night of it, and it was not until morning had dawned that we separated.

The next day I returned to Chicago, and brought down the necessary assistance, and captured the whole gang of counterfeiters in the very act. This den was broken up forever, and most of them were condemned to serve a term of years in the State Prison.

I have those counterfeit half dollars still in my possession, and intend never to part with them, for they were certainly the means of saving my life.

Leaf the Twelfth

The Defrauded Heir

I have already stated that I was brought up to the medical profession although I never graduated as a physician.

My father was a respectable merchant, living in the city of New York. He bestowed as good an education on me as he could afford, and then placed me in the office of Dr. Lignon, who resided in a large country village, for the purpose of studying medicine. I was then eighteen years of age, and was to remain with him until I was twenty-one, and then enter a medical college.

I was very fond of reading, and soon exhausted the doctor's library. From my very boyhood I possessed an analytical mind. I never allowed anything to escape my observation. The most trivial circumstances, which to others would appear unworthy of notice, were recorded by me, treasured up in my memory, and ultimately supplied a missing link in some chain.

Doctor Lignon did a large practice, and afforded a very good school for a student. I had not been with him two years before I was of considerable use to my tutor, being able to visit the poorer classes of patients, and attend to office practice.

Among the doctor's patients was a Mr. Stephen Barton, a wealthy gentleman who lived about three miles from the village. He was a widower with an only son, a boy about four years of age. His brother, Mr. Amos Barton, also resided with him. The latter was reported to be a very pious man, at all events he visited church regularly.

One day Doctor Lignon was sent for in a great hurry to attend Mr. Stephen Barton, who had been taken with a fit. The poor old gentleman, however, died before he reached the house. A few days afterwards I learned from the doctor that young Henry Barton had been left heir to all his immense wealth, and his uncle was sole executor to the will; there was a provision in the will that if the young lad died before he reached the age of twenty-one years, the whole of the property was to revert to the uncle, Amos Barton.

It was about this time that I noticed my tutor paid very frequent visits to Barton Manor House, although there was no one ill there. I noticed this more particularly, as I knew that Doctor Lignon was no great friend to Amos Barton. I had frequently heard him observe that he looked upon Mr. Stephen Barton's brother as a hypocrite. I also noticed that a great change came over the doctor in a few days; his manners were generally open and frank, and he possessed a naturally great flow of spirits; but suddenly all this changed, he became moody and reserved. His health also seemed to give way, he grew pale and sallow. This set me to thinking, and I wondered in my own mind what could be the cause of it.

One morning about a week after Mr. Barton's funeral, I entered the surgery before the doctor was up. The first thing which struck my attention was a glass mortar on the table. I concluded that my tutor had left it there, and must have prepared some medicine during the night. I examined the mortar, and found some small crystals at the bottom of it, which emitted a strong odor of prussic acid. I also noticed that the bottle containing antimonial wine, and the one containing chloroform, were displaced.

"So, so," thought I to myself, "the doctor must have been preparing medicine late last night. But what kind of case in the world can it be that requires cyanoret of potash, chloroform and antimonial wine, for those are the medicines he used? Why there's enough of the first drug left to poison half the village. Well, here's a problem for me to solve, that's all."

I made a note of the circumstance in a copious note book which I carried about with me. I then commenced my daily reading, and continued to be thus unremittingly engaged until evening, when the doctor entered the office.

"Well, James," said he, divesting himself of his overcoat, "busily engaged, I see. What is the subject of your studies to-day?"

"I am very much interested in a curious French book which I found in the library," I returned.

"Indeed, I was not aware you could read French."

"O, yes, I can read it as well as English. I taught myself."

"There are a good many French books in the library. What subject does the one you are reading treat on?"'

"It appears to be a philosophical treatise on different subjects. I am now reading an essay on the 'Art of producing the exact appearance of death.'"

The doctor started and turned pale, he snatched the book from my hand, and hurriedly exclaimed:

"James, you had better be studying the bone. This book is not for you to read just yet. I may let you have it by-and-by."

So saying he hurried from the apartment. I was confounded for a moment or two, and then subdued light entered my mind, and I took my note book from my pocket and made another entry.

A few days after this occurrence a mysterious kind of disease made its appearance in the neighborhood called the black tongue; a great many persons were taken sick with it, and several died. Within ten days of Stephen Barton's death, his little son Henry Barton, was committed to the grave. Every one who attended the funeral thought that it was shocking that father and son should both die within such a short time of each other, and no one appeared more concerned than Amos Barton. His grief was so natural that even his enemies were constrained to acknowledge that in the present instance he had shown himself most disinterested. He could not have mourned more if his own son had died.

After young Henry Barton's funeral, Doctor Lignon returned home for the first time within two days. I had, however, visited the most urgent calls, and had managed very well.

"What a terrible sudden death that of young Barton was," said I, "what was his disease?"

"Black tongue," replied the doctor, curtly, as if he had wished to put an end to the conversation.

"I have heard something about this disease, but know nothing about it," was my reply.

"It is a mysterious disease that has lately made its appearance in this country, supposed to be taken from animals; it affects human beings from the use of the milk taken from cows that have the disease; but look into Copeland's Medical Encyclopedia, and you will find a very able article on it."

I was no sooner alone than I examined the work referred to. I read the article over two or three times, and was entranced by it. I learned how rare the disease was, the strange pathological developments in persons dying from it, and the fine opportunities which were offered for scientific examination.

A sudden idea entered my mind—it haunted me all day—and in the middle of the night I put it into execution. Forgive me, reader, I was an ardent student in my profession, and perhaps might never have an opportunity of investigating this strange malady again. I determined to examine young Harry's body.

The cemetery where he was buried was removed about a mile from the village. The road to it was a dreary one at the best; but especially was this the case when darkness was over the face of the earth.

It was a cold November night when I started on my fearful errand. The wind whistled through the leafless trees, and by its moaning and sobbing I almost fancied it seemed conscious that a grave was about to be desecrated. Until the limits of the village were passed, I got on very well; but when I reached the dark road leading to the cemetery, I must confess my heart began to fail me. I whistled to distract my attention, I sang, I even called out in a loud voice. It was no use, I felt my courage fast oozing away; but shame for my own fears, and an ardent desire to investigate this mysterious disease, made me proceed.

At last I reached the cemetery gate, and with a trembling hand opened the massive portal. The grave where the body was laid was at the further end of the cemetery, and I had, as it were, to walk through a whole city of graves before I reached it. How I reached it I know not, for by this time my fears had almost unmanned me. My legs trembled under me, and various horrible incidents I had read in the course of my life all rushed into my mind in the most vivid manner. I could just trace the form of the white tombstones which lay in my path. Twenty times I had transformed them into spectres, and fancied they were advancing towards me. More than once I turned my back to fly from the spot, but a more powerful feeling than fear prevented me, namely the love of science.

At last I reached the spot where the boy lay buried. I could distinctly trace the form of the newly-made grave. I put my lantern on the ground, and untied the sack I had brought with me for the removal of the body, and which now contained the spade and other instruments necessary for exhuming the body. As I proceeded in my work, my ardor increased, and all my superstitious fears left me. The earth was easily loosened, and in a short time two large heaps were raised on both sides of me. I soon reached the coffin, and a little more exertion served to bring it entirely in sight. I was very strong, and had no difficulty whatever in raising it up, and placing it on the edge of the grave. This done I unscrewed the lid, but before taking out the body I thought I would take a peep at it. I brought the lantern to bear on the face. I started back in consternation; the lantern fell to the ground, but fortunately was not extinguished. I knew young Henry Barton's features perfectly well, and those of the corpse were none of his!

I picked up the lantern, and again examined the features of the deceased. They were entirely unknown to me. I seated myself on one of the mounds of earth, and remained for at least a quarter of an hour absorbed by my reflections. I then rose up, re-adjusted the coffin lid, and again consigned the body to the grave. The hole was soon filled in. The work finished, I hastened home, and in a quarter of an hour I was seated in the doctor's office without any one having been aware of my absence. That night I made another entry in my note-book. This time it was a longer one than usual.

I felt deeply interested in this mystery, and determined to investigate it to the end. For that purpose I asked leave of Doctor Lignon to visit New York on business. I set off next morning, and made some important discoveries which I shall relate by-and-by to the reader; but on one point I was entirely unsuccessful, but I learned sufficient to compromise Doctor Lignon in my eyes, and I determined not to return to him. I wrote to him, stating that I had made up my mind I would adopt another profession. I need not now enter into the reasons which made me turn detective officer, as they have nothing to do with the matter in question; suffice it to say that in a few years I became quite famous, and had as much business as I could attend to. I married and settled myself in the upper part of New York city.

One January evening, eighteen years after I had left Doctor Lignon's, I returned home as usual after the labors of the day. I found my wife seated by a cheering fire, and the tea-urn hissing on the table, on which too was placed the tea service, and the toast, racks fastened to the fender, betokened that the evening meal was waiting for me.

"Home at last, dear James," said my wife. "I have been waiting tea for you some time."

"Yes, I was engaged longer at the office of the Chief of police than I expected to-day. By-the-by, who do you think I met on Broadway to-day?"

"I don't know. Who?"

"No other than Amos Barton." I should have said that my wife came from the village where Doctor Lignon lived, and was well acquainted with all the parties mentioned in this history.

"Indeed," she replied, "did he speak to you?"

"O, yes; it appears he intends running for Congress. He solicited my influence; but of course I did not promise it to him."

"It is very strange, but father never liked that man. There was something in his countenance or his manner which was very repulsive to him."

"A great many people share his prejudices, my dear," I returned. "Amos Barton is by no means a general favorite. I remember when I was a pupil at Doctor Lignon's I used to hate him."

"And yet no one can tell why they dislike him. They can bring no immoral act against him. Did you ever hear anything tangible proved against him?"

""Never."

"Do you remember how strange he came in for his property? I was but a little girl then, still I recollect distinctly the sensation it made. His brother and nephew died within ten days of each, other. It was very curious."

"Very."

I suppose I uttered this word in a very peculiar manner, for my wife put down her cup which she was in the act of raising to her mouth, and glanced curiously at me.

"What do you mean by that 'very?'" said my wife.

"Now, James, I know by your manner that you have a secret to tell me."

"My dear, what secret should I know?"

"I don't know; but you are so different from other men—you have such an extraordinary faculty for tracing matters out—I am certain you know more about that affair than you pretend."

At that moment there was a ring at the bell, and the servant girl entered almost directly afterwards and handed me a sealed envelope. I glanced at the outside, and saw that it had "House's Printing Telegraph Company" printed on the outside of it. I hurriedly broke the seal, and drew from the red envelope a long slip of paper, on which was printed the following message:

> Come to me immediately. I am dying, and have something of importance to communicate to you.
>
> DOCTOR LIGTON
>
> *A——, New York.*

I handed the despatch to my wife.

"Must you go?" said she, with a shade of disappointment in her voice.

"I must indeed," I rejoined. "I have some idea as to the nature of the communication he has to make, and leaving out of consideration my duty as his former pupil, I must go for other reasons."

"Well, dear, of course I can make no opposition; you won't stay longer than is necessary, I am sure."

"Let me see, it is now seven o'clock. The train leaves at eight. I can be at my destination by to-morrow morning."

Kissing my wife good-by, I hurried off. It was bitter cold in the streets, and the snow was falling in large flakes. In spite of the obstruction caused by the snow, I reached the depot in good time, and taking a seat in a car near the stove, in a few minutes I was proceeding on my way to my destination.

The stove heated the cars thoroughly, and I lay back in my seat, and yielding to the relaxation caused by the warmth, I closed my eyes, and in a very short time I was fast asleep. While in this condition I had a curious dream. I thought I was in a court of justice, and that a prisoner was placed at the bar charged with conspiracy and abduction. The prisoner's face appeared to be perfectly familiar to me, although I could not recollect who it was. I also recognized the tones of his voice. I asked myself over and over again who it could be. While endeavoring to recollect, thought some one whispered in my ear that it was Mr. Amos Barton.

The name was pronounced so distinctly that I awoke. I discovered that a man and woman seated before me were conversing in a low tone together, and that one of them had pronounced Mr. Barton's name. I still pretended to be asleep, but examined my fellow travellers with a scrutinizing glance. I found they were common-looking people, evidently past the meridian of life. They were meanly clad. The man evidently was an habitual drunkard, and the woman, with her hard face, led me to suspect that she was an opium eater. Mr. Barton's name aroused my curiosity. In spite of the old adage I determined to listen.

"I tell you," said the woman, in a tone of remonstrance, "you can't deceive him much longer. He'll find out that the boy ran away from us, and then good-by to our allowance."

"How can he find it out," returned the man, in a gruff voice, "if you only keep a quiet tongue in your head? But you always have such a confounded lot to say—"

"It's all very well, Ralph, your talking in that manner; but what would you do when he cross-examines you so closely if I didn't put in my say. I tell you he would floor you directly, and then we might hook for the money that's all."

"I should like to see him dare to refuse it," returned the man in a determined voice; "if he did I'd blow—blame me if I wouldn't—although he has that bit of paper that I signed his name to. I tell you, we haven't lived on him eighteen years for nothing."

"Suppose you tell him his nephew is dead?"

"Bah, that would be of no use. He's such a stingy beggar, he'd stop the supplies at once. No, no, you must leave me to manage him. I'll tell him that I know where he is, and that will keep him in dread, and he'll fork over without a word."

"Now, Ralph, suppose he should be determined not to give you-any more, what would you do?"

"What would I do? I would say to him, 'Look here, Mr. Barton, if you don't send me the money you owe me to 222 East Broadway before three days have expired, then if you don't see the State prison looming in the distance, I'm a Dutchman.'"

"Well, I hope we shall be successful, that's all. I have my doubts, however."

After this they relapsed into silence, and did not speak any more until they reached their destination. I made a few notes of this conversation in my pocket book.

About two o'clock the next day I reached the end of my journey, and was at Doctor Lignon's house. I rung the bell and was at once shown up stairs. The moment I entered the Doctor's bedroom I started back in horror. Familiar as I had been with scenes of suffering, I had never met with one equal to this. Eighteen years had elapsed since I had seen Doctor Lignon, and he was now scarcely recognizable. Time had not dealt very kindly with him, for he was now an old, old man. What little hair he had left was snowy white, even his eyebrows were bereft of every particle of color. His body was attenuated to a most frightful degree. It was plainly to be perceived he was suffering from some painful organic disease. His face was unearthly pale, not a common pallor, but, a sallow, waxy paleness, which it is difficult to describe, but which when once seen can never be forgotten. A dark circle enclosed each eye and by the very contrast with the rest of his face, gave a fearful expression to it. His eyes shone brightly, but were sunk deep in their orbits. His cheeks had fallen in, his chin had become prominent, and his thin, wasted hands shook as if he were affected with palsy.

About a year prior to his present condition, he noticed for the first time a small pimple on his tongue. He thought at first it was occasioned by being grazed against his teeth. He applied caustic to it; but instead of healing it up, it broke out into a small ulcer. This showed no disposition to heal, and by-and-by he experienced strong lancinating pains through it. This alarmed him, and he went to New York to consult Doctor M——, and Doctor P——, the famous professors of surgery. The moment they saw it, they decided that it was cancer, and that all that remained for the invalid to do was to go home and prepare for death, an operation being entirely unjustifiable.

He returned home, and in spite of the surgeon's opinion, and his own experience in such cases, continued to hope against hope. The ulceration, however, continued to spread rapidly. Hectic fever set in, and his digestive powers gave way. He was obliged to keep his bed, and then it was that the conviction was forced on his mind that he must die. His suffering now became frightful to contemplate. But physical pain was nothing compared to the pangs of his conscience. He felt that he must soon stand in the presence of his Maker. He knew he had committed a fearful wrong, and the sole idea of his mind now was to repair it. At last the thought struck him to apply to me, and for that purpose he sent me the telegraphic dispatch, in reply to which, summons I now stood before him.

"I know my days are numbered," said the old doctor, after he had given me the foregoing particulars of his case. "My disease is utterly incurable. But, James, I have a fearful confession to make to you, one which I fear will drag me down to perdition, unless I atone for it by endeavoring to make restitution. O, James, how can I summon up resolution enough to tell you what a guilty wretch I am?"

"Perhaps I already know something of the matter of which you would speak," I returned.

"Impossible! No living soul save one knows it. O God, must I reveal my own shame? Must I tell how guilty I have been? I cannot, I cannot!"And the old man buried his head in the pillow.

I sincerely pitied him, and determined that I would begin the subject myself.

"Doctor," said I, "you had a companion in the transaction to which you refer."

"I had, I had! But how can you know anything about it? Can it be possible that you could have suspected anything at the time?"

"I know all; and to spare you the shame of confessing, I will repeat to you the particulars of the transaction which brings remorse to your dying bed. Eighteen years ago Mr. Stephen Barton died, leaving an only son heir to his immense wealth. Mr. Amos Barton was appointed his guardian. By some means, I know not what, he persuaded you to assist him in his nefarious designs. You administered a preparation to the rightful heir which produced the effect of simulated death. Amos Barton procured a body from the University Medical College in New York. While Henry Barton lay in an insensible condition, his body was removed from the coffin, and substituted by the one obtained from the city."

"Great heavens, how did you find all this out? I had no idea that any mortal man, save the other guilty party, knew anything of the matter."

I here related the manner in which I had ferreted out the truth, with which the reader is already acquainted.

"But what became of the boy, the rightful heir?" asked the doctor, eagerly.

"I don't know. If you remember at the time all this occurred I left your house and visited New York. I made every possible search, but without any success, except obtaining information from where Amos Barton obtained the substitute. I debated a long time whether I ought not to make known what I had discovered to the authorities. But I knew Amos Barton's influence, and feared I should only bring disgrace on myself. Besides which I could not bear the idea of blackening your fair name."

"O, thank you for your consideration, I did not deserve it. But do you think he—"

The old man hesitated, as if he dared not give utterance to his thought.

"Murdered him you would say," I rejoined. "No; this very day I have discovered that he did not make way with him."

And I here related the conversation I had heard in the railway car.

"God grant that he may still be alive," said the old man, "and now, James, listen to my dying words. Promise me that you will use every exertion to discover young Barton and re-instate him into his property. I want you also to draw up a plain statement of the facts of the case. I will sign it, and you shall witness it. In the event of the case coming before a jury, it may aid in establishing the rightful heir's claim. Should you discover Henry Barton to be dead, of course it will be no use to make any movement in the matter, for the present occupant of Barton Manor House would then be heir-at-law."

"I will do everything you require," I returned, and immediately drew up the paper referred to, which Doctor Lignon signed. This done he appeared to be mere easy in his mind, and actually slept some hours, which he had not done for some days before.

Having settled all these matters, I took an affectionate farewell of my old tutor. I would willingly have remained with him until the last moment of his life, but my duties in New York required my immediate presence. Had I known the poor old doctor's end was so near I would undoubtedly have stayed, for he died the next day, and was committed to the grave without one soul being in any way interested in the event. I make a mistake: there was one person interested, and that was Amos Barton, for he saved two thousand dollars a year by the physician's death, that being the sum paid to him for his share in the nefarious transaction.

After I returned to New York, I debated in my own mind as to the means to be used to discover if Henry Barton was still alive; at the same time I set a watch on the premises, 222 East Broadway, giving orders for the messenger to inform me the moment he caught sight of the man who had been called Ralph, and with whom there can be no doubt Harry Barton had been placed after his removal from Barton Manor House.

I had been home two days when my messenger informed me that he had seen Ralph just enter a restaurant in East Broadway. I immediately started for the place, and found the man of whom I was in search, seated in a box, and occupied in gazing very earnestly on a young man about twenty-two years of age, who was seated in another box exactly opposite to him. I placed myself in close contiguity for the purpose of observing all that passed. I was soon rewarded for my trouble.

Ralph at last seemed satisfied with his scrutiny, for he left his own box and advanced to where the young man was sitting. I could overhear all their conversation.

"Young man," said he, carelessly seating himself by the young man's side, "may I ask your name?"

The person addressed started, for he had not seen the man approach.

"What do you mean?" he replied. "Who are you?"

"Never mind who I am," replied Ralph, in a gruff voice. "I ask you again what is your name? Are you ashamed of it?"

"My name is Henry Graham. What do you want with me?"

"No, sir, your name is Henry Murdock, and I am your father. It won't do, you know, trying to disown me; although you did run away from home twelve years ago, I have not forgotten you."

"Silence!"returned the young man, in a subdued voice. "It is true I ran away from your hateful roof. When I lived with you, child though I was, I knew you to be a miserable, drunken loafer, and find after twelve years' absence that you have not reformed."

"Well, come, young man, that's a pretty way for a son to talk to his father."

"You my father! You know you lie. Do you suppose that if I had the sense to discover such was not the case when I was a child, you can impose upon me now?"

"O, it's all very well for you to deny it, but I can prove that you are my son."

"You lie again!" returned the young man with vehemence. "If I thought I had one drop of your ignoble blood in my body, I would open a vein until every particle had ran out. Leave me—your presence annoys me—I wish neither to see nor hear from you again."

"Ah, I see you are riding the high horse. I suppose you are getting on a little in the world, and now want to disown your poor old father."

"Have done, and leave me, or rather I will leave you," returned the young man, rising from his seat, "and listen to me, fellow—if you presume to address me again, I will evoke the protection of the law, and should that not be sufficient to shield me from your persecution, I will take the law into my own hands."

So saying he left the place. Ralph Murdock followed him, and I was not far behind. The young man entered the old Franklin House. In ten minutes I sent up my card, and was at once admitted into his presence. In a few words I explained my business, and was perfectly satisfied that I stood in the presence of Henry Barton. The young man related his story to me, which amounted to substantially as follows:

His first recollection were of living with two persons in Avenue A, in the city of New York. His reputed parents were the very scum of society—the man was a confirmed drunkard, the woman a shrew. The abode in which he lived was wretched in the extreme. He never experienced any kind treatment from his pretended father and mother.

Curses and blows were all they deigned to bestow upon him. His indifference to them soon turned into loathing.

Some years passed away under this wretched treatment, and by the time he had reached ten years of age, he was a poor, depressed, crouching thing, always on the defensive as if he expected a blow to be inflicted on him every moment, in which expectation he was too often correct. He was entirely unlike ether boys of his own age. No children's laugh had ever been echoed in his cars; no children's games had ever released him from the terrible monotony of a miserable existence. His life was at that tender age shrouded over with the dark shadow of despair, and he seemed to have all the miseries of a lifetime developed in the age of a child.

One day the man returned home even in a worse state of intoxication than usual. It was rather late in the evening. When the man entered he gazed around him as if to find some object on which to vent his ill temper. His eyes fell upon the boy who sat shivering with cold in the corner of the room. The man rushed at him, and inflicted blow after blow on the boy's defenseless head. That night he ran away, and managed to reach Boston. He embarked as cabin boy on board a vessel going to the West Indies. He got employment in a mercantile house in Jamaica, and gradually rose to a responsible position. When he had saved a considerable sum of money, he determined to again visit the United States to try and discover his parentage, and was now here for that purpose.

When Harry Barton had finished his history, we entered into a long conversation as to the best means to prove his identity. The task was not an easy one, and I saw but one way, and that was to get Murdock into our power, and make him confess the truth. It was to this end that I devoted all my energies.

The messenger that I had set to watch Murdock informed me, that the day after his meeting with Henry Barton, he had left by the Hudson River cars. I felt certain he had gone to inform Amos Barton of the discovery of the heir. In two days he had returned again.

My mind was made up what to do. I disguised myself as a denizen of the Five Points and threw myself in the man's way, frequenting the same haunts that he did, and ended by making him believe that I belonged to the same class as himself. At last he accosted me, and we became quite intimate. He then proposed to me a bit of business, which was no less than the murder of Henry Barton. I managed to draw out from him the fact that he had been promised five thousand dollars by Amos Barton to effect this piece of villainy. I seemingly entered eagerly into all his plans, and it was decided that he should give me one thousand dollars to assist him. I allowed the affair to progress to a certain point, until I had him completely in my power. I then revealed myself in my true character, and threatened him with immediate arrest unless he would make an instant confession. This he did, after some little hesitation, and it was properly witnessed.

Armed with this document, the confession of Doctor Lignon, and with my own knowledge, I presented myself to Mr. Amos Barton. When I had told my story he at first set me at defiance; but when I read to him the two confessions, he gave in at once. Henry Barton treated him leniently. The uncle resigned all the estates to Henry, and then left the country for France, where he lived on an annuity bestowed on him by his much injured nephew.

Henry Barton is now one of the most respected and wealthy gentlemen in the neighborhood where he resides. Ralph Murdock a few years ago died of delirium tremens in the Bellevue Hospital, and Amos Barton only lived two years after the restitution of the heir to his rights.

Leaf the Thirteenth

The Shadow of a Hand

It is a question that has often been debated, whether man or woman possess most moral courage. I shall not pretend to enter into a discussion of the matter here, but simply relate an incident which came to my knowledge some years since, proving, I think, incontestably, that some of the fairer portion of creation are endowed in an eminent degree with this virtue.

In the autumn of 1846, circumstances called me to Dieppe. To tell the truth I was by no means sorry to visit this fashionable watering place. I had been in Paris for several weeks in search of a cashier of one of the principal New York banks who had committed a heavy defalcation, and the change was a very pleasant one.

It was late in the evening of the 14th of August, when I arrived at the end of my journey, I proceeded at once to the Hotel des Bains (which, by the by, I can recommend to those of my readers who may happen to visit Dieppe), and after a light supper retired to rest.

I have always been an early riser. It makes no difference what time I go to bed at night, I am sure to get up early in the morning. I suppose this is habit, more than anything else. However that may be, the morning after my arrival at Dieppe, I was up by cock-crow. I looked at my watch, and found it wanted a few minutes to four. I determined I would go and explore the town.

When I arrived in the street I was very much surprised to find it full of people. I gave the inhabitants of Dieppe credit for being very industrious, beating their Parisian brethren to nothing, in the exercise of the virtue of early rising, and expected to discover upon inquiry, a practical illustration of the truth of the adage, by finding the citizens of that pretty, but rather slow town, noted for their health, renowned for their wealth, and courted for their wisdom.

I was disturbed from these reflections by observing that the people were all going in one direction, and they hurried forward as if stimulated by some extraordinary curiosity. I addressed inquiries to some of them, but they were too breathless, and in too great a hurry to make any reply to me. All they did was to point before them and nod their heads.

Not being able to obtain any satisfaction from them, I determined to follow their foot-steps, as I was now convinced there must be something to be seen.

We advanced at a very quick pace down a handsome street, which I afterwards learned was the chief street in the town, called the Grand Rue; the crowd becoming more dense, so as to render it very difficult to proceed. We might have gone a mile perhaps, when the street suddenly opened into a large square; this square was densely packed with a great mob. The most distracting noise and confusion prevailed, but I saw something there, raised on a platform at the further end of the square, which engaged my whole attention, and made my blood feel as if it were turned into ice.

It was a guillotine!

Yes, there was the hideous framework painted black, which I had seen once before at the Place du Trone, in Paris. At the moment I turned my eyes on this instrument of death, a man was engaged oiling the grooves, and to enable him to do it more conveniently, the knife was lowered half way down between the two posts, and the morning sun made the blade glitter, rendering it quite distinct to the whole multitude.

Although I had before seen an execution, and was well aware of the painful effect it had upon my mind for months afterwards, morbid curiosity compelled me to remain, and see the conclusion of the tragedy. I had not to wait long, a neighboring bell began to toll, and a cart made its appearance, bearing the criminal. He appeared to take matters very easily, and when I saw him, he was conversing gaily with the two gendarmes who accompanied him. He was smoking a cigar, and glanced around at the multitude with the most perfect *nonchalance.* The populace, when they saw him, raised a veil of execration; a palpable sneer was the only reply he deigned to make.

He ascended the steps leading to the scaffold with an easy gait, and turning sharply around to the mob, stood for a minute or two with his arms folded, and a foot advanced as if defying them. He glanced at them a look of unutterable scorn, and muttered between his teeth the word "*Canaille.*"

It was during this minute or two that I had time to make a note of his appearance. He seemed to be about thirty-five years of age. He was tall and powerfully built, but his features were the very epitome of villainy. His eyes were dark and large, surmounted by heavy eyebrows. He wore a long moustache which extended far beyond his cheeks. Every bad passion seemed to be expressed in his face; in fact, his countenance might be called perfectly devilish. An involuntary shudder ran through me as I gazed upon it.

He resigned himself into the hands of the executioner, and in a few minutes all was over. When the time came for the knife to descend, I had not the courage to look, but turned my head away, and it was only by a shout from the mob that I knew the tragedy was finished.

I inquired of a spectator near me, the name of the criminal and the crime for which he had suffered.

The man stared at me with astonishment, saying:

"Why, it's Jacques Reynauld?"

The name struck me as being somewhat familiar, and I endeavored to remember where I had heard it before. I suddenly recollected the Paris newspapers some months back had been filled with the history of several awful murders committed in Dieppe, and this man's name was in some way connected with them, but in what manner I could not remember. However, my curiosity was now thoroughly excited, I immediately made the most minute inquiries into the matter, and before I left Dieppe had learned the following particulars:

In the Rue des Armes, about four months previous to the time I write, lived a worthy haberdasher of the name of Maurice. His family consisted of himself, his wife, one child, and a servant. They were quiet, respectable people, and very much respected by all their neighbors.

M. Maurice did a good business, and frequently had a considerable sum of money in his house. He had an extraordinary run of customers one Saturday, and when the labors of the day were over he felt very much fatigued. He shut up his shop and proceeded to a small room, where his wife and servant were laying the cloth for supper.

"My dear," said his wife, as soon as he entered the room, "I should very much like some oysters for supper to night."

"I am afraid it is too late," replied the husband, looking at his watch. It was a quarter past eleven.

"Oh no, Justine says there is a shop open round the corner."

"If that be the case, let Justine get some at once, for I am as hungry as a hunter."

Thereupon Justine put on her bonnet and shawl, and went for the oysters; leaving the door ajar, that she might not disturb her master or mistress when she returned.

Now it so happened that the place where she expected to be able to obtain the oysters was closed; but not wishing to disappoint her employers, she determined she would go and seek them elsewhere. In pursuance of this object, she entered the Grande Rue, but had to walk a considerable distance before she could obtain what she sought. She hurried home again, and noticed when she arrived at the door of her master's house that the chimes of a neighboring church struck a quarter to twelve. She had, therefore, been absent just three quarters of an hour.

She was surprised to find the door shut, but supposing that the wind had blown it to, she raised the latch. The door was fastened on the inside. She thought this rather strange, but then again she reflected that it was doubtless only a necessary precaution on the part of her master. She rang the bell, and was very much concerned when, after waiting a few minutes, no reply was made. "They have gone to bed," she said to herself, and felt rather angry with them for having locked her out. She again rung the bell, much more violently than before—still no answer! She now, became alarmed, and rang long and violently—no answer! Her fears were thoroughly aroused, and she related the circumstances to some persons passing along the street. The presence of two or three gendarmes was soon procured, and they proceeded at once to break in the door.

The passage into which the door opened was perfectly dark; but one of the gendarmes stumbled over something, and putting out his hand to save himself, it came in contact with something wet on the ground. A light was immediately obtained, and a horrible sight presented itself.

Lying across the passage was the dead body of Monsieur Maurice, with his throat cut from ear to ear. The floor was swimming in blood. In the little room was the dead body of his wife, presenting the same ghastly wound. Even the little child in the cradle had not escaped, for the merciless assassin had taken its life by the same horrible means. The house was ransacked from top to bottom, and everything of value stolen.

I shall not attempt to depict the horror of the persons who witnessed this shocking sight; it can be more easily imagined than described, and to tell the truth, I don't like dealing in the horrible; it is pandering to a morbid taste, and if have transgressed my usual mode of narration in this sketch, my only excuse is,—it is true.

The most strenuous exertions were made to detect the murderer, but without any success. All that could be learned was, that a man had been seen to look intently in the shop windows about the time M. Maurice was counting out his day's receipts. The whole town of Dieppe was horrified, and when night came many a heart trembled. After a few days the feelings of fear began to decrease, when they were again awakened in a ten-fold manner by another shocking murder.

About ten days after the catastrophe in Rue des Armes, some belated pedestrians were making the best of their way home about two o'clock in the morning. They were walking very rapidly down the Rue Grenard, when they were astounded by seeing a man on the roof of a house, with nothing on but his shirt, crying out with all his strength "murder" "murder!" "murder!" He held a young child in his arms.

They immediately called to him, but all they could gather from him was that murder was committed in the house. They directly made for the door and found it fastened on the inside. They burst the door open with a few vigorous kicks and penetrated into the house. They rushed up stairs, and on the first landing they found the body of a man with his throat cut. He was dead. They entered a bed-room—

hanging half out of bed was the body of a woman, mutilated in the same horrible manner—and stone dead. But they had not yet discovered all the horrors in that house of blood. In the kitchen was discovered the inanimate form of the servant girl, who had been killed by the same means. The assassin was evidently the same who had committed the murder in the Rue des Armes. The wounds inflicted were exactly of the same character, and it was evident the same instrument had been used.

The young man, seen on the roof of the house, was named Pierre Dulon; he deposed before the Procureur du Rio, the next morning, as follows:

> My name is Pierre Dulon; I am twenty-two years of age, and a watchmaker by trade.
>
> For the last two years I have been living as assistant with the late Monsieur Mouton. He resided in the Rue Grenard. His family consisted of himself, wife and child, and servant girl. On the night of the 21st of April, 1864, we all of us retired to bed early. I was accustomed to sleep in one of the attics. In the room next to mine, the servant and child slept. About half-past one o'clock in the morning I awoke. I felt very thirsty and rose to get some water—my pitcher was empty. I went down stairs to fill it. I had nearly reached the first landing when I saw a man stealthily ascending the stairs. I am a very nervous man, and the recent murder had preyed very much on my mind, I had bean living in continual dread ever since. The sight of this man completely paralyzed me; and I stood looking, not able to move hand or foot. He had nearly reached master's door, when M. Mouton opened the door and came out on the landing. The assassin immediately rushed upon him, and putting his hand over my master's mouth, prevented him from calling out. I noticed but one thing, that the murderer had only three fingers on his left hand. I could see no more, but ran up stairs again, and hurried into the servant's room; the child was lying on the bed asleep, but the servant girl was not in the room. I took up up the child in my arms and got out on the roof. This is all I know about the matter.

The excitement in Dieppe was now raised to the highest pitch. No trace of the assassin could be discovered. It was evident that these murders were the work of man—and that he must have been concealed in the houses before they were closed for the night. Government offered a large reward for the discovery of the murderer, and the vigilance of the police was thoroughly aroused.

There lived on the outskirts of Dieppe a widow lady of the name of Beaumaurice. She had no family; but, with one servant girl, lived in a very retired manner. The cottage in which she resided was situated about a half a mile from the city—a little off from the public road.

Madame Beaumaurice had been the wife of an old officer of the Guards. She was an extraordinary woman in every particular; but especially so in respect to a certain coolness of character she possessed, in the midst of danger—which, together with a large amount of moral courage—made her a very notable person. The recent murders had, perhaps, made less impression on her mind than upon any one else in Dieppe,—although it was naturally supposed the retired situation in which she lived would have caused her to be more fearful.

About ten o'clock on the night of the 30th of April, just ten days after the murders in the Rue Grenard, Madame Beaumaurice went up to her bed-room. She was suffering from a nervous headache. She felt very sleepy, and seated herself in a large arm-chair previous to undressing herself. The lamp was placed on a chest of drawers behind her. Opposite to her was a toilet-table, with a cloth on it reaching to the floor. She had already commenced taking off her clothes, when happening to look around her, she saw something which for a moment chilled her blood. It was the shadow of a man's hand on the floor, The hand had only three fingers.

She divined the truth in a moment—the assassin was there, in her house-under that toilet-table. She made not the least motion or sign, but reflected two or three minutes as to the best course to be pursued.

She made up her mind what to do, and advancing to the door, called her servant maid.

"Oh Mary!"exclaimed she, when the girl entered the room. "Do you know where Monsieur Bernard lives?"

"Yes, Madame."

"I have to pay 5,000 francs away very early in the morning. The fact slipped my memory till just now. You will have to run to his house and get the money for me."

"Very well, Madame."

"I will write you a note which you will deliver to him, and he will give you bank bills to the amount."

She wrote as follows:

> "*My dear Monsieur Bernard—*
>
> "The assassin of the Rue des Armes and the Rue Grenard is now in my house. Come immediately with some gendarmes and take him before he escapes.
>
> "HELENE BEAUMAURICE."

And without entering into any explanation with her servant, she dispatched her on the errand. She then quietly re-seated herself and waited.

Yes, she sat in the room with that man under the table for a whole hour. She sat there cool, calm, and collected. She saw the shadow of the hand shift about several times; but the murderer did not attempt to escape from the place of his concealment.

In due time the gendarmes arrived, and Jaques Reynauld was arrested—not, however, without a violent struggle.

I need scarcely add that the most convincing proof of his guilt was found, and in due time he was guillotined, as I have shown in the former part of this sketch.

Leaf the Fourteenth

An Adventure with Italian Brigands

The reader must not suppose that a detective's life is made up only of adventures and hunting after criminals. We, as well as the rest of mankind, have our social hours, and verily believe it has been my lot to meet with as many friends as any one in a similar position in society. I had not resided long in New York before I became acquainted with some capital fellows. We formed a little social circle, and used to meet weekly at each others' houses, where we passed the time most agreeably, relating adventures, telling stories, and playing chess. In the present number it is my intention to give to the reader an adventure which happened to one of my friends.

On the evening that he related it to us there were six of us met together. It was Henry Seldon's turn to tell some event in his life. The night was drawing on apace, and the cozy appearance of our friend Melville's study seemed to invite mutual confidence. It was a December evening, and an unusual silence reigned, broken only by the rumbling of an occasional omnibus as it rolled down the street. The air was chilly and cold outside; but inside a delightful warmth pervaded the whole apartment.

"Well, gentlemen," said Seldon, "to tell the truth, I do not know what to relate."

"Nonsense,"cried our host Melville. "You who have traveled so much have met with plenty of adventures. I have heard you say you lived some time in Rome. Surely something happened to you in that land of bandits and robbers?"

"True, I had for the moment forgotten that. I did meet with an adventure while living in Italy—a terrible one too."

We each of us lighted a fresh cigar, drew our chairs more closely round the fire and placed ourselves in a listening attitude. Our friend Seldon spoke as follows:

"Most of you know that my father was a good, substantial farmer, who resided near Hudson in the State of New York. He was an eccentric man, and one of his hobbies was that everybody ought to follow the bent of his inclination in choosing a profession. I was naturally very fond of drawing, and even when quite a child amused myself with scrawling uncouth figures on every piece of blank paper I could find. This was construed by my father into a love of Art, and forthwith I was destined to become an artist. My taste was fostered, so that by the time I was twenty years of age, I really possessed some talent in drawing. I devoted my time more especially to oil painting, and to perfect my education, I was sent to Rome. This was in the year 1825. Traveling was not so expeditious in those days as now; but after sundry delays I reached my destination. I enstalled myself in comfortable lodgings, and was soon employed in copying the old masters. My life soon became a very monotonous one, and I began to want a change. The solitude of my position began to prey upon my spirits, and my heart yearned for my home again, the banks of the Hudson. I remembered the delightful evenings I had passed there watching the moonbeams play upon the waters—and all the beauties of the Italian sky could not compensate me for my absence from my American home. One night I was pensively walking down a street, when I saw before me an old man who appeared to stagger. I immediately ran towards him.

"'Signor,' I exclaimed, 'you are ill,' and I supported him in my arms.

"'It is only an attack of vertigo, to which I am subject,' he replied.

"I conducted him into a tavern, where, after he had partaken of a little wine, he soon recovered. He was a hale looking man, about sixty years of age, I supposed. His hair was quite gray, and he had a fine open countenance, which instinctively commanded respect.

"'Thanks, Signor, for your great kindness,' said the stranger, after the attack had passed off. 'If I judge correctly, you are not an Italian.'

"'No, I am an American,' I replied.

"This conversation had been carried on in Italian, but the moment I informed him to what country I belonged, a gleam of satisfaction shot across his face—he rose hurriedly from his seat and clasping my hands in his, exclaimed in English:

"'My dear sir, I am delighted to see you. You cannot imagine how much I love your country. I have fought and bled for it.'

"'Indeed' I replied.

"'Yes, I was all through the war of Independence, and had the pleasure of seeing the enemy finally surrender to the immortal Washington. But come, we will not stay here any longer. I must insist upon your coming home with me. I want to introduce you to my family. They will be so delighted to see an American. They have so often heard me speak of that noble people.

"I stammered out some excuses about not being dressed, but it was of no avail, the old gentleman insisted upon my company, and I was obliged to go.

"Signer Morelli, for such was the name of my new-found friend, lived about twelve miles from Rome, on a lonely country road. The old gentleman had his own conveyance, however, and we soon reached his villa.

"It was a magnificent mansion, replete with every luxury. I found his family delightful, and passed one of the most agreeable days I have ever spent in my life. All the inmates of his house were exceedingly friendly towards me, and insisted that I should make a weekly visit to their house. This, after some persuasion, I agreed to do.

"This visit was an agreeable change from my previous solitary life. I found Signor Morelli a most intelligent man. He had been, during our whole struggles for Independence, in daily communication with Washington, and he told me many anecdotes of that great and glorious man. I looked forward to my next visit with extreme gratification.

"During the week strange reports were circulated about Rome. A band of robbers had committed depredations on all the roads leading to the city—nay, they had even the audacity to penetrate into the suburbs. Their leader Velesco, it was stated, was a blood thirsty wretch, who hesitated at no crime. I do not know how it was, but I was very much attracted by these details, and read all the accounts which appeared in the public prints with avidity. I soon conjured up in my own imagination the exact personal appearance of this renowned bandit. I fancied I saw him in his picturesque costume. In fact, his image was scarcely ever out of my mind. This grew so much upon me that I became nervous, and gave a start at every strange sound; especially was this the case at night.

"On the Saturday of that week, I procured a horse and set off on my journey to Signor Morelli's. I had promised to spend the day with him. I reached his house without any accident, and was surprised to find a large number of gentlemen had already assembled there. It appears he had invited these guests in honor of myself. We sat down to a sumptuous repast, and the wine flowed in abundance. Suddenly there was a pause in the conversation, and one of the guests said:

"'By-the-by, there was a horrible murder committed last night in my neighborhood.'

"'Indeed!' we all cried. 'What are the particulars?'

"'Why you know Velesco is on the road again with a band more numerous than ever. His audacity has increased ten-fold since his last visit. It has become a scandal to the government. Signor Algero, a magistrate living near me, particularly signalized himself by making great efforts to arrest the bandit. He scoured the whole country with a troop of soldiers at his heels. But it was all to no purpose,Velesco and his band were securely concealed. But would you believe it, last night Algero and his whole family were murdered—they were all stabbed to the heart. In the magistrate's body the poignard was left, pinning a piece of paper to it, on which was written: '*This is how Velesco avenges himself*'

"A shudder of horror ran through all the guests, and it was sometime before we recovered from the effects of this recital. A long conversation ensued in which various exploits of this fearful assassin were related. These only served to increase my curiosity, and I longed to see the redoubtable bandit.

"Signor Morelli saw the gleam that the history of the horrid murder had cast on all his guests.

"'Come, gentlemen,' said he, 'let us have some champagne. We must not dishonor our guest by these gloomy faces.

"The champagne was brought, and we all of us indulged pretty freely. We soon forgot all about Velesco and his companions. An animated conversation followed, and time flew rapidly away until I was surprised to find it already night.

"I had an important engagement the following day which I was compelled to fulfill, so it became necessary that I should depart for Rome that night. My host pressed me very much to stay, but I was obliged to refuse. Seeing that I was determined to go he insisted on me taking two of his pistols. I mounted my horse and started on my journey. I had not ridden twenty paces before I discovered that I had drank quite enough. My head was a little giddy and I had some difficulty in holding myself straight on my horse. It was a cold November night, and the wind blew in gusts presaging a coming storm. I could even then hear the murmurings of the thunder in the distance, and an occasional flood of lightning forwarned me to make as much haste as I could. I had not proceeded more than a mile when the effects of the wine I had taken began to leave me, and I realized the loneliness of my situation. All the stories that had been told of Velesco returned vividly to my mind, and I began anxiously to look around me, transforming every bush into a bandit. The thunder roared and the lightning flashed, lighting up the road at some distance before me. The rain fell in torrents, and I was soon drenched to the skin. I had great difficulty in making my way on the now muddy roads. Every step my horse took seemed to plunge him deeper in the mire. It was only with the greatest care that I kept my seat. Excepting when it lightened it was intensely dark. I continued to ride on but soon lost all landmarks. I then discovered that I had mistaken my road. I did not know what to do, the storm was every moment increasing in violence, and both my animal and myself were in a pitiable condition. I saw it was useless to attempt to proceed further. I determined to look out for some place of security. Fortune aided me, for in the distance I saw an old tower, made visible by an extra vivid flash of lightning.

"I made the best of my way to this building, glad enough to procure any shelter from the terrific storm. I soon reached the tower. The door was dilapidated, and I had some difficulty in forcing an entrance through the mass of broken stone blocking up the way. When I had effected my purpose I found I was in a stone building which was evidently the ruin of an old castle. The walls were broken and blackened by time. A stone staircase led up to the upper stories. Here and there windows were pierced through the masonry. They were now, however, destitute of glass, and the wind rushed through the apertures with a hollow, moaning sound.

"The loneliness of the situation, the howling wind, the terrific storm, all produced a sedative effect on my already depressed feelings. But what was my horror to find embers still glowing on the floor. It was evident the tower had been lately occupied. Perhaps even now some one was in the upper stories. I involuntarily shivered, and listened attentively. Save the warring of the storm, no sound reached my ears. The thought of Velesco and his band recurred with double force to my mind. After remaining in a listening attitude for at least a quarter of an hour, I began to be a little reassured. I determined I would make a last survey before taking up my quarters for the night.

I made my way out of the ruin and looked about in every direction. The night was so dark that I could see nothing. It was in vain that I listened; the wind howled around the old tower with such violence that it shut out any other sound.

I began to recover myself a little, and walked round the old fortress. I discovered nothing excepting a species of outhouse in which I put my horse.

I was now convinced that I was the only inhabitant of the tower. I felt that I had nothing to fear, and re-entered the room I had just quitted. But I determined that I would prosecute my search still further, and I ascended the broken steps to the next story. I found this chamber to be the counterpart of the one below. There were the same broken discolored walls, and the same stone staircase led to another story.

I examined my pistols, cocked them, stretched myself on the floor, and determined to watch all night. The wine I had taken and the fatigue I had undergone were, however, too much for me, and I felt my eyes close in spite of myself. I was fast relapsing into a deep slumber, when suddenly the sound of footsteps reached my ears. In a moment I was wide awake and on the alert.

I noiselessly crept to the staircase, and by leaning forward I could see into the lower apartment without being myself seen.

Ten persons had just entered the tower. They were men of swarthy complexions, sombre countenances, and robust limbs. They were all of them clothed in brigand costume, and armed to the teeth.

They heaped some wood on the burning embers and seated themselves round the fire. They conversed in a rapid tone, every now and then casting covetous glances on two large chests which they had placed in a corner of the apartment.

The first words they uttered convinced me who they were. They formed part of Velesco's band.

Their features were animated. They frequently carried their hands to their weapons. They began to quarrel about the booty contained in the two chests. Their disputes at length reached a point that I saw the wretches were about to attack each other. They rose up in a tumult, drew their knives, and were about to commence the fight when their chief appeared. In a moment I recognized Velesco, from the published description of him.

He was a man of about forty years of age, of lofty stature, and strongly built. His large shoulders and muscular arms bespoke extreme vigor. His harsh features, ferocious looks, and the fantastic reflection of the fire gave a strange expression to his face which was rather increased than otherwise by a cruel smile which played about his lips.

"Quarreling and fighting again," said he, in a harsh voice. "Diavolo! it seems impossible for you to live quietly together as honest brigands ought to do."

One of the bandits attempted to justify himself. Velesco interrupted him.

"Silence!" he exclaimed, "I won't hear what you have to say. Great God! here you are taking your ease by the fire, like so many idiots, without any more thought of our safety than if we were the only people in the world. Fortunately I always keep my eyes open. Where is the man whose horse I found in the stable?"

At these words I shuddered, and cursed my unlucky chance for placing me in such a terrible situation. In fact I considered myself as lost. There was no way of escape. I knew. I had nothing to hope for from the bandits. Their ferocity was too well known for me to have the slightest doubt as to my lot if I fell into their hands. I determined to sell my life as dearly as possible.

The brigands had seized their carbines, when they heard their chiefs words.

"We know nothing of the man you speak about," said one of the band. "When we entered the tower was unoccupied."

"It may be so," replied Velesco, "but two of you had better go and search outside, he may be hidden near by."

Two of them went out; during their absence Velesco walked impatiently up and down the apartment.

In a minute or two they returned. "Well?" asked the chief. "We can find no trace of him," replied the brigand. "The horse is still in the stable."

"Indeed!" said the captain, and he continued his promenade.

A dead silence now reigned in this apartment, before so noisy. I breathed more freely, supposing all immediate danger was passed. I was wrong.

After a moment or two the chief stopped.

"Has any one examined the interior of the tower?" he asked.

"No!" replied the bandit. "No one would be fool enough to come in the lion's den in that manner."

"Who knows?" said Velesco, shaking his head. "Perhaps he arrived here before you, and has taken refuge in the upper stories. At all events we will go and examine them."

Velesco began to ascend the staircase, followed by his men.

I immediately ascended to the third story. I soon heard the brigands searching every corner of the chamber I had first left.

"No one here!" exclaimed the chiefs voice. "Let us visit the next floor."

The tower had only three stories, terminating by a platform, which I reached in a breathless condition, and a prey to profound terror.

I saw I was lost—lost without resource. No human aid could reach me. I ran to and fro on this cursed platform, like a caged wild beast. From the place where I stood I saw a precipice at least a hundred feet deep.

My teeth chattered, a cold perspiration bathed my face, and a convulsive trembling seized all my limbs. I heard the bandits' step on the stairs, and I shudderingly calculated how many moments yet remained to me.

At last, rendered crazy by fear, I resolved to precipitate myself from the top of the tower rather than fall alive into the hands of the wretches, who, I knew were accustomed to inflict unheard of tortures on their victims.

Before accomplishing this desperate act, I mechanically leaned my head over the top, doubtless for the purpose of measuring the abyss into which I was to fall.

It was then I perceived, about two feet below me, an iron bar three feet long and an inch and a half thick. It came out horizontally from the tower, and appeared to be firmly fastened. A sudden idea entered my head and gave me hope that I might escape the assassins.

Time pressed, and I had not a moment to lose. So, without further reflecting, I climbed the wall, seized the iron bar with both my hands, and dropping down, allowed my body to hang in space.

I had scarcely taken this position when the bandits, tumultuously reached the platform, which they immediately searched in every direction.

The storm still continued, the rain fell in torrents, and the wind blew so violently that I had the greatest difficulty in maintaining my hold.

"You see, captain, there is no one here!" cried one of the brigands.

"So it appears," replied Velesco, in a disappointed tone.

"Diavolo! it is anything but pleasant up here," exclaimed one of the bandits. "Let us descend," said the Captain. A deep sigh escaped my breast. I believed I was saved. I prepared myself to remount the tower.

The position in which I was placed was anything but agreeable, and now that danger was passed, my arms and wrists felt terribly tired. I did not know whether it was illusion or reality, but it appeared to me, that the iron bar on which I hung, was too weak to support the weight of my body for a long time, and in all probability eaten by rust, began to bend and incline towards the abyss.

It was necessary that I should make as much haste as possible. A deep silence reigned on the platform.

Collecting all my strength, I raised my head in order to calculate the distance from the top of the tower.

"So, so," said he.

"Devil!" I exclaimed in a rage. Without making any reply, Velesco leaned forward in order to seize me.

I let go the bar with one hand, and seized one of my pistols, which I had placed conveniently in the breast pocket of my coat.

"You shall not escape me, my lad," said the bandit, sneeringly.

"I will nail you," I murmured covering him with my pistol.

"At that moment I felt the bar bending, the single hand I held on with was slipping, my weapon escaped from my grasp and by a tremendous effort I clung to the now almost perpendicular bar with both my hands.

"Oh," cried I, in despair; "anything rather than such a death." And raising myself by superhuman strength, I made a spring and gained the top of the wall.

"No," cried, the Captain, with a shrill and harsh laugh. "You shall die like a dog." And he pushed me back again.

At that moment I suffered terrible agony. The bar had become perpendicular, and could no longer sustain me. In spite of my frantic and desperate efforts, I felt my stiffened fingers glide slowly along the iron. I heard an infernal laugh, uttered, no doubt, by the bandit, who enjoyed my torture. Then losing all hope, I shut my eyes, so that I should not see the fearful gulph in which I was about to be precipitated, and —

"And?" we all cried, interested to the last degree, and not understanding why Seldon had stopped in his narrative.

"And I awoke, gentleman," he continued, "for all this was only a dream. Heated by the wine I had taken, my head full of stories and robbers, I had slept and dreamt all I have told you, while my horse, happily for me, knew the road, and had gently taken me back to Rome. I assure you, no one ever felt more happy than I did when I recovered from that terrible night-mare."

Leaf the Fifteenth

A Satanic Compact

In the course of my professional life I had passed through some very strange scenes, and met with some very strange personages. It is my intention, in the present number, to relate an adventure which occurred to me some years ago while on professional business in the Northern States.

It was a dark November day, and the thick heavy clouds overhead seemed as if they must soon relieve themselves by pouring on the already saturated earth, the accumulation of waters contained within their bosom. At length the wind began to rise, gently at first but it was not long before it increased in violence until it blew a perfect hurricane. Large drops of rain commenced to fall, and in a short period a most fearful storm raged. There were two of us tracking a dishonest clerk, who had robbed his employer of a large amount of money. At the time the storm came up we were about a mile from the village of Castleton, in Vermont. We made the best of our way to the village in question, and with some difficulty reached it, not, however, without being drenched to the skin. This misfortune was easily remedied by a change of clothes, and by the bright fire burning in the principal room of the chief hotel in the place.

There was only one other guest in this apartment besides ourselves. When we entered he was seated in front of the stove with his elbows resting on his knees, and his face buried in his hands. For a moment he did not appear to be aware any one had come into the room, for he remained in the same position without looking up. My companion, however, addressed some remark to him, he then raised his head, and I had an opportunity to notice his appearance.

There was something very strange about him; not so much in any single feature as in his whole appearance. His face was deathly pale, and his eyes and hair were intensely black. His white teeth, black moustache, and white face, formed such a contrast that it could not fail of being remarked by everyone who saw him. He was clothed in deep black, but he was evidently not in mourning, for his hat, which was placed on a chair beside him, was destitute of crepe. He did not seem to be more than five and twenty, but an expression of melancholy, ill-suited to his years, was plainly to be traced on his features.

He courteously replied to my companion's remark, and made room for us beside the stove. We endeavored to draw the stranger into conversation but found it a very difficult task; it was evident he was naturally very taciturn.

The storm continued to rage until the night was far advanced. After we had partaken of an excellent dinner we resumed our places in the sitting room, and heaping fresh wood on the fire, took pleasure in listening to the howling wind, and the beating of the rain against the windows. I do not know how long we sat there but I was aroused from a kind of reverie, by the lamp, which lighted the apartment, suddenly going out. My companion was asleep but the stranger sat there gazing intently on the sparks as they fell from the grate into the ashes.

"*Sic est vitu,*" said the stranger, moralizing—"We burn brilliantly for a moment and then are extinguished forever."

"You are a philosopher, sir," I replied, feeling called upon to say something.

"Every man who thinks must be a philosopher," replied the stranger.

"Eh! eh! what's that," said my companion suddenly waking up. "What is that about philosophy? Philosophy is all humbug, humbug, sir," continued he rubbing his eyes and yawning.

I should here say my friend was a very practical man, shrewd enough in business matters, but without a particle of imagination. He believed in none of the *isms* of the day, and utterly scouted everything apart from the routine of every day life.

There was a pause in the conversation after my friend's remark. The stranger gave him one look and shrugged his shoulders and that was all.

"Philosophy!"continued my practical friend, in a sneering tone. "Who believes in philosophy? It is a fine thing to talk about, but a hard one to practice. Why I would as soon believe a man could sell his soul to Satan as that a man can be a philosopher."

The stranger's eyes glistened, and he moved his chair a short distance from stove.

"And do you suppose a man cannot sell his soul to Satan?" said he, in a hollow voice. "Let me assure you to the contrary."

"Hum—,"my practical friend was about to reply, but he only uttered half the word, the remainder of it died away on his lips, as he gazed on the stranger's countenance.

In truth, there was something very extraordinary in his features at that moment. From some cause or other his face was contorted, and as the flickering light fell upon it, it was rendered hideous. After a moment or two it subsided into its natural expression.

"Gentlemen," said he, "listen to my story. I promise not to detain you long, and you will then learn there are more things in Heaven and earth than are dreamt of in your philosophy."

We put a fresh log of wood on the fire, each of us lighted a fresh cigar, and my friend and myself put ourselves in listening attitudes. The stranger glanced cunningly around him, as if looking for some one, and then commenced as follows:

"I am a physician by profession, and have been in practice five years in New York City. I soon obtained a reputation, and I can safely say without any egotism, that whilst I devoted myself to my profession, no one obtained a larger share of public support.

"One night, after an arduous day's work, I had returned home in the evening thoroughly tired. I put on my dressing gown and slippers, seated myself by the fire-side, and delivered myself up to all the luxury of repose after the great fatigue I had undergone. I was soon plunged into a reverie. I was suddenly aroused from it by the loud ringing of my office bell and almost immediately afterwards I was informed by my domestic that I was wanted by a person in the hall.

"I obeyed the summons, and found a servant girl who informed me that her mistress was sick and wanted to see me immediately.

"Your mistress' name!" said I.

"Miss Moril, No. 79 Lexington avenue," was the reply.

"I did not know her, but of course I had no option but to go, however much disinclined I felt to leave my comfortable fire-side. I hurriedly put on my coat and boots, and followed the messenger. My patient's residence was not a long distance from my office. In ten minutes I was before the door. The house was a magnificent one, in short, a perfect palace. Massive stone steps, which glistened in the moonlight, led up to the entrance. In answer to my summons, the door was noiselessly opened by a footman in livery and I was shown into a gorgeously furnished drawing-room. It might truly be called the abode of luxury, for everything the heart could desire was to be found in that apartment. I seated myself on a velvet-covered sofa and waited until I should be summoned to see my patient. I was not detained long, for in a few minutes the same messenger who had fetched me appeared and requested me to follow her. I did so, ascending a massive flight of stairs after my guide. In another minute I was in my patient's bedroom. It is impossible for me to convey any idea of the splendor of that apartment. A delicious perfume stole through the room, and a gilded lamp hanging from the ceiling shed a subdued light around. A thick tapestry carpet covered the floor, and the whole appearance of the chamber conveyed the idea that it was the dwelling of some goddess rather than that of a human being. I entered noiselessly, for the floor was too thickly covered to allow the slightest sounds from footstep, and glanced towards the bed. Great Heavens! What a magnificent sight I beheld! How shall I attempt to describe it? I feel it is beyond by powers to convey the slightest idea of the reality of that scene.

"In the midst of a mass of lace reclined my patient. But her beauty was not human, it was divine. Imagine to yourself the sweetest countenance in the world. Eyes of the deepest blue, a skin so dazzling white that it could compete with the purest alabaster, teeth chiseled from the whitest ivory, lips red as the carnation and a form so beautiful and so voluptuous, that when I gazed on her I felt the blood dancing through my veins. Her night dress was partially open in front, revealing the contour of her swelling bosom. No statuary, however subtle the hand which executes it, could give the slightest representation to the divine beauty of her whole form. I approached the bed and seated myself in a *fauteuil* placed conveniently by its side. The beautiful girl extended a small snowy hand to me and I felt her pulse. I found it to be slightly accelerated, but there evidently was not much the matter."

"'Doctor,' said she, in a sweetly musical voice, 'I am not very well. I experience a general feeling of *malaise.* I have no doubt, however, you can soon cure me, for I have heard much of your skill.'

"I made a suitable reply and wrote some simple prescription, at the same time giving her some directions as to diet. In about a quarter of an hour I took my leave.

"When I returned home I could think of nothing else but the beautiful girl I had just visited. I could not sleep that night, I was restless, feverish and uneasy, and I rose in the morning as unfreshed as when I laid down at night. I anxiously awaited the hour when I could with decency again call upon my patient. I sat watching the clock, and each minute appeared an age. At length the time arrived, and I actually ran to the house in Lexington avenue. I was immediately admitted, and found my patient sitting up in her bed-room, looking even more beautiful in her morning negligee. She received me cordially and I saw that she was much better. She conversed with me long and freely, and I discovered her mind to be very much cultivated. I retired from her presence with her image engraven on my heart. Yes! I was hopelessly in love.

"From this time she became the star of my destiny. I could think only of her. Her image was constantly before me and I only lived for her. I visited her every day for a month, although she no longer required my professional services, but she received my visits in good part and I had not strength of mind to tear myself from her.

"One evening I paid her a visit as usual. The moment I entered the room I saw there was something on her mind which she wished to say to me. After the courtesies of the day, she addressed me as follows:

"'Doctor, I have some news to impart to you. I feel that we are old friends now, and I can freely tell you anything. Well, then, I am to be married in a week!'

"'Married!' I exclaimed in a voice of anguish, and turning pale as death.

"'Yes, is there anything very extraordinary in that?' she returned laughing. 'One would suppose from your tone, that it was the last thing in the world likely to take place.'

"My brain was on fire. I reeled from my chair and prostrated myself at her feet.

"'Oh, Eleanor! divine, beauteous Eleanor' I frantically exclaimed, 'recall those words—do you not see that I love, worship and adore you—do you not see that I live only on your smiles—do you not see that I exist only in you! Angel of brightness, spurn me not from you! No one can love you as I love you—no one can worship and adore you as I do—You are my God, my Heaven, my Eternity!'"

"My passionate words appeared to have some effect upon her, for she covered her face with her hands and murmured 'Too late!'

"I dragged myself at her feet. I seized her knees. I pulled her hands from her face and impressed a thousand kisses upon them.

"'Hear me, Eleanor!' I almost shrieked, 'By the Almighty Power above, if you are not mine I must die without you, the world would be a hell to me. Oh! say you will be mine.' Again her voice murmured, 'Too late.'

"Again I entreated her—again I prayed to her—but all to no purpose—'Too late' was all the reply I received. I left her home in a state of mind bordering on madness. I remember, my domestics when I entered my own dwelling, looked at me, curiously, and seemed half-frightened at my appearance. They even shrank from me. I felt that I was going mad—Yes, I felt madness seething in my blood. I felt it mount my brain. At last it came! I was delirious—I danced—I foamed at the mouth—My brain was on fire. They put me to bed and fastened me down to it. Oh! how I glared at them!—how I clinched my fist at them!—How I cursed them! I grew worse. Doctors came to see me; great professors but they could do nothing. With all their skill they could not drive the madness from my blood. They endeavored to let it out and for that purpose they leeched, bled and cupped me, but it was no use, I was so thoroughly saturated with madness that it set them at defiance. I continued to grow rapidly worse, my breath began to fail me, my extremities grew cold, the death rattle was heard in my throat, and that night I died!"

My companion and I gave a violent start at these words, and gazed wonderingly on the monster.

"Died!" we exclaimed simultaneously.

"Yes, died!"returned the stranger in an almost peremptory voice. "They laid me out and an old woman watched by my body. I took pleasure in watching all the preparations of the funeral. How noiselessly they trod about the house, as if afraid of awaking the dead! The next day I heard a strange step on the stairs and *she* entered the room. Great Heavens, how beautiful she looked! She bent over me and tears fell from her eyes on my cold cheek. She was left alone with me!

"'Oh, Eustace!' she exclaimed, 'why did I not know you before?' God preserve your soul, Eustace, and may we meet in another world.'

"I heard that, and yet I lay cold and motionless in my coffin. She bent down and pressed her warm lips against my icy cheek and bade me adieu.

"I was buried that evening. What a grand funeral it was! How everybody discussed my character and merits—thank God! after all, there is some goodness in the world, for people are generally charitable to the dead. They lowered me into the dark vault destined for my reception, and I was left alone. It was then that the agony of devotions came over me. It was then that my soul wept tears of blood. It was then that I thought of all that I had left behind. Her matchless form was continually before my eyes. Oh! how I struggled to break the bonds of death, that I might again behold her, converse with her, and worship her. 'Oh, spirit of Evil,' I inwardly exclaimed; 'come to my assistance. Grant me but the earthly possession of that divinity for a limited time, and my soul is thine for all eternity. I had no sooner given utterance to this thought, than I heard a sound like the napping of wings, and roaring of a mighty wind. I felt a current of cold air blow on my cheek, and almost immediately afterwards a voice reached my ear:—

"'I am here, mortal, at your bidding. What would you?'

"I repeated my wish.

"'I will give you two years of life, and the gratification of all your desires,' replied Satan; on the condition that after that time you become mine for ever.'

"'Agreed! agreed!' I eagerly exclaimed. I again heard the napping of wings and the roaring of a mighty wind, and I felt I was alive again. Yes, the blood again began to circulate in my veins. My chest began to heave, and my heart to beat. The coffin opened and I stood erect. I soon scaled the vault, and reached the open air.

"It was fortunately midnight when I was released from the grave, and it was quite dark. The cemetery where I had been buried was not removed a very long distance from my dwelling. I managed to reach it without being discovered, and gained my own chamber unseen by the domestics. I dressed myself, and immediately bent my steps to Lexington avenue. By this time it was two o'clock in the morning. I tried the door of the house in which my divinity lived, and to my supreme joy found it open. I penetrated into the house, and was about to open the drawing room door, when the sound of voices suddenly reached my ears. I stooped down and looked through a small crevice in the panel. A fearful spectacle met my gaze, which made the blood recede from my heart, and caused it to stop beating.

"Eleanor was seated on a sofa, and beside her was a young man, gazing with a look of rapture on her countenance. I heard him address the most passionate language to her. She replied to him in a subdued tone, and her countenance bore traces of sorrow. I could scarcely refrain myself from rushing into the apartment, and wreaking my vengeance on the intruder, who, I had no doubt, was her intended husband. But I restrained myself, and determined to wait patiently. They conversed long together, the conversation, however, was mostly sustained by him. Her attention appeared to be absorbed by her own thoughts, and the answers she returned to him were, for the most part, only monosyllables. The thought entered my heart, 'could she be thinking of me?' A few minutes after that, I distinctly heard her murmur, as if to herself—'Poor Eustace!'

"Oh! why did I not then snatch her in my arms? Why did I not then bear her away? Some irresistible power held me back, and I still waited. Her lover soon after took his leave. I followed him stealthily; I never lost sight of him for a moment. He reached Broadway, and turned down that thoroughfare. It was entirely deserted and as silent as the grave. I could hear his footsteps resound on the pavement, while mine were inaudible. When he had gained White street, he paused for a moment, and then slowly turned off from the main thoroughfare into it. Now was my time, I hastened my steps and soon reached him. He did not know me—in another moment I had his throat in my grasp. I could feel it crunch between my fingers. He made desperate efforts to escape, but all to no purpose; I had hold of him too tightly for that. I appeared to have superhuman power bestowed on me.

"I could feel him growing weaker and weaker; at last I felt something warm issuing from his mouth on my hand. I looked down, and by the moonlight I saw it was blood. I then knew all was over—in fact, he was dead! I threw his body from me, and hurried back again into Broadway. I had not gone far up the street when I heard the City Hall alarm bell ring; it was followed by twenty others, and suddenly the whole aspect of the street was changed. From being deserted it became teeming with life. The words, 'fire!' 'fire!' were echoed on all sides, and before me I saw the heavens lighted up with a livid glare. I commenced to run with the rest, and, oh! God of Heavens! how shall I describe the agony I felt when I discovered it was the house in which which my divinity lived that was in flames! I scarcely know what passed. I have a distinct recollection of seeing a black, charred corpse on the pavement which they said was my angelic girl. Then there was a long dreary blank. When I regained my senses I found myself in a large house. They treated me harshly. I supposed it was on account of the murder I committed. Satan did not keep his compact with me, and I had great hopes I should be able to set him at defiance at last. Two weeks ago I escaped from the large house, and I have wandered miles upon miles. All my desire now is to escape the penalty of my compact. I would freely die a second time if I were sure of eluding Satan's clutch. But—"

The stranger was here interrupted in his narration by the sudden opening of the door and the entrance of two men. The latter leisurely walked up to the stranger and exclaimed!

"Lo! Doctor, we have found you at last!"

"So it appears," said the doctor in a resigned tone.

"Well, gentlemen," said one of them, "we hope he has entertained you."

"He has told us a wonderful story," I replied. "Oh! yes, we know about it. It was about a beautiful patient, and about his being dead and coming to life again; about him selling himself to the devil; about him committing murder, and lastly about the body of his 'divinity' being burnt to a cinder."

"Exactly his story," I replied. "I need not ask you if it is true."

"No, not a word of it. His history can be summed up in two or three words; he is, as he states, a doctor, and has practiced in New York City. But he has studied too much and it turned his brain—in short he is deranged, and has been confined in the State Lunatic Asylum for four years. He must either have read or imagined the wonderful story he relates—at all events he implicitly believes in its truth and repeats it to every one who will listen to it.

Two weeks ago he escaped from the asylum, and a pretty chase we have had after him I tell you, but, thank heavens! we have found him at last. Come, doctor," continued the keeper addressing the stranger who sat with his arms folded, scowling at the fire, "I have got a carriage waiting for you outside; let us be moving."

The doctor rose without saying a word, and allowed him to be conducted away.

"There!" said my friend after they had all left the room, "did I not tell you it was all hum—"

I prevented him from finishing the word by pushing a fresh cigar into his mouth.

Leaf the Sixteenth

MR. STERLING'S CONFESSION

My father was a respectable merchant, living in New York city. He met a terrible end, perishing by fire. I was studying medicine at the time, with Dr. Lignon, when I received intelligence that my father's house, in White Street, had been burned to the ground, and that he had perished in the flames. My mother was rescued. I immediately left for New York, for the purpose of consoling her under her great affliction. When my father's affairs came to be investigated, it was found that he had left my poor mother almost penniless, although I had been led to believe that he was quite wealthy. It was partially this reason that made me give up the medical profession, for I knew from my mother's scanty means she could ill afford the expense necessary to prosecute it vigorously.

It was about a year ago that my friend, Mr. M., the well known New York attorney, sent for me, begging my immediate presence. I immediately hurried to his residence, supposing that he wished to consult me on some case. I was shown at once into his study, where I found him poring over a parchment.

"Brampton," said he, after, he had shaken hands with me, "do you know a Mr. John Sterling?"

"Sterling—Sterling," said I, endeavoring to recollect; "I cannot say I do. But stay," I continued, "I remember a Mr. Sterling, a banker, with whom my father did business."

"Exactly," replied Mr. M., "he died last night."

"Indeed," I continued, supposing, of course, there was some mystery about his death to be investigated.

"Yes," continued Mr. M., speaking slowly, "and he has left you by will seventy-five thousand dollars."

"What!" I exclaimed, starting up from my chair, as if I had been shot.

"He has left you seventy-five thousand dollars," repeated Mr. M., in a quiet tone.

"Impossible!" I returned; "I did not know Mr. Sterling personally; I never spoke to him in the whole course of my life; in fact, I do not remember ever to have seen him."

"That may all be true, but he has nevertheless left you this money."

"But how can I take it when it rightfully belongs to his wife and family?"

"No, Brampton, it rightfully belongs to you."

"You are speaking enigmas to me. Mr. M. How it is right that Mr. Sterling should leave me such a large sum of money is more than I can fathom."

"Listen to me attentively, Brampton, and I will soon convince you that you are rightfully entitled to the money. You are aware that there is no profession which penetrates so deeply into family secrets as the law. The hiding place of the skeleton, which they say is to be found in every man's house, is readily entered by the family attorney, and all the secrets of his clients are necessarily revealed to him. During my professional career I have had confided to me some extraordinary secrets, which, if I were to reveal, would make the world stand aghast. Parties who have held situations of honor and trust, who have been held by the public as model husbands and fathers, who have been looked upon as the very epitome of integrity, would appear as scoundrels, forgers, and some even guilty of the highest crime known to the law. But the sacred nature of my profession closes my lips; I dare not bring to light the hidden skeleton, and stamp on it the impress of truth by revealing the facts to the world."

I could not understand what the exordium meant, and could only bow in reply.

"One of my best clients was Mr. John Sterling," continued Mr. M.; "a man of considerable fortune, and who was supposed to have led a most exemplary life. He was a member of a church, and noted for his charitable donations to the funds of the cause he espoused. No one had ever presumed to breathe a word against his private character, and he was cited as a model of philanthropy and just dealings by all who knew him. When I first became acquainted with him he was a widower with no family. I had known him for several years without discovering anything in his past history which led me to suspect that is contained any thing of a remarkable character. I always thought that he was unusually reserved and silent, but supposed that it arose more from his natural disposition than from any secret preying on his mind. I hope you are listening attentively, Brampton?"

"Certainly," I replied; "I hear every word."

"Three days ago, I was summoned to his house in a great hurry. The messenger stated that my immediate presence was necessary. Somewhat surprised at this sudden call for my services I lost no time in obeying it. When I reached his house, which was situated in Fourteenth Street, near Fifth Avenue, I found his household in great confusion; several doctors were in attendance, and alarm was expressed on every feature. It appeared that Mr. Sterling had been seized that morning with a paralytic stroke, and no hope whatever was entertained of his recovery. I was immediately shown into his bedroom, where I found the sufferer reclining on a sumptuous couch. He presented a sad spectacle; one half of his body was dead, and his mouth was distorted. He did not, however, suffer much physical pain, but his face wore an expression of intense anxiety. The moment he saw me a smile flitted across his distorted features. He made a sign for me to approach his bed-side.

"'I am glad you have come,' said he in a hoarse whisper; 'I want you to make-my will. It is a duty I ought to have attended to before. Set about it at once, for I feel that my end is fast approaching. Who knows how soon this feeble flicker of life may leave me?

"'I procured writing materials and set about my duty. I soon finished the preliminary writing, and paused for him to instruct me as to the disposal of his property. The invalid anxiously awaited for this moment, and then, in a tone of voice which was firmer than when he first spoke, he said:

"'I bequeath the sum of seventy-five thousand dollars to Mr. James

Brampton, detective officer, son of Mr. Thomas Brampton, late of White Street, in the city of New York.'

"'But your relations,' I ventured to suggest.

"'Do as I bid you,' continued the dying man. 'I leave my relatives the rest of my property, to be divided equally among; them.'

"I had no course left but to obey, and drew out the will as he requested. At the same time I thought it very strange that he should leave such a large sum to you, Brampton. The will was properly attested. When all was completed, a load appeared to be taken off the invalid's mind; a placid smile overspread his features, and he made a sign that all should leave the room but myself.

"'Mr. M.,' said he, as soon as we were alone, 'draw your chair close to my bed-side, get your writing materials, I want to make a confession to you. I can see that you are surprised at the provisions of my will; but hear my history, and you will then learn that I have only performed an act of reparation.'

"I remonstrated with him, and advised him to remain quiet and not excite himself by conversation; but he insisted, and said that if he did not ease his mind he would suffer fearful torture in his dying moments. Seeing that he was determined, I drew close to his bed, as he requested, and took down the words as they fell from his mouth. Here is his confession."

So saying, Mr. M. handed to me a dozen pages of MS., and begged that I would read them. I did so, and the following is the strange history:

"Fifteen years ago I was engaged in Maiden Lane as a banker. I did a large business, and soon accumulated a considerable amount of money. But reverses came; I speculated, and soon found myself involved beyond redemption. There was no other course open to me but to flee the country. I made my preparations, and soon arranged everything to my satisfaction.

"The very evening before my intended departure, as I was examining my books after bank-hours were over, I was interrupted by a knock at the door of my private study. In answer to my summons to 'come in' the door opened, and a friend of mine, Mr. Thomas Brampton, entered.

"How are you, Sterling?" said he advancing and shaking me by the hand. 'Excuse my calling after banking hours, but the fact is I want particularly to see you on a little business. You know the mortgage I had on Blanchard's property; he paid it off this afternoon. I want you to invest it for me.'

"'Certainly,' I returned. 'You know anything I can do—'

"'O, yes, I know all about that. I would rather put this money in your hands than in the United States Bank. There is the amount, fifty thousand dollars. Give me a certificate of deposit,'

"I made out the receipt and handed it to him. He placed it in his pocketbook, saying:

"'This is all my dear wife and boy have to depend on. Thank God! it is now in safe hands, and I can sleep easy in my bed at night.'

"'How came Blanchard to pay off the mortgage?" I asked.

"'I suppose he wanted to free his property. I have not mentioned the matter to my wife yet, nor shall I until you have made a fresh investment. You know what a nervous body she is.'

"'You are right,' I replied; 'women don't understand these things. But I will make your mind easy on that, now. To-morrow I will look out for some good security.'

"After a little further conversation, my visitor left. When he had gone, I seated myself by my study fire, and pondered long anxiously. This fifty thousand dollars, so opportunely placed in my possession at such a critical moment, would release me from my most pressing embarrassments. But then it was impossible for me to use it. I must invest the amount at once. I could not take the sum with me, for I had given a certificate of deposit, and to appropriate the money to myself would be felony, and I could be pursued and arrested for it to the very ends of the earth. I did not know what to do. The golden bait, so temptingly placed before me, stifled as it were every good sentiment in my heart, and I felt that I could be guilty of every crime to further my ends. While pursuing these reflections, a sudden thought entered my brain, and to show how lost I was to all moral rectitude, my soul did not fall back appalled at the suggestion made me by my depraved heart. I might get rid of him and appropriate the money to my own use. Then I dwelt on all I could do with such a sum. It would preclude the necessity of my leaving the country. Yes, I made up my mind that

I would put him out of the way. I said that it must be done speedily, too.

"After I had thought over the matter in every possible light, I went home. I lived at that time in Canal Street, which was then the fashionable part of the city. I suppose my countenance must have expressed my anxiety, for my wife no sooner saw me than she interrogated me very closely. And here, Mr. M., I must make another confession. I have been a bad husband. The world gives me credit for having been affectionate and loving to my wife, but it only shows how mistaken the world oftentimes is. I hated my wife, and in private treated her very brutally; and yet she was a kind, devoted woman. I have often seen her eyes fill with tears at some cruel speech of mine; and yet not one word of reproach fell from her lips, and God knows she had cause enough. Poor Emily! I broke her heart.

"But I am digressing. I replied surlily to my wife's interrogation and bade her hold her peace. I knew it was only love for me that prompted her interference. She did not refer to the subject again.

"I went to bed that night turning I over in my own mind my plan of action; one thing I had firmly settled namely that, Mr. Brampton must be sacrificed. The only thing that I could not decide upon was how the deed was to be done. In the midst of these murderous thoughts, I slept. My dreams were of a varied character that night. Suddenly, in the midst of my slumbers, a thought occurred to me, which, for a moment, completely paralyzed me. I started up in bed, and exclaimed:

"'Fool that I am! I forgot the certificate of deposit!'

"'What is the matter, John?' said my wife; 'what do you mean by a certificate of deposit?'

"'Peace, woman, with your ceaseless, babbling,' I returned.

"'How can you be so unkind to me, dear?' sobbed my wife.

"'Have done with your useless repinings!' I answered.

"'O John, once you loved me, and now verily believe you hate me! yet God is my witness to do my duty to you as a wife. Do tell me, John, what can I do better?'

"'Will you hold your cursed tongue!' I replied, and I kicked her. Yes, Mr. M., I brutally kicked her. The poor thing shrank away close to the wall, and I could hear her endeavor to stifle her sobs by thrusting the sheet into her mouth. God has now punished me for my inhuman conduct. The lower portion of my body is dead, and I can feel death gradually creeping upwards.

"But to return. The sudden thought that Mr. Brampton had the certificate of deposit in his possession completely nonplussed me. If I were to kill him, he had in all probability deposited the paper in some secure place in his house, and after his death it would be brought to light, and I should be no nearer my end than before.

"It was after turning this matter over and over again in my mind that a hellish thought entered my head. I would destroy the house and all its contents by fire! The idea was no sooner conceived than it was matured, and the next night I determined to put it into execution. I went about my business the following day as usual. No one that saw me had the least idea that I was harboring any thought of so desperate a character. I do not know how it was, but it seemed to me as if I were a plaything of some mysterious power. The thought of two innocent people perishing in the flames gave me no concern whatever. The only aim and end that I had in view was to destroy the certificate of deposit. To do this I would have sacrificed all my relatives and friends. I believe if I had any children, and knew that by throwing them into the flames I could have accomplished my wish, I should have done it.

"Mr. Brampton called on me during the day. I told him that I was in treaty for a splendid investment for his funds, and that there could be no doubt but I should succeed in making the arrangement in a day or two. He appeared to be perfectly satisfied, and left me after an hour's conversation on indifferent subjects, during which term I learned that he had said nothing to his wife nor any other person about the matter. I passed through that day as usual. I had the same smile on my lips as if my heart were as guileless as a child's. And yet the hellish thought was harbored there, festering its way to the innermost core.

"Evening came, I retired home as usual. I found my wife had been weeping all the day, for her eyes were red and swollen. The sight maddened me. I no longer hesitated to use personal violence, and vile, cowardly blows followed each other in quick succession. She rushed to her own chamber and locked herself in. This was exactly what I wanted. It left me a free field for action.

"At midnight. I left the house and started for Mr. Brampton's residence. It was a cold winter's night, and the wind blew violently from the northeast. The very elements seemed to conspire in favor of my diabolical design.

"Mr. Brampton lived in White Street. I soon stood before his house. Not a soul was in the street. A small alleyway ran by the side of the house, and some wooden shanties leaned against one of the gable-ends.

"With the aid of a flint and steel, I easily procured a light. I then thrust a quantity of shavings through a small window, and set fire to them with a brimstone match. I also set fire to the shanties in two or three places. This done, I retired exultingly away to the corner of the street, to witness the effect.

"When I came to analyze the feelings I experienced at that time, I found they were actually feelings of pleasure. For some minutes no manifestation appeared—then came a bluish smoke—then smoke of a much more dense description, and lastly the whole building burst out into a sheet of flame. Even then the alarm was not given for some time. At last, I heard footsteps on the pavement, and suddenly the words, 'fire!, fire!' broke the stillness of the night. These words were uttered by others in the distance. Watchmen's rattles were sprung, and the street was soon a scene of bustle and confusion, as the engines began to arrive. But amidst all this din there was one sound which could be heard above all others, and which proceeded from the burning dwelling. It was a woman's shriek. You may judge of the condition of my heart at that moment when I tell you that these cries of agony and suffering fell mute on it.

"The scene which followed was so quick and rapid in its execution, that I can scarcely remember it. One part of it, however, is indelibly impressed on my mind. I saw one of the heroic firemen place a ladder against the burning pile, and fearlessly ascend it. A woman appeared on the balcony, clothed only in her night dress. She was conveyed safely to the ground. Mr. Brampton perished in the flames. The receipt was undoubtedly destroyed, for I have heard nothing more about it.

"When Mr. Brampton's affairs were investigated it was found that he had been paid a large sum of money; but no one knew what became of it. It was afterwards supposed that some robber had entered the house, and appropriating the funds, had set fire to the dwelling for the purpose of destroying the evidence of his crime.

"Fortune prospered with me after this diabolical act. Money flowed in fast, and I became a millionaire—but I had no happiness. The gnawing tooth of remorse has been undermining my existence ever since. But still the demon of avarice had taken such possession of me that I could not refund the wealth I had so criminally obtained.

"Mr. M., I have done. In leaving Mr. James Brampton the sum I have done, I only perform an act of retribution. It is a tardy act of justice, and can by no means wipe out my sin. My only hope now is in a merciful God—to him I commit my soul."

Thus ended Mr. Sterling's confession. I need not say how deeply I was affected by it. The sum restored to me was sufficient to enable me to give up my profession, and since the day I came in possession of it, I have ceased all business.

Leaf the Seventeenth

The Knotted Handkerchief

(I neglected to take any notes of the following case in which I was engaged, but at my request a friend of mine, who was concerned with me in it, has supplied the deficiency. I give the story in his own words—J. B.)

About ten years ago I was studying medicine in New York. I had been working very hard, having specially devoted my attention for the last six months to pathology. This is a tedious study, demanding the most determined mental attention. I threw myself into it with all the ardor of youth, and consequently at the end of six months I had completely exhausted my mental energies.

One day I was sitting listlessly in my room endeavoring to master Bayle's "*Recherches sur Phthisie Pulmonaire,*" but I could not comprehend what I was reading; my thoughts unbidden reverted back to my own home, and it rose up in all its neatness and charms before my mental vision. My heart yearned to see my family again, and I knew that two more long years must elapse before my wish could be gratified. A sudden knocking at the door interrupted my reverie. At my summons to "come in," the door opened, and my particular friend Charles Seldon entered the room.

"What! still pouring over your books?" said he.

"Yes," I replied, "I am trying to master Bayle, but I don't make much progress."

"I tell you what it is, my dear fellow," said my friend, good naturedly, "you will make yourself ill. You don't know how pale you look. Now take my advice, throw your books on one side."

"It's all very well talking," I replied; "but I want to perfect myself in pathology, and it is impossible for me to do so without application."

We then entered into a discussion as to the necessity of an intimate knowledge of pathology to practice medicine, and ended as these discussions usually do, by neither of us being convinced.

"Well, old friend," said he, "the fact is, you must have some relaxation. I am going home to-morrow for a month. Now I propose you accompany me. You have no idea how delighted my friends will be to see you. We live in a homely style, 'far from the busy haunts of man,' but I am sure the change will do you a world of good. Come make up your mind and join me."

I reflected a moment—the temptation was too strong for me, and I agreed to accompany him. The next morning we started off. His father was a farmer, and lived in the western part of the State of New York. I shall not dwell on my visit. Suffice it to say that I was received with the greatest kindness, and treated with genuine hospitality, and I passed there four of the happiest weeks of my life. I had been there about a week when I went out one day for a long walk by myself. Seldon had a headache and preferred to stay at home. I walked several miles, and growing tired, I entered a country tavern, and calling for a glass of ale and a cigar, I sat down to rest myself.

While thus engaged a slight cough attracted my attention, and I glanced at the spot from whence it proceeded. Seated at the further end of the barroom was an individual I had not noticed before. He was a man between thirty and forty years of age. There was something very peculiar about his features which immediately arrested my attention. I do not know how to describe it, but it gave me an idea that he possessed a very acute mind. This impression was further increased by his movements. They were quick, and it was evident that he did not allow the slightest circumstance to escape him. I am not naturally inclined to make friends with strangers, but there was something in this man which attracted me to him. I drew my chair nearer his and commenced a conversation.

"A pleasant day," said I.

"You are right, sir," he replied; "it is very pleasant indeed, considering the time of year. One would expect to find it much colder than it is in this part of the State."

"I should judge from your remarks that you do not live in this neighborhood," I ventured to observe.

Before replying he gave me a scrutinizing glance.

"I live in New York," he replied, after a moment's pause. "My name is James Brampton; my profession is a detective officer."

I was delighted to meet Mr. Brampton. His name had lately been very prominently brought before the public in more than one instance. He was a man of extraordinary sagacity, and had succeeded in discovering the perpetrators of crime, when to ordinary men all clue appeared to be lost. His faculty in this respect was evidently owing to his keen observation, his acute mental analysis and determined perseverance. No difficulty daunted him, in fact his powers seemed to increase in proportion as the case was enveloped in mystery. He was a man of great courage, and what was still better for his profession, extraordinary coolness.

We grew quite familiar, and in the course of conversation I asked him what brought him so far from New York. He told me he was in pursuit of a burglar, and had laid a trap for him, and expected to arrest him that very day. Our interview lasted some time, when I arose to go. He then gave me his address in New York, and stated that he should be happy for me to call and see him. After the time for our visit had expired, Charles Seldon and myself both returned to New York together, and I applied myself to my studies with renewed energies. It might have been about a month after this, that one morning I took up the *New York Herald*, and the following paragraph caught my attention:

> HORRIBLE MURDER.—The inhabitants of Lispenard Street were yesterday thrown into a terrible state of excitement, by the discovery of one of the most fearful murders it has ever been the lot of humanity to witness. It appears that No. 121 is let out into lodgings. An apartment on the second floor is occupied by a young medical student named George Wilson. It was noticed yesterday that he did not make his appearance

> as usual. It was supposed that he was sick, and the owner of the house, who occupied, the ground floor, went up to his room to see if he had need of anything. When he entered the room a dreadful sight presented itself. The young man was lying before the fire-place quite dead. His throat was cut in a fearful manner. Some of his hair which had evidently been pulled out by the roots, lay scattered about the room. The motives for this horrible deed are entirely unknown. The property of the deceased did not appear to have been disturbed. We are happy to say that the probable murderer has been arrested. We refrain from giving more particulars to-day, as it might defeat the ends of justice.

I was very much shocked to learn that poor Wilson had met with such a dreadful end. I knew him well, as he was studying at the same college as myself, and although I could not exactly rank him among my friends, still the little intercourse I had had with him had impressed me very favorably as to his general character. I had only spoken to him the very day before in the chemical lecture room, and it seemed so shocking to know that at that moment he wag lying dead. I went down to the college as usual, and the first person I met in the hall was Mr. Dolman, the worthy janitor.

"Have you seen poor Wilson's body?" said he, after we had been conversing a few minutes about the murder.

"No," I replied; "I suppose it is a shocking sight."

"It is, indeed—but there is one consolation—the murderer is arrested."

"So the paper said, but it did not give his name—who is it?"

"One you know very well. It's no other than Charles Seldon."

"Seldon!" I exclaimed. "Impossible! why, he is my dearest friend!"

"I am sorry to hear that, sir, because there can be no doubt about his guilt."

I begged Mr. Dolman to enter into full particulars. His statement divested of all extraneous matter amounted to substantially as follows:

George Wilson and Charles Seldon had at one time been great friends. They had been inseparable, and it appeared as if nothing could occur to disturb their friendship. But one day they had a quarrel in the dissecting room about the origin and insertion of some muscles. High words took place, and threats were freely indulged in on both sides. But by the interposition of some friends they were reconciled.

After this quarrel they became as firmly attached to each other as ever. They constantly visited at each other's rooms, and were frequently seen together in public.

On the evening of the murder, they had attended the theatre together, and Seldon had returned home with Wilson. The owner of the lodging house testified to their both returning about twelve o'clock at night. He did not know what time Seldon had left. The police immediately proceeded to search Seldon's rooms. They found the student absent. After a strict search they discovered in one corner of his sleeping apartment, a handkerchief saturated with blood, and a dissecting knife also smeared with blood. In a drawer was a letter containing a challenge to Wilson to fight a duel; this letter had no date to it. This evidence was thought conclusive, and Charles Seldon was immediately arrested, charged with the willful murder of George Wilson.

I must confess when all this was told me, the case appeared a very black one for my friend Seldon. It was proved that on the night of the murder he had accompanied the deceased to his rooms that it had not been noticed when he left; that the strongest evidences of his guilt were found in his rooms, but still I was not satisfied. I knew Seldon so well that I could not persuade myself he had been guilty of so atrocious a crime. I at once determined to pay my friend a visit in prison, and easily obtained a pass for that purpose. In an hour I was at the prison door. On delivering the pass I was immediately admitted. When I entered the cell, I found my friend sitting on the edge of his iron bed, with his face buried in his hands. As soon as he heard my step he looked up.

"My dear fellow," said he, rising, "this is indeed kind of you."

"I should indeed be wanting in friendship," I replied, "If I were not to visit you when in trouble."

"You know about the dreadful crime with which I am charged, but as surely as there is a God in Heaven, I am guiltless of this bloody deed."

The poor fellow could restrain himself no longer, but letting his face fall on my shoulder, he wept and sobbed like a child. I had no doubt whatever of his innocence now.

"Come, come," I said, trying to console him; "cheer up, Charles. I am perfectly satisfied as to your innocence, and so shall the world be before many days are over."

"It is not for myself I care," he exclaimed, between his sobs—"but my poor dear mother, it will break her heart when she hears of her son's disgrace."

"My dear fellow," I answered, "you let your fears get the better of you. There can be no disgrace when there is no crime; but come, compose yourself, I want you to tell me a few particulars regarding this matter. Do you suspect anybody of having committed this murder?"

"No, I have not the slightest idea who did it. You well know that poor Wilson and I had settled our quarrel; we were as good friends as ever, and even on the fatal night we went to the theatre together. We returned about midnight, and I accompanied him to his room, where I stayed with him upwards of hour, smoking a cigar and talking about old times. I let myself out without disturbing any one and went immediately home. This morning I was arrested on the charge of murder, and this is all I know about the matter, so help me God."

"Have you employed any one to look after your interests?"

"Not yet. Everything was so sudden that I appear to be in a dream."

"A sudden thought has struck me. You remember my telling you about meeting with a famous detective officer, named Brampton, when I was on a visit to your house?" Now if anybody can find out the truth, he is the man."

"You are right—see him at once, my dear fellow. There is no time to lose."

I agreed with Seldon, that it would be better to see Brampton immediately, and hurriedly bidding him good-by, I proceeded at once to the address the detective officer had given me, and which, fortunately, I had preserved. I found him at home, and in a few words I explained to him all that had occured. He appeared I thought to take the matter very coolly, but consented without any hesitation to examine into the affair.

"What are the proofs against the young man?" asked Brampton.

I then told him about the bloody handkerchief, the dissecting knife, and the challenge which had been found in Seldon's room; at the same time I upbraided myself that I had not mentioned anything about the supposed proofs of his guilt to my friend when I visited him in prison.

"The first thing we have to do," said the detective, "is to examine these things; we will then visit the scene of the tragedy."

He put on his hat and we went at once to the police office. The articles were shown us without any hesitation. Mr. Brampton scrutinized the bloody handkerchief and compromising note very closely.

"If this is all the proof they have got against your friend, it does not amount to much," said he. "With respect to the handkerchief, you see it is only bloody in spots; had it been used in murder it would have been saturated equally through the whole fabric; the blood on the knife is at the least two weeks old, and the challenge was evidently written two or three months ago—you see the paper looks quite yellow, and the ink has already faded."

I was rejoiced to hear him give this opinion, which, when he pointed out to me the reasons for it, was evidently well founded. We left the police office, and started for Lispenard Street for the house where the murder had been committed. It was the middle of January, and the day was bitter cold. A considerable quantity of snow had fallen, which somewhat impeded our progress. In half an hour's time, however, we reached the house which had been the scene of the assassination.

It was quite a modern building situated in the heart of a populous street. One would suppose it to be the last place in the world where such a deed could be committed without instant detection. We had no difficulty in obtaining admission into the fatal chamber. The room remained exactly in the same state as when first discovered. Wilson's body, however, had been removed into another apartment. Mr. Brampton proceeded to examine the room narrowly, determined if possible to discover some clue to the murder. I must premise by stating that the apartment was the middle of three on the second floor. The one on the right was occupied by a lawyer's clerk the one on the left by a clerk in a drug store.

"The first thing to I observed," said Mr. Brampton, "is that it is very singular how this murder could have been committed without any alarm having been given to the inmates of these other two apartments. The natural inference is that the victim must first of all have been deprived of consciousness—this must have been produced by either ether or chloroform. I should judge it must have been the latter, as it is much more rapid in its effects."

I did not agree with the theory of the detective, for it appeared to me that a violent struggle had taken place. The room was in extreme disorder, and the floor was strewn with the murdered man's hair. I mentioned my doubt to Mr. Brampton.

"The very thing you mention only serves to confirm me in my first opinion," said he, with a smile, and he picked up a lock of hair from the carpet. "In the first place," he continued, "there is too much study and regularity in this to satisfy me, and look at this lock of hair, you see the ends are all even and stained with blood, evidently showing that it was not torn out by the roots, as would be imagined at first glance. The even ends show that it was cut off with some sharp instrument, and the fact of their being stained with blood proves that the hair was cut off after the murder was committed, and with the same instrument. This instrument must have been very sharp, and I conclude it was either a razor or a scalpel."

Mr. Brampton now proceeded to search every corner of the apartment, and discovered under a heap of bedclothes a pocket-handkerchief. He picked it up and found that the two ends were knotted together. He raised it to my nose, and I could distinctly trace the smell of chloroform. It was a large white pocket handkerchief, and evidently belonged to a gentleman. In one corner of it were the initials J. D.

"An important discovery," said the detective, putting it into his pocket.

We next proceeded to view the body. The mortal remains of George Wilson were stretched on a low bed in an empty apartment on the next floor. The first thing that Mr. Brampton pointed out to me was that one of the ears of the deceased was almost black and the other was grazed. On the back of the head the hair was matted and pressed.

The detective pulled the handkerchief he had found in the other room out of his pocket, and discovered that it exactly fitted round the head of the deceased, and where the hair was matted the knot had been tied. The pressure had been so great as to stop the circulation of the blood, and this accounted for the peculiar appearance of the ears. Mr. Brampton next proceeded to examine the mouth of the deceased. After separating the lips we both of us perceived a piece of white or transparent substance adhering to one of the front teeth. He detached it.

"What is it?" I asked.

"It is a piece of human skin," he replied.

"What do you infer from it?"

"I will tell you directly, but it is necessary first that we should again visit the room where the murder was committed."

We did so, and Brampton walked straight up to a large cupboard which he had neglected to examine before. He threw open the door, and he had no sooner done so than an expression of satisfaction escaped his lips.

"I suspected as much," said he—"do you see anything peculiar in that cupboard?" he asked.

"No," I replied. "I only see that it is half full of soiled linen."

"Don't you see that the linen is indented in the middle, evidently showing that some one has been concealed there?"

When he pointed it out to me it was plain enough, and I wondered it had not struck me before.

"I think we are now in a very fair way of discovering the murderer," said he. "Your friend is undoubtedly innocent. The murderer, whose initials are in all probability J. D., concealed himself in this closet. He must have been there during the whole of the interview between Seldon and Wilson. When the latter was left alone, he crept stealthily from his hiding place, and first saturating his handkerchief with chloroform, he applied it to the mouth of his victim. A very slight struggle ensued in which the hand of the murderer was bitten by the deceased. The chloroform, however, soon produced unconsciousness; the deed was then committed; the cutting off of the hair, and the disorder in the room, were effected afterwards, as I before told you."

It was perfectly plain to me after his explanation, that everything must have taken place exactly as he stated, and it appeared such a simple and natural conclusion to arrive at, that I wondered I had not come to the same conclusion myself.

"What is the next lecture at the university medical college?" said he.

"Professor P— lectures at five o'clock this afternoon on Materia Medica," I replied, somewhat surprised at such a question.

"Will you allow me to accompany you?" he asked.

"Certainly," I returned, more and more surprised.

We left the house, and it was decided that I should call for him a quarter before five. He gave me no reason why he wished to attend the lecture. At the hour agreed upon I was at his door, and we both proceeded to the college together. When we entered the lecture room he very closely scrutinized every student present, and then he appeared satisfied, for he sat down and listened attentively to the end. When it was over he pointed out a young man to me.

"What is that young man's name?" said he.

"His name is Joseph Davis."

"Do you know him?"

"Yes, I know him very well."

"Do you know where he lives?"

"Yes."

At that moment Davis came up conversing with four or five other students. They stood quite near us, and we could overhear their conversation.

"What is the matter with your hand Davis?" said a student.

I now noticed for the first time that his hand was tied up in a handkerchief.

"I pricked myself while dissecting," replied Davis.

"You ought to be careful of yourself such injuries are frequently very dangerous," returned another student.

"What a shocking thing it is about poor Wilson," said another of his companions.

"It is, indeed," returned Davis. "I suppose there is no doubt about Seldon's guilt!"

"Not at all. By-the-by Davis, it is a good thing the murderer is discovered, for you had an awful row with him yesterday morning."

"I know I had. You know he accused me of cheating at cards, and I could not stand that. I own I used some very harsh language, which I now regret."

The young man now passed on. Mr. Brampton followed him. At last the student who had referred to a difficulty between Davis and Wilson, separated from the rest. The detective officer hurried on and overtook him before he turned the corner of the street.

"What is that young man's name?" he asked of me.

"Herman Doyle," I returned.

"Mr. Doyle," said Brampton, as he came up with the student, "I wish to ask you a question or two. I am a detective officer. You referred just now to a quarrel between Mr. Davis and Mr. Wilson—will you be good enough to give me the particulars?"

The young student appeared to be a good deal astonished at being thus addressed, but replied without any hesitation.

"Yesterday morning, Davis, Wilson and myself were playing poker in my room. There was a dispute between the two persons, Wilson accused Davis of cheating."

"What followed?" asked Brampton.

"Davis, who is a southerner, was very indignant, and swore he would have Wilson's life."

"I thank you. I am much obliged to you," replied the detective, and wishing the medical student good morning, we walked away.

"Now, then, we must go to Davis's lodgings," said Brampton. "Introduce me as your uncle, and ask him to lend you a scalpel."

I did not presume to dispute anything he advised. We had not to walk far before we reached the house in which he boarded. He had only arrived a few minutes before us. We were shown at once into his room, and I introduced Brampton as my uncle as had been agreed upon. When the ceremony of introduction was over, I said: Davis, will you be kind enough to lend me a scalpel for a day or two?"

"Help yourself," said he, pointing to a box on the bureau. Brampton took the box as if for the purpose of handing, it to me. He opened it and glanced at the contents.

"What is the matter with your hand, Mr. Davis?"said Brampton, looking at him as if he would read his very soul.

Davis began to grow uneasy, and moved restlessly in his chair.

"O, it's nothing," he answered— "I pricked myself while dissecting the other day."

"Will you let me see it?" I asked; "perhaps I can suggest something for it."

"It is really not worth while," he answered. Then he added, after reflecting a moment, "but if it will afford you any gratification, you can see it."

He pulled of the handkerchief and showed us his hand. It was as Brampton had expected—his hand had been severely bitten, and the marks of the teeth were plainly perceptible. We then knew that we stood in the presence of George Wilson's murderer! Brampton suddenly rose from his seat, shut the door, and putting his hand on Davis's shoulder, exclaimed:

"I am a detective officer Joseph Davis, I arrest you for the murder of George Wilson, and here is the knife with which you committed the deed," he added, taking one of the scalpels from the box— "see, some of the hair of the victim still adheres to it."

This sudden action succeeded. He gazed for a moment wildly around him as if meditating flight, and then fell back speechless in a chair. The assistance of some policemen was immediately obtained and he was removed to the Tombs.

Two days afterwards he committed suicide in prison by opening the femoral artery, leaving behind him a written confession of his guilt. In this confession he acknowledged that he had concealed himself in Wilson's chamber, and attacked him exactly in the manner stated by Brampton. Charles Seldon was of course honorably discharged.

Leaf the Eighteenth

The Phantom Face

James Bartlett was a particular friend of mine. I always regarded him with the most sincere affection. He possessed many good points. I never knew him to do a mean dishonorable act. When I first became acquainted with him he always enjoyed the best spirits, and was the life and soul of all our little *reunions.* A change, however, suddenly came over him; he grew moody and absent; his lips no longer even smiled, and he would often start as though some secret thought troubled him. He grew pale and thin, so much so that I several times interrogated him as to his malady; but he always treated the matter lightly. In the evening I have especially noticed that he would oftentimes be strangely affected—a violent trembling would seize his whole body, and he would catch me convulsively by the arm, giving utterance to some such phrase as "there! again! again!" I thought that his nervous system was out of order, and recommended a change of air and scene.

One day I learned to my grief and amazement that my friend was dead. I immediately ran to his lodgings, and found him exactly as he had been first discovered, for his body had not been touched. His face was horribly convulsed. On the table were a few pages of MSS., of which I took possession. When I returned home I read them, and now give them to the reader without altering one word.

My poor friend was pronounced to have died of disease of the heart, and his remains now lie in Greenwood Cemetery, Brooklyn.

There! there it is reflected in the mirror, opposite which I am writing. A face so fearful, so horrible that I will not attempt to describe. How the eyes gleam upon me! What a hideous smile lurks about the toothless mouth! Avaunt, thou accursed! Avaunt, I say!

It is gone! The mirror now only reflects my own image. For a few hours I shall be free from this damning spectre. Let me in that time, if I can sufficiently command my thoughts, relate my story.

Edith Clarkson! My pen has written the name almost without my being aware of the fact. Poor Edith! God is my witness that I loved her with my whole soul. But she is dead! Killed by my hand! That glorious form is now mouldering in the grave. That voice, the music of which still lingers in my ear, is still for ever. Poor Edith! Dear sainted spirit now dwelling in Heaven look down from this blessed abode and forgive me!

Edith and I was cousins—brought up together from our earliest youth. How well I remember the poetry-time of our life! Those days of happy youth when we wandered hand in hand together and plucked the wild flowers, which I wove in her auburn tresses. What a beautiful world it was to me at that period. But we separated—separated with natural vows of constancy and devotion. Edith remained in the country, and I came to this Babylon. But Edith I did not forget thee. My letters to thee told thee how much I loved thee. And thy letters, sweet girl—what tenderness—what devotion! Oh how often did I reperuse those precious epistles! I traced thy sinless soul in every line.

Time sped gaily on with me. My studies were nearly completed. I had obtained honors in the profession I had chosen, and in a few months more I should obtain the height of my ambition—a diploma authorizing me to practice as a physician.

Twelve weeks only were between me and the realization of all my hopes. I had been studying hard. I needed relaxation, and by the advice of the professors themselves, I was recommended to visit home for a change. With what alacrity did I seize on the idea, for I should see Edith, my Edith, my best beloved again!

That eventful morning when I entered the Hudson river cars, which were to convey me to my old home, will never pass from my memory. The cars rattled on—old familiar landmarks came in sight—here a shady nook where I had breathed my first vows to the idol of my soul—there an overhanging rock from which I had in my early days gazed with wonder on the swollen flood below. Then came nodding corn fields, the spire of the old church, and lastly the quaint old gables of my boyhood's home. The cars stopped. I leaped from them—almost flew up the noisy bank, and in another minute I was at home.

Edith was there, waiting for me in the hall. I caught her in my arms and pressed her to my heart, while with my lips I stifled the words of welcome, she addressed to me.

"Edith! darling—dearest Edith!" I murmured.

"Dear, dear James," was the soft reply uttered by the blushing girl, as she hid her heavenly face on my breast.

The following day we resumed our old habits. She accompanied me in my rambles, and hand in hand we gazed on the beauties of the glorious scenery of that part of the Hudson. What a happy, happy time! Before us flowed the silver river murmuring the softest music in our ears; behind us rose, towering hundreds of feet above our heads, green sloping banks, thick with umbrageous verdure. On the other side of the river the great Catskills reared their lofty heads to a towering height. And then the glorious sensation of having by my side that angelic being whose every word fell like balm on my throbbing heart. What Paradise could equal this? But why dwell on these, scenes—the recollection of them only makes my present condition more dark and gloomy.

One, two, three weeks passed, and my soul was over burdened with happiness—my physical nature appeared ready to succumb to so much joy—when a change, so sudden, so violent, occurred, as to bereave me of my senses.

One day my cousin received a letter; with that letter set the sun of happiness, and in its place rose the gloomy phantom of despair. What that letter contained I do not know to this day, but I judge it must have been some malicious statement from some one who knew me in New York. With that letter a change came over Edith—sad and bitter change. She would walk with me no longer; she turned her eyes away from me when I spoke to her. She treated me coldly, if not disdainfully. I implored her, I besought her to let me know the reason of this revulsion of feeling on her part. Her only reply was disconnected sentences.

I felt that I was judged wrongfully, mid this sense of wrong grew upon me. I invented a thousand things to account for it. Three days after the receipt of this letter, a young gentleman, whose father lived in the neighborhood, paid us a visit. Edith received him and treated him very graciously. The next day I saw them together in the woods.

The demon jealousy was then lighted up in my heart. This was why she had deserted me; this was why she had scorned me; she loved another! Horrible, soul-destroying thought! Madness now crept into my blood. How that day passed I know not. I have some recollection of wandering miles from home, and shrieking and shouting in the wood. I returned home late at night. The moon was at its full, and even now I remember distinctly noticing the gleam of silver made on the water by its slanting rays.

I went to my chamber without saying a word to a soul, and then I saw it for the first time. Yes, there it was, gleaming and gibbering at me in evident derision. But such a ghastly, such a horrible face as no mortal man had ever seen before. My blood turned to ice. I followed the phantom. It went before me, and I found myself in the open air. The phantom face dissolved away in the moonlight. Reaction had set in, and now I was hot and burning. I walked to the river side, and who should I meet but my cousin Edith, standing on a grassy knoll, with her eyes fixed on the night queen.

"Edith, dearest Edith," I murmured, approaching her, "hear me, Edith. Why—why do you treat me thus, darling? My own dear girl, speak! speak!"

"Leave me, sir," said Edith. "I do not wish to speak to you. I have done with you forever."

"Give me a reason. Do you no longer love me?"

"I do not."

"I know why," I returned, jealousy taking possession of my heart. "You love another. Yes, you are false—false as hell," I shrieked.

Edith looked alarmed, and turned to escape me.

"By the Heavens above us," I exclaimed, "you shall not be his."

And I seized her in my grasp.

"Unhand me, sir," she exclaimed, now thoroughly alarmed, "or I will call for assistance."

My only reply was a mocking laugh. The echo returned to my ears, and I could almost fancy it came from my detested rival.

What followed I cannot tell. The next thing I heard was a dull and heavy splash, and a smothered cry, and I saw something white floating down the stream.

I had pushed Edith into the river!

I returned home and buried my head in the bed; but that splash and that cry rang in my ears. I lifted up my head, and there was the hideous fire right before me, gazing with diabolical malignity into my eyes. That look scorched my brain, and I was seized with a brain fever.

When I recovered, days and weeks had elapsed. It was then broken to me by degrees that Edith had been found drowned, and it was supposed that she had missed her footing, and fallen into the river.

I got better, but that devilish face visited me every night. No repose, no sweet slumbers; if exhausted nature were cheated into a few hours forgetfulness, when I opened my eyes, if day had not already dawned, there was the hideous, horrible face. My days are numbered; this accursed phantom is dragging me to the grave.

Great God! there it is again—more terrible, more fearful, more horrible than it has ever been before. Away you accursed phantom! avaunt, I say! What! wilt thou not obey me? The face approaches. Great God! I feel its toothless jaws pressing against my face—an icy chillness seizes my heart—I faint—I die—oh God—pardon—par—

Here ended my friend's MSS.

Leaf the Nineteenth

THE BROKEN CENT

(A leaf from a Lawyer's Note-Book. I am indebted to one of my friends for this incident, as well as for the other two which follow. —J. B.)

I never was in a gambling-house but once in my life, and that was many years ago. I might have forgotten the circumstance, had it not been connected with an affair that made an indelible impression on my mind. It was in the year 1841, that professional business called me to the city of Baltimore, in the state of Maryland. I was engaged in a patent case, and expected to be there a week. One of the witnesses in the case was a young man named George Broughton, a particular friend of mine, so that the trip promised to be an agreeable one, as we were to travel and room together, during our absence from home.

It was a beautiful spring day when we started on our journey and reached Baltimore the same evening. We drove to Barnum's Hotel, and were soon installed in comfortable quarters. After supper, we strolled about the beautiful city; we could but admire its cleanliness, and the picturesque appearance of the streets. I remember very well, we were struck with the view of the city at night, from the elevation on which the Washington Monument is erected. It was a glorious moonlight night, and not a single cloud obscured the blue vault of heaven. Here and there, the sky was dotted with some large star, which shared the glory of the silver moon. The air was balmy, and the city as calm and still as if we had been in a desert. We sat down on the parapet surrounding the monument, and turned our faces to the south. We both uttered an exclamation of admiration at the same moment. Before us lay no American city, but we were suddenly in Italy's classic land. There were the minarets, towers, steeples, villas, cupolas and domes, belonging to Florence or Venice, rather than a North American city. There was the same hazy atmosphere, the same bright sky, the same delirious feeling of "*dolce far niente.*" George and I lingered over the scene for more than an hour, and it was only by an effort that we at last tore ourselves away. We returned to the hotel, and after a social cigar together, retired to bed.

The next day the trial commenced; it was a most uninteresting case to the general reader, so I shall pass it by. I was very much fatigued when the court adjourned for the night, having been cross-examining witnesses the whole day. A good dinner and a glass of wine soon restored me.

After I had dined, I walked out on the balcony, and found George speaking to a stranger, whom he introduced to me as a Mr. Purcell, of Virginia. The latter was a gentleman about forty years of age, with a fine open countenance, and genial manners. He had arrived that afternoon at the hotel, and was on his way to New York. I entered into conversation with him, and found him to be an intelligent man, and a pleasing companion. We conversed on different subjects for some time, when Mr. Purcell suddenly remarked, turning to me:

"Mr. Mansfield, you are a lawyer, a member of a profession which is purely practical—tell me, do you believe in good and bad luck!"

"I scarcely understand your question," I replied; "if you mean by it, do I believe that some persons are lucky and others unlucky in this world, I answer in the affirmative."

"That is not exactly my meaning," replied Mr. Purcell. "Do you believe that luck is governed by fixed laws?"

"Your question is a metaphysical one, and would involve a long argument, but why do you ask it?"

"I will tell you I have visited Baltimore twice before in my life. The first time was about five years ago. Some one proposed that we should visit a gambling-house. I had never been in one, and wishing to see a little of life, consented. We entered one in Old Town, and I risked a small sum—a five dollar bill, I think it was. I won—I placed the whole amount on another card and won again. I went on playing, and strange to say, won every time. At last the bank declined to play any more, and I left with $10,000 in my pocket. Three years afterwards, I visited this city again. I had never entered a gambling-house since my first visit; but now I determined I would try my chance once more—it was more a motive of curiosity than anything else that impelled me, for I have really no passion for gambling whatever. Exactly the same thing took place. I first of all staked five dollars, and won every time. Again the bank declined to play any more, and I left this time with $15,000 winnings.

"Certainly there is something strange in this," replied George. "Have you ever been in a gambling-house since?"

"Never," returned Mr. Purcell, "as I before told you, I have no love for gambling. But I have something further to confess, and here I am afraid I forfeit my claim in your eyes to the possession of common sense. I know you will think I am superstitious, when I tell you that I ascribe all my luck at the gaming table to the possession of this."

And Mr. Purcell drew from his pocket a broken cent, bearing the date of 1815, which he handed to me to look at.

"You are jesting," said I.

"No, indeed," he returned. "I know it is contrary to common sense and reason, but I have tried the experiment over and over again at cards. When I have that cent in my pocket, I invariably win; when I am without it my luck is the same as other persons, sometimes I win and sometimes lose."

"But that is purely a coincidence," said Broughton.

""No, it is no coincidence, because it is invariable. I have tested it more than five hundred times."

"Where did you get that cent from?" I asked.

"That is the most curious part of the whole story," replied Mr. Purcell. "Some eight years ago, an old family servant of ours, a gray headed negro, sent for me in the middle of the night to visit him at his bedside. He had been ill some days with pneumonia, and our family physician had pronounced his recovery hopeless. I had always been the old man's favorite, and of course obeyed his summons with alacrity. I found the negro fast sinking. The moment he saw me, he stretched out his hand to me and slipped this broken cent into mine. 'This will bring you luck at cards, Massa Charles,' he murmured. 'Keep it for my sake.' To please the old man, I put it into my pocket, but thought no more about it. He died that night. During the winter, we played whist almost every night at home to while away the time. The next time we played after this incident, an extraordinary vein of luck seemed to have fallen to my share, for I won every game. But even then I never thought anything about the talisman I possessed. The same thing occurred night after night—I could not understand my extraordinary good fortune, when one morning, happening to feel in my waistcoat, pocket, I found the cent. I then remembered what the negro had told me, and commenced a series of tests, which convinced me that this coin possesses all the virtues I have ascribed to it. The first time I came to Baltimore, I thought nothing about my talisman, although I always carry it in my pocket. It was not until I had returned to my hotel with my winnings from the gambling house, that I remembered it—I then knew to what I owed my good fortune."

Mr. Purcell spoke so earnestly, that I saw it would be no use attempting to combat the extraordinary delusion under which he labored. I contented myself with saying that it was very strange.

"Now, gentlemen," said Mr. Purcell, "it is my intention to visit the gambling house again to-night—if you would like to accompany me I should be glad of your society."

At first, I declined—I had lived forty years without entering a gambling house, and felt no particular desire to do so now—but George appeared disposed to go. The thought struck me that this Mr. Purcell might be a plausible sharper, in the employment of some of the gaming-house keepers, to get victims into their dens. When I saw that my friend Broughton was determined to accompany Purcell, I altered my mind and resolved to go too for I knew that I had a great deal of influence with my friend, that a word from me would prevent him from playing deeply. We sat a little while after supper and then started off. It was exactly ten o'clock when we left the hotel.

It was a glorious night; the moon was fast rising to the zenith, while the gorgeous Orion was sinking in the west. Near the moon was the regal Jupiter, a little further east the pale Saturn, and within a few degrees of the western horizon was the king of the long winter's night, Sirius. I have always been a lover of the wonders of the heavens, but the recollection of the magnificent spectacle the sky presented on that eventful night is indelibly impressed on my memory. We proceeded along Market Street, over the bridge, and were soon threading the narrow thoroughfares in Old Town. At last we stood before a house in Bond Street, which our conductor informed us was the dwelling we sought. It was a long, low dark building, with but few windows, facing the street. It had the appearance from the outside of being unoccupied, and such at first was really my idea—but Mr. Purcell soon undeceived me, for he advanced to the door and knocked at it in a peculiar manner. The door was immediately cautiously opened by a negro, who scanned us carefully before he admitted us.

"All right, Sam," said Mr. Purcell. The porter doubtless remembered the Virginian, for he threw the door open and we entered. We had no sooner passed through an inner green baize door, than a flood of light burst upon us, proceeding from a chandelier, which served to illume a staircase. Our conductor ascended the stairs and we followed. The flight was a short one, and we found ourselves in a long room, handsomely furnished, and brilliantly lighted. In the middle of this apartment was a table, on which were printed representations of thirteen cards. In front of the table sat the dealer, a flashy looking man, with an impassible face, and superabundance of jewelry. He had before him a spring box in which was placed a pack of cards, from which he kept continually taking the top one and placed it on one of two heaps. I knew nothing of the game, but learned that it was a faro table. A large number of persons surrounded the table, who, from time to time placed bank notes or checks on the cards painted on the cloth, and as a card was turned up, the dealer either took the amount to himself, or paid an amount equal to that placed on the card; the point being decided by the fact whether the card turned up belonged to the dealer's pile or the players. If my description of the game is meagre and unsatisfactory, my ignorance must plead my excuse, for as I said before, I knew nothing about the game. I only describe what I saw.

The moment Mr. Purcell entered the room, he was accosted by a stout redfaced man, with a singular unprepossessing cast of countenance, who advanced and shook him cordially by the hand.

"I am glad to see you, Mr. Purcell," said the proprietor of the gambling-saloon, for such I afterwards found him to be. "Have you come to break us again?"

"I have come to try my luck," replied Purcell.

The latter now advanced to the dealer, and handed to him a pile of notes, and, received in exchange a number of red checks, which he informed me each represented five dollars. George Broughton bought a few white checks representing one dollar each.

They now commenced to play. I watched the game with much interest. Purcell placed a dozen or so of his red checks on the queen. After the dealer had turned a few cards, I saw that the Virginian had won, from the fact that an equal number of checks was placed beside his stake. Every one supposed that he would now bet on another card, but he left his stake there—he won again, Purcell appeared to be entirely careless about the matter, not even looking, at the table.
"Your card has won the third time," said Mr. Emery, the proprietor of the saloon. "Luck has not deserted me, it, seems then," was his only reply.

"You had better take down your funds," said George Broughton whispering in his ear.

"O, no, I'll let them be."

"But the queen has won three times—and everybody is betting against it."

I glanced at the table and saw a large number of checks piled on the queen—but all of them were topped by a cent except the Virginian's. This cent I afterwards learned, denoted that they played against the card winning the next time.

"You will certainly lose," said Broughton, perceiving that his new friend took no notice of what he had said to him.

"I shall win," returned the Virginian, with the utmost confidence.

And he did win, for again the queen was turned on the player's side. I need not prolong the description of the scene; suffice it to say, that the Virginian won every time. He changed his check for those of larger denominations, and according to old gamblers, he played in the most reckless manner, but always with the same result. He soon absorbed the attention of the entire company. One man in particular—a thin, cadaverous looking individual, who I afterwards learned was an actor at the Charles Street Theatre, gazed on him with wonder and astonishment.

I began to get tired of it, and proposed to Broughton that we should return to our hotel. But he was fascinated, and did not want to leave. I then bade him good night. I felt the necessity of retiring to bed, as I had a hard day's work before me on the morrow, and I left the gambling-house. I soon reached East Baltimore Street, and turned as I supposed, in the direction of my hotel. I continued to walk until I found myself in a very wide street which I did not remember to have seen before. A watchman fortunately passed me at that moment, and I inquired my way to Barnum's Hotel; I then learned that when I left Bond Street I had turned to the right when I should have turned to the left, and by this means had absolutely been proceeding in an exactly opposite direction to the one I ought to have taken. The watchman, however, setting me right, I hastened to repair the mistake I had made by quickening my steps. But with all the speed I made, I lost at least three-quarters of an hour by my want of knowledge of the points of the compass.

At last I reached Jones' Falls. It is necessary that I should inform those unacquainted with Baltimore, that Jones' Falls is a small stream of water, dividing the city into about two equal portions—that part on the eastern side of the Falls is called Old Town, while the western portion is Baltimore proper. The stream of water is crossed at the foot of every street by a bridge, there are Pratt Street bridge, Baltimore Street bridge, Fayette Street bridge, etc.

I stood on Baltimore Street bridge, and leaning over the parapet, paused a few minutes to admire the beauty of the scene. Before and behind me lay the sleeping city; to the right and left of me was the winding stream of which I have just spoken. The moon was shining on the surface of the waters, turning it into liquid silver, while a short distance off I could see the Fayette Street bridge—the moonlight enabling me to trace even the open ironwork of the parapet. It was such a clear beautiful night, the air was so soft, and the moon was so bright, that I was tempted to linger on the bridge, as I have said before—but I at last tore myself away, and was on the eve of leaving my resting place, when a sudden shriek made me start. It came from the Fayette Street bridge, and I immediately turned my eyes in that direction. What was my horror to see a man's body deliberately raised to the top of the parapet, and then thrown into the Falls. I was even near enough to hear the splash as the body fell into the water. There was one more shriek, the sound of running footsteps as the murderer crossed over to the western side of the city, and then all was still. I immediately ran as fast as I could down Front Street, in the direction of Fayette Street. I met a watchman on my way, and hurriedly told him what had occurred. He sprung his rattle, and we soon had plenty of assistance.

We commenced a strict search for the body, but without any result; the stream had doubtless taken it down the Falls. "We then examined the place from which the man had been thrown over the bridge, but, excepting a pool of blood on the pavement, there were no evidences to be found. Two or three watchmen started in pursuit of the murderer, while the rest continued to search for the body. I remained with the latter for more than an hour, but we met with no better success than at first. Finding that nothing could be done until daybreak, I gave my name and address to one of the watchmen, and started for my hotel.

When I reached the hotel, I went directly to my chamber, and found that George Broughton had returned, and was already in bed and fast asleep. At first I felt half-inclined to wake my companion and tell him what I had seen, but then I thought it would be such a pity to wake him out of his sound sleep, and that the morning would do as well. I undressed myself and went to bed.

The terrible sight I had seen kept me awake some hours, and it was not until the first rays of the morning sun shone in my window that I fell asleep. How long I slept I know not, but I was awakened by a loud knocking at my chamber door. When I opened my eyes I found that it was broad daylight. I turned my eyes to my companion's bed and found that he was still fast asleep—in fact, George Broughton was always a sound sleeper, and I was not surprised that the knocking had not awakened him. I immediately rose up and opened the door. It was one of the waiters of the hotel, who informed me that two constables were below and wished to see me directly. I ordered them to be shown up to the chamber. The sound of voices awakened George, and he sat up in bed.

"What is the matter?" said he, rubbing his eyes.

"There are two constables down stairs, who want to see me. I have sent for them to come up here."

"What in the world can constables want with you?" said Broughton.

"I will explain all by-and-by," I replied, putting on a few articles of dress.

I had hardly finished a hurried toilet when the door opened and the two officers entered.

"Is there a Mr. George Broughton here?" asked one of the men, advancing into the middle of the apartment.

"That is my name," said George.

"Is this your card?" asked the man, showing one of George's visiting cards.

"Yes, that is my card—why do you ask?"

"It is an unpleasant business, sir; but we shall be compelled to search you."

"I really don't know what this means," replied George—"but you are at perfect liberty to search my clothes—there they are on the chair."

The officers began to examine the pockets of my friend's clothes. From one they took a gold watch, from another a large quantity of bank notes and gold. As these things were brought to light, I could see a peculiar smile flit across the countenances of the officers.

"Does this property belong to you?" asked one of the officers.

"You are very inquisitive," said George. "Why do you ask?"

"Only duty, sir. Of course you are at liberty to tell or not, as you think fit."

While this conversation was going on, I stood as if thunderstruck. I immediately asked myself the question where did George get the watch and all the money from—for I knew that they did not belong to him.

"I have no objection to tell," replied George, "although I do not recognize your right to ask me the question. That money and that watch belong to Mr. John Purcell, of Virginia."

"Exactly," said the officer, with a sagacious nod, and then, he added: "you were with him last night?"

"I was."

"You left the gambling-house in Bond Street together, at one in the morning?"

"We did."

"Then, sir, it is my painful duty to arrest you for the wilful murder of Mr. John Purcell."

"Good God!" cried George, starting from the bed; "what do you mean?"

"Simply what I say. You must accompany me at once to a magistrate's office, and we shall want your company, Mr. Mansfield."

I was dreaming. I did not know if I was asleep or awake.

"My company,'" I stammered, "what can you want me for?"

"You are an important witness, sir. You are the only witness to the murder."

"What! do you mean that the body I saw thrown over the bridge—" I hesitated to finish the sentence.

"Was Mr. Purcell's," replied the officer. "His body was found below Pratt Street early this morning. And on repairing to the scene of the tragedy we found Mr. Broughton's visiting card on the pavement. It was overlooked in the search last night. We received information that Mr. Broughton was lodging at Barnum's, and came here at once. I need not tell you that we have found corroborative testimony," added the speaker, pointing to the watch and money which still lay on the table.

"Mansfield, you cannot believe me guilty," said George, turning as pale as death.

"No, my dear fellow," I replied, "I do not believe you guilty—in fact, I know it is utterly impossible that you could have committed this crime. I have no doubt an explanation at the magistrate's office will set all to rights."

George hurriedly dressed himself, and we proceeded to the nearest magistrate. We found several witnesses already assembled there, and the case was at once gone into. The first witness called was the keeper of the gambling house. He deposed that the deceased, accompanied by Broughton and myself, visited his saloon on the previous night, that the deceased won very largely, and partook of supper a quarter of an hour after I had left. He further deposed that the deceased drank a great deal of champagne during the meal, and soon after left the house accompanied by the prisoner.

Henry Dornton, a private watchman, was the next witness called, and deposed that he had seen the deceased in company with the prisoner going down Fayette Street together, about a quarter of an hour before the murder occurred. He identified them positively because his attention was called to them by the fact that the deceased appeared to be intoxicated, and the prisoner was half forcing him along the street.

I was next witness called, and gave the statement with which the reader is already familiar. The constable was then called, who deposed as to the finding of the prisoner's card on Fayette Street bridge, and the discovery of the property of the deceased in the pockets of the prisoner. Patrick O'Neal deposed that he was a porter at Barnum's hotel, and that the prisoner returned to the hotel at half past one in the morning, and appeared to be very much out of breath, and somewhat excited. When it is remembered that I had previously stated that it was twenty minutes past one by my watch that I had seen the body thrown over the bridge, it can easily be surmised how this fact told against the prisoner.

This was the whole of the evidence. The magistrate then asked George if he had any statement to make. The poor fellow, who appeared utterly confounded at the mass of circumstantial evidence brought against him, replied in the affirmative, and made the following statement.

"The deceased, accompanied by Mr. Mansfield and myself, visited Mr. Emory's establishment yesterday evening. The deceased won largely. At about a quarter past twelve, as near as I am able to judge, Mr. Mansfield bade us good night, stating that he wanted to get to bed, and left the gaming-house. Fifteen minutes after that we went down stairs to supper. The deceased partook largely of champagne and afterwards drank some brandy. After supper the proprietor declared that the bank would play no more that night, and we left the house. It was one o'clock when we returned to the corner of Bond Street. The deceased was very much intoxicated and declared that he would not go home. I used every effort that I possibly could to induce him to proceed quietly along the street, but it was all to no purpose, he became more obstreperous every minute. At last, when within about a square of Fayette Street bridge he sat down on the steps of a dwelling, and declared he would hot advance another step. Again I begged and entreated him, but in vain. I then tried to pull him along by force, but he grew very angry, so I desisted. I then told him he had better give me his money and watch, and he could return to the hotel when he pleased. To this he consented, and confided to my care nearly all his winnings. I then ran to my hotel and retired at once to bed. I knew nothing whatever about the murder having been committed until the constable informed me in the morning. This is all I know about the matter."

"Mr. Broughton," said the magistrate when he concluded, "I have but one duty before me. Your explanation may be satisfactory to a jury but truth compels me to say that it is not so to me. I now commit you to jail for the wilful murder of John Purcell, there to await the action of the grand jury."

I whispered a few words of comfort in my friend's ear while the commitment was being made out but he shook his head and murmured the words, "my poor mother!"

Broughton was removed to jail, no bail being of course admissible in his case, and I went with a heavy heart to the U. S. Court to prosecute my patent claims. To my joy it was brought to a conclusion that day, the judge deciding in my favor some objection I offered which ruined my opponent's cause. I was left at liberty to devote my whole time to my poor friend, for in spite of the evidence a doubt of his innocence never for a moment entered my mind.

When I returned to my hotel in the evening I sat down seriously to consider the case. I must confess I was appalled at the weight of circumstantial evidence against him. Every link seemed to be perfect. There was the motive for the deed, the possession of the property, and the damning fact of his card having been found on the scene of the tragedy, everybody of course supposing that in the struggle it had fallen from his pocket. How was I to meet facts like these? I felt certain that some one had followed Broughton and the deceased, and that when the former left Purcell, the assassin had attacked him almost immediately. But how to discover this person? It was but natural to suppose that the murderer was one of the visitors to the gambling house, and I saw that my first inquiries must be directed in that quarter.

The next morning I visited Mr. Emory's establishment and had a long conversation with him, for to tell the truth, I suspected him very strongly. A few minutes' conversation, however, convinced me that I was in error. He proved conclusively that he had never left the house on the night in question. I then interrogated him as to his visitors. He knew them, and gave me such a character of them that I could not suspect them. I left his house no nearer a solution of the mystery than when I entered it.

My next visit was to Fayette Street bridge, and I made a most minute inspection of the place where the body had been thrown into the water. Here I met with a little more success, for wedged in some of the interstices of the iron work of the parapet I found a vest button. It was a peculiar round button of black jet, and I felt certain that it must either have come off the murdered man's vest or that of the assassin. To decide the former point, I immediately went to inspect the body of the deceased. One glance was sufficient to tell me that the vest button had never belonged to him, for his vest was a cloth one and the buttons were of the same material. A minute examination of the body also convinced me that he had been struck from behind. The wound it is true was on the right side, but the direction was such that it could not have been given in front.

This button, then, was the first clue I had to the real assassin. It is true it did not amount to much, for the chances of my finding the man who wore the particular vest with those buttons in a city of two hundred thousand inhabitants were very slight, to say nothing of the fact that hundreds of people might wear just such buttons. But still it was something, and I felt encouraged. In the afternoon I visited my poor friend in prison. I found him calm and hopeful. He was so conscious of his own innocence, that he felt it almost an impossibility that other people could believe him guilty. His greatest anxiety was on his mother's account. He entreated me to write to her and tell her the true facts of the case, for he felt unequal to the task. I promised to do so. We conversed together more than two hours, but I found that he could give no solution of the mystery.

"By-the-by, George," said I, as I was about to leave, "there is one thing that tells very much against you, and which I am at a loss to explain, and that is the fact of your visiting card being found on the spot where the murder was committed."

"I can explain that easily enough," he replied. "When I first saw Purcell we conversed together a few minutes, and finding him very agreeable, I introduced myself by handing him my card; he placed it in his waistcoat pocket, and in his scuffle with the assassin it must have fallen to the ground."

"Did any one see you give him your card?"

"Certainly—a waiter was in the room at the time."

"If he can only remember the fact," I returned, "the chief link in the chain of evidence against you is broken."

"I am sure he will remember it, for he was handing a glass of water to Mr. Purcell at the very moment I presented the card."

"This is very encouraging," I returned.

Our conversation lasted a little time longer and then I bade him farewell. My first duty on my return to the hotel was to call the waiter to me. I found my friend was correct—he remembered all about the card. For the next two weeks I devoted all my time in hunting up additional evidence. I will not detain the reader with an account of my proceedings. I used all the ruses so well known to our profession, but they every one failed. I could not obtain the slightest clue to the real perpetrator of the crime. I visited my friend almost every day, and endeavored to keep up his spirits by representing his case in a more favorable light than really existed but he could not fail to gather from me that I had met with no decided success.

I began to grow very much discouraged, for unwilling as I was to admit the truth, I could not disguise from myself the fact that my poor friend must inevitably be convicted unless I could discover the real assassin, and of that there did not appear to be the slightest probability. George's mother had come down to Baltimore, and was staying at the same hotel with me. Every evening I had to report progress to her, and, as with her son, I was obliged to disguise my own dreadful forebodings.

One night, weary in mind and body, as I was passing the Charles Street theatre, my attention was attracted by a huge poster at the door. I do not know what impelled me, for God knows I was in no mood to seek amusement, but I entered the theatre, and paying the price of admission, took my seat in the parquette. The house was very full. I glanced at the bill and found that the first piece to be played was "The People's Lawyer," the principal part, that of Solon Shingle, being filled by a Mr. Denner. The performance was advertised to commence at a quarter before eight. It was now eight o'clock, and the curtain had not yet risen. The audience began to be very impatient, stamping, whistling and calling at the top of their voices. It was in vain that the orchestra continued to play. At last, at a quarter after eight, the drop curtain was moved on one side and the manager advanced to the footlights. The house became so quiet that you could have heard a pin drop.

"Ladies and gentlemen," began the manager," I have to throw myself on your indulgence. The piece has been delayed, owing to the absence of Mr. Denner. We expected him every moment, but we have just received information that Mr. Denner is ill. Under these circumstances Mr. Cowly at a few moments' notice has kindly undertaken the part. I have to bespeak for him your kind indulgence."

All American audiences are good natured, and this little speech was received with applause. One individual behind me did not, however, appear to be satisfied with it; for I distinctly heard him utter the word, "gammon." I turned round to him, and found myself face to face with a seedy-looking individual who was busily engaged chewing tobacco.

"You don't believe that statement to be true?" said I.

"I know it aint," he replied.

"Why?"

"Because I saw Denner myself at the Eutaw House, this afternoon."

"What do you suppose, then, is the reason he does not play?"

"He's above it now."

"Above it—how do you mean?"

"Why, you see, sir, this Denner is a great gambler, and he has had an extraordinary streak of luck lately, he's broke half the faro banks in town."

"What!" I exclaimed in a loud voice, starting from my seat, and drawing the attention of the entire audience on me. I became sensible of my ridiculous position, and sat down again.

"You seem mightily concerned, stranger," said the man—"I repeat what I said before, this Denner's been and broke half the faro banks in town lately; he is all the talk among the sporting men."

"What kind of a looking man is he?" I asked, in as calm a voice as I could command.

"He's a thin, lanky, slabsided sort of a man, with a face pale enough to make one think he had lived on tallow candles all his life."

"Do you know where he lives?"

"Yes, he boards at the Western in Howard Street."

I said no more, but in a few minutes left the theatre. I remembered that on the night of the murder I had noticed a pale, sickly-looking man gazing with a peculiar look on Purcell when he won so largely. If this Denner should prove to be the same man I felt certain that it must be he who had committed the murder. His extraordinary luck at gaming-houses must be owing to the possession of the broken cent which he had taken from his victim's pocket, in all probability without knowing its value. I determined on a *coup de main*, and went to the police office and procured the services of two officers.

We started for the Western Hotel in Howard Street, and when we arrived there, I was delighted to be informed in answer to our inquiries, that Mr. Denner was in his room. I inquired the number, and stated that I would go there without being announced. I placed the officers outside the door, and told them not to come in until I clapped my hands. I dispensed with the ceremony of knocking, but opening the door entered the chamber. I found Mr. Denner all dressed, in the act of drawing on his boots, evidently preparing to go out. When he raised his head I could not prevent giving a start, for I recognized, not only that he was the man I had seen in the gaming-house, but that he wore a vest with buttons exactly resembling the one I had found—one of which was wanting.

"Mr. Denner, I believe," said I.

"That's my name," said he, in a surly tone, "what do you want?"

"I want to see you on important business," I answered.

"I suppose you come from the theatre—tell the manager I won't come."

"No, sir, I do not come from the theatre," and I clapped my hands. The officers immediately entered the room. The actor turned very pale when he saw the stars, but he recovered himself almost directly.

"What means this intrusion?" said he.

"It means this, Mr. Denner," I replied, "that on the 28th, you visited the gaming-house of Mr. Emory, in Bond Street."

"Well, what then?" asked the actor, growing livid.

"That you followed Mr. Purcell and Mr. George Broughton—that when you saw the latter leave his friend, you rushed forward and stabbed the unfortunate victim of your avarice. You rifled his pockets, but found very little to reward your crime—you then threw his body into the Falls."

"It is a lie!" said the man, but his countenance proved that I had told the truth for it turned almost green, and a convulsive quivering seized his limbs.

"It is the truth," I returned, "and what is more, I hold the proof in my hands. Search him, officers," I continued, turning to the latter; "you will find on his person a broken cent bearing date 1815, which I can swear belonged to the murdered man."

"I have got no broken cent," returned the assassin, doggedly.

"That we shall soon see," was my reply.

The officers began to search Denner. From a corner of his waistcoat pocket they produced the broken cent with the date 1815. The accused gazed first at the officers and then at me with open mouth, and with wonderment and astonishment depicted in his face. It was evident that he did not know he possessed the cent.

"That is not all," I added—"when you dragged your victim to the bridge he was not dead, and struggled. In that struggle one of your vest buttons came off. Here is the button," I continued, taking it from my pocket, and going up to him I pointed to the place where it was wanting, "and here is where it belongs."

My *coup de main* was successful. The man thought I knew a great deal more than I really did, and at once made a confession. He was committed forthwith to prison. The next morning George Broughton was released. I shall never forget the meeting between mother and son to the last hour of my life. That same evening we all left for New York.

Denner's trial took place three months afterwards. He was found guilty and condemned to be hung. He evaded the sentence, however, by committing suicide.

I never knew what became of the broken cent.

Leaf the Twentieth

An Adventure at an Inn

(A Leaf from a Physician's Note-Book.)

I shall never forget to the last day of my life, my emotions of joy when I was called up, on the evening of the Commencement of the University Medical College, in the city of New York, to receive my diploma authorizing me to practice as a physician. The idea of my being able hereafter to write John Merrifield with M.D. after my name, was a sufficient reward for all my hard study and I remember the next day I did nothing else but write it on a piece of paper to see how it would look. This vanity is perhaps pardonable, when it is remembered that for three years I had been looking forward to that happy day; that it was the end of all my ambition; that for this privilege I had burned the midnight oil, and that I looked upon it as a stepping-stone to a respectable position in the world, if not to fortune and renown. I little knew the trials and difficulties a young physician has to undergo to gain even a moderate competence; but I suppose I expected that I should jump into practice at once, and rich patients, large fees and successful cures formed the staple of my thoughts.

I determined that I would settle in the city, as affording me a larger scope where to exercise the abilities I thought I possessed. The very next day I hired a suitable office in Bleecker Street, fixed my "shingle," in all the glory of gold letters on a black ground, to the side of the house, furnished my apartment in a very moderate style, and then sat down in my office to wait for patients.

And I had to wait days, weeks, nay, even months elapsed, and no patients came. My small means were slowly dwindling away, and I saw no prospect of time effecting any improvement in my circumstances. I began to despair, and resolved several times that I would give up my profession and seek some other employment, which would at least afford me a means of support. At last I came to a fixed resolution on the subject, and determined that if another week did not bring me a patient, I would at once take down my sign, scratch out M.D. from my name, and endeavor to procure a situation my previous education qualified me.

Six days passed, and not a soul came; the seventh (it was Sunday, how well I remember it!) dawned. It was a bitter cold day in March, and the streets were covered to some depth with snow. I advanced to my office-window and gazed listlessly into the street. It looked so hopelessly cheerless outside that it struck a chill into my heart, and I sat down in my "Boston rocker" utterly dispirited. I attempted to read, but the words swam before my eyes and I threw down the book. I could only gaze into the fire, and endeavor to read my future in the glowing coals.

I might have been thus occupied an hour or more, when I was aroused by a violent ring at my office-bell. At first I thought it was only my imagination, and rubbed my eyes to see if I had not been dozing. A second ring, even more violent than the first, caused me, however, to start to my feet. I ran to the door and opened it, and found standing there a young girl about seventeen or eighteen years of age. The passage was rather dark, so I could not see her features well.

"Does Doctor Merrifield live here?" she asked, in a sweet musical voice.

"I am Doctor Merrifield," I replied.

"Would you be kind enough to come and see my father? He is very sick, and wishes you to come immediately."

At last, my first patient had come.

"Where does your father live?" I tremblingly asked.

"He lives in Third Avenue, near Sixteenth Street. I will accompany you, if you have no objection. You might not find the house, as there is no number on the door. I have a hack at the door."

To put on my hat and overcoat was the occupation of but a moment, and in another minute I found myself seated by the side of the young girl in the hack. It was only then that I had an opportunity of seeing her features, and I was immediately struck with her extreme beauty. As I have before said, she was about eighteen years of age. She was above the medium height, and her features were faultlessly regular. Her hair was bright auburn, her eyes dark blue, and her long eyelashes gave that dreamy expression to her face so charming in woman. She evidently possessed a fine mind, for her forehead was lofty, and her actions and motions showed that she had been endowed with a refined education.

We spoke but little while in the carriage. She answered my interrogations as to her father's symptoms, with an eagerness which showed that her whole thoughts was centered in him, and perceiving her pre-occupation, I did not attempt to discuss any other subject.

At last we stopped before the door of her father's house, and I descended from the vehicle and having assisted the young lady to alight, I glanced at the building in which my first patient resided. It was a substantial-looking edifice, standing a little back from the street, and everything around it betokened easy circumstances, if not wealth. The young lady led the way, and in answer to her summons at the front door, it was speedily opened, and we entered a spacious hall. Requesting me to remain in the parlor for a moment or two, my fair companion tripped nimbly up stairs.

While she was gone I had an opportunity of examining the apartment. It was elegantly furnished, and gave the same evidence of more than a moderate income which the exterior did. The walls were decorated with handsome oil paintings, and from the large number of sea subjects, I judged that my patient had been a sailor. While I was examining the pictures, the young lady reentered the room and informed me that her father, Captain Linton, was ready to receive me. Escorted by Miss Linton, I ascended the stairs and was shown into the captain's bedroom. The bed on which my patient reclined was at the further end of the chamber. The moment I entered, he stretched out his hand, and I took my place by his side.

He was an elderly man, and at first glance did not appear to be very sick. His face was full, and excepting an anxious expression to be traced on it, bore evidence of good health. The moment, however, I placed my fingers on his pulse, I discovered the secret of his malady, for it was intermittent. I knew even before examination, that he was suffering from organic disease of the heart. He answered all my questions calmly and to the point. After an interview of about half an hour, I prescribed a sedative and returned to my office.

The next day I visited him again, and found that he was something better. I conversed with him longer than I had on the first day, and found him to be a highly intelligent man, full of anecdote and valuable information. It was as I had previously supposed; he had followed the sea as a profession, and had been the captain of a privateer during the war of 1812. He had taken many valuable prizes, and from his successful career had amassed quite a fortune.

I need not dwell on this part of my history; suffice it to say that I attended Captain Linton for three weeks. During this time I had frequent opportunities of seeing his daughter, and my acquaintance with her only served to increase the favorable opinion I had entertained on our first interview. She was a charming girl, full of grace, gentleness, and what the French call *esprit.* It was, therefore, with no small degree of pleasure that I heard Captain Linton, when he was able to dispense with my professional services, request me to drop in now and then and pay them a friendly visit. Helen Linton had frequently when I was alone with her, asked me my opinion of her father's condition. Without wishing to alarm her seriously, I thought it my duty to intimate in pretty plain language that his heart was organically diseased, and that he might be taken away at any moment. She heard my opinion with tears in her eyes, and begged that I would do everything in my power to persuade him to follow a strict regimen. This I promised to do, and really think my advice had some weight with the hardy old seamen, for I noticed on subsequent visits that he indulged much less in stimulants than he used to do.

I do not know how the feeling crept on me, or what fostered its birth, but I seemed as it were to find myself suddenly in love with Helen Linton. I suppose it was the thorough awakening of my mind to all her noble qualities, that caused me to draw the conclusion that she would make me an excellent wife. Be that as it may, I found myself visiting there every night, and really looked upon myself as one of the family. Helen always received me with *empressement,* and yet I could not tell whether she simply viewed me in the light of a dear friend, or entertained any tender feelings in her heart.

One day, however, I determined to know my fate, and taking advantage of her father's absence, I poured into her ear a flood of impassioned eloquence which proceeded from my heart. I had the supreme happiness of imprinting on her lips the seal of an accepted lover. That same evening I asked her hand of the captain, when he returned home. The only reply was to place her hand in mine and repeat a prayer for our happiness. I shall not attempt to paint our joy. It was decided that in a month from that time we should be married. Since my first attendance on Captain Linton, patients began to drop in, and I was getting together quite a good practice.

Three weeks passed on, and the preparations for our wedding were all completed, when I suddenly received a message from Helen, begging me to come immediately, as her father was very sick. I obeyed the summons, but before I got to the house he was dead! Instead of a wedding we had a funeral. Helen was terribly affected by her father's death. Of course our wedding was postponed, and it was decided that she should go and spend a few months with an uncle who lived at a small village called Industry, on the banks of the Ohio. Our parting was an affecting one, but we were cheered by the hope of soon meeting again; for it was agreed between us that after she had been visiting there a month, I should go and see her.

She had been gone about a week, when, to my great surprise and consternation, I received a letter from her uncle, Mr. Henry Linton, stating that she had not arrived at his house, and begging some explanation of the delay, at the same time expressing a hope that it was not occasioned by sickness. I did not think it necessary to answer this letter, for I determined at once to go on. I made a hasty arrangement with a follow practitioner to attend to my patients during my absence, and that same evening I procured a through ticket to Wheeling, and in a few hours had left New York far behind.

When I reached Wheeling, I made the necessary inquiries at the various hotels, and succeeded in tracing Helen there. I also discovered that she had taken passage in a boat to Wellsville. To this last place I hastened with all the celerity I was capable of exercising. Here, however, I lost all trace of her, and nothing was left for me but to go on to Industry, for I thought that perhaps she might have arrived at her relative's house since the letter had been dispatched to New York.

When I reached Mr. Linton's house, I found to my consternation that she had not been heard of. Her uncle was extremely surprised to learn that she had left New York, for he had supposed something had detained her. He immediately dispatched messengers in every direction to search for her. I would have accompanied them, but I was physically unable to do so, for I was so thoroughly exhausted that I could scarcely stand. Mr. Linton insisted on my resting for the night. Much against my inclination I was compelled to comply with his request.

I woke early the next morning, very much refreshed, and hurrying on my clothes descended into the garden, where, through the window, I saw my host walking up and down one of the paths in an agitated manner.

"Good morning, doctor," he said as soon as he saw me. "I suppose you are off again."

"Yes. I will search the earth through but I will find her."

"God grant you may be successful!"

"You speak doubtingly—you cannot think anything serious has befallen Helen."

"I hope not—I trust not, but we live in strange times."

There was something so peculiar in the tone in which he spoke, that I gazed earnestly at the speaker.

"You are alarmed and agitated," I exclaimed. "Tell me what it is you fear."

"Doctor, I ought to tell you, and yet I am afraid of exciting your fears needlessly, but on reflection it is perhaps better that you should know all."

"You do indeed alarm me. You have heard some bad news. Speak, I conjure you."

"No, I have heard no bad news, I have heard nothing at all of Helen. But, doctor, there is something very mysterious transpiring in our neighborhood. No less than four or five of our best citizens and several strangers have suddenly disappeared from our midst, and nothing more has been heard of them, and all this within six months."

"But have they been sought for, and is it certain they did not leave of their own free will?"

"If only one or two had disappeared, it would be a very just suspicion, but it is impossible that five respectable farmers and merchants would desert their wives and children, as these men have done. You ask me if search has been made for them. The most minute and careful search has been instituted; in fact, the whole country has been scoured for miles, but not the slightest trace of the missing individuals could be found."

"How strange! What is supposed to have become of them?"

"Heaven only knows! There are a hundred rumors afloat, but nothing reliable in any of them. The thought struck me this morning that perhaps Helen may have disappeared in this manner."

"That is scarcely possible," I returned—at the same time I felt a chill strike my heart. "Surely no one would harm a young girl. Your suspicions will, however, stimulate me to fresh exertions. Is there any particular locality where these people who have disappeared were last seen or heard of?"

"As I before told you, these parties who disappeared were farmers, and most of them were returning from Rochester, a town eight miles from here, where they had been to dispose of their produce. They were traced to Rochester, where they did their business, and were then traced out of that town; then all their further clue was lost."

"It is certain then that the ambuscade or whatever may be the cause of their disappearance, lies between Rochester and Industry?"

"So it would seem, but every foot of ground has been thoroughly explored without any success at all."

A domestic now came to inform us that breakfast was ready. After a hurried meal, I jumped on the back of the horse which I borrowed from Mr. Linton, and determined that I would explore for myself the road between Industry and Rochester.

It was a beautiful spring morning, and in spite of my anxiety, I could not help noticing the charming country through which I passed. On one side of me was the silvery Ohio, flashing and sparkling in the beams of the morning sun, as if it were greeting its bride. The trees were musical with birds, and covered with the bright green verdure which they assume in the spring of the year. While I was pursuing my journey, I could not help thinking on all I had heard, and the more I reflected on it, the more extraordinary it appeared; at the same time it did not seem to me to be at all probable that Helen had shared the same fate, whatever it might be.

It was while indulging in these thoughts that I reached Rochester. I visited every portion of the town, but could not learn that any one answering to Helen's description had been seen there. It was night by the time I had concluded my search, and I must own my mind was considerably relieved that I had heard nothing of Helen—for the conversation I had with some of the inhabitants of the town, only served to confirm all that Mr. Linton had told me.

It was quite dark when I left Rochester for Industry, but as I had only eight miles to travel I set off at a gallop, expecting to reach the latter place in less than an hour. I had, however, not proceeded more than two or three miles, when my horse fell suddenly lame, and I found that he could proceed no further. I dismounted, and leading him by the bridle, walked for a half a mile, when I came to a large inn or tavern, which I had noticed in the morning when I passed along the road.

It was now about ten o'clock, and I determined I would leave my horse there for the night and try and procure another animal from the landlord, which would convey me to my destination. I advanced to the door of the inn, and knocked loudly. Although I could see a light burning in the interior, no reply was made to my summons. I knocked again more loudly then the first, and after a minute or two the bolts were withdrawn, and a man appeared. I made known my request to him; he informed me that he could not let me have another horse, but that I could sleep there until the morning, when a stage would pass the house.

I debated a minute or two in my own mind as to what was best to be done. It was late, and I knew that Mr. Linton would scarcely expect me at that hour, and the idea of walking five or six miles on a road concerning which such terrible stories were rife, was by no means an agreeable one. Not that I felt afraid, for I had taken the precaution to arm myself with a revolver. I finally made up my mind to accept the landlord's offer, and consigning my horse to his care, I entered the house and made my way to the parlor, where I found a woman seated by the fire, whom I afterwards learned was the landlord's wife. I sat down after making a few general remarks, and was soon rejoined by the landlord.

He was a strong, healthy-looking man, with a remarkable mild face and pleasant smile, the very impersonation of a jolly host. His wife was also a very fine-looking woman, with an excellent expression of countenance. I felt perfectly at home in a minute, and we conversed on a hundred different topics.

"By-the-by," said I, after a pause in our conversation, "the road between here and Industry bears a bad reputation, if I am to believe all the reports concerning it."

"You may well say reports, sir," said the host of the White Swan. "The fact is, I don't believe there is a word of truth in the matter. I have lived on this road now going on twenty-two years, and I never saw anything wrong here. It's my belief that the first man who disappeared went out West, and anybody that wants to leave takes advantage of the excitement, and by this means conceals his flight."

"That supposition is very reasonable," I returned; "but I am informed the men who have disappeared were all of the highest respectability."

"That may be, sir, but there's no fathoming the human heart—a man may lead a seemingly virtuous life, and yet in his heart may be everything that is bad. What makes me think that any supposition in this matter is a correct one, is the fact that a man was here the other day and stated to me that he had seen one of the missing men in Wisconsin."

"If that is the case, it certainly goes far to explain the mystery. It is a pity the fact is not made public and positive proof adduced; it would tend to disabuse the public mind."

"If the truth could be made manifest, it would do me a great deal of good, for I assure you, sir, since these reports have been circulated, my business has suffered terribly. Formerly my house used to be always full, now scarcely anybody visits it. If it were not for what I make at my business as a carpenter, we should starve."

We prolonged the conversation for some time longer, when I expressed a wish to retire to bed. I noticed for the first time a peculiar glance pass between the man and woman, which afterwards returned with terrible significance to my mind, but at the time I paid little heed to it.

"The white room," suggested the landlord's wife.

"No, the red room," returned the landlord, knitting his brows—which action had the effect of silencing her, for she offered no further objection.

The landlord handed me a lamp and ushered me into my chamber. It was a large, old-fashioned apartment, with a high ceiling and polished floor, for strange to say, it was without a shred of carpet or matting to cover it. The bed was a heavy four-poster, with thick red curtains drawn close all round it. The furniture in the room was old but strong and substantial, and the walls were covered with several large sporting prints. The landlord bade me good night and left me to my own reflections.

When he had gone, I went to the window and looked out on the night. A glorious sight met my gaze. The moon was at its full, and rode through the heavens in all the majesty of its solitary splendor. Through the trees I could see the waters of the Ohio flashing in the moonlight. I put out the light that I might better enjoy the scene, and fastening the curtains back, seated myself close to the casement, and supporting my head with my hand, delivered myself up to my own reflections.

In what I have written, I have dwelt but little on the condition of my own feelings since Helen had been lost, but the reader must not imagine on that account that I did not feel this trial poignantly. It was now, especially as I gazed on the beautiful scene before me, that the recollection of her glorious character, of her noble heart, of her devotion, all came back in a flood to my heart, and unmanly though it may seem, the tears coursed each other down my cheeks. Although her disappearance was most mysterious, I could not bring myself to believe that any accident had befallen her. I thought that perhaps, instead of getting off the boat at Wellsville, she might, through accident, have gone on to Pittsburgh, and be detained there from some unavoidable cause.

It was while plunged in the midst of these reflections, that I distinctly heard a stealthy step on the stairs, and almost directly afterwards the door opened gently, and the landlord's wife put her head in.

"Did you want anything?" I asked, rising up in a standing posture.

"We thought you called," said the woman, withdrawing her head.

"No," I returned, "you are mistaken, I did not call. I want nothing."

"I beg your pardon, sir. Good night."

"Good night."

And the woman closed the door, and left me alone again. It was now that suspicion began to creep into my mind. There was something very strange in this woman's visit to my apartment. I could not believe that they thought I had called. The night was too still and calm to admit the possibility of such a mistake. Then recurred to my mind the look which had passed between them when I expressed a wish to be shown to my chamber. Still, my suspicions took no tangible shape, but only determined me to keep all my senses about me. The thought certainly did strike me once or twice that perhaps this innkeeper might have something to do with the mysterious disappearances, but when I remembered his honest face, I repelled the idea as being most chimerical. After a little time, I dismissed the subject from my thoughts, and resumed my occupation of gazing on the silver river.

One sense I possess in a very acute degree, namely, the faculty of hearing. Ever since I was a boy I have been able to distinguish sounds, while to the majority of persons a complete silence reigns. I suddenly became conscious that some one was listening at my chamber door. It may be that I was more on the alert than usual. My plan was immediately formed. It was evident that for some purpose or other, the worthy host and his wife wished me in bed, so without making any preparation whatever, I threw myself, dressed as I was, on the bed. I was immediately conscious that the person left the door, retreating down stairs.

It was now my turn to exercise a little diplomacy, for I was by this time assured that there was something very unusual in all this. I rose quietly from the bed and concealed myself in the folds of the window-curtains, determined to watch and wait. I remained in this position for at least half an hour, without a single sound reaching my ear, and was about to go to bed in good earnest, when I heard the clanking of iron in the room immediately underneath the one I occupied. It was very faint and resembled, as near as I could tell, the hooking of one iron chain to another. I now felt certain that something extraordinary was about to occur. Another long pause, however, followed. It might have been perhaps half an hour, when happening to turn my eyes in the direction of the bed (on which the moon was shining), I saw the top of it oscillate, and then, to my intense surprise, it began to sink slowly through the floor, a large trapdoor having opened for that purpose.

More determined than ever to penetrate this mystery—for I was now satisfied that the mysterious disappearances were in a fair way of being explained—I stole gently forward, and before the bed had wholly disappeared, I had clung firmly to one of the bed-posts, the bed-curtains concealing me from a casual observer.

The bedstead continued to descend so gently and slowly that its motion was scarcely perceptible, and I am certain had I been asleep, I should not have felt it. I was not aware at the time how far we went, but it seemed to me to be a considerable depth. At last the motion ceased, and I watched with some anxiety to see what was next to be done. I had not to wait long, for suddenly a heavy iron plate, which appeared to come out of the top of the bed, fell with tremendous force on the bed itself. It is certain if I had been lying there, I should have been instantly killed. As it was, I was shaken from my hold and fell on damp earth. I was not hurt, however, and was immediately aware that I must be in a species of cellar, or cave, from the softness of the ground. I rose on my feet, and endeavored to penetrate the darkness which surrounded me, but I was unable to see a single ray of light.

I groped my way along an uneven wall, until at last I came to a round projection. Passing round this by the aid of my hands, I saw the glimmering of a light which proceeded from an opening in this subterranean chamber, for such it proved to be. I cautiously advanced to this opening and glanced through it, and who should I see there but the landlord and his wife! They were conversing together, and their voices distinctly reached my ear.

"You will not, hey? Take that for your trouble then."

And I heard the villain give her a blow which evidently felled her to the ground, for she was silent after it.

I now saw the innkeeper, with a bowie knife between his teeth, stealthily leave the cell, and with a candle in his hand, direct his steps towards the further end of the cavern, where I saw, by the rays of the candle, a circular projection similar to the one he had just left. His fearful purpose was only too apparent. I followed, close to his heels, the soft ground preventing my footsteps being heard.

Another thrilling and heart-rending shriek reached my ears. My only wonder now is, that I did not seize the assassin there and then. But I suppose I was afraid I should never be able to find Helen in that accursed place, unless guided to her place of confinement at all events, I thought it better to allow him to proceed. He unlocked a grated door and entered a dismal-looking cell. I glided in after him, and saw my beloved girl bound hand and foot to an iron bedstead.

"Young girl," said the villain, as he entered, "I will give you two minutes to say your prayers in—you must die!"

"O, spare me—spare me!"shrieked Helen. "O, John, John, why are you not here to protect me?"

"I am here!" I exclaimed, seizing the villain by the throat, and almost choking the life out of him.

The moment he saw me, he was completely paralyzed, for I suppose he thought I was some one risen from the dead. I bound him hand and foot, and then proceeded to release Helen. I shall not attempt to describe our meeting, for any words I might use would but feebly portray the delights of us both. The cause of her appearance there was explained in a few words.

By some mistake, she was landed at Rochester instead of Wellsville, and on inquiring on the wharf the way to Industry, he told her that he was going there and would take her to the stage. This man was no other than the landlord of the inn, and he conveyed her and all her luggage to his dwelling and confined her, as the readers have seen, in the cell underground. His sole motive appeared to have been plunder. He would doubtless, however, have murdered her at once, had it not been for his wife, who had not yet lost every particle of humanity from her heart.

I locked the villain up in the cell where Helen had been so lately confined, and then went to where his wife was lying, still insensible. I found in this apartment a winding staircase, which led to rooms up stairs. I carried the landlord's wife up these stairs and confined her in a bedroom, and then, accompanied by Helen, as soon as it was light, we returned to Rochester.

In a few hours both the man and his wife were in custody, and they were tried a few months afterwards. They attempted no defence, for the remains of all the missing men were found, and the proof was overwhelming. The man was hung and the woman sent to State Prison for life.

The inn, until it was burnt down a year or two ago, was a place of great curiosity, and the proprietor of it reaped a handsome fortune from showing its mysteries. It appeared that the criminal, who, as the reader knows, was a carpenter by business, possessed great mechanical skill, and began the alterations in his house more for his own amusement than for any evil design, but when he had finished them, the thought struck him that he might make them subserve his own private purpose. One thing led to another, and the first crime committed, all remorse was stifled and he plunged boldly and deeply into every description of iniquity. The mechanical contrivances were perfect, and defied ordinary penetration to discover them. There was no other outlet to the cave, excepting through the lower floor of the dwelling, and the trap-door was so ingeniously concealed, that when the secret was known, but few could distinguish the spot where it opened.

I will not attempt to paint Mr. Linton's joy when I confided his niece to his care. His advice to us was to be married immediately. We were of the same opinion, and before I returned to New York, I called Helen by the endearing name of wife.

Leaf the Twenty-First

My First Brief

(A Leaf from a Lawyer's Note-Book.)

With the exception of medicine, there is no profession so difficult to obtain a footing in as law. It frequently happens that the best years of a young man's life are passed in some obscure street waiting for a stepping stone which is to lead him to professional honor, and what is more important still, put money in his purse. No one knows but those who have had stern experience for their mentor, all a young man has to go through before he can obtain a respectable position in this world of competition and cares. None but these can tell the heartsickness, a thousand times worse than any bodily ailment, which these strivers after reputation are obliged to suffer. But there is one satisfaction. With a steady purpose, sterling integrity, and unflinching perseverance, the day of fortune will come, it may be delayed—but come it eventually must, and then, when the end is gained—the struggles to attain it appear much less than they really were.

In 1846 I was admitted to the bar. I shall never forget my feelings of pride when I saw for the first time my name,

Henry Melton, *Attorney at Law*,

in gilt letters on a black label, nailed to the front of a dingy looking house in Chamber Street, in the city of New York. Know then, gentle reader, my offices were situated in that same house. They were two in number; the first being a kind of reception room, and the other my sanctum. I remember how the latter was furnished distinctly, although so many years have intervened since then. The principal articles of furniture were two large bookcases, containing my library—the lower shelves were filled with large books, bound in sheepskin and backed with a red title. The upper shelves contained works of a little lighter description, and if the truth must be told, the latter were taken down much oftener than the former.

Well, I seated myself at my desk the same day that the before mentioned shingle was exhibited outside, and expected that I should soon be overwhelmed with business, but I soon found my self deceived; day after day passed, and not a soul called. I was in despair, my small means were slowly oozing away for, in spite of all my economy, I was obliged to eat.

Six months passed away and I had not a single client. One day I heard a ring at the bell, but I took no heed of it now; when I first occupied my offices such a peal as that would have caused me to pass my hand through my hair, straighten down my vest, and seize one of the pale, yellow-bound books with red titles—but I had been so often deceived, that I scarcely notice it now, or only expected my boy to enter stating "that a man wanted twenty-five cents for the *Herald*," or some other demand upon my purse. What, then, was my surprise, when the boy opened the door, saying with a smile:

"If you please, sir, there's a lady wants to speak to you?"

I started, and was completely dumbfounded for a moment; but the boy looked at me with such a curious glance, which appeared to say "first client," that I immediately recovered myself, and assuming all the dignity I could command, I told the boy to inform the lady that I should be disengaged in a few minutes.

Having arranged some paper on my desk, and taken down one of the aforesaid sheepskin bound volumes, I requested the lad to show the lady in.

Immediately afterwards she was ushered into the room. I had no opportunity of judging whether she was old or young, as she was closely veiled. It was evident she had recently suffered some loss in her family, for she was dressed in deep black. I invited her to be seated and placed myself in a listening attitude.

"Have I the pleasure of speaking to Mr. Melton?" she asked, in a musical voice.

I bowed affirmatively.

"I wish to consult you, sir," she continued in the same clear voice, "on a matter which nearly concerns my happiness. I will at once lay the case before you for your opinion. I should first tell you my name is McLeod, Margaret McLeod—"

"McLeod!" I interrupted with a start. "Not any relation to the gentleman who last week was—" I hesitated to finish the sentence.

"Murdered you were about to say," she continued. "Yes, sir, I am his daughter." And she lifted her veil from her face as she said this, revealing features of unsurpassed loveliness.

I gazed with increased interest on my fair visitor, for the fact is, the murder of James McLeod had made a great noise. The papers had been filled with the details of it during the past week.

"You are aware," continued Miss McLeod, "that a young man named Harvey Johnston, is arrested on suspicion of having committed the deed; but I know him to be innocent."

"Indeed!" I returned, "how is that? Appearances are very much against him, if we can judge by newspaper reports."

"I tell you he is innocent, innocent!" she exclaimed, bursting into a flood of tears. "Harvey could never have committed a crime like that! O, you don't know him, sir, if you did, not the slightest shade of suspicion would remain on your mind for a moment."

By the vehement tone in which she addressed me, I immediately penetrated her secret, that she was in love with Harvey Johnston. I gently hinted that such was the case to her; she delicately acknowledged it to be the truth.

I besought the young lady to lay the whole facts of the case before me as she knew them. This she proceeded to do, and the substance of her statement was us follows:

Mr. James McLeod was a retired merchant, living up town, as Bleeker street was then called. He was a widower, his family consisting of himself, his daughter—the only child he had—a middle-aged lady, who acted as a kind of governess, and two female servants.

Mr. McLeod was a very stern man, who never changed an opinion, and would be obeyed to the letter in his household. He scarcely ever smiled, but passed through the world unloving and unloved.

It is true his only daughter, Margaret, sometimes appeared to soften him, but still he never seemed to regard her with the fondness of a parent. He was polite to her, and that was all. As for Margaret she loved her father as much as his cold nature would allow her; but never having received any token of love from him, it can scarcely be wondered that her affection was more a matter of duty than feeling.

Up to within a year of the date of this history, they had lived a very retired life, seeing little or no company. Their house in Bleecker street was a very large one, so they could only occupy a small portion of it, and I remember the impression of loneliness conveyed to my mind by Miss McLeod, when she was describing the uninhabited part of the house.

One day her father informed her that he had made an engagement for her and himself to spend the evening with a former partner of his. It was here she first met Harvey Johnston, and they were soon attached to each other. They became firm friends, and the friendship soon ripened into love. For a length of time they met clandestinely, Margaret not daring to make her father acquainted with her passion. At length Harvey persuaded her to allow him to make known his suit to Mr. McLeod. He did so, and met with an indignant refusal; in fact, Margaret's father had gone so far as to insult him, and forbid him from ever speaking to his daughter again. It is needless to say this his orders were disobeyed—the lovers corresponded and met as before. At last Margaret McLeod, made up her mind that if her father would not give his consent to her marriage, she would marry without it, but she wished Harvey to make one more effort.

This brings us down to the day of the murder. On that night Harvey paid Mr. McLeod a visit about nine o'clock in the evening—high words were heard to pass between them, and then there was a blank.

About eleven o'clock that same night a policeman was walking down Bleeker street, and discovering Mr. McLeod's front door open, he mounted the steps in order to close it, when he fancied he heard the noise of footsteps in the house. He entered and ascended the stairs. When he reached the front drawing-room a terrible sight met his gaze. Mr. McLeod was lying all his length on the floor stone dead. A pool of blood was beside the body, as well as a knife with which the deed had evidently been committed, for it was proved upon examination that his throat had been cut from ear to ear. But the strangest part of the story was, that Harvey Johnston was discovered in the room with the murdered man. When the policeman first entered the room he discovered him groping round the walls, for the apartment was quite dark until the policeman brought his lantern. Of course Johnston was arrested, and the proof against him appeared overwhelming, for it was found that the knife with which the murder had been committed belonged to him. A coroner's jury was summoned and Harvey Johnston was committed to take his trial at the ensuing assizes for the wilful murder of Mr. McLeod, and every one who read the details of the coroner's inquest appeared to be perfectly satisfied of his guilt.

Such was the substance of Miss McLeod's statement to me; of course in her relation she frequently wept, and made repeated asservations of her lover's innocence.

"Now, Mr. Melton," she added, as she concluded, "I want you to undertake his case—and for Heaven's sake do everything you can for him, for I confess to you that all my hopes of happiness in this world are wrapped up in him."

"But, my dear young lady, I am afraid his case is desperate. What is his explanation?"

"I have neither seen nor heard from him since his arrest, but I feel he is innocent."

"I am confident such evidence as that will be of but little avail to him in a court of justice; however, I will call and see him, and hear his statement; I will then let you know the result."

With a reiterated request that I should spare no expense, and promising to call the next day, the young lady took her leave.

The moment she had gone, I put on my hat and wended my way to the Tombs. After making my business known, I had no difficulty in obtaining access to the prisoner, and was immediately conducted to him. I found myself in the presence, of a very fine young man about five and twenty years of age. He was possessed of a fine open countenance, and I sought in vain to discover the slightest indication of guilt in any one feature. All was placid and serene there. I made known my business to him, at the same time stating that I had been sent there by Miss McLeod.

"Poor girl!" exclaimed he, the moment I mentioned her name, "she believes in my innocence then. Yes, yes, I know it must be so, she knows me too well to suppose for a moment that I could be guilty of committing such a horrible deed!"

He paused an instant and hurriedly wiped away a tear, supposing that I did not notice him.

"I have now been incarcerated here for more than a week," he continued, after a pause, "and yet I cannot realize the fact, it appears like a hideous dream to me. I ask myself is it possible I can be arrested for *murder*? And for the murder of the father of my own dear girl! But no jury can bring me in guilty."

"Mr. Johnston," I replied, "truth compels me to state that the evidence against you is fearfully strong."

"Why, Mr. Melton, you surely do not believe me guilty of this hideous crime?" said he, his face flushing with indignation.

"Let me hear your statement," I replied, "and then I will answer your question. You are aware of the nature of the evidence against you. It can be summed up in a few words. A gentleman is found murdered in his drawing-room—a policeman enters the apartment and discovers you there alone with the murdered man—and the deed is found to be committed with your bowie-knife, besides your clothes being sprinkled with the victim's blood."

"Mr. Melton," replied the prisoner, lifting up his hand to Heaven, "I swear before God that I knew nothing of the murder until the policeman entered the room with his lantern. The discovery of the horrid deed inspired me with as much surprise and terror as it did him."

I looked at Johnston as he uttered these words, to see if he were not deranged. But no, his countenance was perfectly calm and collected.

"Explain yourself," I exclaimed," for the life of me, I cannot understand you. You appear to me to be speaking paradoxes."

"I will give you a plain statement of what I know of the matter. You can form your own opinion as to how far I am implicated in it. On the night in question I went to pay Mr. McLeod a visit, in order to obtain if possible his consent to my marriage with his daughter Margaret.

"I found him in the front drawing room. I suppose it was about nine o'clock when I visited the house. Mr. McLeod received me very haughtily. I should say some months ago I had an interview with him on the same subject, which passed off anything but satisfactorily. The moment I broached the matter again to him he became very violent, and used very harsh language to me—at length my blood was up, and I believe I retorted in very strong words. I have no idea how long this interview lasted; it must have been sometime, however, for I felt it my duty to enter into considerable explanation, and to free myself from various charges he brought against me. At last I took up my hat to go, and had already turned towards the door, when, I felt a stifling sensation, and suddenly became senseless, and God is my witness that I am utterly ignorant of all that passed in the room after that. I only recovered my senses a few minutes before the policeman entered the room with a light. And this is all I know about the matter."

While Johnston was making this explanation, I scrutinized his face closely, but could not detect the slightest appearance of deception in his features.

"But how do you account for the murder having been committed with your bowie-knife?"

"It must have been taken from my pocket while I was insensible; for I acknowledge the knife is mine, and that I had been accustomed to carry it about me for one month past."

"Have you any idea who could have committed the deed?" I inquired, after a pause.

"None in the world," he replied; "it must have been some one from the outside, for there were none but women in the house."

After a little further conversation on the matter, I took my departure, without giving him any decided opinion as to my belief in his innocence. When I reached my office, I seated myself in my easy chair, and pondered over the matter long and seriously. I was well aware that Johnston's statement was an improbable one, and would of course have no weight in a court of justice; but there was something in his manner of telling it me—something in his frank, open countenance, which impressed me strongly in his favor, and after mature consideration I came to the conclusion that the statement might be true. But it is one thing to believe in a person's innocence, and another to prove it. The next question to be decided, was, if Johnston was innocent, who was the murderer? Here, I must confess, I was totally at fault, I had not the slightest clue to guide me. It appeared certain to me that none of the inhabitants of the house could have done it, for as I have before said, they consisted only of Miss McLeod, Miss Leroy, and an old maid who acted as a kind of governess to Margaret, and the two servant girls. I made up my mind that it must have been some one from without, and the door having been left open, favored the supposition. I began to invent a thousand different theories as to how the murder was effected, until my brain grew dizzy. The thought then entered my head to go and search the house where the deed had been committed, to see if I could discover any clue there. I immediately acted upon it, and in a few minutes found myself before the door of the late Mr. McLeod's residence.

It was a large, gloomy looking house, bearing anything but an inviting aspect, and just such a place as one would imagine to be the theatre of some dark deed. I knocked at the door, and requested to see Miss McLeod. I was immediately shown into a parlor, and in a few minutes she entered the room.

I then informed her as to the result of my interview with Harvey Johnston. I also told her that I believed in his innocence, but did not seek to disguise from her the fact that there was much to be done before we should be able to convince a jury such to be the case. I then requested permission to search the house. It was immediately granted.

My search did not amount to much. I noticed, however, one thing—the drawing-room door was so situated that when any one stood on the threshold of it he could not see a portion of it on account of the projecting fire-place. I was further satisfied that a person might easily have entered from without, and ascend the stairs. I was about leaving the house, when the thought struck me I had not examined Mr. McLeod's bedroom. I hastened to repair my forgetfulness. I found it to be an ordinary sized chamber, with nothing special in it except an old bureau, which immediately struck my attention from the fact of my father having possessed one exactly like it. I opened the top of it, and found that it contained two secret recesses like ours at home. I opened these recesses, and discovered one to be empty, the other contained a single paper, which proved to be an old letter, yellow with age. I felt justified in opening and reading it. It ran as follows:—

> ALBANY, N. Y., MAY 19, 1826. You have basely deserted me, and deceived me; all my burning love is now turned to bitter hatred; but do not imagine you shall escape me with impunity. By the living God, I swear to be revenged! I can wait for years—ay, years, to accomplish my purpose! Think on it and tremble!
>
> HELEN MORRIS.

On the outside it bore the superscription, "Mr. McLeod, 52 Front Street, New York." I read the letter over several times; it was to say the least of it, a curious document, and I decided to keep it in my possession, not expecting that it would lead to any discovery—it appeared to be written too long ago for that, and the chances were that Helen Morris was long ago summoned to her long, last home.

I returned home, weary and unsatisfied. For the next three weeks I made every possible exertion to clear up the mystery without the slightest success. The day of trial approached, and I had not discovered the slightest evidence to corroborate the prisoner's statement. Scarcely a day passed but Miss McLeod either called herself, or sent to know what progress I was making. I could give her but very slight hope of being able to save Harvey.

On the evening before the day fixed for the trial, I seated myself in my office, utterly dispirited and worn out. I had now no hope of being able to convince a jury of Johnston's innocence. I was well aware that his statement would be laughed at, and the only witnesses I could bring forward, would be as to character. I was miserable at the idea of bringing such a lame defence into court—and my first case, too.

I thought I would smoke a cigar, and try if it would have any effect in soothing my irritated nerves. I tore a piece from an old *New York Herald,* in order to light it, when by some strange circumstance, what, it is difficult to explain, the following advertisement among the "personals" caught my eye:

> If the lady who purchased the chloroform of Messrs. R. & C., apothecaries, 201 Broadway, will call upon the latter, she will have the purse restored to her which she left on the counter.

I snatched the other portion of the paper for the purpose of discovering the date, I found it to have been issued the very day after the murder.

To throw away my cigar, put on my hat and rush from the house, was the work of a moment. I had not far to go, and soon found myself in Messrs. R. & C.'s store.

"A lady bought some chloroform of you about two months ago," said I to a gentlemanly looking clerk behind the counter.

"Yes, sir."

"She left a purse on the counter?"

"Yes, sir."

"Will you be good enough to inform me if you she has never reclaimed that purse?"

"She has not, although we advertised it several days."

"Who served her with the chloroform?"

"I did."

"Did you notice her appearance?"

"She was quite elderly. I was surprised at her buying so much at a time; but she stated she wanted it for her husband, who is a physician, and so I let her have it."

"Would you know her if you were to see her again?"

"I believe I should. I noticed that she wore a blue shawl with a red fringe—it struck me particularly because it had such an uncommon appearance."

I could obtain no further information from the clerk, and returned to my office with even my last hopes swept away.

The next day I was in court early. I determined to do all I could for my client; but without the faintest hope of success. The case was soon called on, and the prosecuting attorney commenced his address; he stated to the court what he intended to prove, and as he recounted the fearful array of evidence against the prisoner, I could not help turning my eyes to the latter, and observed he stood perfectly aghast at the strong case made against him. Not a single event that had transpired during his intercourse with the McLeod family but was turned into the strongest evidence against him.

Miss McLeod was the first witness called. Her testimony made fearfully against the prisoner. She acknowledged there had been a violent quarrel between Harvey Johnston and her father some time previous, and that the former had been very much irritated by some epithets bestowed on him by Mr. McLeod, and had even vaguely threatened vengeance.

By the cross examination of the witness, I elicited the fact that the prisoner's disposition was good, kind and amiable; but her anxiety to say as much as possible for her lover did him more harm than good. And when she descended from the stand, many reproachful glances were cast after her.

The two servants followed, and gave much the same evidence as Miss McLeod. I declined to cross-examine them. Witnesses were then called to fix the ownership of the knife on the prisoner at the bar. I elicited nothing on cross-examination; and it was the same with the policeman, who first discovered the murder.

The governess, Julia Leroy, was next called on the stand. For a moment or two she did not reply to her name, it had to be repeated two or three times. At length she made her appearance, and ascended to the witness-box. The moment I cast my eyes upon her I saw something which made my ears tingle, and sent the blood coursing like fire through my veins; but I had sufficient command over myself to say nothing.

"Miss Leroy," said the prosecuting attorney, "you, I believe, were a friend of the deceased, and lived in the same house with him?"

"Yes, sir."

"You opened the door for the prisoner at the bar on the night of the murder?"

"I did."

"Relate what passed."

"I showed Mr. Johnston into the front drawing-room where Mr. McLeod was sitting, and I returned to the back drawing-room, where I was at work, sewing, when the prisoner rang the bell. The two drawing-rooms are only separated by folding doors, so I could hear nearly all that passed. Mr. McLeod and the prisoner soon got to high words—and I heard the former call the latter a 'villain' and a 'scoundrel.' Mr. Johnston retaliated, and swore he would be revenged on him on some future day. And then their voices lowered, and I could not make out what they were talking about. I went to bed at ten o'clock, leaving them still in the room together, and was roused about half past eleven by the intelligence that Mr. McLeod had been murdered. This is all I know about the matter."

"I suppose the counsel for the prisoner will not cross-examine this witness," said the district attorney, seating himself, "this, your honor, closes the case for the prosecution."

"Stay," said I, rising, "I wish to ask the witness a few questions, if she has no objections."

The witness, who had already descended from the box, took her place again on the stand.

""Madam," said I, "you are unmarried, I believe?"

"I am."

"What is your name?"

"Julia Leroy."

"Would you have any objection to write it down for me on this piece of paper?"

"None at all,"she replied, doing as I had requested, and handing back the paper to me. I glanced at it and placed it before me.

"Miss Leroy," I exclaimed, slowly, "I am about to ask you rather an ungallant question, but you must forgive it. Will you be good enough to tell the court your age?"

She hesitated a moment, and then replied:

"Certainly, I am forty-five next birthday."

"Thank you," I returned. "Will you be good enough to answer the next question as explicitly—have you ever had any use for chloroform?"

She turned fearfully pale, and for a moment or two made no reply—at last, she said:

"I appeal to the court if I am to answer such stupid questions?"

"It appears to me," said the worthy judge, "that the cross examination is entirely extraneous to the matter in question, but of course if the counsel insists, the witness must answer the questions he propounds."

"I reiterate my question," I replied, quietly, "do you ever use chloroform?'"

"I do use it occasionally for the tooth-ache," was the sullen rejoiner.

"Now, madam, listen to me, and answer the question distinctly. Did you, or did you not purchase four ounces of chloroform on the day of the murder, at Messrs. R. & C.'s drug store, Broadways?"

The witness reeled in the box, and had to support herself by catching hold of the side of it. She turned as pale as death, and could not speak for more than a minute. I kept my eyes fixed on her as if I would read her very soul. She partially recovered herself and replied in a firm voice:

"Well, I did buy four ounces of chloroform on the day mentioned—and what then?"

"I simply wanted to know, that is all."

"Very well, I have answered your question. Have you anything more to ask me?"

"Yes—were you ever known by another name then Julia Leroy?"

The woman glared at me and made no reply.

"I insist on an answer," I continued.

"No,"she replied boldly, summoning up all her courage.

"Now, madam, answer me," I replied in a stern voice, "did you not live in Albany in 1826 and was not your name then Helen Morris? It is no use your denying the fact, for I know all," I added.

She gave one shriek, and exclaimed in a heart rending voice:

"Yes—I acknowledge it—I committed the deed—I am guilty! I am guilty!" And then she fainted away.

An indescribable scene of confusion took place in court. Harvey Johnston was remanded, and the witness, Julia Leroy, was taken into custody.

The fact is, the moment she had entered the box I knew I stood in the presence of Mr. McLeod's murderer, for she wore a blue shawl with a red fringe. The true facts of the case passed through my mind like lightning, and I immediately divined that this Julia Leroy was no other than Helen Morris, and after she had written her name, I was certain that such was the case. Why such an idea should have entered my head, I know not, it appeared to be inspiration.

That same night Julia Leroy made a confession. It appeared when she was a girl, Mr. McLeod had become acquainted with her, and by his wily arts effected her ruin. She lived with him some time, and then he deserted her, and it was then she wrote the letter I had found in his bed-room. From that time she lived only to accomplish her purpose, and after a lapse of some years, obtained an introduction into his family. She waited for twenty years, until a favorable opportunity occurred to put her scheme into execution. At length the time seemed come. She obtained a supply of chloroform, and first rendered Harvey Johnston insensible by its influence, and before Mr. McLeod had time to give the alarm, she took away his life in the manner before referred to by means of a bowie-knife, which had fallen from Johnston's pocket, as he fell. She used the latter weapon in preference to the one with which she had provided herself, as being more likely to fix suspicion on the young man.

In one month she was found guilty, and only saved herself from an ignominious death by taking poison.

About three months after the events described, Harvey Johnston and Margaret McLeod were married, and I have reason to know that they have lived happily ever since. As for myself, this case was a stepping-stone to renown, and amid all the favors of fortune with which I am now surrounded, I always regard the hand of Providence in the success I experienced with my first case.

Leaf the Twenty-Second

The Walker Street Tragedy

A few years ago there might be seen in Walker Street, in the City of New York, two old houses remarkable for their peculiar style of architecture. They were built entirely of red brick, and their pointed gables and Gothic windows immediately, carried the mind of the observer back to the days of good queen Bess, when that peculiar style of building was in vogue. No one knew when they were built, but it must have been long, long time ago, before even Walker Street was in existence, and when the ground around them was a verdant meadow. In all probability they were originally the country residences of some staunch Dutch yeomen, who lived on their own land, a pleasant ride from town. Perhaps they were originally built by two brothers, for they were close together, a narrow alley-way only dividing them.

The strange history I have to relate in connection with one of these houses is, however, of a much more modern date. It was when every vestige of country was removed far away, and when, as I have before said, these dwellings attracted universal attention from their strange appearance in the midst of more modern buildings that the house nearest West Broadway became the theatre of a fearful tragedy, which caused it to become one of the lions of New York, until it was demolished some two years since.

In the year 1844, this dwelling was occupied by a Mr Stephen Alford, a gentleman of means, who had purchased the property some years before. Mr. Alford was a widower without any family. His establishment was under the superintendence of a niece, who had lived with him ever since his wife's death, and for whom he appeared to have the greatest affection. And she well deserved his love; for, according to all appearances, she returned his fatherly attachment with the devotion and obedience of a dutiful child. For many years nothing transpired to disturb the calm tranquility of their lives. They seemed to be perfectly happy and contented, and saw little company. Clara Alford was, at the time this history opens, twenty years of age. She was very beautiful; her features were regular, her hair a glossy auburn, her skin dazzlingly white, and her large deep blue eyes, fringed with long eyelashes, gave a peculiar dreamy expression to her face which could not fail to arrest the attention of every beholder.

In the summer of 1843, I had worked very hard investigating a forgery case. I had to give my entire attention to it, for the case was a very important one, involving immense interests. I worked at it day and night for six weeks, taking very little sleep during the whole of that time. At last, after tremendous mental exertion. I succeeded in discovering the guilty party—but I was so utterly worn out that I became seriously ill. The excitement of the case had kept me up during my investigation, but, the end attained, my nervous system entirely gave way. In this condition I was ordered by my physician to go into the country for a change of air. I resolved to go to Niagara.

It was here I became acquainted with Mr. Alford and his niece. I was completely fascinated by the latter. I do not wish the reader to make a mistake. I was by no means in love: I was fascinated by her intellect and superior attainments—with respect to her beauty, I regarded her as a beautiful piece of statuary, realizing all the poets have sung in praise of woman's loveliness.

I shall never forget the first time I saw her. It was in the drawing-room of the Clifton House. It was evening at the time, and the apartment was filled with guests. There was that continual hum of conversation always prevalent in large assemblies. Seated apart from the rest, I noticed an old gentleman and a lovely girl engaged in earnest conversation. Her beauty attracted numerous eyes towards this couple, but no one seemed to be acquainted with them. Suddenly she rose from her seat, evidently in obedience to the request of the old gentleman, and sat down at the piano. She nimbly ran her fingers along the keys as trying its tone, and then commenced to play the Prayer from Moses. She performed so exquisitely, and with so much taste, that suddenly every voice was hushed, and the most miraculous silence fell over that large assembly. She appeared to have the power of making music enter the souls of people—I looked around me to see the effect of the *chef d'oeuvre* of Rossini on the assembled guests, and was not surprised to see the eyes of many of them filled with tears. It was a great musical treat for the boarders of the Clifton House that night. She played for more than an hour. Her execution was perfectly marvelous, and when she left the piano there was not a single person who had the slightest "music in his soul," who did not regret.

The next day I had the good fortune to render her some trivial service while viewing the Horse-shoe Fall, which dispensed with the necessity of a formal introduction, and for the next two week I had the gratification of enjoying society every day. I found her, as I have before intimated, charming in the extreme. She was well read, and could converse on almost every subject. Alford made no objection to our intimacy. I had good opportunities to read her uncle's character during this time. There could be no doubt he loved his niece. While to others he was touchy and irritable, with her he was all gentleness. Yet with all this he watched narrowly. He seemed jealous of every young man who sought to become acquainted, with her. Many, attracted by Clara's loveliness, made the effort but they were always repulsed by her Argus-eyed uncle. Mr. Alford was anything but an amiable man. The least thing would cause him to fly into a passion; and there were moments when it was dangerous to speak to him at all, unless a person did not mind to run the risk of being insulted. Clara, at this unpropitious time, always had the power to calm and soothe him. I have seen his face, distorted with rage, at a word from her become smooth and placid as a sleeping infant's.

My stay at Niagara completely restored my health, and we all three returned to New York together. Here our intimacy did not end. I frequently spent an evening at Mr. Alford's house in Walker Street.

This continued for about a year, when one evening I visited my friends, and was as usual cordially received. But still I could see there was something wrong. There was a gloom hanging over both uncle and niece. Instead of Clara being full of life and spirits as was usually the case, she was constrained and silent. Mr. Alford, too, was in worse humor than I had ever seen him. He abused everybody and everything, and to my great surprise, Clara made no attempt to sooth him.

Miss Alford soon excused herself under the plea of a headache, and left her uncle and myself alone together. There was a pause of a minute or two after she had gone. Mr. Alford appeared to be debating with himself, if he should confide something to me which weighed on his mind. I am an acute observer of countenance, and I noticed that several times he was about to speak, and then checked himself. At last he said:

"Brampton, I have been very much annoyed to-day."

"Indeed," I returned. "I am sorry to hear it. What has occurred?"

"Clara and I have had a quarrel for the first time in our lives."

"You and Miss Alford quarrelled," I replied, in the greatest astonishment; "impossible!"

"I would have said so too, if any one had asked me this morning, but it is nevertheless true."

"I can even now scarcely believe it."

There was a pause. Mr. Alford hesitated to continue.

"Do you know a young man named Albert Seyton?" he asked.

"I know him well," I replied, "a young physician."

"Yes," he returned, bitterly, "a physician without patients."

"I believe he has only lately commenced practice. It takes some time for a physician to establish a name."

"Well, sir, what do you suppose this beggarly young doctor has had the impudence to do!"

"I am sure I cannot guess," I returned smiling at the old man's vehemence.

"He has had the impudence to fall in love with my niece."

"Indeed," I returned, "not such a very great crime after all—perhaps the poor fellow could not help it."

"Don't tell me he could not help it," cried the old man, getting more and more excited. "I should like to know what the miserable pill-prescribing beggar means by his impudence."

"Does Miss Alford know of his passion?" I asked.

"Aye, sir," he returned, striking the table with his fist—"she not only knows it—but, by heavens she is in love with him too."

"If they were really fond of each other, why should you object? It is true Doctor Seyton is poor, but he is one of the most honorable, good-hearted young men I ever knew."

"Don't speak to me about his honor or his good heart, and as for his poverty—I care nothing about that. Were he as rich as Croesus he would never marry my niece."

""I suppose, you would object to any one marrying her."

"You are right—I would. Mr. Brampton, you have no idea how much I love that girl. I can never, never part with her."

The poor old gentleman's eyes filled with tears as he spoke.

"How did Miss Alford become acquainted with him?"

"I only discovered to-day. It seems some two months ago, Clara was crossing Broadway, when she was in danger of being run over by an omnibus. This young man rushed forward, and seized the horses by their bridles, and by backing them, Clara reached the side-walk in safety. Of course Clara felt very grateful to her preserver. He saw her home, but she did not dare to ask him in, for she knew I would send him off in double quick time. But since then they have frequently met stealthily, and have corresponded together. I intercepted a letter of his this morning, when the whole truth came out. Of course there was a scene—a violent one, too, I forbade her ever to think of this young Episcopalian again. She wept, I stormed—in short, as I before said, we had a violent quarrel, although I must do the poor girl the justice to say, all the quarreling was on my side. All that she did was to entreat and shed tears."

"But, my dear, sir," I ventured to suggest—"You cannot surely expect that she will never get married."

"Not while I live, not while I live." repeated the old man with energy. "At my death I shall leave her rich— she can then please herself."

I said it was no use to urge the matter any further, and after extending the conversation a little longer, I took my leave. On my way home, my mind was filled with what I had heard. I sincerely pitied the young couple, for I knew it was utterly useless to attempt to soften the uncle. If they married secretly, there was no possible hope of extracting a cent from Mr. Alford. He was obstinate in the extreme, and although he sincerely loved his niece, if she once disobeyed him, I verily believe his pride would prevent him assisting her, even if she were dying of starvation. I wished to assist them, and turned over every possible method in my own mind—I could not come to any satisfactory conclusion. I retired to bed that night utterly undecided as to the best course to be pursued under the circumstances.

The next day business called me away to a distant State. It was a very important matter, and engrossed all my attention, so that I had no time to think about the love affair of Clara and the young physician. In about a week my business was finished, and I returned home.

The day following my return, I rose early, and while seated at breakfast, I took up the morning papers to read, as was my custom. I believe it was the *New York Tribune* which first claimed my attention. The moment my eyes fell on the paper they were attracted by a paragraph which made my blood recede from my veins, and which sent an icy chill to my heart.

It ran as follows:

> SHOCKING MURDER.—The inhabitants of Walker Street, yesterday, were horrified by the discovery of one of the most horrible murders it has ever been the lot of humanity to witness. The old fashioned house in Walker Street, situated near West Broadway, was the scene of the tragedy. This house has been occupied for some years past by Mr. Alford, a wealthy gentleman who lived on his means. It appears that a Mr. Merrill had some private business with the proprietor, and went early yesterday morning by appointment, to call on Mr. Alford. He was surprised to find the house was fastened up. This was specially remarked, as it is known Mr. Alford always rose very early in the morning. He knocked at the dour some time, but not being able to obtain admission, he became alarmed, and calling the aid of two policemen, the door was forced, and a number of persons entered the house. There was nothing on the ground floor to indicate that anything unusual had occured. But when they entered Mr. Alford's room, a fearful spectacle met their gaze. Mr. Alford was discovered on the floor stone dead.

> The wound was in the region of the heart and had evidently pierced the great artery known as the aorta. Death must have been instantaneous, the victim not being able to utter a single cry. It is satisfactory to know that the person whom suspicion points out as the perpetrator of this fearful deed is arrested. We refrain from giving more particulars, as it is supposed there may be accomplices, and the ends of justice might be defeated. A coroner's inquest will be held today, when it is expected some important revelations will be made, the particulars of which will be given in tomorrow's issue.

When I read this paragraph I was utterly astounded. I did not know what to think or what to do. I mechanically seized my hat, determined to visit the scene of the tragedy, and had already made a step towards the door when my servant entered.

"If you please, sir," said she, "there's a gentleman below wants to speak with you."

"Tell him I can't see him now—that I am engaged, and he must call again."

"He says his business is most important."

"Did he give his name?"

"Yes, he told me to tell you his name was Doctor Seyton."

"Doctor Seyton!" I almost shrieked, much to the surprise of my domestic, who I verily believe thought I was mad. "Admit him directly."

The servant left the room, and almost immediately afterwards the young physician entered the apartment. He looked fearfully haggard and pale, and trembled in every limb. He staggered up to me and shook me by the hand, and then fell exhausted into a chair.

"My dear Doctor, compose yourself," I cried, the sight of his excitement restoring me to my self-possession.

"Oh, Mr. Brampton," he exclaimed, "you have heard the fearful news."

"Yes," I returned, "I suppose you allude to the Walker Street tragedy."

He bowed his head, but seemed too much overpowered to speak. His conduct appeared very strange to me. I could not understand the intense feeling he manifested. It was true it was a fearful murder, and one sufficient to horrify any one. But it was evidently not this feeling which caused him to act as he did. He appeared like one completely overwhelmed by some astounding misfortune. So far from Mr. Alford's death being a misfortune to him it would, in all probability, advance his interest, for it removed the only obstruction to his marriage with Clara.

"It is indeed a fearful deed," I added; "it is satisfactory to know, however, that the person who committed the deed is in custody."

The young man gazed at me with the utmost wonderment expressed in his countenance; and then letting his face fall between his hands he wept like a child.

"Oh God!"he exclaimed in the utmost anguish of voice, "my last hope has failed."

"What do you mean?" I cried, astonished more and more at this extraordinary conduct. "Has not a person been arrested who is suspected of having committed this murder."

"Alas, it is only too true."

"For the life of me I cannot understand what all this means—is not the party arrested, guilty?"

"Do you—can you believe it?"

"I know nothing more about the matter than is stated in this paragraph," I returned, handing him the *Tribune,* and pointing out to him the item in question. He eagerly perused it.

"What!" cried he, when he had finished, "do you not know whom the police have arrested on suspicion of having committed this murder?"

"No, indeed; who is it?"

"Clara Alford, the murdered man's niece!"

"Who?" I cried, starting on my feet, and supposing that I had not heard correctly.

"I repeat," said he slowly, "that the police have arrested Miss Clara Alford on suspicion of having murdered her uncle."

Again I asked the question, and again I received the same answer. I could not believe my senses. Had a thunderbolt fallen through the roof at my feet my astonishment could not have been greater. "What!" thought I to myself, "she, the gentle and confiding girl who would not harm a worm, murder her uncle in the dead of night—impossible! absurd! there must be some mistake." I glanced at Doctor Seyton, and saw that he was watching my face with the utmost eagerness. The sight of his, pale anxious countenance calm and collected.

"My dear Doctor," said I, "I now understand your excitement and anxiety—but this charge must be frivolous in the extreme. I suppose the police thought they must arrest some one, and so took the first person they happened to meet."

"Thank God that you hold such an opinion!" exclaimed the physician. "I was afraid, at first, that you, like every one else, was convinced of her guilt."

"Do you mean to tell me that any one has expressed an opinion that she is guilty?"

"Oh yes, everybody that I have heard speak about the matter; but, of course, they are entire strangers to her."

"I should think so, indeed," I replied; "but come, tell me what you know about it."

"I know no more than the paper states; the inquest is to be held today. My motive for coming here is to ask you to attend it."

"That I shall do as a matter of course. But tell me, when did you see Miss Alford last?"

"Only yesterday. I called to see Mr. Alford. Clara begged me not to do it, but I was determined to know the worst. I should tell you I am a suitor for Miss Alford's hand."

"I am aware of that," I replied; "tell me what passed in your interview with Clara's uncle."

"When I called. I found them both in the drawing-room. Mr. Alford appeared very much surprised to see me, and received me very coldly. The moment I mentioned my business to him he broke out into a most violent passion. He heaped every opprobrious epithet on my head, and ordered me out of his house. It was a violent scene. I left, utterly confounded and dismayed."

"What did Clara do during this scene with her uncle?"

"She wept, and entreated her uncle to calm himself."

"Nothing more passed than this?"

"Nothing."

I looked at my watch, and found it only wanted a quarter of an hour to the time appointed for the inquest. I informed Doctor Seyton that such was the case, and we both left the house together for Walker Street. When we reached our destination the jury had already assembled, and when they had viewed the body they proceeded at once to their investigations.

Clara Alford was not present. The first witness called was Martha Donovan.

"Martha," said the coroner, "you were a servant in the employment of the late Mr. Alford?"

"Yes, sir."

"Were you in Mr. Alford's house the night before last?"

"No, sir."

"How was that? Did you not usually sleep there?"

"Yes, sir; I had never slept out before ever since I had been there."

"How came you to be absent on this particular night?'

"My young Missus told me that evening that if I liked to go and see my friends I might, but to be sure and come back the next day."

"Where do your friends live?"

"At Harlem."

"Did you ask for leave to go and see your friends?"

"I asked a week or two ago; Miss Clara then said she would see about it, but as she did not refer to it again I thought she did not wish me to go."

"I believe you were the only servant in the house?"

"The only one, sir."

"Now, Martha," said the Coroner impressively, "listen to me. On the day that you left for Harlem did you hear any quarrel between Miss Alford and her uncle?"

"Well sir, I can't exactly say there was a quarrel, but I heard high words in the drawing room. Doctor Seyton came to see Mr. Alford, and there was a great noise. I heard Master abuse the Doctor."

"Did you hear Miss Alford say anything?"

"Yes, sir. I heard her say to her uncle that he would live to repent his conduct."

"That will do, Martha. You may stand down."

I saw in a moment, from the course of examination, that the Coroner was fully persuaded of Clara's guilt, and that he shaped all his questions to make the chain of evidence complete.

Doctor Seyton, to his own great surprise, was the next witness called. The Coroner interrogated him as to his recent visit to Mr. Alford, and drew from him his motive for going there, and the whole particulars of the reception he met with.

"And now, Doctor," said the Coroner, as he was about concluding with this witness, "answer me one more question. Did you hear Miss Alford say to her uncle that he would live to repent his conduct?"

Before replying the poor fellow glanced at me. I made him a sign to tell the truth.

"I believe she did make some such remark," he stammered out.

"That will do, Doctor," said the Coroner; "just sign your deposition."

Mr. Merrill was next called. He deposed that he had gone to see Mr. Alford, by appointment, on the morning the murder was discovered. That he found the door fastened, and having knocked some time without obtaining admission he became alarmed. He then procured the assistance of some policemen, and they broke open the door. He then gave the same statement as to the discovery of the body, which had appeared in the newspapers.

Nicholas Crouch, a police officer, was next called.

"You are the policeman who forced the door of Mr. Alford's house?" asked the Coroner.

"I am, sir."

"State what you found."

"I found Mr. Alford dead on the floor of his chamber."

"Who was in the house at the time of this discovery besides those who had entered with you?"

"No one but Miss Alford."

"Was there any evidence of any one having broken into the house?"

"None at all, sir. The fact is, all the doors and windows, with the exception of one attic, through which it would be impossible any one could enter, were securely fastened on the inside."

When this answer was made, I could see the jury look at each other with that peculiar kind of glance which told me that their minds were already made up.

""Did you discover any traces of blood on the floors of the house?"

"There were no traces of blood on the second story, excepting those on the bed. On the upper story, however, there were distinct traces of blood on the floor which led to the door of one particular chamber."

"Who occupied that chamber?"

"Miss Alford."

The jury again glanced knowingly at each other.

"Did you examine Miss Alford's chamber?"

"I did, sir."

"Did you find anything there?"

"I found, this dagger concealed under the carpet," replied the policeman, handing the weapon to the Coroner.

I glanced eagerly at it. It was a small ivory handled dagger, evidently of foreign manufacture. It was stained with blood. I must confess when this terrible proof was adduced I was confounded. I knew not what to think, the evidence appeared so overwhelming. The answer to the next question did not tend to enlighten me.

"When you first went to Miss Alford's room was the door fastened or not?"

"It was fastened on the inside."

A physician was next called, who testified that he had made a cursory examination of the body, and was of opinion that the deceased came to his death from a wound in the region of the shirt. He further testified that the dagger found in Miss Alford's chamber exactly fitted the wound—in fact, that there could be no doubt whatever that it was the weapon with which the murder had been committed.

The investigation here ended, and the Coroner here summed up the evidence. He began by stating the important character of the evidence they had heard. The first point to be established was that the deceased had died by violence. Of this there could be no possible doubt. The next point to be settled was, who did the deed. He thought that the evidence they had heard settled this point also. He dwelt particularly on the facts of the servant girl having been sent away the night of the murder, the doors and windows being all fastened on the inside, and lastly, the discovery of the murderous weapon under the carpet in Miss Alford's room, while the door was fastened on the inside, thus precluding the possibility of any one having entered and placed it there. He then dwelt on the motive for the deed. He showed that Miss Alford was engaged against her uncle's consent to the young physician, Doctor Seyton. That there had been a quarrel the day previous to the murder, in which the niece of the deceased had used something like a threat. After enlarging on these points he left the case to the jury.

I was not surprised, after all I had heard, to see the jury, after deliberating a minute or two, turn round and deliver a verdict to the effect "that Stephen Alford had met his death by a dagger wound, inflicted on him by the hands of his niece, Clara Alford."

She was immediately committed to the Tombs for trial on the charge of wilful murder.

The developments made by the coroner's inquest completely bewildered me. On one side was the most damning evidence—circumstantial—it is true—but there was not a single link wanting in the chain. On the other side there was my own knowledge of her character, temper and disposition; and I must confess when I recalled all I knew about her to my mind, the idea that she could commit the crime of which she was accused seemed preposterous and absurd in the extreme.

I determined in the first place to examine narrowly the theatre of the tragedy. I thought perhaps that I might find something there that would give me a clue.

I soon found myself in the old house where I had before paid so many friendly visits. I do not know why, but the extreme old-fashioned character of the rooms appeared to strike me more forcibly than ever. The large hall, the wide stair-case, the immense lofty rooms, the small windows, and the air of solidity in every thing, called my mind insensibly back to times long gone by. For some time I discovered nothing to give me the least enlightenment. A cursory glance at the doors and windows convinced me that no one could possibly have entered by them.

It will be remembered that when the policeman entered the house, he had found only one window unfastened—namely, that of the attic. After having thoroughly searched the lower part of the house, I made my way to this apartment, and examined the window in question. I found that it looked into the alley-way situated between the two old houses. Just underneath the window was a beam or support, the extremities of which rested on the gable-end of each house, evidently for the purpose of support. When I gazed from the dizzy height into the narrow alley, it seemed utterly impossible any one could have entered by that means. The window was far too much elevated for any ladder to have reached it, and as for any one climbing up the sides of the house, that was entirely out of the question.

My heart sunk within me when I saw my last hope fail me. I was almost tempted to leave the house in utter despair. Still after a little reflection I determined to finish my search.

My next visit was to Miss Alford's bed room. I had not been three minutes in that chamber before my countenance cleared up, and the discovery I made served to dissipate all my gloomy forebodings. I was now certain that some one had entered the house by some means as yet undiscovered, and committed the crime.

It will be remembered that the most damning proof against Miss Alford was the discovery of the bloody dagger concealed under the carpet in her bed room. Yet this very fact now proved to me beyond doubt that she was entirely innocent. This may appear a paradox, but the explanation is very simple.

The reader will bear in mind that the house was a very old one, and consequently the doors had shrunk a good deal. This was specially the case with the one opening into Miss Alford's room. In fact a piece of list had been nailed along the bottom of it to keep out the cold air. I was first attracted by a single spot of blood on the *outside* of the piece of list. I thought it very strange it should be there, and stooping down I turned it up. I found there was a space of more than an inch between the bottom of the door and the floor. I then turned up the carpet in the room, and found a long scratch on the boards, extending from the door to where the dagger was found concealed. The whole truth flashed on me in a moment; the murderer after committing the deed had thrust the dagger under the door and pushed it with a stick as far as he could under the carpet.

This discovery, as far as it went, was very satisfactory and stimulated me to fresh exertions. I next proceeded to visit the body of the deceased. I found him lying just as he had been discovered by the police. I am something of an anatomist, having studied medicine when young. When I saw the wound I was convinced that the blow had been struck by some one who had a profound knowledge of the human frame. It was impossible such a wound as that could have been given by chance. It was directly over the arch of the aorta, and must have cut into the artery, producing instantaneous death.

I was about leaving the apartment when I noticed in a desk, which I opened, a packet of letters, yellow and worn by time. I picked them up and glanced curiously through them, but finding they referred only to private matters I replaced them from where I had taken them.

I could discover nothing more and left the house.

I had gone a block or two on my way home when the thought struck me I had not examined the alley. I was half inclined not to go back, but something prompted me to do so. The search was soon made and not entirely without success. In the middle of the alley I found a single sleeve stud. It was a peculiar one, being made of blood stone with a forget-me-not raised in gold in the centre.

I put it into my pocket, thinking it might lead to something by and by, and had just entered the street again when I was accosted by an old friend of mine whom I had not seen for some years.

"Brampton, how are you?" exclaimed Mr. Duvall, for such was his name; "why it's an age since I saw you."

"I have lost sight of you for some time, and did not know you were in the city. Where do you live?"

“"Why, I live here," he returned, pointing to the house adjoining the one where the murder had been committed. In fact it was the other old fashioned dwelling referred to in the commencement of this story.

"Indeed!" I returned; "then you are the very man I wanted to see. Did you hear any noise on the night that Mr. Alford was murdered?"

"Not a sound."

"Did any one in your house?"

"No one that I am aware of."

"Did any one beside your own family sleep in your house that night?"

I asked this question on the impulse of the moment—a sudden thought having struck me.

"Let me see," returned Duvall. "Yes, I remember now; a Dr.

Seroque, a dentist, and distant relative of my wife, slept in the house that night."

"Seroque, Seroque," I muttered to myself; "where have I seen that name. Oh, I remember now," and hastily bidding my friend adieu, I again entered the house I had just quitted.

The fact is, in running my eye over the letters which I found in Mr. Alford's chamber the name of Seroque had struck me. I now hastened to take possession of these letters.

I seated myself in the drawing-room and perused them all. I found them to be old letters from Mr. Alford's late wife addressed to her husband. In them she complained of the persecutions of a Frenchman named Seroque, and afterwards gathered from other letters that Mr. Alford had taken summary vengeance on the persecutor by chastising him publicly.

I now began to see my way clear, and putting the letters in my pocket I again left the house. This time, however, I walked directly to the front door of the house occupied by Mr. Duvall and rung the bell violently. The master of the establishment opened the door himself.

"What, back again, Brampton?" said he. "I am delighted to see you—walk in."

"Mr. Duvall," said I, "I want you to do me a favor."

"You may command me, what is it?"

"Just to let me see the room which was occupied by that Dr. Seroque you mentioned just now."

"With all the pleasure in life," he returned, "but I tell you, you will have to walk up a good many steps, for our house was full that night, and we had to put him in the attic."

The light grew brighter and brighter.

Without further parley, Mr. Duvall led the way, and we mounted to the top of the house. As I expected, the attic was the exact counterpart of the one in which the window had been left unfastened in Mr. Alford's house.

The moment I glanced out of the window my mind was made up.

"Where does Dr. Seroque live?" I asked.

"He practices as a dentist, and lives at No. 51 Canal street," replied Mr. Duvall, evidently not knowing what to make of all this. "But come," he continued, "now your curiosity is satisfied—for it can be nothing else that brought you up these stairs—let us go down and smoke a cigar together, and have a talk about old times."

"Thank you," I returned, "you must excuse me—the fact is I have got a bad tooth-ache, and must go and see a dentist. I think your friend, Dr. Seroque, will do for me."

"Well, he's a good dentist—another time you must promise me to come."

I made the required promise, and having procured the assistance of two brother detectives, soon found myself in Canal street. Directing the officers to wait outside, I entered the French dentist's establishment.

I was received by a dark looking foreigner somewhat advanced in years, with a bushy black beard, which had evidently been dyed.

"Dr. Seroque, I believe?" I observed.

"Yes, sir," he returned, with a very slight foreign accent.

"I have a tooth which troubles me, and wish your opinion as to whether it had better come out."

"Let me see, sir," he returned, turning up his coat sleeves after having placed me in the operating chair. I did not wait for anything more, but rising hurriedly from my seat, to the intense surprise of the dentist. I went to the door and called in my friends. When they entered I said:

"Secure that man—I charge him with the wilful murder of Mr. Alford!"

They gazed first at me and then at the dentist. Dr. Seroque turned ghastly white, but he recovered himself in a moment.

"What do you mean, sir," he said, "by this extraordinary conduct?"

"I simply mean that you are the murderer of the unfortunate gentleman who lived in Walker Street. To show you that everything is known, I will detail to you how you committed the deed. Some years ago Mr. Alford publicly chastised you. Since that time you have been burning to be revenged."

"How do you know that?" exclaimed Seroque, gazing on me with the utmost astonishment.

"Never mind how I know it, such is the fact. At last an opportunity presented itself. On the night of the murder you stayed in Mr. Duvall's house. Some time in the course of that night you rose from your couch, and opening the window of the attic in which you slept, you cautiously let yourself down on the beam which forms the gable-end of Mr. Duvall's residence to that of Mr. Alford. You cautiously crept along this beam until you reached the opposite window. Through this window—you entered Mr. Alford's house. You then descended to your victim's chamber and committed the fearful murder. The deed done, you went to the door of Miss Alford's room and pushed the dagger with which you had committed the deed underneath it—in all probability using this very cane for the purpose," I continued, going to one corner of the apartment, and taking from it a thin walking cane.

The Frenchman's countenance was now piteous to behold. He was pale as a corpse—his face was perfectly livid—he muttered something.

"Allow me to finish," said I, interrupting him "After you had as you supposed, fastened the blame on an innocent person, you departed the same way that you came. But during your passage across the beam you lost something. See—this is what you lost; and see—here is the place where it is wanting."

So saying I held up the sleeve stud I had found—and then pointed to one of his shirt sleeves, in which there was no button—and then to the other cuff, where the exact fellow to the one I had found was to be seen.

This overwhelming proof was too much for the Frenchman. He threw up his arms and murmured:

"Guilty! guilty! Yes, I did the deed—I did the deed."

After taking the precaution of putting the hand-cuffs on him, I immediately conveyed him before a magistrate, where he made a full confession.

I lost no time in procuring an order for the release of my fair acquaintance. It was the happiest day of my life when I opened the prison door for her. I conveyed her to my own house, where I had arranged a pleasing little tableau. I then opened the door of my drawing room, and who should be sitting there but Doctor Seyton. The moment Clara saw him her joy was so great that, throwing all prudishness on one side, she rushed into his arms, which were stretched out to receive her.

I no sooner saw them locked in each other's embrace than I thought it prudent to leave them together.

It may be asked how I came to the conclusion that Seroque was guilty of the murder. The simple truth is that when I visited the chamber in which he had slept, I noticed on the outside of the window still the bloody marks of four fingers, where the murderer had evidently placed his hand as he got in the window.

Two months after Seroque was hanged—and one year after I witnessed the wedding of Doctor Seyton and Miss Clara Alford.

Leaf the Twenty-Third

Buried Alive

(The stories which follow and conclude this series are not details of my own experience, nor are they strictly of a detective character. They are the adventures of various personal friends of mine, and I am certain they are for the most part strictly true. In two or three of them perhaps, the relators may have allowed imagination to supply the place of facts. I have thought them sufficiently interesting to deserve a place in this collection.—J. B.)

"Come, Grafton, it is your turn to tell us an adventure."

"Oh, nothing has happened to me since I was buried alive!"

"What!" we all cried, in accents of the greatest astonishment.

There were half a dozen of us young fellows on a visit to George Grafton who was doing a first-rate practice in a small town in the State of Maryland. He had insisted on us visiting him for "Auld Lang Syne," and this was the second evening we had passed at his house. The simple fact is, George was to be married in a day or two and we were there to assist at the ceremony, as the French say. George Grafton was as good a fellow as ever breathed; and we, his fellow-students, loved him with all our hearts.

"I repeat," said George, "that nothing has happened to me since I was buried alive."

"Oh, you're joking," said one of us.

"Why, I must have told that story over and over again," returned George.

"We never heard it," we all cried.

" Is it possible? Well boys, light a fresh cigar, fill up your glasses, and I will tell you all about it."

We all followed the advice given us by our friend, and fixed ourselves into listening attitudes.

"Eight years ago," began Grafton, "I was studying my profession in the University Medical College of New York. I was a hard student, and having obtained the situation of clinical clerk to the great surgeon Dr. M—t, I determined to merit the good opinion of my master.

"In my zeal I was accustomed to sit up late at night making researches in anatomy on the dead subjects.

"One night I was alone in the anatomical theatre, tracing the relative anatomy of the femoral artery. I grew sleepy over my task, and I suppose it was owing to this fact that I pricked myself with my dissecting knife.

"All of you know the fearful effects which frequently follow the inoculation of the poison from a dead body into a living one. I, however, was not frightened, and sucking my finger, I resumed my work.

"It was early in the morning when I returned to my boarding-house. It was then I felt for the first time pain in the wounded finger. This grew worse, my arm began to swell, and by the middle of the next day I was in a high fever and delirious.

"All the professors of the college came to see me, but they shook their heads and said there was no hope. I gradually grew weaker and fainter, and before twenty-four hours had elapsed, I supposed I was dying and finally became unconscious.

"When I came to myself again, there was a dim light burning in my chamber, and an old woman was seated by my bedside, dozing in a chair. I endeavored to stretch out my hand to awaken her, when to my horror I discovered that I could not move hand nor foot. I tried to speak, but could not utter a sound. My body was dead, but my mind was living!

"At first I thought I was really dead, and that the soul had not as yet quitted the body. I was perfectly conscious of everything passing around me; and yet I was utterly unable to make the slightest motion or give the slightest sign.

"And thus the night passed away. The old woman continued to doze in her chair, refreshing herself every now and then by sundry drinks from a bottle, but never once casting a glance at me. I thought this was a very strange way to treat a patient, but supposed she thought I was asleep and did not wish to disturb me.

"The morning at length dawned, and the sunlight came streaming through the casement. But one thing surprised me very much, there was such an air of quietness through the whole house, usually so noisy the moment day-light appeared. As I lay there I could distinctly hear the ticking of the clock on the stairs—a thing I did not remember to have heard in my room before. Even the old nurse walked about the room on tip-toes.

"By and by I heard some stealthy soft steps approaching the door, and almost immediately afterward two men entered and approached the bed.

"They gazed on me in silence for a moment, and then one of them began deliberately to measure my body.

"He makes an elegant corpse!" said the man when he had finished, surveying me with the eye of an artist.

"The fearful truth then broke on my mind. They thought I was dead, and yet there I lay as living as any of them, but in a cataleptic state. No words that I could use would express my mortal agony at this conviction; but my body refused to act, and I remained motionless and silent.

"The day wore on; several persons with whom I was well acquainted came in to see me. They sat by my bedside and expatiated largely on my character. My little failings were all glossed over, and numerous virtues ascribed to me which I did not possess. The professors of the college came, too, and mourned over the sad fate of one so young.

"At last they all left, and no one remained in the room but the old woman whom I discovered had been hired to watch the body.

"Towards evening I heard two men ascending the stairs, evidently carrying something between them.

"The door opened, and to my horror there entered two men, bearing my coffin.

"They placed it on trestles by the bedside, and then they carefully placed me in it.

"In the evening more friends came to take a farewell look at me. Again I heard them discussing my character.

"I learned that I was to be buried the next day!

"One by one they left the room, and by night I was left alone in my coffin, with no one but the old woman for my companion.

"I could not see her, but heard her every now and then walk across the chamber. Oh! the mortal agony of that night! Some of you have doubtless suffered from night-mare. Increase the agony you felt on such an occasion ten fold, and you may in some degree realize my sensations.

"That night of agony at length ended—only to be followed by agony still more fearful; for the next morning the house was filled with those who were to follow me to the grave. Once more they leaned over the coffin—and then the lid was adjusted, and I could hear the grating of the screw-driver as it was firmly fastened down.

"I was now in utter darkness—but the undertaker (God bless him!) had not made the coffin air-tight, so that I was not suffocated.

"I felt myself carried to a hearse, and felt the jolting over the stones as the funeral *cortege* proceeded to Greenwood Cemetery.

"The ride seemed interminable to me; at last the vehicle stopped and I was lifted out. Then after an interval, I heard the clergyman read the burial service over me. This over, I was conveyed I know not where. I heard a key turn in a rusty lock, and I was left alone, as near as I could judge.

"For two hours I remained in the same condition, when suddenly I felt a tingling in my arms, beginning at the fingers. Gradually I recovered power over my muscles, I could first move my arms, and then my legs, and lastly my whole body.

"It was then that the appalling horror of my situation was fully realized. I moved my arms, they came in contact with the sides of the coffin. I moved my head, it struck against the lid. I could breathe comfortably enough; but fearful lingering death, stared me in the face.

"A sudden calmness came over me. I lay quietly and began to speculate how long I should live. I began to analyze my own feelings, and determined to watch with the calm philosophy of utter hopelessness the approach of each symptom of dissolution.

"But I soon began to get thirsty and all my philosophy was put to flight. The feeling at length became intolerable and I screamed—my voice did not penetrate beyond the coffin, but returned as it were on myself.

"Then began the combat between life and death. I struggled. I kicked. I beat my head against the coffin-lid. I hit the sides of my narrow prison-house with my arms, and endeavored to force out the end with my feet. This I continued for an hour or two, when I began to grow exhausted. A film came over my eyes, a dizziness seized my brain, and this time I thought I was dying in good earnest. During the last two hours I had suffered excruciatingly from thirst. My tongue was swollen in my mouth, and my throat was dry and parched. My breath too, began to fail me. I was suffocating. I was dying!

""I made one more terrible effort, using my arms, legs and body at the same moment. I then felt a sudden sinking, and a moment afterwards the coffin came in contact with the stone floor with a terrible crash. It was shivered to atoms and I was free without even a scratch.

"I stood up and found myself in the receiving vault of Greenwood Cemetery. The coffin had been placed on a ledge—my continued exertion had forced it to the edge, and my last desperate effort had tipped it over.

"In a few minutes I recovered myself. It was evening. I now went to the grating and began to use my voice to the utmost of my power. I soon attracted the keeper, at first he was frightened, and thought I was a veritable ghost; but a few words explained every thing, and he immediately conducted me to the lodge, where suitable restoratives were administered and clothes provided for me.

"In an hour I felt as well as ever I did in my life, and returned to New York that very night.

"When I got to my boarding-house, I found some of my fellow-students sitting in one of the fellow's room discussing a bottle of claret. I crept closely up to the door and listened.

"'Well,' exclaimed one of them, holding up his glass, 'here's to the memory of poor Grafton.'

"'I will drink to that, boys,' I returned, opening the door and taking the glass from his hand.

"I can give you no idea of the scene that followed. At first they were frightened, as the lodge-keeper had been; and when they discovered how matters really stood, their joy, knew no bounds.

"This, gentlemen, is how I was '*Buried Alive.*'"

Leaf the Twenty-Fourth

The Mystery of Darewood Hall

Some months ago, while crossing Broadway, I fancied that I saw before me an old friend whom I had known many years before. I ran up to him, and it was as I expected. His name was George Elliot, and he had been a college chum of mine. I had not seen him for a long time. When I first became acquainted with him, he was the picture of health; but now I was grieved to see that all his former robustness had disappeared, and his whole, appearance indicated very indifferent health. Of course, I offered him the hospitality of my house, which he at once accepted. After we had dined and were seated before a cheerful fire, I inquired of him what had occasioned the great change in his appearance. He drew nearer to the fire, and in a singularly musical voice, told me the extraordinary story. Did I not know the friend's unimpeachable character for veracity, I should hesitate to lay it before the public. I shall make no further preface, nor attempt any explanation of the phenomenon witnessed by him, but give it to the reader in my friend's own words.

Soon after graduating in the Columbia college, New York, I accepted a situation as tutor in a family who lived near Columbia, in South

Carolina. The compensation offered me was very liberal, and I thought myself fortunate in procuring so eligible a situation. After several days' travel I reached my destination, and was soon installed in my new home. My pupils were two boys—the elder, twelve, and the younger nine. They were very diligent, and made rapid progress in their studies. I was treated with great kindness and consideration by the members of Mr. Clare's family, and my time passed very agreeably.

Mr. Clare was a planter, and possessed great wealth. His family consisted of himself, his wife, the two sons I have just referred to, and a daughter, eighteen years of age.

Ada Clare was one of the most beautiful young girls I had ever seen. Her hair was soft brown, while her eyes were a dark hazel. Her form was exquisitely moulded, and her handsome features were not only faultless, but revealed high intellectual culture. She had a beautiful mind, which was filled only with the highest aspirations—no groveling thoughts ever obtaining an entrance there.

It is scarcely to be wondered, that isolated as I was in that lone house, I should be attracted to Ada Clare. We were necessarily thrown much together, and I could but admire her high intellectual attainments. There was a communion of thought and feeling between us which soon generated into love. One day—how well I remember it—I took her hand in mine, and poured into her ear a flood of impassioned eloquence in which I revealed my love. The looks she gave me when she turned her face to mine, and with tears of happiness in her eyes, is deeply engraven on my heart—I see it always. I need scarcely say I was accepted, and it was decided that I should at once explain the position of matters to her father. But the happiness of knowing that I was beloved by Ada, made me defer the explanation day after day. Oh, that happy, happy time! It was the glorious summer of my life. After my labors of the day were over, we would wander in the various pretty walks in the neighborhood, and build up Utopian dreams for the future. When the shade of evening came on, we would sit down on some rustic bench, and with my arm encircling her taper waist, we would gaze on the wondrous sky, and endeavor to read our destiny in the rolling orbs above us. A strange superstition seized us—we each chose a favorite star and called it after ourselves. She chose the white star in the constellation of the "Harp"—Lyra. We would sit and watch it for hours together. It is a pure star—as pure as her own virgin soul, and even now when I gaze upon it, I feel as if she were looking down upon me from her abode of bliss. You may call it childishness, but not a single clear night passes without my holding communion with my lost Ada through her star. But to my story.

Days, weeks, months passed away, in the intoxication of my love. To say that I adored her would be but to feebly express my feelings; there are no words in the English language sufficiently strong to paint one tithe of my devotion for that angel of purity and goodness. At last I summoned up courage and went to her father, and opened my whole heart to him. He listened to me very attentively and quietly, and told me he would give me an answer that same evening.

How anxiously I waited for the time no one but those who have loved as madly as I did can form any idea. At last the time came, and he called me into the parlor, and made known to me his determination. He spoke to me very kindly, and while he did not positively discountenance my proposal, he stated that he thought Ada was too young to enter into a decided engagement, and made known his intention of sending her on a visit to a sister of his who lived at a place called Darewood Hall, a short distance from Wilmington, in North Carolina. She would there have an opportunity of seeing the world, as his sister led a very fashionable life, and received a great deal of company; if, after a year's probation, Ada should remain in the same mind, he would offer no further objection. He concluded by informing me that his daughter would leave the next day, as he did not think it necessary that a letter should be sent to announce her intended visit. Invitations had been extended so often that her arrival would not take them by surprise.

I will not attempt to portray the anguish of mind I experienced at the thought of this separation. I was consoled, however, with the reflection that a year would soon pass away, and I felt so certain of Ada's constancy that I already considered her as mine for ever.

That night our last interview took place. Every word that was uttered, every look bestowed upon me is as vividly present in my memory to-day, as if the interview had taken place an hour ago. It was a glorious autumnal evening. The sky was decked with its myriads of burning gems, among which shone the star of my beloved brighter than all. We sat down on the old rustic bench, and in low sad voices spoke of our separation. The thought of our meeting again after the year's probation soon raised our spirits, and in anticipation of the future we forgot the present.

"George," said Ada, after a pause in our conversation, "is it not the soul that lives in us?"

"Certainly, Ada," I returned.

"Then why can there not be a union of soul between us—in that event, death cannot ever separate us."

The strangeness of the idea made me think, and the more I reflected the more feasible I thought the compact. We then lifted up our hands to the blue arch above us, and made a vow that we would be true to each other body and soul, and that even death should not lessen our love. We further agreed that whoever should die first, the other should appear to the survivor. This strange oath appeared to be all that was wanting to dissipate the feeling of anxiety at our approaching separation. We conversed more calmly after it; at last the time arrived for us to part. I drew her frantically to my breast, and imprinted a thousand kisses on her rosy lips.

The next day, at an early hour, she took her departure, and I was left alone. I do not know how the next few days passed; I only know I wandered about the house and grounds like one bereft of all hope. Vague anxieties which I had not experienced while she was present agitated me, and an inward dread of some impending misfortune took possession of my heart.

One night, a week after Ada had left me, I wandered in the garden alone, and cast up my eyes to her star. The sky was beautifully clear, and the stars shone with peculiar brilliancy; but a strange change had taken place in the white Lyra—*it was blood-red!* At first I could not believe my eyes, and shielded them for a moment with my hand—I looked again, but there it was shining with a red lustre. At that moment one of my pupils entered the garden.

"Ernest," said I, pointing out the star to him, "do you see that star?"

"Certainly," he replied, "you have often shown it to me—it is Lyra in the constellation of the Harp."

"What color is it, Ernest?"

"It is a pure white."

"And yet to my eyes it appeared a deep bloody red!"

I tried to persuade myself it was some hallucination of my senses. I looked at the other stars; they all shone with their natural color.

I returned slowly to the house—my mind distracted with evil forebodings, and my heart oppressed with vague fears. What could this strange circumstance mean—was it a warning—was it Ada's soul speaking to me through her star? I retired to bed, and tossed about several hours unable to sleep. At last I fell into an uneasy slumber. I was suddenly awakened by a shriek—a shriek so piercing that it still rung in my ears when I assumed a sitting posture. I thought at first it was only some hideous dream; but this idea was dissipated by a recurrence of a shriek still more terrible than before. I distinctly recognized Ada's voice, and jumped from the bed in a state of mind impossible to be described. I rushed to the window—the sound of that dear loved voice appeared to be borne on the breeze until it was lost in the far off distance. I mechanically gazed on the star of my beloved. It still continued the same hideous color, but there was a dark sharp-pointed cloud in its vicinity, to which my heated imagination gave the form of sword or dagger.

It was rapidly approaching my beloved star, and in another instant it had hidden it from sight. At the moment of conjunction, another fearful shriek saluted my ears, as distinctly as if uttered by some one in the chamber. I could not disobey this third warning, but hastily packing my carpet bag, and leaving a note on my dressing table, informing my employer that particular business called me away, I left by the omnibus, which started at an early hour in the morning for Columbia. From thence I took the cars to North Carolina, and by traveling night and day reached Wilmington in two days.

Darewood Hall was situated about fifteen miles from this town, and I hired a horse to convey me there. It was late in the evening when I arrived, and I was immediately struck with the desolate appearance of the house. There was not a single light to be seen in any of the windows, and the carriage-way to the house was overgrown with thick and rank weeds. I advanced to the hall door, and knocked long and loudly, but received no reply. Now thoroughly alarmed, I directed my steps to some neighboring negro huts. Here I obtained information which somewhat re-assured me; for I was told that the family had been absent for three months on a visit to the North, and I was further informed that no visitor had been there; in fact, that the house was shut up. I then thought that Ada, by some means, must have learned in Wilmington that her aunt was absent from home, and having numerous friends there, had stayed with them until her relatives should return. Re-assured by the reflection, I was about to retrace my steps to Wilmington, when, some influence which I cannot explain made me return to the hall. I walked round it, and found that the door situated at the back part of the building was open. The same irresistible influence made me enter the house; and I visited every room. The furniture appeared in considerable disorder, and an accumulation of dust was visible on everything. The last room I entered was a bed-room, in which the bed appeared not to have been made since the last person slept in it. A strange feeling, which I could not define, came over me when I entered this chamber; it seemed as if I had seen it before, and that all the objects in it were familiar to me. Whilst examining this apartment, I could hear the wind howling outside the house, and in a few minutes the rain came pattering against the roof in large heavy drops. I glanced out of the window, and saw it had set in wet for the night. I therefore determined that I would sleep there, and return in the morning to Wilmington. I threw myself, dressed as I was, on the bed, and the fatigue and want of rest from which I had suffered, soon caused me to fall into a deep slumber.

How long I slept I know not, but I was awakened by the sound of footsteps. I opened my eyes, and the moon's rays were streaming in the window, by which fact I knew that the weather had cleared up. I glanced round the room, but saw no one, and yet I heard the pattering of feet; but the sound appeared to come from an adjoining chamber. I was in the act of rising from the bed, when I saw some object darkening the doorway. It advanced slowly forward until the moonbeams shone directly upon it. Great God! what was my horror to recognize Ada—*my* Ada! but so white, so ghastly, that my blood froze, in my veins. As she stood there, she pointed to a spot on her breast, which to my horror I saw was red and dripping with blood. I have often asked myself since that fearful night, if this was merely a vision or a reality, and I am compelled to state that it was all real.

I made a spring towards her for the purpose of clasping her in my arms, but stretching forth both hands, she made me a motion to stop.

I obeyed her gesture, then an ineffable smile moved her lips, and she raised her hands to heaven. She then stretched her hands toward the door, and waved them as if wishing me to follow. I obeyed, and she passed out of the house, down the stairs, through the back entrance, and led the way over some fields. At last I saw some water shining through some trees, and in another minute we came to the banks of a large river, the existence of which I was unaware of before. We proceeded some distance along the banks until we came to a small triangular piece of ground, which was covered all over with thick sedge grass. Ada glided through this grass until she reached the centre of the plot. She pointed to one particular spot, and again smiling sweetly on me, she pointed to heaven and disappeared.

The moon rendered everything distinct, and I could see the ground which she had pointed had been recently disturbed. I looked about for something to dig with, and found a short distance from the spot a spade, which bore evidence of having been recently used. I immediately began to dig, and had soon made a considerable hole. My spade at last came in contact with something soft, which proved to be clothes. You can judge of my horror when I at last dug out the dead body of my beloved Ada. Any words that I could use could not express the anguish I felt at the sight. I threw myself on the inanimate body, and frantically pressed it in my arms. I called her by every endearing name. I then perceived there was a frightful wound in the region of the heart. I was about conveying the body to the house, when I saw something glisten in the grave. I took it out, and found it to be a hackman's badge, with the number 94 engraved upon it. I now knew that I had discovered the murderer of my angel. I conveyed the body to the hall, and then mounting my horse, rode as fast as the animal could gallop to Wilmington. In half an hour after my arrival, the driver of the hack number 94 was in prison. When he was acquainted with the evidence before him, he made a full confession. It appeared that he had driven Ada to the Hall, and finding it shut up, she had ordered him to return to Wilmington; but the sight of the jewels she wore, and a well filled purse, had inspired him with the hellish idea of killing her. He carried out his purpose, and buried her in the piece of waste ground; as he was filling in the grave, by some accident his badge had fallen into the hole, and he had covered it up with earth. Two months after his arrest he was tried, convicted and executed.

I caused Ada's body to be conveyed to her father's house, and she was buried in the family vault.

Since that day, my health has visibly failed. I long to die that I may meet my Ada again. I have told you the exact truth, and all that I ask is, that you will not make it public until I shall be dead.

My friend then finished his story, and the next day left the city. Last week I received a letter, from which I learned that my poor friend had died. My promise of secrecy being now removed, I have related this strange episode in his life.

Leaf the Twenty-Fifth

The Artist's Story

After a long residence in the country, I returned to New York. The exhibition of the Academy of Arts was then open, and being very fond of paintings, I hastened to visit it. On the very threshold of the door I met my friend George Herbert, one of our most charming landscape painters. After shaking hands we entered together.

I asked Herbert if he had anything on exhibition, and on his replying in the affirmative, I begged of him first to show me his pictures. But modest as usual he led me to some of the best paintings, and pointed out to me beauties of detail not usually appreciated by the mass of visitors. He thus passed in review the works of his friends, rivals and enemies, and was equally just with them all. It was not until an hour had elapsed that he placed me opposite one of his own pictures, which was surrounded by a considerable number of ladies.

"I can make no remark on this picture," said he, "look and judge for yourself."

The moment I cast my eyes on it, I could not suppress an exclamation of surprise and joy, which made all the persons looking at it turn round their heads. One only remained motionless. She was a lady elegantly dressed in black, and who with her elbow leaning on the balustrade, appeared to be entirely absorbed in the contemplation of my friend's picture. I profited by the departure of several of the spectators to approach closer myself, in order to explain if possible the impression the first glance at this picture had made on me.

Nothing could be more simple than the subject of the painting. It represented a white house, festooned all over with green vines; in front of it two beautiful children were playing together.

Seated on a green bank at the entrance of a long avenue of old trees was a lady, watching the children with a tender and loving glance, while a piece of embroidery just fallen from her hands showed her distraction. In the foreground a young man was pushing off a boat which was half hidden by a bed of roses. His eyes were fixed on the house, the children and the lady, and from the expression of his face they appeared to sum up his whole happiness. The work was executed with marvelous detail, and simple though it appeared, it was really a remarkable *chef d'oeuvre.*

I turned to my friend to express the sympathy and admiration with which his picture had inspired me. He cut my praises short by pretending that he had forgotten to show me an important painting, and drew me away for that purpose. But when, after another walk through the galleries, we passed through the apartment in which Herbert's picture was placed, I cast another look at it, I was a little surprised to find the lady in black still gazing on it.

"That lady's admiration," said I to Herbert, "is very flattering to you, if her face only corresponds with the elegance of her shape and toilet."

"Pshaw! what matters it to me?" he replied, in a tone of utter indifference.

"It matters to me, though," said I, laughing, "I like to see that my friends are appreciated by those whose good opinion is worth having."

And letting go his arm I advanced towards the unknown. She was at that moment referring to her catalogue, doubtless for the purpose of discovering the painter's name. But at the moment I leaned forward for the purpose of catching a glimpse of her face, she uttered a cry, and fell fainting into my arms.

Scarcely noticing her marvellous beauty, I had just untied her bonnet strings, when I heard another cry which appeared to be an echo of the first one behind me. I turned quickly round, and saw Herbert reel forward and catch hold of the balustrade for support. Leaving the strange lady in the hands of her friends, I ran to him.

His eyes were half closed, and he was frightfully pale. He could not articulate a single word. When he had somewhat recovered, his first glance was directed to the spot where the lady had stood. Not perceiving her, Herbert's first impulse appeared to be a determination to follow her; but reflecting a moment he stopped, and I heard him murmur:

"What woe would it be? It is well she did not see me."

This scene, which no one understood, drew a concourse of people around us. I drew Herbert into another gallery, and after a little time proposed that we should leave the place. He followed me without making any reply. At the door we got into a hackney-coach, and I ordered the coachman to drive us to Herbert's residence. During our progress there he did not utter a single word.

"You are suffering, Herbert," said I, when he pointed with a mute gesture to a bunch of cigars on the mantle-piece of his studio.

"No, it is nothing," said he, shaking his head, as if to chase away a painful thought. "I thought at first I should have died, but I feel much better now."

"You know that lady?" I asked, after a moment's silence.

"And you are always on the alert for stories, even if they are about your own friends," he replied, with a resigned smile. "Well, so be it. You, at least, are not '*bete*' enough to laugh at a love affair."

And handing me a cigar, Herbert sat down by my side on the sofa, and related to me the following history:

During my last visit to the little estate owned by my mother near Albany, I met my uncle, Major C——, of the United States army, many times. He was home on leave of absence, and resided near my mother's property. He told me marvellous stories of his campaign in Mexico, and with the Indians, and as I was a good listener, I speedily ingratiated myself in his favor. His leave of absence expired about the same time that I proposed to return to New York. We had to proceed twenty miles by carriage before we could reach the boat that was to convey us to New York, and the major proposed that I should accompany him. Of course I could not refuse, although to tell you the truth, his society somewhat bored me. The day before our intended departure I called upon him to know the exact time that he would start. I found him fuming and fretting as only a military man can fume and fret.

"The deuce take all women!" he cried, the moment he saw me, crushing up in his hand a note that he had just read.

"That is not a very gallant speech, uncle," I returned, offering him my hand.

The major looked at me a moment without speaking, and then pushed away my hand.

"I suppose you are a gallant man," he replied. "If so, to-morrow you will have a chance of showing off your gallantry to the greatest perfection."

"How is that? Do we not start tomorrow?"

"Yes, and that is precisely the reason I am out temper. Would you believe it, that I, who will not take the trouble to look after my baggage when traveling, have been requested to take charge of a young boarding-school miss, who is returning to her mother?"

"You appear to me to be a very proper escort."

"Thunder and lightning! I wonder if they take me for a nurse?"

"How old is your charge, Major?"

"Seventeen."

"In that case, if she be not too ugly, I will relieve you of your duties."

"On the contrary, she is represented to be charming."

"You have not seen her, then?"

"I suppose I may have seen her at her uncle's, who is one of my old friends, although it is not very amiable of him to impose this task on me."

"What is her name?"

"How should I know? I believe it is Miss Vane."

"A pretty name."

"Yes, a pretty name and a pretty face; but not a cent of fortune," returned my uncle, with a sneer. "Do you like girls without fortunes?"

"That depends on circumstances. I know many heiresses who would not suit me, even to mix my colors."

"I tell you what it is, Mr. Artist, with such ideas as you have you will ultimately die of hunger. But take your own course, marry this girl, if you like. But, come, we will pass the day together, and you shall go with me to take an answer to this cursed letter, for I am expected there to dinner, and you can be introduced to your future dulcinea."

"Thank you," I returned, smiling, "I am not in such a hurry to run after my chains. It will be time enough to-morrow, if you are really determined to yield your right to me."

"Go to the deuce, then," said the major, taking up his hat and approaching the door; "but remember, if I do not see you again to-day, we leave to-morrow at eight o'clock. Confound all women, I say!"

So saying, my worthy uncle disappeared, leaving me to my own reflections. I returned home, and having finished packing my trunks, and made a few farewell calls, I was somewhat embarrassed to know how to spend the remainder of the day. I determined at last that I would pass it amidst the green fields, and take a last view of the face of nature, for I was well aware that I should be exiled from it for many months in New York. I took my sketch-book and pencil and soon reached the fields.

It was towards the close of September. These last days of summer possess a serene splendor which, to my taste, more powerfully affects the mind than the beauties of spring. Never, did I perceive their glory so much as on that day. I strode on, forgetting that I was a painter, and so much captivated by the charms surrounding me that I lost all idea of reproducing them. I was awakened from my ecstacy by the rustling of a dress on the other side of a rustic hedge, after a walk of several hours. A single glance convinced me that this hedge enclosed a park, in the midst of which stood a large mansion. Another glance revealed to me a young girl walking slowly along an avenue of gigantic oak trees. She approached the spot where I was concealed by the thick bushes. She hid her eyes fixed on a letter which she held in her hand, so that I could not see her face. But at last she finished reading the letter, and let it fall in her lap; it was then I beheld for the first time her glorious beauty, and I could scarcely restrain an exclamation of surprise.

But why was her charming face bathed in tears? They were not furtive tears, but bitter and burning tears, which rend the heart and redden the eyes. What could that letter contain which appeared to have provoked them? Was it the death of a relative? She would not have isolated herself in this manner to weep. Was it the treason of a lover? She was too young and too beautiful to have been deceived What could it be, then?

She was sitting on a grassy bank facing me, and as I have before said, the letter had escaped from her hands. Her eyes were fixed on the ground, her breast heaved with sobs, and she seemed to be oblivious to everything around her. Sometimes her lips moved as if she would speak, but a stifled sob prevented her uttering a sound. There was something dreadful in this poor young creature's despair. My first impulse was to run to her, and I should probably have done so had not the sound of voices, evidently approaching reached my ears. The young girl also heard them, for she hurriedly picked up the letter, concealed it in her bosom and re-entered the avenue. If I moved I should betray my presence, and the young lady would know that she had been watched. From motives of delicacy, therefore, I determined to remain where I was. My mysterious heroine joined a group which had already advanced within a few yards of where I was concealed.

The group consisted of a middle-aged gentleman, a lady, who was doubtless his wife, and a young girl, decidedly plain. The young lady whom I had seen a minute before plunged into such violent grief, took the arm of the latter and walked by her side, and listened to the conversation of the middle-aged gentleman, who spoke with much animation. I could easily understand what a violent effort she must have made over herself to effect such a complete transformation, for all trace of sorrow had disappeared from her face. Calm, and if not gay, at least tranquil, she smiled at some observation addressed to her in the course of conversation, which I could now hear distinctly.

"He is playing at billiards," said the gentleman, doubtless in reply to a question I had not heard; "but the essential point is that he accepts, and we are thus saved great embarrassment, and yet had it not been for your mother I should on account of this young man have waited for another opportunity."

"But why?" said the elderly lady. "This young man is of a good family, and I do not see what inconvenience can arise—"

"What inconvenience, madam!" replied the gentleman, somewhat tartly. "Have I not already told you that he is an artist, who, instead of following his father's lucrative business, must needs settle in New York under the pretext of art, and waste his means, heaven only knows how?"

"But, uncle," said my heroine, in a voice so clear and musical that it almost made me start, "I think I have heard that this young man possesses a great deal of talent."

"And where will his talent lead him?" said the old gentleman, with bitterness. "Most likely to die in the hospital. I tell you these artists are a curse. Their morals are bad, and they bring trouble into the bosom of our families."

"Take care of yourself, Laura," said the daughter, addressing my unknown.

"O, I fear nothing," she replied, with a sad smile, in which I saw traces of the grief she had so promptly suppressed.

"Come, let us go to dinner," cried the enemy to artists, hearing the sound of a bell from the direction of the house. And they all left the spot, leaving me at liberty to emerge from my concealment.

"Laura!" said I to myself, as I continued to walk along the hedge which skirted the park. "Her name is Laura. What a charming name, and what an adorable girl! But why the deuce did that frightful old man rail so against artists? Could he be referring to me, and yet that is scarcely possible, for I never saw him before in my life. Why did she weep so much, and why conceal it when her friends approached? Her grief must have a secret cause. Could it be love?"

This last supposition was by no means an agreeable one to me, but I was ashamed to confess to myself the interest with which this young girl had inspired me. The continued ringing of the dinner bell at the house made me remember that I had taken nothing since morning, and yet I hated to leave the spot where my fair unknown lived.

After considerable hesitation I decided to seek for a farm house in the neighborhood, where I could appease my hunger, and then return to the garden of Eden where my Eve lived.

I immediately began the search. But whether it was that I took the wrong direction, or that there were no farmhouses in the neighborhood, I discovered none. Night came on during my fruitless walk, and I was very glad at last to meet with a countryman who directed me to my uncle's residence, that being the nearest, I reached it, harassed and famished, at eleven o'clock at night.

The major had returned an hour before, and while they were preparing supper for me I entered his chamber. He suddenly awoke, but scarcely recognized me, and when I asked him if he knew a young lady named Laura living in the neighborhood, he uttered an exclamation, doubtless not very parliamentary, but so energetic as to forbid all hope of getting any information from him.

I passed a very uneasy night. The image of the young girl under the tree appeared unceasingly before me, and I felt that I must penetrate the secret of her tears. It was daylight before I fell asleep, and I must have slept but a very short time, when a servant came to inform me that the carriage was waiting at the door. I dressed hurriedly, and went down stairs with the firm intention of telling the major that I had changed my mind, and could not be his travelling companion.

He was already in the carriage. I advanced to the door, and had already commenced to make my excuses when I caught sight of a beautiful face. I was immediately silent, and asked myself if I were not dreaming. But the driver, who had become impatient, pushed me in and closed the door. The carriage drove off, and I found myself sitting by the side of my fair unknown of the previous evening, Miss Laura Vane.

Surprise doubtless imparted to my face a singular expression, for the young girl could not help smiling, while the major reproached me for my want of punctuality. I sought to excuse myself, not for delay, but for my bewilderment, which must have appeared incomprehensible, so after I had been introduced to the beautiful girl, I exclaimed:

"Your presence here, Miss Vane, explains to me many things which were complete enigmas yesterday."

"What enigmas do you refer to George?" said my uncle.

"O, they are much too complicated for you, major," I replied glancing at Miss Vane.

"Pshaw!" he replied, with indifference.

Perceiving that I made no reply to his attacks, he ensconsed himself in a corner, and closed his eyes. I profited by this opportunity to examine more attentively the beautiful girl whom chance had thrown in my company at the very moment when I thought I should never behold her again. Her beauty was increased by being viewed closely. Her eyes were large and pensive, of that deep blue which the summer sky could only rival; her hair was a golden auburn and shaded a forehead as white as alabaster. When she smiled she revealed teeth so white and regular that they might have been cut out of a solid piece of ivory, and they could not have been excelled. Her form and figure were perfect. One of her little hands was ungloved, and I had an opportunity of observing how beautifully it was formed. Her toilet, though simple, showed exquisite taste. Whilst I was making this examination, she was looking out of the carriage window as if for the purpose of viewing the surrounding country; but a few furtive glances cast towards me convinced me that she knew she was being observed.

The major, Heaven, forgive him! commenced to snore. Perceiving that silence, if more prolonged would become more and more embarrassing, I determined to break it. I commenced with some commonplace remark, and we were soon on terms of frank intimacy. After conversing on different subjects for some time, I suddenly remembered that I had certain mysteries to clear up, I resolved to introduce less general subjects.

"Are you fond of paintings, Miss Vane?" I asked, abruptly.

The young lady doubtless thought that this was a very vulgar way to commence a conversation on art, and looked at me with surprise. But I renewed my question. Perceiving that I was determined to have an answer, she replied with a smile:

"I am compelled to make you a humiliating confession, Mr. Herbert, and that is, having been brought up in the country, I have never been able to obtain the necessary knowledge to judge of art."

"What matter, if you are able to feel its beauties, and that I am sure you are?"

"What gives you that certainty? Very flattering for me, I must confess, but I am afraid quite unmerited."

"Probably the desire I have to consult some one on the subject of a picture which has teased me since yesterday, and I thought that perhaps you would be that some one."

"Very willingly. Let me hear your idea, and I will give you my opinion of it, which you can accept for what it is worth."

"This is it, then: Under the trees of a park, a charming young girl—"

"Of course," interrupted Miss Vane, with a smile.

"Is surprised by a group of persons advancing to the spot where she is seated," I continued, without heeding the interruption; "at the moment she is reading a letter, her eyes being filled with tears. The instant she hears the footsteps she hides the letter in her bosom, and chasing away her grief advances to meet the approaching group."

On hearing me describe a scene in which she had been the principal, or rather sole actress, Miss Vane showed great emotion. She regarded me with a sort of fright, and appeared to ask me by her looks by what right I had mixed myself up with her secret. But the affected indifference of my attitude doubtless re-assured her, for she asked me, hesitatingly:

"Is it since yesterday that you have entertained the idea of this picture?"

"Yes," I returned, "it was a scene of which chance made me a spectator some time ago; but it came back, to my memory last night, and I thought that that beautiful girl, surprised at the moment she was reading a love-letter, would make a good subject for a painting."

"Why a love-letter, Mr. Herbert—how can you tell it was that?" asked Miss Vane, quickly, who, a little re-assured by the first part of my last speech, in all probability felt herself attacked in the latter portion.

"Why, Miss Vane, how could a young girl conceal herself in a secluded, spot, and weep so violently when reading a letter, if that letter did not speak of love? That was my impression, as it would be that of everybody else."

"Everybody else, like you, often judge wrong," replied Miss Vane, in a tone so serious that her sincerity could not be doubted. "Is not the real cause of the tears of those who weep in secret sufficient for them, without having them interpreted according to the fancy of the first indiscreet person who may chance to surprise them in their grief?"

A cloud settled on the young girl's face as if these last words recalled some pitiful reminiscence to her mind. My curiosity as to the cause of my travelling companion's secret grief, although far from being completely allayed, was in some measure satisfied by the discovery that it was not love that had caused her tears to flow, and I was so overjoyed by this fact that I determined she should pardon the indiscretion of which I had been guilty. I so far succeeded as to restore to Miss Vane's countenance its accustomed calm and serious look.

We were conversing very gaily when the major awoke. He first glanced ahead of us, and then actually greeted us with a smile, and even deigned to address a few words to Miss Vane. I was very much surprised at this great change from his usual surly demeanor; but it was explained when I saw that we had already reached Albany.

We drove immediately to the wharf, where we landed and had to wait some little time until the "World" should start. The major shrugged his shoulders when he saw me offer my arm to Miss Vane, and pointed significantly to a cigar which he had just lighted, and then disappeared in a bar-room. Miss Vane and I took two or three turns up and down the wharf, when she said with some hesitation, doubtless having remarked the major's significant gesture:

"I do not like to see you, on my account, deprive yourself of the pleasure of smoking a cigar."

My first impulse was to state the truth, and that was, that all the cigars in the world were not worth the gentle pressure of her hand on my arm, and the proud satisfaction in having such a beautiful creature by my side; but I was afraid of frightening her, so I determined to make myself a victim, and replied, with a shade of bitterness in my tone:

"Is that a polite way to rid yourself of my company, Miss Vane? Have I been too presumptuous in hoping that you would accept my services?"

"How could I entertain such an idea?" she replied, with a graceful gesture, of impatience.

"You know artists have such a bad reputation."

"Which is, perhaps, undeserved."

"Allow me to thank you, Miss Vane, in their name and mine, for the flattering opinions which I know you entertain of them."

"And how do you know that?" she exclaimed, with an uneasy look.

"I guessed it."

"Nay, you heard me express myself so."

"I confess that chance made me hear you speak in their favor."

"Then," she replied, "that picture of which you spoke to me just now, was taken from a scene in real life?"

"I cannot deny it."

"You are acting unfairly. Was it not enough to have committed an indiscretion—involuntarily, I fully believe—without aggravating it by endeavoring to penetrate the secret of a grief which has never been confided to you?"

"I am satisfied to know that that grief was not caused by love."

"And what interest can it be to you to know whether the first girl you meet loves or not?"

"What interest? Is not the woman who loves, a precious flower under a glass shade?—a rare bird in a cage?—a ripe fruit in an inaccessible garden? All these things possess only sweetness, perfume and harmony for those who possess them. Is it not natural one should prefer the wild flower of the woods, the bird of the heavens, and the fruit of the hedges which belong to the hand bold enough to take them?"

In spite of the sadness which had fallen on Miss Vane, she could not help smiling at my comparisons. Although I did not then comprehend the secret bitterness which she had in her railery, she replied:

""Yes; but the fruit of the hedges sometimes grows beyond reach, the wild flower sometimes blooms on inaccessible rocks, and the bird of the heavens does not allow itself to be caught."

"Ah, Miss Vane," I replied, "you want to intimidate me, and I must not show myself less courageous than you are."

"How am I courageous?" returned the young girl in a tone of unaffected surprise.

"Did not some one say to you yesterday, 'Take care of yourself?' And did you not reply, 'I fear nothing?'"

The young girl became quite serious, and made no reply. She bent her head down, and I felt her hand tremble on my arm. She appeared for the moment to be overpowered by some painful reminiscence, which I had before remarked had several times excited its influence over her. At last she raised her pure eyes to my face, and said, gravely:

"No, Mr. Herbert, I fear nothing, because I possess a talisman which I trust will never fail me."

"And what is that talisman?" I asked, with an ironical smile.

"It is duty!" she returned, with a proud glance. "And now I beg that we cease this conversation, which doubtless has no more interest for you than for me."

So saying she hurried on board the steamer, which had just come up to the wharf. I followed her, and took my seat by her side after a little delay in procuring tickets. Her head was perched over the railing, and she appeared to be watching the water through which we were now gliding. But in spite of all her efforts to hide it, I detected a furtive tear stealing down her cheek. This touched me to the heart. What had this poor girl done to me that I should harass her thus?

"Have I offended you, Miss Vane?" I asked, in a whisper. "If so, I beg that you will forgive me, for I assure you it was unintentional."

"Let us say no more about it," she replied, her countenance becoming serene again. "I am exceedingly sensitive, and perhaps it is good for me to be subjected to ridicule."

I was about to reply, when the major made his appearance. He did not stay with us long, however, but meeting a fellow-officer on board, they moved to another part of the vessel, and began to fight their battles over again. Miss Vane and myself were again left alone, or rather isolated in the midst of half a dozen passengers. Among the latter I noticed a lady very elegantly dressed and quite young. She was accompanied by an old man, who appeared to overwhelm her with his attentions, which she tolerated rather than received. This lady displeased me very much, even more than the little dog which she carried in her lap, and which annoyed us all by its continual barking. She went into ecstacy about the beauty of the scenery, and by pretentious exclamations uttered in a loud voice appeared to wish that everybody should hear her. While I was annoyed at this lady's remarks, I could not help admiring the beauties of the panorama spread before us. The steamer was between two hills covered with verdure, relieved here and there by white cottages which gleamed through the trees. It was most beautiful; every mile we made offered to us some new delight. Now it was a rustic village, descending to the very edge of the water, now it was green sloping, banks, with the spires of country churches peeping out from a mass of foliage, now the giant Catskills looming up to the very heavens.

Everything appeared so calm and beautiful that I felt its serene influence over my spirits, and had it not been for the noisy demonstrations on the part of the lady I have referred to, I should have been perfectly happy. I cast my eyes on Miss Vane and found that she was completely absorbed by the beauty of the scenery. I gently touched her shoulder.

"Is it not beautiful?" said she, without turning round. "There is no necessity for one to travel in foreign countries to find the true poetry of nature."

I perceived at that moment a white cottage hidden like a nest among leaves. The river at this point was somewhat inland, forming a miniature bay in front of the dwelling. The front of the house was covered, all over with a grapevine, while a carefully kept flower-garden extended around it. An avenue of beech trees skirted one side of the cottage. At the entrance of this avenue a lady was seated on a grassy bank employing herself with embroidery, at the same time watching two handsome children who were playing in the garden. A boat was fastened to the bank in front of the dwelling. All seemed so fresh and so pure that I could not restrain an exclamation of pleasure. Miss Vane had also noticed it, and appreciated its beauties, for she pointed to it and exclaimed:

"That is the place for one to live in."

"Not alone?" said I, intentionally.

"O, no," she replied, without thinking what she was saying; "but—" she stopped and blushed.

"With a companion, then," said I, quickly, without allowing her time to be frightened at the sense my words might convey. "Yes, it would be very pleasant to be awakened in the morning by the singing of birds, and to walk into the garden while yet wet with dew—"

"And gather flowers for the breakfast table," said Miss Vane, interrupting me.

"Yes, and after breakfast, work, for a little work would be necessary. During the hot hours of the day—"

"Read under the shade of the avenue."

"And dine in that pretty arbor—"

"After dinner row in that boat to yonder green hill."

"And in the evening have music in the drawing-room, with the windows open, and, with no other light than that given by the moon, sing—"

"Norma."

"You like Norma?" I cried, happy to find in her preferences a new point of contact with mine.

But this question appeared to dissipate the dream in which she had indulged. She cast down her eyes with some embarrassment, and a bitter smile replaced the look of serene gaiety which had before animated her face.

"Are you already tired of your pretty cottage on the Hudson?" I asked.

""No," said she, with her eyes filled with tears; "but it is dangerous to indulge in castles in the air."

"Why should it be a castle in the air, when a single word can make it a reality?"

Was it a flash of joy or anger which for a moment illuminated Miss Vane's countenance? I cannot tell; but whatever it was, it immediately fueled away, and was replaced by that look of grief and discouragement which I had often seen before. She silently moved away, and walked to the other end of the boat. I dared not break in on her reverie, but sat still and indulged in my reflections.

My thoughts, of course, were fixed on but one subject. I had never met in any woman the irresistible charm which had attracted me towards this ravishing creature. What, then, could be the cause of her secret grief? Evidently it was of recent origin, for her expansive nature repulsed it energetically, only allowing it at certain times to obtain an influence over her. I interrogated my own heart. I asked myself, supposing that she were free, could I in justice to her, offer her marriage? This young girl had no fortune, and I in pursuit of my studies had expended the modest patrimony left me by my father. It is true I was beginning to find a resource in my talents; but this was still so uncertain that I was often obliged to have recourse to my mother's small income. Could I expose this young girl to the hardships of an artist's life, and without making her happy, compromise my future by domestic troubles? But, then again, was it nothing to find in a devoted and faithful heart a refuge in the hours of doubt and discouragement? Was it not worth trusting something to chance? Does not faith in destiny often make our destiny?

While making these reflections I directed my eyes towards my traveling companion. She was still contemplating our white cottage in the woods, which was fast fading from view. In another moment a turn in the river hid it altogether. Miss Vane turned round, and her look met mine.

Had she thought of me as I had thought of her? Had our souls met and revealed themselves to each other while we were apparently separated? Who can say? But no human language could more clearly have expressed what our looks said during the eternal minute they were confounded together. Intoxicated, I advanced towards her, and I should perhaps have kneeled at her feet, and have offered her my life, had she not repulsed me with a gesture which had more despair in it than fright. She then put her hands to her face, and appeared scarcely able to stifle a sob.

But I only saw in this emotion the modesty which makes a woman blush at the avowal, the knowledge of which makes her happy in secret. I wished to allow Laura time to forgive me for the happiness she had bestowed upon me. I glanced around me without fixing my eyes on any particular object. I saw the green banks, the gliding water, the fleecy clouds, and birds, singing in the heavens. Everything appeared to smile, and I heard a voice which spoke to my soul, and which said, "Love!" Not wishing to disturb Miss Vane, I lit a cigar and joined a group of passengers, who were evidently farmers.

"Look," said one of these, pointing to the old man who accompanied the lady who was so loud in her praises of the scenery of the river, "see how attentive the old fool is to his young wife."

"Wife!" said I, in amazement. "You must be mistaken. You mean grandfather?"

"No, indeed, I mean wife. I come from the same town that they do. He is very rich, and that is why she married him."

I left them, and turned back. As I passed before the loud-talking lady avoiding to look at her, she uttered a cry and her umbrella fell close at my feet. I picked it up and returned it to her, bowing to the old man, and casting a disdainful look on the woman.

"What have you done to that lady!" asked Miss Vane, whom I had rejoined and who had seen this little scene.

"Nothing," I replied, smiling; "she let her umbrella fall, and I returned it to her."

"From the look you gave her, one would say that you hated her."

"No, indeed. I am only of the opinion that when a woman has courage enough to sell herself, she should at least have the honesty to keep to her bargain."

Miss Vane uttered a cry of suffering which I could have understood if the words had been addressed personally to her. She then gazed on the woman and then on me, and her eyes evinced so much pity for her, and so much reproach for me, that I felt myself blush, and could not utter a word.

By-and-by we conversed on general subjects, and continued to do so until we reached New York. When the time came for me to leave this beautiful girl, without the hope of seeing her again, I felt how much I was attached to her, and how the bonds so easy to bend were so hard to break. I approached her, and in a low tone of voice which emotion made to tremble, said:

"May I hope to see you again?"

Miss Vane was silent for a moment or two—her head fell on her heaving bosom—there was evidently a struggle going on, and I anxiously awaited her answer. At last a shiver ran through her frame, and raising her humid eyes to mine, she murmured, in a voice which she in vain endeavored to make firm, "No!"

I was about to protest against the decision, when Laura cried out with a feverish joy, mingled with terror:

"Henry! Henry!"

A young lad fifteen or sixteen years of age, approached, accompanied by my uncle, and having first embraced Miss Vane, turned towards the major and myself, and said:

"My mother, gentlemen, not being able to come to meet my sister, begged me to thank you in her name, and to beg that you will call on her and receive her thanks in person."

He then left us to see after his sister's baggage; the major accompanied him. I was transported with the invitation which had been given me, but I did not long remain so.

"Mr. Herbert," said Miss Vane, "you have been very good to me, full of kindness and indulgence; you can still, however, acquire a new claim on my gratitude."

"O, speak, Miss Vane—what must I do?'

"Do not mention my name during your residence in New York, and above all, do not accept the invitation which my brother has given you."

"But that would be very impolite," I returned.

"I will make your apologies. Do this for me, Mr. Herbert." Then seeing her brother and the major returning, she pressed my arm and whispered in my ear, "I beseech you, for my sake!"

The pressure of her hand on my arm, her breath in my hair, and above all her tender words, almost overcame me. When I recovered myself, Laura and her brother had already disappeared. I rushed to the side of the boat to catch a last glimpse of her. They were already on the pier. Laura turned her head and fixed a look of gratitude on me, and then the sweet vision vanished from my sight.

"I am much obliged to you for relieving me of a disagreeable duty," said the major, when they were gone. "What do you think of her, nephew?"

"I don't know," I replied.

Should I yield to Miss Vane's desire, and was she really sincere when she made it? Such were my thoughts when walking the next day down Broadway. At that moment I saw Miss Vane, accompanied by her brother, within a few steps of me. The young man recognized me, and made a movement as if he would stop, and speak to me, but his sister prevented him, and they rapidly passed me, as if they had not seen me.

This determination to avoid me wounded my vanity, and made me feel quite angry, and I at once determined to respond to the invitation sent me by her mother. The same evening I directed my steps to Mrs. Vane's residence.

She resided in the upper part of the city, almost in the country. The house was quite large, with a garden which was kept with great care, extending in front of it. The iron gate was open and I entered. The windows of the front room were open, and I heard the notes of a piano. It was evidently played by a practiced hand. Suddenly I heard the sweet prayer of Norma, "*Casta diva che inargenti,*" etc. I had arrived there angry, but this plaintive and sad melody found an echo in my heart, and love only spoke in me. I fancied I again heard the prayer that Miss Vane had addressed to me, and perhaps I should have retired, had not a suppressed cry interrupted the song, and if Laura herself had not suddenly appeared at the entrance. She advanced toward me, and said, with a sad smile:

"You here? I hoped too much from you, then."

"Why are you without pity?" I replied. "And why cannot you understand that if I come here in spite of you, in spite of myself, it is because I love you—"

"O, utter not those words," she cried, hiding her face with her hands.

She trembled, and her face became so pale, and betrayed so much suffering and fear, that she frightened me. I rushed forward to support her, but suddenly, by an energetic effort of will recovering herself, she said to me, calmly:

"Enter since you will have it so. I will go and inform my mother."

And pointing out the door of the drawing-room to me, she left me. I entered—the apartment was full of her presence—a vague perfume of flowers freshly gathered greeted my senses. I saw the book she had lately been reading, the open piano, and the piece from Norma still open, placed before it. I perceived on the table a little glove which belonged to her. I seized it and carried it to my lips, but the sound of approaching steps and voices made me conceal my modest treasure.

Three persons entered the drawing room—Miss Vane, who appeared very serious, and with a dignity about her which was almost solemn; her mother, a woman still handsome, and an old man, on whose arm Mrs. Vane leaned familiarly. Whilst I inclined my head, Laura, after having murmured my name, introduced me to those two personages.

"My mother, Mr. Herbert," said she, and then raising her limpid eyes to my face, with a look which seemed to ask for pity, she added, in a more feeble voice, hesitating between each word, "Mr. Emory, my affianced husband!"

These words struck me like an electric shock. So many confused sentiments burned in my heart at the same time that I could find no expression for a single one of them, and I remained overwhelmed with dismay. Whilst Mr. Emory surveyed me from head to foot, and whilst Mrs. Vano was thanking me for the attention I had paid her daughter, Laura, as if she had spent all her strength in pronouncing her own sentence, reeled rather than walked to the door. Before leaving the room, her supplicating eye sought mine. Whether it was my look revealed ironical disdain and cold contempt, I cannot say; but she appeared to be entirely overcome, and it is with great difficulty that she dragged herself away.

I do not know what the lookers-on thought of this scene; I do not know what I said during the few cruel moments I remained in the room. At last I got away with suffering, rage and hatred in my soul. While crossing the garden, my hand came in contact with the glove I had taken. A few minutes before it had made me tremble with happiness, now it burned me. I threw it from me in disgust. I heard a stifled cry behind me, and turning round, I thought I saw the vague form of a woman standing against the window. But without stopping to heed it, I hurried on, and reached my own lodging, and passed an agonizing night.

The next morning a letter was handed me It was a woman's handwriting.

After a moment's hesitation I broke the seal. I burnt this letter long ago, but every expression of it remains so deeply engraved on my heart that I can repeat it word for word. It was as follows:

> Alas! yea, I also have had the courage to sell myself, but I shall keep to my bargain, for I shall never forget my duty. I wished that our rapid journey should remain for you as it will always for me—a pleasant reminiscence; but you did not understand me. But if I must lose your love, if I myself entreat you to look upon it only as a dream, I do not wish that you should blush at having confessed it. It is for that reason that I write to you. I also have dreamed a sweet poem of an obscure life, in which labor was compensated by love; I also have upbraided those women who believe, or feign to believe, that riches alone are necessary, and who stifle their hearts under their vanity, and the expiation of my error is come—I only feel contempt when, perhaps, I ought to have felt pity. Who should have said then that I should have bent my head under the same reprobation that bestowed on others? O, why did you come to the house? I should have so loved to remain to you one of those dreams which, if they have no morrow, at least have no regret. Could you not understand by my sadness that I had no happiness to bestow? What have you gained by your obstinacy? Instead of a fugitive vision of love, you entertain only contempt for me. But the burden is already sufficiently heavy, and I am not resigned enough to bear more. You may forget me, pity me, perhaps; but your contempt is more than I can endure. God forgive me, if I do wrong, but

> you must know the truth. In seeing me here, surrounded, if not with luxury, at least with comforts, you doubtless thought it was only ambition that caused me to give myself to an old man. Alas! my only ambition is to secure an asylum for those I love, for in a year misery would enter our home, perhaps in a few months. My poor mother, by her imprudent tenderness, gave us an education suitable to our birth, instead of preparing us for labor, which the state of our fortune at my father's death should have destined us. I have taken the step for my mother's sake, for my brother's, that noble boy whom you know, and for my young sister's, whom necessity, perhaps, in a few years would have compelled to pursue a similar course to mine. It was this thought, especially, that one of us was fatally predestined, that gave me strength enough to be resigned to it. If a sacrifice is necessary, it is for me, who am the eldest and strongest, to make it. I know the task is a hard one, and I sometimes fear my own weakness; but I hope, in seeing my mother without care for the future, my brother launched in an honorable career, and my sister free through me, to choose for herself, that I shall find in the sentiment of duty accomplished that resignation and calmness which is all that I can aspire to. Adieu! Do not visit me again! I trust you will not seek to take from me the strength of which I stand so much in need to tread my sad path. May you be happy! May you become famous! And if you ever think of me, pray to God that he will give me oblivion and repose!
>
> Laura

My first impulse on reading this letter was to visit Laura again. But reflection soon came to obscure the charming mirage which the certainty of her love had for the moment caused to pass before my eyes and my heart. It was then, that I could not succumb to the temptation which assailed me to pursue my love even at the price of Laura's repose, that I determined to travel. I visited Europe. But while sailing on the calm or agitated waters of the Adriatic, or of the Ganges, whether in the palaces of Venice or Calcutta, my dream everywhere was that little white cottage on the borders of the Hudson, with its vines, its flower-garden, avenue, and the young wife, who with tender glances watched her two children playing on the grass; and this young wife always assumed to me the lovely and elegant form, the blue eyes, and the resigned smile of Laura Vane.

Two months after Herbert had told me this history, a lady of my acquaintance informed me that Mr. Emory had received a few days before a package containing a picture, without any indication where it came from. From the description she gave me of this painting I recognized it as my friend's work.

"The most singular thing about it," she continued, "is that when Mrs. Emory saw the picture she was seized with an emotion which she in vain endeavored to dissimulate."

The next day I called on Herbert. The moment I entered, he handed me a letter to read. It contained only these words, "I thank you!"

Leaf the Twenty-Sixth

A Churchyard Adventure

(I am indebted for the following to one of my oldest and best friends, and I know every word of it to be strictly true.—J. B.)

I was born among the green hills of Vermont. My father was a respectable farmer, and fully intended that I should be brought up to follow the plough. But I had a soul above corn and potatoes, and determined I would adopt some other means of obtaining a livelihood than the healthy unintellectual occupation of farming.

A simple incident soon decided me in the choice of my profession. I had a favorite dog which exhibited unmistakable symptoms of hydrophobia. I had him tied up and muzzled, but could not bear to have him killed. I looked into my father's library—a very small one, by-the-by—to see if I could find any book from which I could gain information what to do in the case. The only medical book we possessed was "Buchanan's Domestic Medicine." I thought what was good for human beings would also be good for dogs, and eagerly turned it over to the article on hydrophobia. I read and became fascinated. Eureka! I had found it! Of course my dog died, but I was consoled for its loss in the treasure I had discovered. I perused, reperused, and almost committed to memory the whole of that work. I soon became perfectly at home in the symptoms, diagnosis, regimen and treatment of all diseases that flesh is heir to—of course I mean theoretically. However my determination was now taken, I would be a doctor and nothing else.

My father endeavored to reason me out of the notion. He painted to me in vivid colors all the hardships, discomforts and trials of a physician's life. But it was all to no purpose. It only served to make me more determined. My father, seeing all further opposition was useless, at last gave his consent, and in due time I was sent to Dr. Colburn, of Burlington, to read in his office. Dr. Colburn was an Englishman who, however, had passed the greater part of his life in America. He had gathered together a large practice, and was very much liked by every one who knew him. He had a fine library of books, and among them a large quantity of old English novels of the Minerva press school, written in that peculiar style so common to all works of imagination which deluged the country before Sir Walter Scott introduced a new era in novel writing.

I was always very fond of reading. I perused everything that came in my way, and this library was for me the land of promise. I was soon deep in the "Ruins of Rigonda," or endeavoring to solve the "Mysteries of Udolpho." I trembled over the "Three Spaniards," and shuddered over the "Italian." Old castles, ruined abbeys, spectres of murdered brides, and black-bearded villains with gleaming daggers in their hands were my constant companions. I began to grow nervous and timid. When night came, and I had retired to my own room, I peopled the darkness with hideous spectres, and sometimes fancied I could hear the death-groan of some assassinated victim under my bed. This state of things at length grew so bad that it rendered me unfit for my studies. I then determined to break through the superstitious net by which I was surrounded. I shut up the novels, and endeavored to dissipate their effect by going into society. I succeeded in some measure in effecting my purpose.

One night, after I had retired to bed, I heard some one ringing violently at the office bell. Dr. Colburn had gone some miles in the country to see a patient, so it fell to my lot to answer the summons. I crept to the window and found a man before the door.

"What is it?" I asked.

"You must come and see Mr. Jenkins directly, he is very ill," replied the messenger.

"Very well, I will be there in a few minutes," I returned in no very good humor, for this Mr. Jenkins was an old patient of the doctor's, and an unprofitable one too; he had never paid a cent in his life. Besides which, he was a hard drinker and had had several attacks of *delirium tremers.* I thought it very probable I might be detained there all night, as he was usually very violent when suffering from these attacks. I dressed myself hurriedly, and slipping a bottle of laudanum into my pocket (opium is the best remedy for *delirium tremers*), I made the best of my way to Mr. Jenkins' dwelling.

He lived a short distance from town and I confess some of my old superstitious feelings returned when I had left the lights of the town behind. I was not sorry when I stood before my patient's residence.

In reply to my summons, an elderly woman opened the door, the moment she saw me she exclaimed:—

"Oh, Doctor, I am so glad you have come, for Mr. Jenkins is very bad indeed, worse than he has been yet."

I followed the woman up stairs and entered the patient's bed room. A terrible sight met my gaze. The invalid was a raging maniac. He was sitting upright in bed, his countenance expressing intense alarm. His eyes were rolling in his head, and appeared to be very much injected. His hands trembled and picked at the sheets with convulsive grasps. The moment he saw me he glared at me like a tiger about to spring upon his prey.

"Back! back!" he cried, "I will not come! Will no one free me from this persecutor?"

"Hush!" whispered the woman, "it is the Doctor!"

"The Doctor!" he exclaimed, with a vacant stare. "Give me brandy—brandy, I say! The room is filled with serpents—they are hissing round the bed! Take them away! For God's sake take them away!"

I approached the bed and took hold of his hand.

"Your hand is ice—cold—cold!" said he with a shudder. "Ah! see that snake, it is coming here, keep it off!"

His raving increased, and he became very violent—requiring force to keep him in bed. After a time his physical powers began to fail. Just before his existence terminated he raised himself in his bed, and in a hollow voice shrieked out:—

"Fool that you are! I will haunt you after death!"

With these words he fell exhausted on the couch—a gurgling was heard in his throat—a convulsive spasm seized his limbs, and he was dead!

I returned home very much shocked with what I had seen. It was the first fatal case of *delirium tremens* I had ever beheld, and perhaps it would be impossible to find anything more appalling or horrifying to the feelings. The last words of the poor wretch made a deep impression on my mind, and I was haunted by them for several days.

About a week after this event, I was summoned to the chief hotel of the town to meet some college chums, who were on the road to Canada, and took advantage of passing through Burlington to spend the day with me.

I dined with them, and we passed what is called a jolly time—which means, that we drank a great deal more wine than was good for us, and acted as ill became rational beings. In the course of conversation, I related to my friends the particulars of Jenkins' death, dwelling especially on the evil effects of intemperance, at the same time that I was certainly not practicing what I preached. By some turn of the conversation the subject of physical courage was introduced. The brandy had made me very eloquent.

"Well, for my part," I exclaimed. "I think it all nonsense for any one to be afraid. Nothing can be more unphilosophical than to indulge in so debasing a passion."

One of my friends looked curiously at me, and replied:—

"Whereabouts is that Jenkins buried?"

"In Mount Clare Cemetery."

"How far is that from the city?"

"About a mile."

"Well, old fellow, I will bet you the price of a champagne supper that you dare not go at twelve o'clock to-night, stick a penknife in his grave and leave it there."

"Nonsense," I replied, "I should be robbing you."

"Will you take up my bet?"

I was by this time in a state of demi-intoxication, and felt that I was equal to anything; therefore, without a moment's hesitation, I cried out, "Done!"

The moment the word had passed my lips I repented my foolish wager; but it was too late to retract. My friend looked at his watch, it was then half-past eleven. It was therefore time I should set out. It was agreed that I was to go to the grave and wait there till the cemetery clock struck twelve, with the last stroke I was to plunge my penknife into the grave and leave it there.

I took another large tumbler of brandy and water to keep up my courage, and started off on my foolhardy excursion.

Until the last house of the town was passed I got along very well, but when I reached the dark road leading to the cemetery my heart began to fail me. I whistled to distract my attention, I sang, I called out, but the only answer I received was a dull echo. It was no use. I felt my courage fast oozing away, but shame made me proceed.

I forgot to say it was a windy, blustering November night, and so dark I could scarcely see my hand before my face.

The moaning of the wind amongst the huge trees lining the road did not tend to reanimate me. I plodded on in a state of miserable, abject fear.

At length I reached the cemetery gate, and with a trembling hand swung open the massive portal.

Jenkins' grave was at the farther end of the cemetery, and I had, as it were, to walk through a whole city of graves before I reached it. How I got there I know not, for by this time I was completely unmanned, and my legs trembled under me as if they were afflicted with palsy. All the horrible incidents I had ever read in romances came back to my mind in the most vivid manner. I could just trace the forms of the white tombstones which lay in my path. Twenty times I transformed them into spectres, and fancied they were advancing toward me. More than once I turned my back to fly from the accursed spot; but a more powerful feeling than fear prevented me—namely, the dread of derision. At last I reached the spot where the drunkard was buried. I could distinctly detect the form of the newly made grave. I pulled out my penknife and held it in my hand, ready to plunge it into the grave when the clock should strike twelve.

I do not know how long I waited; it appeared an age to me. All the time I was there the wind moaned and whistled round the old tombstones, as if interrogating me as to my business there.

Suddenly a sound vibrated through the air. I gave a start, and then, even in the midst of my fears, smiled at my folly. It was only the cemetery clock striking twelve. I waited until eleven strokes had been sounded, and while the last was still ringing I stooped down and plunged the penknife deeply in the brown earth. I then attempted to rise, but great heavens! I was fixed—immovable. A hoarse sound of mocking laughter rang through the cemetery, as if it proceeded from some being deriding me. Again I made the attempt—and again something held me back. I was dragged down—down, until I lay all my length on the grave; I felt the cold earth against my face. The laughter was repeated; it was now distinct and perceptible, and grated in my ears. Perspiration poured from my brow like water, my hands trembled, and there was such an oppression about my heart that it appeared as if it must cease to beat. The last words of the miserable wretch came forcibly into my mind—"*Fool that you are, I will haunt you after death*!" It was true then, I was in his power, and spirits did revisit the earth.

While I lay down I no longer felt the invisible *thing* holding me. It must have relaxed its grasp. I began to reason with myself—could I have been deceived—was it simply a hallucination of my senses? As I asked myself these questions I began to gain a little courage. I cautiously got upon my knees and the blood began to return to my cheek, for no hand held me back now.

I remained in this position for a minute to collect my energies, and then made a movement to attain a standing posture—but oh! horror of horrors! the *thing* was holding me again. Yes—it was no dream—it was no hallucination—it was palpable, stern reality. The drag was steady, continuous—down—down again on the mound of earth which covered the body of the wretched drunkard. At this moment too the wind increased in violence; again the horrid laughter greeted my ear—it was even intensified in harshness. I could bear no more. I shrieked aloud in agony, and made desperate efforts to get free; but it was all in vain. Exhausted nature could hold out no longer—my energies failed me, and I sunk into a state of unconsciousness.

How long I lay there, I know not; but when I came to myself it was broad day-light. I made a movement to get up, but found I was held fast as before. The day-light, however, gave me courage, and I began to look around me. A single glance convinced me there was no visible spirit at work. I began to examine the ground, and the mystery was explained to me in a moment. When I had thrust my penknife into the grave, I had also passed it through the lapel of my coat! The mocking laughter I had heard was also explained by a half broken branch hanging from a tree in the vicinity. The wind every now and then caught it in such a manner that it creaked and grated against the trunk of the tree.

I was thoroughly ashamed of myself for my fears, and arose up very much crest-fallen. I made the rest of my way home, and the incident afforded me a lesson which I have never forgotten.

Leaf the Twenty-Seventh

A Terrible Night in Baltimore

A year or two ago I was dining with an old friend of mine, Jonathan Gunby. After dinner, when the wine was on the table, he asked me to relate him some of my experiences as a detective officer. Willing to do anything in my power to amuse I told him of my adventure in Dieppe, which I have already given to the reader.

"A very good story that, Brampton," said Gunby when I had finished, "but I know something better which occurred to me."

"Indeed, pray let me hear it," I replied.

He thereupon related the incident which follows, and which at my request he afterwards wrote out for me and which I now give to the reader *verbatim et literatim.*

I am no politician. I am a provision dealer—a wholesale provision dealer, doing business in New York City. Having commenced my veritable history with the above assertion, it is necessary that I should inform the reader how it was that I was a member of the New York delegation to the Democratic Convention held in the city of Baltimore last year.

One evening in the latter part of May; I was seated with my wife in our pretty house in Eighth Street, enjoying a fragrant cup of tea, for if there is one thing that I'm a good judge of it is tea. My wife had been shopping, and while I was sipping my Hyson flavored with Orange Pekoe, she was showing me her purchases. She was expatiating on a "love of a bonnet," when we were both startled by a violent ring at the bell; and in a minute or two afterwards a servant entered, informing me that Mr. Lawrence Ardew wished to see me immediately. As Ardew was a particular friend of mine, I immediately ordered him to be admitted.

"Gunby." said Ardew, as soon as he had paid his respects to my wife. (I should have told you before that my name is Jonathan Gunby), "Gunby, I want you to do me a great favor."

"What is it, my dear fellow?" I replied. I could afford to be affectionate, for I knew that Ardew was too rich to want money.

"You know I am a politician," said Ardew.

"I know you are," I returned, "and much good has it done you. To my certain knowledge you have not received a cent benefit from it yet; on the other hand you have spent a good many hundred dollars."

"Just wait till —— is elected president, and then you will see what you will see; but, that is not the question. I am a delegate to the Baltimore Convention, and I want you to act as my substitute."

"What!" I cried, jumping up from my chair in excitement, "I, Jonathan Gunby, wholesale provision dealer, act as a member of a political convention! Never, my dear friend, never!"

"But you must. I will pay all expenses, and the trip will do you good. I have noticed that you seem to be a good deal thinner than you used to be a change is the very thing for you. Baltimore is a beautiful city. The fact is, I have an important law suit coming on, and it is utterly impossible that I can leave New York. You must do this favor for me, my dear Gunby."

"But, Ardew, I never attended a political meeting in my life," I replied, somewhat softened by the fact that all my expenses would be paid. "I should make a blockhead of myself, for I know nothing of the rules and regulations of such assemblies."

"You don't want to know anything; all that you have to do is to vote through thick and thin for ——."

"But I don't like the man."

"You have nothing to do with that. I do like him and you will be voting for me."

"You are right—I forgot that."

"Jonathan shall not go to that awful rowdy city, Baltimore," said my wife. "He will be killed by the 'Plug Uglies,' 'Blood Tubs' or 'Black Snakes.' It's not safe to walk the streets there. I'll never consent to his going."

"You need have no fear on that head, madam," said Ardew; "they have got a new police there, and Baltimore is now one of the quietest cities in the Union."

I need not detail any more of the conversation, suffice it to say, that Ardew persuaded me to act in his place, and a hint of a handsome present from the monumental city, so modified my wife that she too gave her consent.

On the appointed day, provided with the necessary vouchers, I started on my journey—having first faithfully promised my wife that I would not venture in the streets of Baltimore after dark. I shall not detail the particulars of my journey; were I to do so, I might describe how crowded we were; and how annoyed by a squalling infant that it was utterly impossible to silence; how we were delayed in the crossing of the Susquehanna by some accident to the ferryboat; how everybody talked politics until I was perfectly sick of it; how I tried to read, but could not on account of the perfect Babel around me; how I endeavored to make fun of the boys who sold apples, and had the laugh turned against me by those youthful venders of that wholesome fruit. All this, and a great deal more, I might tell, but as every traveler goes through the same experiences it would only be repeating an old story.

We reached Baltimore at last, and I was immediately driven to Barnum's Hotel. I had some difficulty in making my way up to the clerk's counter, the hill was so crowded with people.

"All full, sir," said the gentlemanly clerk, as I pulled the book towards me to enter my name.

There was no help for it; I went to the Gillmore House, and received the same reply. It was the same with the Eutaw, the Howard House and half a dozen other hotels. It was getting dark, and my case began to get desperate. I began to think that I should have to sleep in the hack all night.

"Try Old Tom, Bill," said a friend to the hackman, who saw my dilemma.

"There are only third and fourth rate inns there," said the driver, "and perhaps the gentleman would not like to lodge there for a night?"

"Anywhere that I can get a bed, my good fellow," I returned. "It is no use being particular at such a time as this."

The horses' heads were turned round, and we proceeded down Baltimore Street over a bridge which spanned a muddy stream of water, called Jones's Falls, I believe. We then plunged into a mass of intricate, narrow streets, and at last stopped before the door of a very ordinary looking tavern. It bore a nondescript looking sign which I was told represented a golden angel, by which name the tavern was known.

I entered and made my stereotyped inquiry whether I could have a bed there for the night. The landlord, a thick, burly looking man with a gleam of latent humor in his face, shook his head and repeated to me the hateful words—"all full."

I turned to go away, but was recalled by the voice of the host.

"Would you mind sharing a bed with another party?" said he.

I glanced out of doors; it was quite dark, and a cold wind had arisen from the north.

"If there is no help for it, I suppose I must," I replied, "although to tell you the truth, it is by no means agreeable to me," and I inwardly heaped denunciations on Ardew's head for persuading me to be his substitute.

"Your bedfellow is a quiet fellow when he is asleep—although I must say he is rather violent when annoyed. He sleeps very soundly, and all you have to do is to be careful not to awake him. He has been in bed some time."

I must make a humiliating confession to the reader; I am not a brave man. I have often tried to persuade myself that I am, but stern truth compels me to state that a greater coward does not exist than myself. The landlord's description of my bedfellow was anything but assuring, and I was on the point of declining, when the proprietor of the Golden Angel, no doubt reading what was transpiring in my mind, exclaimed:

"You are not afraid, are you?"

"Afraid! I should think not, indeed," I returned, for I was too much a coward to brave being thought one. "I accept your offer of half a bed. Bring some brandy and water and a cigar."

I sat down at one of the little tables in the bar-room, and puffing away at my cigar I tried to persuade myself that I was very jolly. It was a miserable attempt, however. I had previously supped at a restaurant in a more modern part of the city. After my cigar was finished I asked to be shown to my chamber. The landlord took upon himself the task of being my conductor, and I followed him up a narrow, rickety staircase. We kept on ascending until we reached the top of the house, when we entered a moderately sized room, but much cleaner than I had expected to find it. The ceiling was very low, and inclined in front to the slope of the roof. The apartment contained but one bed, which was placed against the wall near the door. At the opposite end of the chamber was a table, placed between two windows which looked out on the roof.

The landlord placed the lamp on the table, and I noticed that he shielded the light with his hand as he passed near the bed.

"Be sure and don't take the light near him," whispered the proprietor of the Golden Angel; "nothing wakes him sooner than that. You see, I don't know how he might like my putting another man with him; and he's a very ugly customer when he's riled, I can tell you."

"I shall be careful," I replied.

"That's right! Good night," he whispered, and left the room.

He had no sooner gone than I cautiously sat down, taking care not to make the least noise, I then calmly surveyed my position. It was certainly not a very enviable one. According to the landlord's account, my companion for the night was anything but an amiable character. If I should chance to awaken him, I knew not what might occur. He might assault me dangerously before I could enter into any explanation. I half resolved to pass the night in the chair, and not retire to bed at all. But it was one of those old-fashioned, high-backed chairs, and made such an uncomfortable seat that I soon got tired. I then ventured to glance round the room. My eyes naturally fell on the bed. There was one thing that consoled me, my companion appeared to be in a deep sleep, for he did not even move. I could see the ridge made by his feet at the end of the bed, and that was all. I also noticed that the bed was a very large one. The man who had possession of it lay near the wall, and there was plenty of space between him and the outside for me to lie without touching him. I screwed my courage up, and began to undress—but I suddenly remembered the landlord's words, that the stranger was "an ugly customer when he was riled," which made me desist. The thought struck me that I might manage to lie on the floor, but a moment's examination settled that question in the negative, for the floor was entirely bare, and the wind blew very cold through the wide chinks in the planking. I cast my eyes up to the ceiling, and noticed for the first time that a heavy beam studded with numerous hooks ran through the apartment; but as I was not a bird and could not perch there, this discovery was but of little use to me.

Half an hour passed away in this state of indecision. I stole cautiously to one of the windows, and gazed on the beautiful city bathed in the light of a full moon. How quiet and calm everything looked.

But the air felt fresh and cold, and I closed the window and resumed my seat on the chair. I then found myself wondering what a vocation my friend in bed followed. I had forgotten to ask the landlord. I suddenly cast my eyes on a heap of clothes which lay on a trunk, covered over with a handkerchief, no doubt belonging to the sleeper. My curiosity got the better of my politeness, and before I scarcely knew what I was about, I found myself examining his apparel. The handkerchief which covered them was a coarse cotton one, and his clothes were of a coarse homespun, and were such as are usually worn by drovers. My companion then was evidently a drover—a rough class of men who usually stand upon very little ceremony.

Partially undressed as I was, I began to feel very cold—but before I ventured into bed I determined to try an experiment to see if the drover slept soundly or not. I took off one of my boots, and holding it up let it fall to the floor. I had taken the precaution to leave the bedroom door open, so that I could make a run for it if necessary. I fixed my eyes on the bed as I let the boot fall. The drover was evidently a sound sleeper, for, although the noise made was considerable, he did not make the slightest motion. This decided me, and I hastily finished undressing and crept into bed.

Of course I was very careful not to touch my companion. I do not know how long I lay awake, but the novelty of my situation drove sleep from my eyelids for some time. By degrees, however, the strangeness of my position wore off. I felt reassured by my bedfellow's sound sleep, and the gentle murmuring of the breeze outside caused me to follow his example.

I have no idea how long I slept before I commenced to dream. I suddenly, however, thought that my companion woke up, and sat upright in bed; that he glared around him, and at last his eyes fell upon me. He then uttered a terrible cry and threw himself upon me. In spite of my natural cowardice I saw that if I did not struggle I should be killed. I thought I seized him by the throat, and tightening my grasp, I saw him getting black in the face. His hands fell powerless by his side, a smothered groan escaped him, but still I pressed his throat tighter, and tighter—his face grew blacker and blacker.

In agony of fear I awoke, and what was my horror and dismay to find that my hand was really pressing my companion's throat! He did not move nor stir, and his body felt as cold as ice.

"Good God!" I exclaimed, aloud. "Can he be dead?"

I jumped out of bed. Morning had dawned, although the sun had not yet risen. I rushed to the window and pulled back the curtain. I then ran to the bed again and looked at my companion. My worst fears were realized.

He was dead—black in the face—strangled in my sleep!

I shall not attempt to describe my sensations at this horrid spectacle. My body was bathed in a cold perspiration, my hands trembled, and for a few moments I believe I was bereft of my senses. I recovered by degrees—but it was only to realize in a more acute degree the horrors of my situation. There lay my victim—and I was a murderer! My trial, conviction and the hideous gallows all passed in rapid review before me. What defence could I make? Who would believe me? I sat down, buried my face in my hands, and sobbed like a child. My wife, my own comfortable home, should I ever see them again?

What was to be done? Should I arouse the house and make a clean breast of it? But what could I say? Tell them I had killed a man in my sleep? Not a soul would believe the story, Could I effect my escape? Impossible—the crime would be discovered before I could leave the city, and I should be arrested—and then the law would take its course and I should be hanged by the neck until I was dead.

"Hanged by the neck!" Yes, that would be my fate. As this terrible thought crossed my mind, I cast my eyes round the chamber, and they fell up on the beam with the hooks in it. From thence they wandered to the handkerchief covering the dead man's clothes. A means of safety suddenly suggested itself to my mind. Suppose I could make it appear that the man had committed suicide. I determined to put it in execution.

I took the dead man's handkerchief and advanced to the corpse with a great deal of repugnance, but with more courage than I could have anticipated, my own fearful situation no doubt animated me to an extent I should never otherwise have dreamed of.

I made a noose in the handkerchief, and slipped it over the dead man's neck. I then lifted the body out of bed, and standing on a chair fastened the other end of the handkerchief to a hook in the beam. I now let the body go, and I it swung in space!

I jumped into bed, and shut my eyes to close the horrid sight from my gaze. I determined to wait there until somebody should come into the room, and then pretend that I knew nothing at all about it, but that the man must have got up in the night and hanged himself.

I lay quaking and trembling for over an hour. It grew broad daylight. I felt the sun shining directly on the bed, but I dare not open my eyes for fear that I should encounter the dangling corpse. Suddenly I heard the steps of two men on the stairs. They appeared to be carrying something heavy between them.

The long anticipated moment was approaching. In a few seconds more they would discover the body. My life depended in a great degree upon their opinion. If they were deceived by my *ruse,* others might be also.

The door opened, and two men entered the chamber, placing something heavy on the floor.

"Well, I'm blessed if the man hasn't bin and hanged himself again," exclaimed a voice, which I recognized to be the landlord's.

"By golly! that's true," said the other man. "No, I see how it is, the stranger found out the trick you played on him, and not liking the idea of sleeping with a corpse, he tucked him up there to get him out of the way."

"You're right," replied the landlord; "well, he's a cool 'un anyhow, and would you believe it, last night I thought he was a coward?—that only shows how easy it is to be mistaken in people. And now he sleeps as sound as a church; let's be careful not to wake him."

I breathed freely; for I immediately understood the whole matter. The landlord had put me to sleep with a dead man. I heard them take down the body and put it into a coffin—for it was that they had brought with them. They carried it away, and I was left to myself. With my mind thus relieved I fell asleep, and enjoyed two hours delicious slumber. I then got up, dressed myself, and proceeded cooly down stairs.

"Good morning," said I to the landlord, who was behind the bar.

"Good morning, sir," he replied sheepishly; "I hope you slept well."

"Splendidly," I returned; my bedfellow gave me some trouble at first, but I soon got rid of him."

"I know you did," returned mine host, with a knowing wink. "Well, I must say you are the coolest chap I ever saw."

Not another word passed between us with reference to the affair. I afterwards learned from the conversation of people while I was at breakfast, that my companion for the night was a drover, who, having made a ruinous speculation in cattle, had committed suicide by hanging himself in the chamber the night before.

I left the Golden Angel that morning, having obtained quarters at Barnum's Hotel. I went to the Convention, voted six hundred times for ——, and returned home, having given full satisfaction to Mr. Ardew.

I told my adventure to my friends—not as I have told it to you, reader, but with the same construction that the landlord of the Golden Angel put upon it. Everybody thought that I had displayed extraordinary coolness and intrepidity. There is one thing, however, to which I have fully made up my mind, and that is, I will never attend another political convention as long as I live.

Leaf the Twenty-Eighth

Magnetic Influence

(I am indebted to Doctor Macfarland for the following strange story.—J. B.)

I am an old man now. My hair was is silvered with gray years ago. My days on earth cannot be many. My memory begins to fail me. Events which occurred in the early part of my life are fading from my mind. And yet, strange to say, every now and then recollection appears to be lighted up in my brain, as it memory were not extinct, but only slept. Perhaps the vehicle for the expression of the thoughts of the soul is becoming dull—age having impaired its usefulness.

Yesterday I was reading in a French journal an account of some recent extraordinary chemical discoveries. How strange it is that a word will sometimes call up a whole flood of reminiscences which have entirely passed from the mind! It would seem as if memory is something material imbedded in the brain, and that is only reproduced when another thought enters the organ, and acts upon it in some subtle manner. Of course this is purely an hypothesis incapable of proof; but certain it is, that reading about the recent chemical discoveries in France, awoke in my mind the recollection of an event which transpired many years ago, and in which I acted a subordinate part. Years ago I almost determined to make the matter public, but the fear that the improbability of the history would convey a reflection on my veracity, restrained me. With age has come obtuseness, and I care nothing about the opinion of the world, now. I know what I relate is true, and this is sufficient for me. Nor shall I attempt to explain the extraordinary phenomena of which I have to speak. I have no doubt a natural explanation could be given, but I am too old now to attempt it. Without further digression, I will relate what I have to tell.

Thirty-five years ago I was practicing as a physician in the State of Virginia. It was a rustic spot, and in spring and autumn it was really beautiful. The village on all sides was surrounded by majestic trees, which had braved time for many a year, and which every summer embedded the white cottages in a mantle of greenery. This village boasted of its country tavern, its parsonage, its blacksmith's shop, its country store, and other buildings usually found in such places. But the great pride of the place was a large building, which went by the name of the Grange.

It was a very old mansion—having been erected in the days of the early settlers of the State. It was situated about one mile from the village in question, and was at the same time the pride and fear of the inhabitants. It was an Elizabethan structure—rambling, large, and commodious. One side of it was completely embedded with ivy, and the windows—around which the evergreen had been trimmed—resembled paths cut through the foliage. The front was gray and discolored; the windows were small, gothic, sloped, and latticed. It was situated on a beautiful eminence, so that it was a conspicuous object for miles. The Grange was surrounded on all sides by a species of park, which extended at the back of the dwelling for several acres, and was terminated by a beautiful stream of water, which rippled gentle music over its pebbled bed all the year round, excepting a short time when it congealed under the baleful eye of the dread king of winter. The rooms were lofty, the staircases wide, and the oak, so plentifully used in its internal construction, was almost black with age.

When I first went to live in the village of Daughton, the Grange was occupied. The owner had lived in it for years, but had resided most of the time in New York. One day, however, the whole village was in a state of commotion by the arrival of workmen, who had come to put the Grange in a condition of thorough repair. A hundred rumors were immediately afloat, but which all eventually were absorbed in one report—namely, that Mr. Templeman was about to be married and would bring his bride home to his family mansion. This rumor proved to be a correct one, for in a short time the house was repaired, the old-fashioned furniture was dusted, the cobwebs were removed from the picture-gallery, a bevy of black servants were installed there from one of Mr. Templeman's Southern plantations, the building was declared to be ready, and it received the owner, and his bride.

The village was immediately all excitement. Who had seen the bride? Was she pretty? Was she young? Did she seem happy? These, and a hundred other questions were asked, but no one could give a satisfactory reply to any one of them. The fact was, no one had seen her face, for she was closely veiled when she arrived.

Days, weeks, months passed away, I and Mr. Templeman had never been seen, excepting by persons in his own household. It was noticed when he first returned to the home of his father he appeared to be in excellent, indeed, it might be called robust health; but by degrees a change came over him; he grew pale and visibly declined. His eyes, too, had a strange expression about them; usually they had a dull, dreamy look,very different from the light of intelligence which shone in them when he first came home; but then again they would suddenly lighten up in the most surprising manner, and he would then seem to be bewildered, and scarcely knew what he was doing.

One day he called upon me at my house. I was not burthened with many patients at that time, and was generally at home.

"Dr. McFarland," said he to me, "I wish to consult you respecting myself. I have something the matter with me, it is undermining my health, but what it is I know not. All that I do know, is that I am getting weaker and weaker every day."

"What are your symptoms, Mr. Templeman?"

"Well, doctor, to tell you the truth, I don't know myself. I only am aware of the fact, that I am declining every day. I cannot sleep at night; I lay and toss about for hours together. I do not suppose I get more than three or four hours sleep on an average."

"To what can you ascribe this want of sleep—have you no mental trouble?"

"None at all.'"

"Is your mind fixed on any one particular pursuit?"

"I indulge a good deal in chemical experiments, and devote a considerable portion of my time in investigating that beautiful science, but this soothes, rather than irritates me."

I examined my patient, and found that every organ of the body was in a normal condition. The heart and lungs were perfectly healthy; digestion was good; in fact, it was impossible for me, after an hour's careful investigation, to discover the slightest vestige of disease; and yet he was evidently failing; he was losing flesh, and if some remedy were not discovered, he must ultimately die.

"Mr. Templeman," I exclaimed, after I had finished my examination, "your affection is evidently one of the nervous system. You must———"

While I was yet speaking he rose suddenly from his chair, and his eyes, which before had been dull and heavy, suddenly grew brilliant as two diamonds.

"Excuse me," said he, advancing towards the door; "SHE is calling me. I must go."

"She!"I exclaimed. "Who do you mean? No one has called you."

"My wife!" he replied, and rushed out of the house.

I was very much astonished at this strange conduct, and was at a loss how to account for it. I immediately followed him to the door; there was not a soul in sight. My first impression was that his brain was affected.

The next day I received a message from the Grange, requesting my immediate presence, as Mr. Templeman was seriously ill. I obeyed the summons at once, and was shown into a very large bed chamber, the heavy old-fashioned furniture of which contrasted strangely with the modern carpet with which the floor was covered. On a stately four-post bedstead reclined my patient. His eyes were wild and haggard, and his cheek was as pale as a corpse.

"Doctor," said he, as soon as he saw me, "I am glad you have come. I am, sick—very sick."

I examined his pulse, and strange to say, I found that it was quite natural; his respiration too was quite easy, and had it not been for his wild gaze and pallid face, I should not have thought there was anything the matter with him. I asked him a few questions, to which he responded in a natural manner.

"You appear to be suffering very much," I exclaimed, after he had replied to all my enquiries—"is there any fear oppressing your heart?"

"Doctor, you are right. You have guessed it—there is fear oppressing my heart—one that haunts me night and day—a demon that never quits my side—riding or walking, awake or asleep—it is my constant guest—it is the demon of self-destruction!"

"Self-destruction! what mean you?"

"I mean that I am haunted day and night with the idea of suicide. I feel an almost irresistible impulse to lay violent hands upon myself."

"Have you no reason for this feeling?"

"None at all. I am wealthy, enjoy every comfort. I——"

At that moment his features assumed the same expression they had done the day before in my office.

"Oh! God of Heaven!" he exclaimed, pointing towards the door; "she has just left her room—she advances along the corridor—she stops to adjust her hair—she comes to the door—she is here!"

With that he gave a shriek and fell back on the bed insensible. At this moment the door opened and his wife entered the room. I had not time at this moment to even glance at her; my whole attention was occupied by my now unconscious patient. In a very short time I succeeded in restoring him to life, in which office I was assisted by a pair of milk-white hands, which, when they touched mine, sent a thrill through my whole system.

After we had restored him to consciousness, he fell into a deep slumber, and Mrs. Templeman beckoned me out into another room. It was now for the first time that I had an opportunity of examining the woman about whom report had been so busy. She led the way into the picture gallery, and we sat down on a sofa. When I gazed on Mrs. Templeman, a strange feeling which I could not account for took possession of me. A mist at first appeared to float before my eyes, through which I could see the dim form of my companion. This, however, cleared away by degrees, and I could gaze upon her without emotion. She was gorgeously beautiful, such beauty as I have never seen before nor since.

Her hair was as black as the raven's plume, her eyes were intensely black, but they were large, lustrous and piercing in their size. They seemed to enter one's very soul, and when she looked straight at me,

I felt deprived of all power or strength. She was of tall and commanding stature, but her form was gracefully moulded. Her skin was as white as the purest alabaster, her neck and shoulders might have served as a model for the Titan Venus; her cheek was tinged with the hue of perfect health, and her long eye-lashes gave a peculiar expression to her face which it is difficult to describe. It must not be supposed from my description of Mrs. Templeman, that I experienced anything like admiration for her beauty. It was entirely the reverse, and even now when I try to analyze my feelings I cannot do it. I felt at the same time attracted and repelled by her presence. It was certain when she gazed on me I felt the influence much more than at other times. When she appeared to be thinking of something else. I could look upon her and be in her presence without the slightest emotion.

"What do you think of Mr. Templeman's case?" said she in a voice so peculiar, that I could compare it to nothing else than the notes given forth by Aeolian harp.

I told her my opinion, namely, that I considered he was suffering from some nervous disorder, and that a change of scene would be more likely to restore him to health again than anything else. She fully agreed with me, and promised to exert her influence to make him take a trip to Paris. After we had discussed this matter fully, I was attracted by the pictures and stood up to examine them. I walked from one end of the gallery to the other. When at the lower end I was struck with a full length portrait of Oliver Cromwell, but through the canvas were the distinct mark of two bullet holes. I thought it rather strange, and turned round to Mrs. Templeman, and made some inquiry in reference to it. I fancied she appeared confused, for she changed the conversation. In a short time after that I left, promising to return the next day.

The next morning I was there early, and was immediately shown into my patient's bed chamber. I found him something better, but very weak and nervous. I had reflected a great deal on his case, since the previous day, but could only come to the conclusion that his wife's presence had a mysterious influence over him; but how, or in what way this could occur I did not attempt to explain. I resolved to converse with him on the subject.

"Mr. Templeman," I began, "Mrs. Templeman's presence appears to have a strange effect upon your nervous system?"

"You are right, Doctor," he replied, "she is killing me."

"Killing you! what do you mean?"

"I repeat it, she is killing me, not by poison or by any physical means, but simply by the influence of her mind."

"The influence of her mind?"

"Yes; my mind is completely subjugated to hers; what she wills I must do. I am perfectly satisfied if she were to will me to put my hand into that fire, I should be compelled to do it."

"You can scarcely be serious in what you say."

"Alas it is only too true. Listen to me while I tell you something, for I feel to keep this matter secret any longer would be death to me. I met Mrs. Templeman in New York for the first time some three years ago. At that period she was married. I was introduced to her, and was struck with her superb beauty. I lost sight of her for three years, but when I met her again she was a widow. I was attracted by her magnificent appearance, and married her. I had not been married a week before I was conscious that there was some strange influence at work with my mind. Whenever my wife looked fixedly at me, thoughts and feelings would arise which did not seem to emanate from myself. It was some little time before I found out the exact truth of the matter, but when I did discover it—when I did find out that I was a slave—that I no longer possessed will, mind, or power, a terrible feeling of desire to rid myself of life, haunted me. With this feeling I have contended for months, and I find each day it becomes stronger and stronger. That it will ultimately end by my committing suicide—if this spell is not broken—I am perfectly satisfied."

"What makes you so certain on this point?"

"I will tell you. I find Mrs. Templeman has been married twice before."

"Indeed!"

"Yes, and both of her husbands committed suicide!"

There was something very strange and fearful in this revelation. When I remembered the influence this strange woman had over myself, I felt my blood turn to ice.

"But does she not treat you kindly?" I asked.

"Kindly—yes. The same kindness that a serpent shows the bird when he is sure of his prey. He does not attack him, but remains at the bottom of the tree, until the bird falls directly into his mouth.

"Do you suppose this influence is voluntary on her part?"

"I know it is. When her mind is occupied with something else, she loses influence over me, and for that time I feel myself a man again. It is at such moments that an irresistible desire to kill her rises up in my mind. I have thought of a thousand different ways— sometimes it is poison—at others I will slay her while she sleeps—but she paralyzes me in a moment by her will."

"Hush, my dear sir, such thoughts as these will lead me to suspect that your brain is disordered."

"But it is not, doctor. I thought I had effected my purpose the other night. I was in my study, reading, when I fancied I heard voices in the picture gallery. It was near midnight, and my first idea was that robbers had broken in. I took my gun, and accompanied by my two dogs, I entered the picture gallery. I saw, as plainly, as I see you now, my wife stretched on the floor, and the form of her late husband bending over her in a threatening attitude. Although I had seen him only twice in my life, I knew him perfectly. The desire to free myself from my cursed thraldom was too powerful. I raised the gun to my shoulder and fired. When the smoke cleared away there was no one to be seen; and almost immediately afterwards my wife came running into the gallery by the same door that I had entered, to inquire what was the matter. I am now inclined to think that the whole was a hallucination. The next day I examined the spot to which I had pointed when I discharged the gun. I found that the bullet had pierced the portrait of Oliver Cromwell."

"You are right in your supposition; that must have been an optical illusion."

"I suppose so; but what course do you recommend me to pursue?"

I then told him that he had better at once leave the country, and recommended Paris to him as the place where he would most likely meet with persons and events that would restore his nervous system to a healthy condition again. He agreed to the proposal, and in a week he started off to New York, and left by a packet sailing from that city to Havre. A week passed on without anything occurring, when one day I received a message from the Grange, requesting my immediate presence there to see Mrs. Templeman. I thought by the urgency of the message that she must be very sick. I was, therefore, very much surprised to find her sitting in her boudoir, apparently in perfect health.

"Doctor," said she, as soon as I entered the room, "I have not sent for you professionally. I wish to consult you on another matter."

I bowed, but made no reply.

"You are aware," said she, "that my husband has devoted himself a great deal to chemical pursuits. For days together he has been at work in the vault underneath this house; especially was this the case a few days before he left for Paris. Now I will confess to you that I have an irresistible curiosity to know what he has been doing there. At the same time I am not free from a species of superstitious dread about descending into that cold, damp, dark, place. Will you examine the vault for me?"

"Did Mr. Templeman express a desire that no one should enter it during his absence?"

"He gave the most strict orders to that effect and especially begged *me* not to visit the vault. It is that very fact which makes me so desirous of seeing it. I should never have thought of it, if he had not been so earnest in the matter."

"Madam," I replied, "I regret that I cannot comply with your request. Mr. Templeman's wishes must be law with me."

She tried in vain to combat my resolutions, but I was determined, and soon after left her, anything but pleased with me.

The next evening a report was current in the village that Mrs. Templeman had suddenly disappeared, that she had not been seen since the evening before, when she retired to bed. Search was immediately made in every direction for her, but it was all fruitless. It was then that I suddenly thought about the vault, and suggested that some one should search it, relating the particulars of the conversation I had had with her on the subject.

The necessary search was made, and to the horror of every one she was found on the floor of the vault stone dead. There was no wound visible, and a jury of inquest returned a verdict of "Death by the visitation of God." the vault contained nothing particular, and there were certainly no evidences of any occupation followed by Mr. Templeman there. A few bottles and vials containing chemicals was all that could be found. I noticed, however, that there was a strong sulphurous smell plainly apparent.

This sad termination of the life of such a beautiful woman was a nine days wonder, and a vast variety of opinions were given on the subject. By degrees, however, it ceased to be talked about, and in a month or two it seemed to be entirely forgotten.

It was about three months after the occurrence that I was seated in my little parlor one night, resting myself after a long country ride. I was informed by my black boy that a gentleman wished to see me. I gave orders that he should be admitted, and almost immediately afterwards Mr. Templeman entered the room, but oh! so changed that I scarcely knew him. He was wasted to a perfect shadow, his arms appeared to hang helpless by his side; his eyes were sunk deep in their sockets, but still shone with an unearthly glare; his features were pinched and his face was as colorless as that of a corpse; in fact, his whole appearance was more that of a living corpse than anything else. He sat down, and for a moment or two he did not utter a word. At last in a hoarse whisper he exclaimed:

"She is dead!"

I proceeded to condole with him at his wife's sudden decease, but he interrupted me.

"I murdered her—I killed her; her blood is on my soul! It has been eating into my heart ever since that fatal night. I have not slept for weeks."

"Compose yourself, sir," I replied, "you accuse yourself wrongfully, she died while you were on the road to Paris."

"True, but I killed her notwithstanding. Listen. I will tell you how. You are aware that I have been devoting a considerable time to chemical experiments. In the course of my investigations I discovered an explosive substance which would ignite at the slightest friction, being even more explosive than fulminating mercury, but it also possessed this property, namely, that when it exploded any person near it would be, struck dead, as if from a stroke of lightning, and no mark or wound would show how the person had met his death. The truth is, that it kills through the nervous system. I prepared some of this terrible chemical and placed it in the vault in such a manner that whoever should open the door would explode the compound and must meet with certain death. I then told my wife on no account to visit the vault, but I knew that the very fact of my telling her this would make her do it. You know the result—I am a murderer!"

I tried to soothe him as well as I could. Suddenly he rose up in his chair; his eyes assumed a fearful expression. Stretching forth his hand he exclaimed:

"She calls me! From her cold, dark grave she calls me! I cannot resist—I must go."

And he fell back again into the chair—dead!

Leaf the Twenty-Ninth

A Story of a Pack of Cards

In the beginning of the month of June, 18—, I left New York in pursuit of a criminal among the Allegheny Mountains. The weather was very beautiful and all nature decked in her complete spring apparel, offered a thousand charms to a traveller's gaze.

The Baltimore and Ohio Railroad was not completed at that time, and I made my journey from Baltimore on horseback. After a few days' journey I reached the foot of the Alleghenies, and commenced my ascent. The scenery through which I passed was wild and grand. Here I saw immense forests in which, perhaps, the foot of man had never trod, and mountain streams forcing their way through precipitous gorges next attracted my attention.

One day I rode five miles without meeting a living soul. Towards evening I reached the hut of a wood-cutter. He received me cordially enough, and offered me a bed, but he knew so little of the country that he could not direct me where to find a shelter for the next night.

The next morning I started at hazard, keeping beside a mountain river as long as I could. At last I left its banks, and after continuing my journey for some hours I fancied I entered into a less wild-looking country.

Already the day began to decline, the setting sun was enveloped in a cloud of gray vapor, and I felt one of those melancholy moods stealing over me which a solitary traveller at the close of day frequently experiences.

Every now and then I cast uneasy glances around me, for I had no idea where I was going. At last I perceived a path before me. My heart beat with hope. It was doubtless one of those paths that are often to be seen through the mountains—paths which always lead the traveller to some hospitable roof.

Soon the lowing of a cow changed my hope into a certainty, and a turn in the path brought to my view a wreath of smoke, and another turn brought me in front of a charming dwelling, surrounded by a carefully kept garden, and with well cultivated fields all around it.

It was a much superior habitation to what is generally met with in the mountains, and although it had evidently been built for many years, it was the very perfection of neatness. The front of it was entirely covered with honey-suckle, through which the little Gothic windows peeped. The interior was in harmony with the exterior. Everything bespoke cleanliness and care; it is true the furniture was old-fashioned, but it was none the worse for wear.

In the sitting-room two muskets were suspended against the wall, some powder flasks and several game bags, and above these as if it were the only object worthy of that honor, was a pack of cards fastened to the wall. This singular ornament was fixed there by a large nail which penetrated the entire pack, and the black head of which rested on the ace of hearts.

Before the door of the house sat an old man about eighty years of age; his white hair full in curls around his shoulders, and his whole exterior revealed health and strength. His face was nearly free from wrinkles, and the natural gaiety of his disposition was reflected in his blue eyes as well as in every movement of his lips. He was one of those men, the winter of whose life is so blessed by heaven that it is calm and serene.

The old man's family consisted of three persons—his only son, a man of forty years of age, his son's wife and their child. The latter about ten years of age, resembling neither his father nor his grandfather. Instead of their blue eyes, his were black; his hair was long, silky, and very dark.

I was received at the door by the old man, who bade me welcome, and invited me to enter. I accepted his invitation without any ceremony, but with that easy nonchalance which a sense of superiority always imparts; but my pride received a great reproof when, having entered the cosy sitting-room of the family I found myself in the presence of the mistress of the house.

She resembled so little the woman I expected to see in such a place, that I bowed to her quite timidly. Instead of a course country-woman, with red cheeks and homely garments, there stood before me a lady, in every sense of the word. Her face was pale, her eyes black, and she was excessively beautiful, not so much from the regularity of her features, as from a nameless grace which ornamented every action.

The old man's son presented her to me as his wife, and I learned that her name was Rachael. She spoke but little, but followed with interest the conversation entered into by her father-in-law, her husband and myself. Every word that fell from her lips revealed a superior education. Her husband listened to her with evident respect, often interrogating her with a look, and then changing the common-place expression which he had uttered into a more delicate and agreeable phrase.

The child sat on a stool at its mother's feet. He was eagerly reading a book, every now and then raising his eyes to his mother's face with a look beaming with love and affection. There was something touching in the picture. The two men evidently watched him with emotion. It is scarcely necessary for me to state that such a strange spectacle vividly excited my curiosity. I suspected there was some mysterious history concealed in all this, and I was very anxious to have my host tell it me.

After supper we gathered round the hearth on which a bright hickory fire was burning. I endeavored to amuse the company by recounting my travelling adventures, and while doing so my eyes wandered about from one object to another, and fell by chance on the pack of cards, I have referred to above. I thought at first it was a painting, but rising to satisfy myself, I saw it was really a pack of cards, and the nail which fixed them to the wall was a real nail. The discoloration of the edges of the cards by smoke was a sufficient proof that they had been there for a long time.

"You have a singular ornament there on the wall," said I, smiling on my host.

No one replied to my question, nor my smile; a cloud of melancholy on the contrary spread over all their countenances, and a moment afterwards the young wife disappeared. When she had gone her husband approached me.

"It is in truth," said he, "a singular ornament. I will tell you the history of it after prayers."

Rachael returned with a Bible in her hand, which she placed on the table before the old man. Such was the daily custom of the house. The old man opened the book at the page marked by his spectacles, then put on the latter and read a chapter. After which they all kneeled down, and he prayed in a loud voice. A few moments afterwards, in the midst of a deep silence, Rachael rose, took her son by the hand, and having wished us good night, returned to her chamber. The old man soon followed her example, and I was left alone with my host, James Carew, for such was his name.

Without any preamble whatever, he pointed to the cards, and told me the following history, which I give in his own language:

~

There is a history attached to those cards (he commenced) which I like to tell to every young man who is about entering the world. You may think it strange, but I look upon them in the light of a Bible, for when I see them it recalls to my mind all the events connected with them, and I fancy I hear a chapter from that holy book which my father read a few minutes ago.

It is twelve years ago since those cards had such a marked influence on my existence, I must therefore, go back to that period. I was not much different then than I am to-day, for I have changed but very little. Perhaps I had more life and vivacity at that time, for the truth is my spirits were always good, rivaling in this respect my dear old father.

We lived in the same house that we do now, without, however, enjoying the same easy circumstances. I was alone with my father, hunting, fishing, and the culture of our farm was sufficient for our wants. An honest laborer, with his wife and two sons, assisted us on the farm. They lived, and still live, near us. We worked hard, and certainly made but little, but our expenses never exceeded our resources, and we enjoyed such robust health that the visit of a physician under our roof was an unknown event. In short, we had every reason to be happy, and to thank Providence for its kindness to us.

One hot July day I mounted horse and proceeded to the little town of Grafton, for the purpose of making some necessary purchases. I executed my commissions, and was returning home, when plaintive and distant cries reached my ears. I pushed on my horse towards the spot from which they proceeded.

About three or four hundred yards off I perceived, in the midst of some low shrubbery, a man calling for help. His horse was extended on the ground, and he was on his knees near the animal, rubbing one of its legs with his hand. Not far off lay a dead rattlesnake. I understood in a moment what had occured. I leapt from my horse and approached the stranger, to assist him if it were possible. But the poison had already conquered, and in spite of all our effort the poor beast expired.

At that moment I examined the stranger attentively. He was a man passed the middle age, with very strongly-marked features, and with very black hair; his eyes were full of fire, and they had such a piercing look about them that I felt myself transfixed by his gaze. His face was pale, and his dress in the height of fashion; he carried a gold watch fastened to his vest by an expensive chain. In his hand was a gold snuff-box, fashioned in the form of a shell. The loss of his horse did not appear to affect him much, and he received my expressions of condolence very coolly.

"Pshaw!"said he, with a half smile, "it is not worth mentioning. You have a good horse there, and you will give it up to me; you appear to be an excellent young man."

The proposition was by no means to my liking. I cast my eyes over my horse, which was in fact a superb beast, and felt by no means disposed to part with him. Having confidence in my own strength, I did not fear that he would attempt to take him from me by force, but still I looked upon the stranger with suspicion; he remarked my perplexity, and explained himself more clearly.

"Young man," said he, "I repeat that your horse is a very fine one. Will you sell him to me? I will pay you what he is worth."

This proposition gave the affair entirely another aspect. It was a simple sale that he proposed. I was willing to accede to this, for although the horse coveted by the stranger really deserved the praise he bestowed upon it, we had others in the stable sufficient for our business, and yet I felt that it would cost me a good deal to separate myself from my faithful companion, and if I had not taken into consideration the stranger's embarrassed condition, an embarrassment I could easily remedy by selling him a superfluous horse, if I had not reflected that we required another cart and other materials for the farm, the bargain would certainly have never been concluded.

"You find my horse to your liking?" said I, hesitatingly.

"Perfectly so, and I am ready to pay you a good price for it."

"What will you give me?"

"Fix the price yourself; you are old enough to know what it is worth."

"Well, then, I ask a hundred and thirty dollars for it."

"That is not enough; I will give you a hundred and fifty. Are you satisfied?"

"Quite so."

"I will give you my dead horse in the bargain. He is a superb animal, and deserves to be stuffed for a model."

So saying the stranger drew from his purse a hundred and fifty dollars and placed them in my hands. I bit them to see that they were good, almost blushing at my suspicions. In fact the appearance of this man should have inspired me with contrary sentiments. A rogue would not have been dressed so elegantly, he would not have worn such handsome jewelry, and he would not have been mounted on such a handsome horse. The stranger watched me attentively.

"Have you ever," said he, "possessed as much money as that at one time before?"

"Never."

"I thought so by the way you looked at it. You seem to me to be very frank and honest. Your horse, I suppose, is sound?"

"I will answer for it with my life; but to be frank with you, I think I do wrong in taking more money than my horse is worth."

"Ah, your conscience is hurt, my honest lad? But I will find a way to satisfy it."

So saying, the stranger drew from his pocket a pack of cards, the same that you see nailed to the wall.

"We will play," said he, "for the twenty dollars which you think you have received too much."

And throwing that sum on the dead horse, which was thus transformed into a gaming-table, he began to shuffle the cards. Although I felt remorse, I could not resist this man, and placed my twenty dollars by the side of his. He showed himself so firm and resolute in all his movements that all contradiction was impossible.

"What game do you play?" said he.

And he named some fifteen, of which I had never heard before. My ignorance appeared to embarrass him.

"You know no game, then?"

"None."

"Very well, we will play at 'Old Sledge,' and I will teach it to you."

The stranger gave me two or three lessons, and I soon comprehended it. He passed the cards to me.

"You begin," said he. I played and won.

"I double the stake," cried the stranger.

And before I understood what he meant he had already placed forty-nine on the horse. I felt a sinking at my heart and did not wish to play. I wanted to lose, but did not know how to resist the piercing glance he bent on me.

In spite of myself I picked up the cards. I won again, and continued to win. I was a prey to real despair. I trembled in every limb. My adversary, on the contrary, was as calm as possible; he drew from his purse all that was left of his money.

"Play," said he, giving me the cards. Fortune favored me again. "You are a favorite child of the fickle goddess," said he. "the money is yours. Here," he added, throwing on the heap of notes and gold his purse, "take this to put your winnings in."

I refused, and leaving the enormous sum I had gained, took only twenty dollars, the amount of my first stake, and rose up to leave.

"Remain," said the stranger, "and sit down."

I obeyed.

"I cannot take back what you have won," said he, "for according to all law and right it is yours. There only remains one way for me to regain possession of it. I will play you for my horse."

My heart beat violently—not that I desired to win back the horse that I had sold; but I felt pity and sympathy for him.

"You are very lucky," said he, "and you appear to be a very steady young man. I do not see why I should not make you my heir. You are not married!"

"No, indeed."

"But you have probably a sweetheart, that is allowable at your age."

"Not yet. In the deserted region in which we live there are but few girls, and among those that I have seen there is none that I should like to make my wife."

"The fault is perhaps in your own self-esteem. You think too highly of yourself to bestow your hand on a poor girl."

"Nothing can be further from the truth; but it seems to me that to marry, one should be in love, and I have not experienced that passion yet."

"You must be difficult to please. So much the better; I approve of it. A marriage made in haste is repented at leisure. But there do exist young girls."

The stranger did not finish his sentence. The cards were dealt and we began to play. How shall I say it? I won again. I cannot picture to you my despair. I rose convulsively.

"Sir," said I, energetically, "do not think that I intend to despoil you of your horse and your money. Keep the latter and give me back the former; or if it please you better, keep the horse and give me the hundred and thirty dollars I asked for it. I will not take a cent more."

"You are a singular personage, my dear James. Do you know that such a proposition from any one else would be an insult? Debts of play are debts of honor, and no one can avoid paying them. There is your horse and your money, but do not think that our game is finished. I have already declared that you are a good and steady young man, and that is why I love you, and intend to make you my heir. In the meantime I hope to win back my horse and my money. If my purse is empty, my resources are not entirely exhausted. I possess, among other things, a brooch and a diamond ring, which are worth double what you have won, I will stake them."

"No," I replied, quickly, "I will stake the money, but not the horse, or if I stake the horse and money, I withdraw a hundred and thirty dollars of the latter."

"As you please; only, my young friend, I have not the ring and brooch with me, and although it appears scarcely fair to play for an object the existence of which my adversary has no certainty, I can act in no other manner; but I give you my word of honor that if you win the diamonds they shall be faithfully transmitted to you."

I did not believe this, but it gave me no uneasiness, for I wanted my adversary to win back his property. I had never played for money in my life before, and what I had won burned my fingers as if it had been stolen. The stranger took a gold pencil-case from his pocket, and wrote on a piece of paper the following words:

"Good for two diamonds—a ring and a brooch—worth eight hundred dollars."

He signed it with two initials. The stranger then showed me what he had written. I asked myself, when I had read it, if the man was not crazy. I was certain of it when I heard him add:

"There is an important condition attached to the possession of these diamonds," said he.

"What is it?"

"If you win them, you will also win a wife."

I could not help smiling.

"Do not laugh, I speak seriously. You are a bachelor, and no doubt some time or other intend to marry."

"Certainly, if I meet a woman whom I can love."

"You are a good fellow, James, and you deserve a good wife. The person I refer to is worthy of you."

"But will she prove to my liking?"

"I hope so—I believe so. She possesses every virtue that can charm a young man. She has mind, a good heart; she is well educated and sings like an angel, and plays the piano and guitar."

"A piano and guitar—what do I know about such instruments? I have no wish to marry a musician."

I said this in an ironical tone. I was persuaded more than ever that the stranger was a madman escaped from some lunatic asylum. But where did he get all his money from?

"Yes, she plays the piano and guitar," he continued, "besides which she draws and paints. Nothing has been neglected in Rachael's education."

"Her name is Rachael, then?"

"Yes."

"And her surname?"

"You shall know it when you win the diamonds."

"But what is her age? What is her appearance? Is she young and handsome. She is nineteen years of age. I wish you well, and that is the reason I play against you. My loss will be your gain, and you shall be my heir."

"I thank you. May I ask if she is your daughter?"

A cloud came over the stranger's features. He replied in a grave tone:

"My daughter! Do I look like a man whom Heaven has blessed with children, and especially with a girl as Rachael is?"

"Here is a lucid interval," thought I to myself. "I must profit by it." And I looked around me to seek for a means of escape.

"No, James," he resumed, "Rachael is not my daughter. She is the issue of respectable and virtuous parents. Have you any other questions to ask me?"

"No."

"You consent, then, after what I have said of Rachael, to take her for your wife, or rather you promise me to marry her if you win her?"

I looked at him with an irresolute air; but he fixed on me his piercing eyes, so that I was compelled, in spite of myself, to lower mine. Reflecting that the man was certainly a madman I thought it better to humor him, and replied in the affirmative. He shook me cordially by the hand, and we commenced our game. Fortune again favored me. I won the diamonds and Rachael.

"I congratulate you, James Carew," said the stranger. "You are really worthy of your reputation. I have found in you the man I have been seeking for a long time. Everything I possess now belongs to you. Lend me your horse so that I can go to Harper's Ferry and fetch your wife."

"My horse is at your service," I replied, "as also is the money I have won. I have resolved not to take a single cent of it. Such an acquisition, obtained by such means, would weigh heavily on my conscience."

"You are crazy," he replied, putting the cards in his pocket. "I will borrow your horse and twenty dollars."

"Take all," said I, and left the whole of the money, with the exception of a hundred and thirty dollars, on the dead horse.

"You are my heir, James, consider yourself as such. Between two persons so closely connected there should be no secrets."

He stretched out his hand to take the money. I turned away my head, that I should not see him. When I turned round again he was already on the saddle, and had galloped off. To my great astonishment, with the exception of twenty dollars he had left all the money on the dead horse. I still thought that he was mad, but I gathered together the notes and gold, and slowly proceeded home.

When I reached the house I told my father that I had sold the horse; but I did not say a word of my gambling exploit, for he held gambling in the greatest horror. I showed him only the hundred and thirty dollars and concealed the rest. I was at first very much distressed about the possession of so much money; but our harvest followed. It was our busy season, and in three weeks time I had almost forgotten my adventure, and recovered my tranquility.

One evening, however, just as the sun was setting, I was seated beside the door of the house, after a hard day's work. I was in my shirt sleeves, I had no coat on, and my face was bathed in perspiration. Suddenly the stranger appeared on horseback, coming directly towards the house. I recognized him at a glance, and my heart beat quickly, for riding beside him was a young girl on a brown pony. I turned towards my father, who noticed my emotion; but he had not time to question me, for the two strangers had already arrived. In spite of my confusion I could not help looking at the young girl with the greatest curiosity. She was exquisitely formed, and sat on her horse like a queen; but her face was veiled. The stranger helped her off her pony.

In my whole life before I had never felt so much troubled. The sight of the stranger was in itself a great surprise; but to see him with the girl I had won at play, put a climax to my agony. I arose to welcome them, and began by making apologies for the negligence of my toilet.

"You need make no excuse, Mr. Carew," replied the stranger, abruptly, "labor is honorable. How are you? Ah, this is your father, I suppose?"

I introduced him to my father as the gentleman who had bought our horse, and then ushered them into the house.

"My ward, of whom I spoke to you," said he, as he entered.

At these words the young girl threw her veil back. I do not know why, but I actually trembled at the sight of her. I shall say nothing to you of her beauty; words are powerless to express what I thought, and what I still think of it.

The stranger fixed on me and on my father an interrogative look. I thought I remarked in his features doubt and uneasiness; but the impression were soon dissipated. I saw his countenance after he had examined my father's face, beam with cordiality and kindness which solicited sympathy and confidence.

"Mr. Carew," said he, to my father, "I am sure I can appeal to your hospitality to give a chamber to my ward?"

"Our house is simple and homely," replied my father; "but it is entirely at your service."

"I thank you; you are a man after my own heart. My name is Alfred Denver. My ward is the daughter of dear friends of mine. Her name is Rachael Herder. Rachael will be very grateful to you if you will conduct her at once to the chamber you design for her. She requires to make her toilet after her journey."

We immediately carried out his wish. Rachael was installed into our best chamber. Mr. Denver unfastened the portmanteau which was fastened behind the saddle, and conveyed it to Rachael's room. I took the horse to the stable. When I returned my father and the stranger were seated side by side, and conversing as confidently as if they had lived all their lives together.

You can fancy my condition of mind. I was like one intoxicated. I did not know if I were asleep or awake. The sight of my horse gave me real pleasure. But these diamonds and that young girl? My pride revolted. I could not allow myself to be made the plaything of a stranger. After a short time I took courage.

"Although I am only a countryman, without much education," said I to myself, "I have, nevertheless, my heart in the right place. No woman ought to make an honest man blush, even although she wears silks and velvet."

These reflections did not prevent me making a change in my clothes before rejoining our guests. When I re-entered the room where I had left Mr. Denver with my father, I noticed that the former surveyed me with pleasure. Supper was announced, and Rachael entered. If she appeared handsome to me in her travel-stained garments, you can judge of the effect she produced on me in her present modest and fresh attire. Once I remarked she cast her eyes on me. I endeavored to interrogate her look. She turned her eyes away without the slightest embarrassment, and then paid no more attention to me. This wounded me; I concluded that Mr. Denver had said nothing to his ward of what had passed between us. Was I then, seriously, to be that man's dupe? "I will wait," said I to myself.

The supper was simple and frugal. The young girl scarcely touched it, and I had lost my appetite. After supper Mr. Denver proposed that we should take a short walk, while Rachael, who had completely captivated my father, continued to converse with him. We entered a neighboring wood. The stranger suddenly stopped.

"Well, my dear James," said he, "you have seen the young girl I spoke to you about. Does she please you?"

"This is an embarrassing question," I returned. "She is certainly the most handsome girl I have ever seen; but beauty alone is not sufficient in a wife, and to pronounce a final judgement it requires time."

"How long do you ask?"

"I do not know."

"Is two weeks long enough?"

"That depends on circumstances. There are characters that show themselves in the first hour—such is mine— there are others on the contrary, that are enveloped in an eternal mystery."

"I trust Rachael's is not one of that kind," replied Denver. "Rachael is easy to read. I will leave her here for two weeks; when I return I am sure your mind will be made up, for your dispositions are the same."

"Then are you serious in this matter?"

"Quite serious; but your question is natural, and I understand it. You regard my conduct as very strange, and so it is, judged from an ordinary point of view. I have reflected long and seriously upon this matter. I am the young girl's guardian; her parents, as I have already told you, were my oldest and dearest friends; when they died they left her to my care. I have treated her with the tenderness of a father, my sole desire is to leave her in the hands of a noble and worthy husband, who can supply my place. I am old, and already on the brink of the grave. In you, dear Carew, I have found the man who can make my beloved child happy. As you said just now, your character is easily read. With my experience of the world I recognized those qualities which distinguish you, and which made me resolve that you should marry Rachael. As yet she knows nothing of my project, and from what I have gathered, I have discovered that you have equally concealed them from your father. Perhaps you have acted right, although as a general thing I do not approve of secrets between parents and children. I shall go, then, and I hope when I return that all difficulties will be smoothed over.

Such was our conversation. I could not help, however, when we were returning to the house, expressing my astonishment that he had not chosen in some city a husband more suitable in worldly position and education for his ward. Mr. Denver replied to this observation in a manner so determined and resolute that, although I was by no means satisfied, I was silent.

"Yes," said he, "your remark is a just one, and any other than myself, perhaps, would have sought for Rachael a rich citizen. But I know her heart; her desires are simple and innocent. I therefore seek for her an honest and virtuous husband."

On the evening of the same day, when Rachael had retired to rest, Mr. Denver asked permission of my father to confide his ward to his care for two weeks, while he went to Baltimore, where he had important business to transact. He pretended that he dared not expose her person to the fatigues and dangers of so long a journey. He presented the matter in so simple a light that my father could do nothing else but consent. And yet, the next morning, when Mr. Denver had started, my father said to me:

"James, when I reflect upon it, it seems very extraordinary that Mr. Denver, who is a stranger to us, should leave this young girl in our care, and in a house where the only woman is an old servant."

"But, father, is she not as safe here as if she were with her own relations?"

"Certainly, James. But she will soon grow tired of this deserted place. She is one of the most charming creatures I ever saw, full of grace and innocence."

I was of the same opinion as my father, but I said nothing, although my heart beat violently, and a secret trouble made the blood ascend to my cheeks; for although my own fate, as it were, seemed to be in my own hands, I forsaw that I should have to surmount terrible difficulties. At breakfast my father announced to Rachael that Mr. Denver had gone. At first she seemed much affected, but by degrees she grew calmer, and appeared to take pleasure in our society.

This intercourse every day, under the same roof, at the same table, soon dissipated the extraordinary timidity I had felt in the young girl's presence; her amiability gave me courage, and when I dared to speak freely, I had so much to say, and she listened to me so willingly, that we might have been taken as friends from childhood. She was so good, and appeared to interest herself in all that I showed her. We took long walks, morning and evening. My father often accompanied us, but he could not go very far and soon left us to ourselves. Thus hours and days slipped away in Rachael's company, and my work was neglected.

I need scarcely add that all my remorse on the subject of my gambling with the stranger had entirely disappeared. I understood marvelously well now what he meant by saying that his loss would be my gain. I do not speak here of the diamonds, I had not as yet seen them, and they gave me no uneasiness; I speak of an object more precious in my eyes than all the treasures of the earth.

I awaited Mr. Denver's return with impatience equal to the fear which his re-appearance had before inspired me with. But his absence was prolonged a week over the time agreed upon. He arrived at last. At the first glance he penetrated my secret.

"Well, Carew," said he to me when we were alone, "I see that all has gone on well. You have convinced yourself by this time. I suppose, that I told you the truth about Rachael. There only remains for us to see what she thinks about you. You have been often with her?"

"Often, that is not the word; I have occupied myself with nothing else but Rachael."

"What! you have neglected your work, your cattle, your horses?"

"They have enjoyed perfect liberty."

"That is bad news for the prosperity of the farm, but good as showing your love. When you are married you will repair the time lost."

"Alas! I fear that will never happen, for how can a girl so gifted and endowed as Rachael love a poor rustic like me?"

Mr. Denver examined me attentively for a few moments. This silent examination was torture to me. My heart beat ready to burst from my chest.

"Rachael," at last said this singular man, "has always followed my advice, for she knows I love her as a father. You, James, possess all the necessary qualities to inspire a woman's love and devotion. You are young, you have an agreeable exterior, and you have that courage and strength which only country life, gives. You are good, and you have a delicacy of feeling and thought, which must certainly recommend you in Rachael's eyes. I will not say that you have already won her heart—that is a slow operation, and does not sometimes occur until after marriage. But I hope my efforts, my influence, and especially my love, will hasten the denouncement we hope for, and which will be followed by such happy consequences for Rachael."

My mind was so full of thoughts of Rachael that I scarcely listened to what Mr. Denver said. I thought I detected in his voice and attitude a sort of melancholy gravity which had escaped me before. This gravity dissipated the idea that he was merely jesting with a simple countryman.

He shook my father cordially by the hand, and having kissed Rachael on the forehead, he offered her his arm and took her on one side.

"What strange people," said my father, "and yet they have excellent hearts. The girl is an angel, but it is easy to see that he is very melancholy."

I could make no reply—my heart was too full.

"How is it," continued my father, "that he could leave her so long with us? There are few fathers who could so abandon their child to strangers in such a wild country as this."

"But you know she is not his daughter."

"But he loves her as his child; and in all probability she has never known any other father. How I pity that poor creature, and how much I wish she could remain always with us."

My father's last words decided me to speak. I then told him what had passed between Denver and myself; our gambling transactions, the money I had won and Rachael's diamonds. I did not omit a single fact. I then told him that the young girl's departure would be a mortal blow for me, and related my last conversation with Denver, and my hopes and fears.

My father shook his head; the passion for play which I had revealed as existing in Denver opened his mind to suspicion. But it did not alter the good opinion he entertained of Rachael. He only pitied her that she was so closely allied to a gambler.

We were interrupted in our conversation by Denver himself. This man, so sombre, so mysterious, had a talent of making himself agreeable in the most eminent degree. He took me by the arm, and said:

"Go and find Rachael, she is expecting you."

I flew to the house, but when I arrived on the threshold, I suddenly stopped. I fancied I heard a deep sigh. I was prey to a violent emotion. I asked myself if it was not a crime to force the inclination of this poor young girl. I felt humiliated that I had not won her love; but this very humiliation remained my resolution and courage.

"Yes," said I to myself, "if I cannot succeed in pleasing Rachael, she shall at least know that I am not a coward, and that it is not my intention to abuse her state of dependence on her guardian."

I entered the chamber, I stood before her, I seized her trembling hand; what I said I do not know. My heart spoke from its most secret recesses, and my lips murmured the words. I only remember that Rachael, her eyes filled with tears, blushed. She told me with a sweet smile, that she acceded to Mr. Denver's wishes, and that, they were in accordance with the desires of her own heart.

Denver joined us; he found Rachael in my arms, I pressed her to my heart. He appeared to have had a satisfactory conversation with my father, but in spite of his apparent joy, I saw there was something strange about him. Since his journey to Baltimore, his eyes had lost their brightness, the furrows in his face had become more distinctly marked, and a great change had taken place in his appearance.

"Dear James," said he, "my desire is that you be united as soon as possible. To-morrow morning we will go to the clergyman's, and the nuptials shall be celebrated."

Everything was done as he wished. And we were married. The day after the wedding, after breakfast, Mr. Denver was to take leave of us.

"Rachael, my child," said he, addressing his ward, "I must now leave you for a long time, perhaps, for at my age we may never meet again. I have fulfilled the promise I made your father, and you are now the wife of a noble and worthy young man. I hope and believe that you will always live happily together, and that you will be as good to him as he is to you. Give me a kiss my dear child; it is perhaps the last."

"O, no, no, father!" cried Rachael, throwing her arms around his neck.

It was a moving picture, of which neither my father nor I understood the true signification. The poor child clung convulsively to the old man; at last overcome by grief, she fainted. Mr. Denver carried her into her chamber and placed her on the bed.

"She will soon come to herself. I will profit by the opportunity to get away. You will join me by-and-by James, I will wait for you."

He left the house before Rachael had regained her consciousness. In my agony and despair I did not know of whom to ask counsel or assistance. At last she came to herself, and seeing that Denver was already gone, she pressed me tenderly in her arms.

"O, James," said she, in a broken voice, "you are now my only support—all that I have to live for in the world!"

I told her that I should have to leave her for an hour while I went to bid adieu to our old friend. She made no objection.

When I rejoined Denver I remarked that he was still on foot, and had made no preparation for his journey.

"Where is is your horse?" said I, very much astonished.

"I have no need of it," he replied. "Besides, I have done. Have you forgotten that you won it at cards?"

"But can you believe that I will take it away from you, my dear benefactor?"

He interrupted me by putting his hand over my mouth.

"Not a word more, James, on this matter," said he. "The horse belongs to you, and you may regard it either as having won it at cards or as a present from me. I have already told you that you should be my heir."

I did not know, in the midst of my trouble, what to reply.

"Will you leave us in this manner?" said I, at last.

"I must."

"But how are you going? Are you going to descend the river in a boat?"

"Perhaps. It is difficult to choose a means of transport when one wishes to leave the world; for such is my design. Life at the best is but a delusion and a snare, and yet most men cling to it. It is not the case with me; a long experience has enlightened me. I am useless in the world, and I leave it. I have prepared everything to this end; my career is finished, and as I have already promised you, you shall be my heir."

I cried out.

"Do not interrupt me. My time is short—let me enjoy it. When I am no more, you can think what you please. But do you not understand what I mean?"

"Great God? You would not commit suicide?"

"Yes, James. But you turn pale, you tremble as if it were you that were about to die," said he, smiling.

I remained mute and felt that I was almost crazy. At last I asked Denver what reason he had to form such a terrible resolution.

"It is a long, very long history," he replied, "but let it suffice for you to know that I am tired of life. Every moment that I live serves to humiliate me more. I have enjoyed an almost princely fortune. I had intelligence, friends and talents. But in the different countries I have visited, I had not strength of mind enough to avoid frivolous company, and above all, I have not strength enough to resist the attractions of a passion, the most powerful and the most terrible of all passions. O! if I alone had been the victim—but this poor girl—your wife, the child whom a dying friend confided to my care, I have dragged her with me to perdition and misery. Do not let these words frighten you. Rachael is as pure as an angel in heaven—I only speak of her fortune which I dissipated with mine. It is true that Rachael is not entirely without an inheritance, but this absorbing passion menaced it without ceasing—it was the fear and torment of my life. Now she is yours, and I have nothing more to fear. She is saved, and I know she will be as happy with you as you will be with her. Do not imagine, my dear James, that I have ever been embarrassed to find her a husband. Many rich and distinguished men have asked her hand in marriage, and an alliance with any of these men would have satisfied the self-love of most mothers. But I knew Rachael's heart, and was determined to do nothing except for her own happiness. In you, my dear son, I have found the man I sought, and my mission is fulfilled. There only remains for me to address one more prayer to you."

And Denver drew from his pocket a pack of cards.

"You see these cards," he continued, "they have been my ruin, my curse—no, it is my own weakness that has ruined me; the cards in my hand were only an instrument without conscience, and is as innocent as the dagger and pistol in the hands of a murderer—a dangerous instrument, and against which I wish to warn you. Take these cards—keep them—but not for use, but to serve for you and your children as a talisman against gambling. Now leave me, adieu, my dear friend—adieu!"

He handed me the pack of cards, while I endeavored to dissuade him from his terrible resolution, but he turned from me and ran in the direction of the river. I seized him and endeavored to retain him, but he disengaged himself by a sudden effort. We reached the bank of the stream, he regarded me fixedly, and cried out in a loud voice:

"I repeat to you, leave me. Return to your wife who is expecting you. She will give you the diamonds you have won, and the book of deposit for twenty thousand dollars, which is placed in your name and hers in a bank in Baltimore."

"No," I returned, "I will not leave you."

Without listening to me, he ran in the direction of the water. I ran across him to intercept his flight, but at the moment when I was about to seize him, he pointed the barrel of a pistol at me which I had not perceived before. I instinctively recoiled.

"You are a good and noble hearted young man," said he, "but you shall not prevent me from taking my last journey."

At these words, he threw the pistol from him and leaped from the rocks into the river.

I rushed in after him. I could swim well. I sought a long time for him in the water, but all in vain. The current had borne him away and left no trace. I returned to the house, trembling. What despair welcomed my return. During my absence, Rachael had found on the table of the room occupied by Mr. Denver a purse full of gold, and a letter revealing his terrible design.

Here, my dear guest, my recital must finish. You have seen my wife. Denver did not deceive me when he stated that she would be happy with me. She has repeated it to me every day for the last twelve years. I am also the happiest of men. Only when she looks on the cards does Rachael become sad, but when she reflects that it conveys an eloquent lesson by which our son will one day profit, she becomes calm and serene again. What will a mother not do for her child?

My host here finished his story. I passed a day or two with him, and then resumed my journey, reflecting on what had been told me, and admitting that they were the happiest family I had ever seen in my life.